TWISTED LEGACY

Greed & Deceit

ASIN: B086SZJ8XJ
ISBN: 9798669687007

JULY 30, 2020

We are easily drawn to greed
when the truth is a twisted legacy of deceit

Chapter 1
Friday

Daniel had just received some exciting news and couldn't wait to get home and tell Alice. His phone rang as he picked up speed, but he was not going to stop and answer it, or waste any momentum, as he tried his best to ignore the annoying vibration.

It was Friday afternoon, the start to another weekend of nights out, drinking with friends and an opportunity to take his mind off recent events.

The vibration stopped and he muttered, 'Thank fuck for that.'

He was already late, and at first angry with his Manager, Old Sniffer for delaying him. The scene replaying itself, as the wind whistled through the gaps in his cycle helmet.

'Whatever you want to discuss, can't it wait?' Daniel had asked on his way out of the office.

'No. You need to know now, so that you are prepared for Monday. Some people need more time than others to digest a change of circumstance,' came the contemptuous reply.

Daniel had dropped his backpack on a nearby chair and squared up to the miserable looking man opposite him. 'You're sacking me, aren't you?' He had challenged.

'No Daniel. Please be patient, this is good news.'

Old Sniffer, the nickname Daniel had lumbered the elderly Office Manager with was not normally as civil, and left him with an uneasy feeling. So, he had hesitated and thought it worth humoring him, rather than making his normal excuses for a hasty retreat.

'You're not sacking me?'

'Quite the opposite Daniel. As from Monday, you will be the new Junior Office Manager. You have been here for six years, coming up for thirty, and in our Chairman's opinion, quite ready to take on a more senior and responsible role.'

The sudden change had been truly out of character and made Daniel search for any sign of this being some sort of weird joke. His boss had never really taken to him, and the change was most unexpected.

'Are you sure about this?' Daniel had asked hesitantly. 'I mean... you and I have never seen eye to eye... and I thought I would be the last person you would want to promote.'

'Firstly, not my choice Daniel,' Old Sniffer had sighed. 'And secondly, out of my hands. Not forgetting that the corporate world operates in the most mysterious of ways... I say no more.' Smiling briefly, he had showed Daniel the door. 'Now that I have delivered your good news, I need to be get going myself.'

Noticing that his Manager had neither congratulated him or even attempted to shake his hand, he headed for the lift with an overwhelming feeling of confusion. Then again, the whole scenario had felt strange, and left him with a range of emotions. From one of elation, to a sneaky suspicion that there was something else lurking in the background.

As he had walked to the cycle stand, his thoughts drifted. His boss had mentioned the Chairman, but he had never met anyone more senior than Old Sniffer in the six years he had worked at WASP. So if not pushed forward by Old Sniffer, then why would the Chairman want to promote him?

Waiting patiently in his study at home for the Berlin Office Manager to report back, the Chairman sat studying a photograph on his desk. A picture of two men on a yacht with a young red headed boy standing between them. Even though he was

2

expecting the call, he jumped when shortly after five thirty the phone rang.

'I have done as you asked Mister Warren,' Daniel's Manager answered, even before the Chairman had time to enquire as to who was calling, or how his task had gone.

'Good... that is all I ask, and remember, not a word of this is to ever get out. I know he was not your choice, but his uncle and I were very dear friends and partners in business. Even though old Harry is no longer with us, I have at least honored one of his dying wishes.'

The Manager's silence was an indication of his annoyance at what he had just been ordered to do, and Warren realizing it, ended the call.

Daniel's phone started to vibrate again, bringing him back to the present, as the wind ruffled at a few strands of uncontrollable red hair that had managed to escape his cycling helmet. He cursed, then thought it might be important and should answer it. His beloved Alice was pregnant and may well have been trying to contact him. However, as he started to apply his brakes, the vibration stopped.

Reaching the bottom of a gentle slope and gaining as much speed as he could for the incline ahead, his phone rang for the third time. Coming so soon after the previous missed calls made him think it had to be urgent. Avoiding several other cyclists careering towards him, he veered to the side of the path and dragged his mobile from his shorts. When he looked at the screen, he knew immediately it was not Alice, but recognized the first four digits as being the code for Berlin.

'Hello?' he answered hesitantly, always on guard against any cold callers.

'Mister Daniel Somersby?'

'Yes.'

'Mister Fischer here.'

'Do I know you?'

'Have you a minute?'

'This had better not be a fucking sales call,' Daniel reared.

His freckled face flushed and blended with the natural color of the strand of hair that stood askew from his helmet.

'Far from it Mister Somersby,' The dignified response caught him off guard. 'If you recall, you had a message from my secretary yesterday regarding the reading of your late Uncle Harry's will. I am the senior partner officiating the process and would like you to attend a meeting at our office tomorrow morning.'

'Uncle Harry? Holy shit. Apologies Mister Fischer, I have thought of nothing else since the call yesterday. How could I have forgotten? Then my promotion today threw me well off course. Yes, your secretary did mention someone would be contacting me.'

'Well, I took the liberty of speaking to your wife when I initially failed to reach you, and she agreed to you both attending my offices tomorrow morning at eight.'

'But tomorrow is Saturday. What about early next week?'

'No, unfortunately not Mister Somersby, the clock is ticking, and the meeting cannot wait.'

'If you don't mind, the clock is ticking on my fucking weekend Mister Fischer,' Daniel replied, clearly annoyed.

He had so many plans for the following two days, however had to concede this was most likely more important, and after Fischer told him he would forward the office address, he pocketed his phone. Then he thought of having a word with Alice about agreeing appointments without consulting him first.

Continuing his cycle alongside the River Spree, he skirted the city and headed on towards their apartment block. He could have done it blindfolded if he had to. It was such a familiar route.

Being in Berlin was not a new experience for Daniel. He had spent the first sixteen years of his life living in the city. Growing up at first in a stable home and attending a local school. Then soon after his sixteenth birthday, on the twentieth of July 1996, a day he would never forget, tragedy struck, and changed his life forever.

His parents had always promised themselves a vacation, and during a lull in their lives had packed their only child off to summer camp before heading for New Zealand to visit distant relatives. However, the Malaysian airline went off radar and in a dramatic turn of events disappeared somewhere over the Pacific Ocean. It took months as search vessels attempted to locate the proximity of the crash site, but then after tracking the flight recorder, decided to leave the plane where it was. The sea currents and depth of water at the site of the crash made the costs of trying to make a full recovery prohibitive, and with the cockpit voice recorder missing, the cause of the accident remained a mystery forever.

A year later, a floating memorial was established to mark the spot. Daniel had stood on the deck of a cruiser with hundreds of other mourners and threw a small bouquet of flowers into the calm blue waters. His Uncle Harry and Aunt Wilma stood close by, and did their best to console the boy.

Soon after the disaster, and while Daniel was still in a state of shock, his uncle and aunt had thought to adopt him. They were feeling sorry for their young nephew, now orphaned and alone in the world. Although they soon changed their minds when he became difficult and abusive, getting into regular fights at school and being threatened with expulsion. And it brought home recent events they were trying so hard to banish from their minds. Terrible problems they had faced with their own twin boys.

Daniel had been raised with certain beliefs which did not always meet with everyone's approval. Having never experienced anything remotely close to discipline, he was anti-social and disruptive to other pupils in his class, and was soon in the back of Uncle Harry's car and off to another school.

'One should be able to do exactly what one wanted, it frees one's mind,' Daniel complained from the rear seat.

The older man had grunted, told the boy to shut up, and enrolled him in a school with more draconian rules.

After two years of trying, and in a last-ditch attempt at salvaging the boy, he paid for him to attend a private academy on the outskirts of New York, where discipline was more rigorously enforced. The angry young boy with wild red hair was not their child, but a nephew nevertheless, and Wilma said she would do whatever she could to help. She felt she had failed her own twin boys and had a need to redeem herself. And while she vowed never to fail Daniel, Uncle Harry compared the wild redhead to the devil, and had serious misgiving about his wife's soft approach.

However, Daniel did change, and he proved the sceptics wrong. He loved being in America, calmed down, and two years before the turn of the century graduated from the military styled academy with honours.

Just as minds were changing and previous doubts extinguished, Daniel got in with the wrong crowd, and as his nearest relative watched from afar, the boy went wild, cruising around California for a year in a campervan and mixing with a crowd of drifters.

Concerned that he was going to go completely off the rails, Harry paid for him to go on and attend university. It helped Daniel, but their relationship soon deteriorated and became difficult as Harry tried to guide and control him. Offers of vocational work at his offices in Berlin during university recess was not what the boy was looking for.

In the end Uncle Harry signed a cheque to cover any remaining expenses and told his nephew to get on with his life, and never darken his doorway again.

Then to Harrys surprise, in late 2002, he received a letter from the university stating that his nephew had graduated with a first-class degree in architecture.

Daniel had never felt confident about returning to Berlin whilst his uncle was still alive. He knew he had let the old man down, but after being notified of his sudden passing and being offered a job by a large firm of architects, it urged him to return to a city he had grown up in and loved as a child. He was also looking forward to being reunited with his only living relative, Aunt Wilma.

Now, with her unexpected death, it marked the end of his family and left Daniel feeling quite alone. Being back where he had witnessed one family tragedy unfold after another was not quite as easy as he had initially thought, and if it had not been for Alice by his side, he was not sure whether he would have coped at all.

Riding under the broad canopy of Beech trees that provided sun dappled shade and shelter from the hot afternoon sun for most of his journey, his spirits lifted as he thought about a possible inheritance. Alice was pregnant and he had just been promoted to Junior Office Manager. Life just could not have got much better, as a broad smile creased his face.

Breathing in a lungful of fresh air he was unable to help himself shout out. 'I am king. I am king of the fucking world.'

Fortunately, it was a quiet stretch of path, and saved any lone walkers from feeling threatened by his outrageous behaviour. But it was quite normal for Daniel, even subdued some might argue, for him to be so restrained.

Looming up ahead was a beer garden, and Daniel veered towards the bike stands where hundreds of bicycles already stood. Although already late, he needed to process the day's events, and as far as he was concerned a pint of beer was as good a lubricant as any.

Then soon after settling down, he felt the familiar feel of his mobile phone as it buzzed and vibrated in his pocket. Hard to ignore, he took a quick sip of beer before dragging the small phone from his cycling pants. It had stopped ringing, but he could see that it had been Alice. A picture of her smiley face was underpinned with *missed call*. He felt a tinge of guilt, a surge of joy and pressed redial.

'Hi, my darling I have some brilliant news,' she said as soon as they were connected.

He was not sure he could bear any more good news; life had been so full of good news lately. A baby on the way, a promotion, and a reading of the will. Maybe he should be sharing it out, he thought, then quickly dismissed the notion as being ridiculous.

'Don't tell me my love, I can't stand it,' he replied.

'What do you mean?' She asked in a subdued tone.

'Sorry Alice, that's not fair of me. I have just had wonderful news myself, which I will tell you about as soon as I get home.'

'Let me guess... you were going to tell me they gave you that promotion you always wanted,' she said excitedly.

'I was rather hoping to wait and surprise you when I got home, but yes it came through today. Say a big hello to the newly appointed Junior Manager, in charge of ten people and an office of my own.'

'That is fantastic, I am so proud of you,' she praised him.

'I was going to surprise you when I got back,' he quickly added.

'Sorry my darling, I should have waited until you got home. But what fantastic news, and by the way, well done. We can celebrate tonight.'

'Listen, don't apologise, just have beers in the fridge, and we can decide on a name for the little chap that's about to enter our lives.'

There was a perceptible pause, and Daniel realised Alice had been calling him and he had hijacked the conversation.

'Sorry Alice, what brilliant news have you got?'

'I had a call from JJ Fischer and Partners, and they want to see us tomorrow morning in connection with your Uncle Harry's estate. Apparently, it has taken a while to sort since Aunt Wilma's death, but they are now keen to move quickly ahead.'

'I know Alice, I got the same message. I vaguely recognise the man called Fischer, but just can't place him.'

'He was the Solicitor we submitted our expenses to after visiting your Aunt Wilma every month.'

'Now I remember. Always questioning our spends.'

'What do you make of it all Daniel? Do you think we may inherit something?'

'Sorry Alice, but I don't think the old goat would have left me much. Other than scowling and moaning, he had little patience and certainly no time for me.'

'Be positive Daniel... come on, sound excited.'

'That *is* brilliant news,' he played along, before following up with an unconvincing whoop. 'Let us see what he wants to punish me with and then we can get back to enjoying our lives once again.'

'We will soon find out,' she replied excitedly.

'But it's Saturday and we were going to have a cycle and picnic with Colin and Debbie. I thought we could have seen the Solicitors on Monday, but this Fischer chap was insistent. Why agree to Saturday?'

'Daniel,' she scolded him. 'This is about your inheritance. The solicitor tried to call you, got no response, and then called me instead.'

'I was cycling,' he replied defensively, 'but I did speak to him eventually. Now, more importantly, what about time with our friends?'

'I have already spoken to Debbie and she is fine with changing to Sunday.'

He said his goodbye with an air kiss, finished his beer and got going again. Hearing Alice's voice had certainly added to his good mood and he found himself whistling and smiling at everyone he passed. It was unusual for Daniel; he normally scowled and swore if anyone got anywhere close to where he was cycling.

There was time to think, and Daniel's brain never remained static for very long, as his thoughts drifted back to that unsettled period in his life.

He had always been under the impression that his father's brother Harry had written him off as a waster with no potential. And this was not just Daniel speculating, the old man had on more than one occasion told him he would never amount to much. 'Like father, like son', he had once ranted in despair, before adding, 'and don't ever expect to see a penny of my hard-earned cash.'

Daniel, if he was honest, would have acknowledged that his uncle had given him more than a fair share of opportunities. But when the young man had eventually pushed his uncle too far, the door that slammed in his face had remained permanently closed from then on.

That was, up until the recent phone calls from the Solicitors.

Chapter 2
The Family

When Daniel arrived back at their apartment block, he found Alice had already received a follow up email from JJ Fischer, confirming their Saturday morning appointment.

The message went on to say that there would be a reading of the will, followed by a meeting to go through some conditions and clauses. It left them both baffled as to what might be waiting for them when they got there.

'Try calling them Daniel. I know it's Friday evening, but they might be working late.'

Having attended the readings of his own parents' will, he found it odd that there should be an initial reading first.

'Why not just read the will?' he said to Alice as he dialed the number given on the email.

Surprised to find his call answered after just two rings, the terse response left him feeling prickly and annoyed. And nobody's hackles rose faster than Daniels.

The solicitor's secretary would not even transfer the call to the Senior Partner, and told Daniel that whatever he needed to know would have to wait until their meeting the following day. The only bit of information she did part with, was that the whole process of disclosing the contents and terms of the will was to follow a due process devised by his late uncle, and would be handled personally by the deceased man's lifelong friend and Solicitor, Mr JJ Fischer.

Daniel thought back to soon after his uncle's funeral when he was informed that probating his estate was to follow many steps, with any beneficiaries collecting only once his widow had died. And the 'healthy old bird', as Daniel had often referred to Wilma, was due to live on for many a year. So, as time wore on, thoughts of inheriting any of his wealth had slowly faded from his mind.

Now his thoughts raced as he tried to guess at how wealthy the old man might have been, however discounted the notion of much coming his way. Or surely, he thought, they would be treating him with a little more respect.

Trying desperately to clutch onto reality, the weight of the loss of Aunt Wilma, mixed with the euphoric feeling of possibly inheriting a bit of cash was not going away. They searched old historical Rich Lists of millionaires on the internet, but his name did not appear anywhere.

'Not that rich then,' Daniel speculated.

'Very nice of him to even think of us,' Alice smiled kindly. 'Don't you think?'

Daniel shrugged and turned away, while scrolling his phone for the latest football results. Then, as always, his thoughts drifted to the coming weekend.

Later that evening Alice snuggled up to him on the couch. 'I don't know much about your family Daniel. Other than what you told me, and of course the bits your Aunt Wilma passed on when we visited, I know very little.'

'A total fuckup,' he replied with a sigh.

'Daniel, I wish you would stop swearing. You know I don't like it…, but explain anyway.'

Daniel fetched another beer for himself and a glass of sparkling water for Alice before settling down next to her.

'I will go back as far as my grandfather and give you the quick version. If that is alright?'

'That will do,' she replied, taking hold of his hand.

'I don't know how much you know about Berlin after the second world war, but grandad was part of the joint allied forces that occupied the city during the aftermath. Then after returning to New York with his regiment, he found it difficult to settle. So he joined a multinational peacekeeping force, and within months was back here in the city. Where he met and married a local girl, who gave birth to two boys; Harry and Arthur.'

'Your father and Uncle Harry.' Alice smiled.

'That's right. Then when the occupation ended in 1955, granddad had no desire to return to the States. Already married to a local girl, being part of the community, and with two sons, he decided to stay on. He then went on to establish a construction company specialising in low cost housing units that were so desperately needed at the time.

Years marched on, and by 1968 Harry had trained as a joiner, while my father did basic bookkeeping. And soon, both were ready to join grandad's growing business.' He checked to see if Alice was still interested before continuing. 'Then two years later, as foreign investment poured into the city, they secured their first major development contract. Before long, many of the tower cranes advertising Somersby Developments made it more than evident they were fast becoming a serious contender during the reconstruction period.'

Alice collected another beer for Daniel, and then settled back on the sofa as he continued.

'Harry was the older of the two, and in the late seventies married a girl called Wilma. While my father struggled to settle and was often seen in the clubs and bars in the early hours, drunk and dishevelled. Granddad put pressure on him to marry an Irish girl called Alma whom he had met locally. The hope being that it would stabilise his reckless and wild nature. And it worked for a while.'

'How long after they got married were you born?'

'I arrived two years later in 1980. The same year Aunt Wilma produced twin boys.'

'You've told me about them,' Alice added with a sigh.

'Yes, they were quite well known at the time. All for the wrong reasons I hate to say. Being uniquely identical, they had caused confusion from the very first day. The eldest by just minutes was Frederick, but it was impossible to tell them apart. Then as they got older, it was discovered that Frederick was mute, while his brother Francis developed normally.'

Alice shifted uncomfortably. 'Was Frederick deaf?'

'No, but nobody at the time could explain his condition.'

'And Francis was normal?'

'Yes, but he soon changed as the boys grew older, when Frederick started bullying his brother.'

'Why would he do that?'

'Whether it was the frustration of not being able to speak while his brother spoke non-stop, or the fact that Francis appeared a lot smarter, nobody knew. But Frederick continued to beat his brother whenever they were left alone. Their parents saw the bruises and noticed Francis changing, becoming more morose and withdrawn by the day. Harry tried to discipline Frederick, but he was too preoccupied with his business. He ended up leaving the domestic duties, including the raising of the boys with Wilma, who tried her best to protect Francis. But she ultimately failed.

'With all their wealth, couldn't they do something?' Alice enquired. 'Weren't they able to get some help?'

'They were extremely wealthy by then. Living in a mansion not far from here, while employing half a dozen servants. They could have had any amount of help, but chose initially to hide their domestic problems.'

'You never told me about a family mansion nearby, maybe we could go and find it one day. I would find it interesting to see where they lived.'

'Manor House was claimed to be haunted, and it was not just the twins that made the place creepy. There was something else about the large building that scared the shit out of most people.'

'Now I am intrigued Daniel. But I can't understand how they lived in a mansion while your family lived in a small apartment in a neighbouring town?'

'A tale for another day Alice,' Daniel dismissed any further discussion.

'Alright then, but you were saying Wilma struggled to cope.'

'Yes. As you know, she was a mild-mannered woman, and was at a loss as what to do, while Harry would wade in and lash out at Frederick with a leather strop. There were of course dedicated staff caring for the boys, but the bullying intensified as Frederick became more aggressive and Francis more withdrawn.'

'Daniel, that is a shocking story, how could anyone be so cruel?'

'That is not the worst of it,' Daniel shook his head. 'Francis soon changed, and by the age of five stopped talking altogether. While Frederick continued to vent his frustration on the more sensitive child.'

'Was there nothing anyone could do?'

'They did eventually call in specialists to treat him. But the more attention they gave Francis, the more Frederick lashed out at his twin. The experts said that Francis becoming mute was brought on by the continued trauma dished out by Frederick, and it was Francis's way of trying to normalise their relationship.'

'That is so terrible,' Alice shifted uncomfortably. 'I would have had Frederick locked up.'

'That was to come,' Daniel nodded. 'However they were identical looking boys. At first Harry shaved Fredericks scalp, so he could tell them apart. But Frederick was rotten to the core, and shaved Francis, so that they were once again identical. Then Frederick resorted to pretending to be the victim, self-harming, so that he could watch Francis getting punished by his father, thinking that he was Frederick, the bad apple. That boy was an absolute master at deception.'

'How did Frederick behave around you?'

'I was beaten by him whenever we visited. Fortunately for me our fathers never got on, so we rarely spent much time together. That at least spared me from my cousin's outrageous behaviour for most of my early years.'

'What did they eventually do?'

'Both Harry and Wilma consulted with specialists and tried being more vigilant. Nonetheless, they were soon at their wits end, as the evil brother taunted and provoked everyone. Then one day, Harry concluded the only way to correctly identify Frederick was to first make certain they had the right child, and then scar his arm in an apparent accident. It was not difficult to do, and if the truth was known Harry enjoyed the moment. The knife he was using close to his son suddenly slipped in an apparent accident, and penetrated the boy's arm, slicing down to the bone.'

Alice sat up in shock. 'What! I can't believe anyone would do that.'

He shrugged. 'They had run out of options. It appeared to have been done more in a moment of desperation, and from what I heard Uncle Harry instantly regretted what he had done. Frederick wailed and made threatening gestures with a small kitchen knife, but at the age of eight, he was no match for his burly father. Although we learned later that Frederick had caught Francis soon after, held him down, and made a similar incision to the one he had received from his father.'

Alice snuggled in closer. 'I would have been so scared.'

'I think they were. Everyone was, as they continued to watch Frederick closely. Then the boy started to outwit them, by disguising himself as Francis and hiding his scarred arm. Even the maids lived in fear, while the Chinese chef locked his knives away in a secure cupboard, after being threatened on more than one occasion. Even the chef's son Ming, who lived with his father in the attic, became the target of Frederick's aggression. He was beaten daily and chased around the large estate on a motorised mower.'

'Oh, how wicked.' Alice shivered at the thought.

'There was hardly a school or learning institute that would consider accepting Frederick. Knowledge of the boy had spread, and always appeared to precede any interview with a School Head. While the wealthy industrialist offered to sponsor the construction of new libraries and extensions, his back-handed approach invariably failed. Often ending with Frederick being expelled, even before the foundations had been dug. So, they concluded that the boy was a lost cause and the only thing they could do to protect Francis and everybody else, was to have Frederick placed in a secure institution. They had him analysed, treated, and then committed. This resulted in huge sighs of relief, as the family home returned to some form of normality.'

'At last,' Alice breathed her own sigh of relief. 'At least they had their lives back.'

'Not for long,' Daniel shook his head. 'A few weeks later Francis disappeared.'

'No!' Alice gasped in shock. 'Where did he go?'

'He went to bed one night, and the next morning after failing to turn up for breakfast, they found his room empty. A travel bag, along with a few bits of clothing was also gone.'

'But why leave?'

'All I can recall of Francis before he went missing was that he behaved in the most peculiar of ways, even after Frederick had been locked up.'

'In what way?'

'On occasion, when we were forced to spend time together as young boys I would try and get Francis to play in the garden. He would stubbornly refuse, and stay put in his dimly lit room with the curtains drawn. When Aunt Wilma banged on the door, he would unlock it, only to return and sit staring at a blank wall. While I was left to play with his expensive toys, lying unused and abandoned around the large stately garden.'

'So, they lost both children?'

'Yes, and with Francis missing, Harry and Wilma were beside themselves. The business faltered and I recall The Mansion being repossessed by the bank. It was a tough time for the whole family..., ours included. Days turned to months and then years, as they started to lose all hope of ever finding him. I can clearly recall the tragedy and whenever I asked my parents for news, all they told me was that Francis must have been abducted. While most tabloids ran front page stories about the struggling ex Tycoon's missing son, with the story even appearing on prime-time television. The fact that one twin was locked up, while the other had been apparently abducted, added to all sorts of speculation.

Along with the fact that their business was struggling, they had no choice but to withdraw from public life for a while.'

'That must have been tough for him.'

'It was. He had been a well-known and respected businessman up until then.'

'Had Francis been abducted?' Alice asked.

'Initial speculation circulated that he was being held for ransom, and the once rich industrialist would be paying out a large sum of money to get him back. Money, of course he no longer had. Theories were rife, and some even suggested it was an abduction gone wrong, and the child would never be found, let alone alive.' Daniel looked at Alice with a grimace. 'But no ransom note or phone call was ever received, and as time went by the media lost interest. They moved on to fresher pastures, while the family was left to be consoled by the authorities and were told to expect the worst.'

'Wow, that is one hell of a tale,' Alice added. 'And I thought my life was complicated.'

'Still two final twists Alice.'

'No!' she exclaimed and sat up.

'Firstly, my father and Harry had a massive fallout. I will not bore you with the details, but it was nasty, with all sorts of accusations flying between brothers. They parted company and Harry re-established the business on his own. Within months he was back on their feet, while my father was left out in the cold.'

'What about the mansion?' Alice asked.

'I am not sure,' Daniel replied. 'I think the bank tried to auction it off, but in the end had to settle for tenants. I never knew the details, or why Harry and Wilma never returned.'

'Most likely all the bad memories,' Alice speculated.

'Possibly, but the final twist was when Frederick escaped. He broke out of the institute and was on the loose. Those who were trying to be supportive and kind, said maybe the boy was trying to find his twin brother. With them being identical, they said there had to be some sort of spiritual connection, where they were drawn together by unseen forces. Those who knew Frederick better, feared he would be hunting Francis, and if he ever found him it would be the end of his brother.

Then in a most bizarre turn of events, there came a loud banging on the stately Manor's front door one evening. The tenants answered and were confronted by a crazed looking man, who held up a sign saying he wanted to see his father called Harry.

It was late in the evening when the tenants in The Mansion phoned. Harry and Wilma were busy readying themselves for bed in their rented apartment when they received the call. The couple rushed over from their neighbouring suburb, and when Harry saw the boy, he gasped. It had to be Frederick, he told everyone. When Wilma drew near, she wasn't sure, and presumed it to be Francis, because he was subservient and quiet, and had a gentle way about him. Then Uncle Harry rolled up the boy's shirt sleeve and saw the scar. Bellowing that it had to be Frederick returning to torment them, he shoved the boy away.'

Alice was startled. 'I don't believe it.'

'Apparently the boy turned and fled back into the darkness just as a storm broke, which only added to the confusion and mystery of the event. The police set up a patrol, and a week later managed to capture him, verifying the person they had was indeed Frederick. Back to the institute he went … and that my dear Alice, is the sorry tale of my family.'

'And no other family?'

'With Frederick cast from the family, Francis presumed dead, and Aunt Wilma gone, I now consider myself the last of the Somersby's.'

'Not much worse than my own sad family Daniel,' she replied mournfully.

Alice was from what was initially a stable suburban home in Vermont. Spending most of her formative years in private schooling, boarding in a hostel and going home twice a year. She excelled, and at the start of her final year was elected Head Prefect. The previous year she had been given an award for her outstanding achievements and volunteering work. She was an only child, and not long into her first annual semester, received a call from her mother, to say her father had been having an extramarital affair with his secretary and left home. Alice could quite clearly recall writing a long letter, pleading with her father to think carefully about what he was doing.

In return, he sent a post card a month later from a tropical island. He complained of being stressed and in the need of space, and wanting to find himself. As time went by Alice thought the space he disappeared into must have been enormous, as she never saw or heard from him again. Or maybe, she surmised, he had never actually found himself.

All the while, her mother continued as a single parent, and everything settled down for a short while. Up until one evening when she made an unscheduled visit to the boarding school in Middlebury.

Mother and daughter sat huddled together in a secluded part of the refectory, as she explained to Alice how a swollen gland had been detected and removed. The diagnosis was acute Lymphoma and she told how the specialist had grimaced when he described the disease progressing from early to late stage four. The tears that rolled down her mother's face told her everything, and Alice knew the end was not far off.

Moving closer to home to continue her studies at a more affordable local school, she found it heart wrenching. She watched her mother go from an independent woman who had worked so hard in life, to an emaciated figure, bed ridden, and reliant on constant care.

Fortunately, she only suffered for a short time, before the illness took her to a more peaceful place.

Friends of her parents who attended the funeral were compassionate, but quick to leave after the service. They tried to explain to one another how it would be difficult taking on an orphaned child, especially when their own children were so demanding.

Completing her final year at school, she spent a while at a friend's house, then when that year was over, she was on her own.

Money left in her mother's estate at least provided some level of security. And just as well, as there was no family other than a father, who was most recently reported to be on a yacht somewhere in the Caribbean. Although even that sighting had been a speculative one.

Taking a year out after finishing school, she put all her energy into helping homeless people. She had witnessed young children being moved from one foster home to another and at times even sleeping rough. She had seen older people sheltering in subways and doorways, while the public walked by.

Then the sheer scale of the problem was brought home when she joined a charity and assisted with their food program. There were hundreds living in deprived and rough conditions. Feeling overwhelmed, the desire to do more grew into an obsession to help those who were destitute, vulnerable, and unable to find accommodation or food themselves. A situation she herself could have quite easily found herself in.

With funds running low, and the charity in need of help in the City, Alice headed for New York, where she spent days doing part time work and evenings at college.

Then an acquaintance introduced her to Daniel. With an instant attraction, or as some whispered, a fatal one, the couple fell in love and the mismatched pair became inseparable.

Having both come from unstable backgrounds, and with no support from relatives, they were left with a feeling that there were no certainties in life, other than pursuing their own ambitions and dreams. And maybe that was all it needed to unite two people, who were so different in so many ways.

Alice believed she could make a change to the world, whilst Daniel was not bothered. She spent a lot of time doing part time work for homeless charities, whilst Daniel filled his time with leisure activities, drinking and eating out.

She believed that not everyone had been blessed with a safe and secure upbringing. That every person should at the very least have a plate of food and a roof over their head at night. Her passion to assist the homeless became an obsession. While Daniel thought they should get their heads out from under their blankets and find a job.

Alice continually questioned why the world was not opening more doors to the unfortunates left out in the cold, while Daniel referred to them as a blight in the parks, and a nuisance in doorways at night. 'They should be taken off the streets', he told her. He was not bothered where they went, just so long as he did not have to look at them.

Regardless of their differences, romance filled the air throughout their college years, and by the time they graduated, the couple were a well-established duo. They appeared ready to tackle the world and everything it offered.

But where to settle? The question occupied most of their conversations, up until when Daniel received the news of Uncle Harry's death. Then a mysterious email from a firm of architects in Berlin called WASP arrived. They were head-hunting graduates for an expanding office, and his name had apparently surfaced. His part time placement in New York was coming to an end and the timing was just perfect.

He applied and was taken aback at how quickly the response was emailed in return. He had an incredibly attractive offer, with all the trimmings. Annual bonuses, housing, relocation allowances, and a particularly good starting salary.

Alice's career as an English teacher was a perfect fit for any foreign country. With every youngster apparently eager to learn the international language, she was very much in demand.

Although she enjoyed the change away from New York, settling in Berlin was difficult. The few friendships she had developed were back in the States, and she had to start getting acquainted with a whole new group. Although it was made easier being with Daniel. He was a lot more sociable, and within a short space of time they had gathered a wide network of acquaintances they called friends. Young people very much like themselves, who had been transient for most of their young lives. They were all enjoying the thrill of exploring the world, working hard, while playing harder.

Colin and Debbie were different, and more reserved. They became their closest friends. While Colin worked alongside Daniel in WASP, Debbie and Alice, both teachers, shared a common interest. They spent their spare time helping the homeless, and as a result, the girls became inseparable.

Chapter 3
JJ Fischer & Partners

Berlin was a busy city. Even at that early hour on a Saturday morning. People rushed by, or stood queuing outside patisseries for fresh pastries and bread. Standing in tight huddles, with scarves pulled high, while breaths of fog rose gently above their heads. Smells drifting out of the open door kept the queues captivated, while Daniel's stomach growled as he cycled by.

However, he forgot all about food when they arrived at the address given in the email. It was an impressive looking block of glass towering high above the street and dwarfing the surrounding buildings, with JJ Fischer and Partners occupying the penthouse suite.

Dressed in casual clothes and trainers they arrived at the entrance of the building and secured their bikes. The vast foyer that greeted them contained a reception desk with a row of turnstiles, a security guard, a couple of large plants, and little else.

There had been no indication of what to expect. Stories of wealthy people leaving everything to charities, or to their pet spaniel, quelled any enthusiasm with a heavy dose of realism.

After being given a pass and directions to the lifts, they travelled the thirty-two floors in silence, holding hands and seeking reassurances from one another, that if nothing else they had each other. Likening themselves to space travellers and the eerie feeling one might experience venturing into the unknown and a world beyond planet earth they headed for the sky. With a gentle movement the lift slowed, the doors opened with a whoosh, and they entered the very plush reception area of JJ Fischer and Partners. Air drifting in from the foyer was fragrant and cool, like a spray of perfumed mist.

Arriving some ten minutes late, they barely noticed their tardy timekeeping. It hardly bothered them. They guessed the formality would be straightforward and they would be out of there within the hour. After all, it was only a preliminary reading and they were not expecting much, if anything at all.

Thick pile carpeting absorbed sound, while their voices were cushioned by the surrounding leather padded chairs and solid oak panels. Daniel thought it compared favourably to the Presidential suite in 'The House of Cards' series they had recently watched on a pay channel.

Reaching the reception area, they were met by a smartly dressed woman in her mid-fifties. She had obviously been expecting them, and came out from behind her desk with a broad welcoming smile and outstretched hand.

'The Somersby's,' she greeted them. 'Pleased to meet you.'

Alice felt genuine warmth radiating from the woman. 'Thank you. We have an appointment to see Mister Fischer.'

Smiling gently, the receptionist turned to Daniel and shook his hand. 'Mister Fischer has been expecting you and is waiting in the boardroom. Would you like to follow me through?'

Daniel returned a confident smile that hid a ball of nerves. Up until then he had been feeling full of himself. Now his knees trembled as they walked down the corridor in silence. Holding hands, they glancing at one another. Daniel gave Alice's hand a squeeze, and when she squeezed back, he grinned with uneasy excitement.

Expensive oil paintings adorned walls on both sides of the wide passage of closed doors, as the receptionist guided them to an open glass panel at the very end of the corridor. Inside was a boardroom with a panoramic view of the city. Dominated by an oversized table and two dozen padded chairs, it took Daniels breath away. He had never been in, let alone seen a meeting room like it. It dwarfed the six austere looking men in suits who sat with files, folders and loose sheets of paper spread out in front of them.

They all stood as if on cue when the couple entered.

'Ah, the Somersby's. Please come in.' The more senior of the men greeted them.

He introduced himself as Fischer, the senior partner, before going around the table.

Greeting each person in turn, they tried to remember the names given. However it was futile and under the circumstances hardly expected of them. They had certainly not anticipated a reception committee or anything of the sorts, and felt overwhelmed as they struggled to comprehend why so many people needed to be present.

One of the men however was familiar to them. He looked different in his pinstripe jacket, and at first barely recognisable. They had only ever seen him before in cycling gear, and it provided a welcome distraction for the young couple.

Daniel smiled as he greeted his weekend cycling colleague. 'Hello Harvey, I didn't know you worked here?'

Clasping his hand firmly, for Daniel it felt like a lifeline in a sea of strangers. Having cycled and spent so much time together over the past year, he had even thought of naming Harvey as second Godfather to their forthcoming child. His best friend Colin was always going to have the primary role.

Formalities out of the way, they settled into their allocated seats, preferred a cup of coffee to tea when offered and looked around the table. They were a serious bunch of suits, Daniel's collective name for the men sitting opposite them. He nervously side-kicked Alice and caught her on the shin. She yelped, and he laughed.

'Are you alright?' Fischer enquired.

'Yes, yes, fine,' she replied. 'He has such big feet, he never knows quite where to put them.'

She sneaked a quick sideways glare and nudging him with her elbow. It raised a few polite smiles and almost as if on cue, they all turned over the first page of the document in front of them.

Fischer passed over pens and blank A4 pads to the couple. 'You may want to take a few notes, but don't worry about the detail. You will be getting a full report straight after the meeting.'

Daniel drew a smiley face on the cover of his pad, which in turn made Alice smile.

'As you are already aware,' Fischer began, while looking at Daniel. 'Your uncle left a will,' he paused, 'only to be probated after the passing of your aunt. It involves a complicated gateway for his wealth to be distributed through an elongated process. Best described as,' he hesitated, 'unusual and quite complex to say the least. That is why the reading is taking place so long after your Aunt Wilma's passing. So if you will bear with me, as I first read a letter he wrote.'

He saw the confusion on the couples faces, and decided to add, 'I am instructed in the will that it should be read before reading the main contents of the will and at this preliminary meeting, so that you will be more prepared for the full reading that follows.'

Fischer then removed a few sheets of paper from a folder, adjusted his glasses, and started to read a handwritten letter.

Dear Daniel, I did not have much to do with you as a child. Saw you occasionally, but mostly on occasion when I visited your father, or when your family came to Manor House. Then of course we had our differences regards schooling and college and ultimately went our own ways. So, you may be surprised to find yourself sitting with my solicitor and friend, listening to the bequest I invested a lot of thought into before putting pen to paper. But most of all, I would like you to first understand why I have made you my major beneficiary.

Daniel raised his eyebrows and glanced sideways at Alice when he heard the word 'major'.

Other than the sums I have divided amongst a few charities, the largest benefactor of my estate is you.

'Largest?', Daniel muttered and shifted a little further forward in his seat.

Frederick disappeared, escaped from the institute and will never be found. And as you know Francis went missing. That quiet boy bullied mercilessly by his twin was lost to us forever. Nobody knew what happened to him, and we may never know. Despite all our efforts we failed to find any trace at the time, and I can assure you it was not from lack of trying. No ransom note was ever received, and the police speculated that it had been a poorly timed kidnapping. With me becoming insolvent around the time he went missing, there was nothing to trade him for. I am afraid the truth may forever elude us.

Ours was not always the happy home we outwardly portrayed.

At the time, due to financial reasons we had been forced to vacate Manor House and rent an apartment.

With the family home repossessed, we became concerned that Francis might one day want to return and find us gone. Although we asked the new tenants and neighbours to be on the lookout for him, and take care of the boy should he ever return, we heard nothing that was truly convincing. I am also sure you were informed about Frederick at the time. Better known as Frederick the Horrid, escaping the institute and returning to The Manor. He was arrested and returned to the institute, from which he soon escaped again and has since never been found. While your Aunt Wilma always thought that we may have got the wrong boy sent back, I was not convinced, but then we had no way of knowing.

More on that later.

Now back to you Daniel.

I am aware that I was intolerant and have prayed for forgiveness. As you are aware, I even tried to make it up by financially supporting you through college and then university.

Your Aunt Wilma was always very fond of you, and I hope you were kind to her after my passing.

'We used to see her at least once a month,' Alice spoke up for the first time.

Their lives had been busy and although the couple presumed there may not be much in the way of any inheritance coming their way, they kept in touch with Aunt Wilma. They paid her regular visits, where she resided in an outrageously expensive Austrian mountain retreat for the elderly.

Although Daniel was initially excited to see his aunt, monthly visits soon intruded on his time, while Alice solicitously enquired after her health and reminded him of his duties. She often thought that if it had not been for her persistence, their visits may not have been as regular, or even happened at all.

So, on the first Saturday of every month the young couple would travel by train and then taxi to the Austrian retreat. The family's solicitor took care of all costs and made sure Wilma's every need was attended to. It was not necessary for anyone to go to any expense, least of all Daniel, who religiously submitted a receipt for the rail tickets and supplementary costs incurred during each trip.

Wilma always appreciated the little they did and as dementia set in; she got Daniel confused with her long-lost sons. During one such visit when she called him Frederick, Daniel became techy, while it made Alice laugh. She thought Daniel's aunt extremely sweet and the old lady must have realised they were genuinely fond of her, regardless of Daniel's irritable and petulant behavior.

Up until her passing, she was the only remaining relative he was aware of, and her death come as a blow. He suddenly felt more alone in the world than he could ever have imagined, and it unnerved him.

'Shush Alice. We will be here all day if you keep interrupting,' Daniel muttered out of the corner of his mouth and jabbed an elbow into her arm.

Fischer smiled politely. 'That was very noble of you to pay your aunt all those visits, but let us continue with the letter,' he added, and focused back on the sheet of paper in his hand.

Our father had become exceedingly wealthy with his business in Berlin. Then he decided to retire and hand over the reins to us boys. We split our roles into Development and Construction. I did one while your father did the other.

29

Not to bore you with the detail, but a year after we took over the business it went insolvent. We were suddenly bankrupt, and it not only astounded me, but blindsided our creditors. I had thought the business to be sound, as nothing had shown up on the annual audits. But during a follow up investigation by a team of forensic accountants, it was discovered, and I hate to remind you of the facts, but your father was the cause of the loss. He had, without our knowledge, or raising any suspicion, gambled the business away. He had embezzled money out of the firms account and when that went into overdraft, used our assets as collateral to feed his gambling habit.

'That's not very fair,' Daniel blurted out. 'My father always blamed his brother Harry.'

Alice turned on him. 'You never told me that part of your family history.'

'I am not here to cause any trouble or judge,' Fischer interjected in a reassuring tone. 'Let us leave the past in the past. I am only acting as executor of the estate... now please if I may continue?'

He found his place, threw a furtive glance at Daniel over the top of his glasses and continued to read.

We were declared insolvent. All our wealth and everything our father had worked so hard for was gone.

We split up. There was little choice, as our relationship was in tatters, and from then on our paths rarely crossed. Your father went his own way and I started up my own development company.

I decided I was not going to remain destitute and used what little funds I could muster to get myself back on my feet.

My timing was perfect. Then later in 1991when the Berlin wall came down it gave me that additional boost, and from then on my success is history.'

'Bully for him,' Daniel cheered.

Harvey looked embarrassed. The remaining suits adjusted themselves in their seats, while Fischer took little notice of the outburst, and only paused, before continuing with the letter.

'So, we come to you, my Nephew Daniel. The only known surviving member of our dynasty, and a chip off the old block.'

'Is he saying I am a gambler?' Daniel was outraged. 'Harvey, you tell them. Have you ever seen me gamble?'

Fischer raised his voice. 'Please Mister Somersby, hear the rest of the letter first, and then we can discuss the contents. We have a lot of material still to get through.'

Daniel looked angry as his face flushed. His eyes darted from one suit to the next, but nobody was willing to engage, and eventually settled back into his seat, as Fischer continued.

'Yes, I can imagine at the reading of the will you may not be particularly happy with me for saying so, but you always appeared to be playing tricks on other people. Not a nice boy, I thought, but better than my son Frederick, so what could I say?

Daniel prickled but held his tongue.

I would love to know that you have taken whatever opportunity has come your way to progress in life and turn it into a positive. Your father never gave you any moral guidance or opportunity, so I am going to try and do that for you from my grave.

In terms of the options I am going to give you...,'

Daniel sat up. 'Options?'

'That is what his letter says Mister Somersby,' the solicitor said firmly. 'Now if I may continue?'

Without waiting for a response, he continued reading.

The option of a brand-new house or the old family Manor House that was repossessed years ago to pay off your father's debt.

Daniel lent forward.

I am acutely aware of not wanting to place a burden on you by taking on a too bigger project, and that is why I have offered you a brand-new house as a much lesser alternative.

But if I have understood you at all, it will be Manor House you choose.

For you, the last known surviving member of our family, I think it is the very least I can do. But it will not be plain sailing, and I want

31

you to earn your corn. And that is why I have structured my will in the manner I have.

Yours Sincerely,

Uncle Harry'

Alice looked at Daniel in confusion.

He in turn shrugged and turned to the Solicitor. 'I don't understand what he is saying.'

'Don't worry, it becomes a lot clearer as we go through the will,' Fischer replied, picking up a second cluster of papers. 'Now for the first reading of the Last Will and Testament.'

He went through all the formalities before coming to the part the couple had been waiting for. The section detailing exactly what they would be inheriting.

'The following section is quite extensive, so I have summarised it for this meeting,' explained Fischer. 'You will be taking a copy of the full transcript with you when you leave.'

Daniel sat still, as an eager look of anticipation creased his face.

Fischer took a deep breath and started. 'Firstly, there will be no immediate access to any cash in this estate.'

Daniel had settled back but lent forward as his face blossomed once again. 'What? What the fuck is this? A joke?'

The lawyers sitting around the room shifted uncomfortably, but kept their eyes fixed on the folders in front of them. Harvey had seen this brash young man perform on many an outing and barely flinched.

Fischer had the measure of who he was dealing with by now, and continued undaunted. 'There is however a substantial amount set aside for an investment in property, depending on the choice you make.'

'That's better,' Daniel exclaimed, as he settled back and gave Alice a smug look.

Fischer continued. 'There are the two basic options previously mentioned, and six clauses that guide us through the process. So, please stop me at any time if you need further clarification.'

The suits around the table were feverishly taking notes, and doing their best to avoid looking across the table. The silence highlighted the sound of rustling paper, as everyone appeared to be busy searching for something in their packs of information, or elsewhere on the table.

'From the options available it will be up to you to choose which property you want, and according to the rules, you must make up your mind and choose one or the other after hearing Part Two of the will. That is, if Manor House is still on the market and you can get it for the right price.'

Daniel looked at Alice and smiled. 'I am still confused, but at least we get a house.'

Fischer split the pack at a marker tag and put the two reams side by side.

'The two options he mentioned in his letter,' he said patting each pack in turn.

Then selecting the smaller pack, he started to read.

'Option one allows you to purchase a brand-new home, valued up to a maximum of one million Euros.' Daniel whistled. 'With all associated costs borne by the estate once you have found the house of your choice. There are only a few restrictive clauses attached to this option. The most relevant being, that the house will only be assigned over to you after the ten-year anniversary date of purchase expires.'

'Ten years?' Daniel blurted out 'Was he fucking bonkers?'

Alice gave his shin a hefty kick. He barely flinched.

Fischer lifted the top sheet from the thicker pile on his right.

'The second option is Manor House which his family once owned on the banks of the Spree. The old family home he mentions in his letter…'

'I spent many a weekend there as a child,' Daniel interrupted. 'It was then sold, and I can clearly recall my father getting terribly angry over the loss.'

Fischer looked like he was enjoying himself as he responded. 'May I just remind you Mister Somersby. The house was repossessed by the bank to pay off part of the debt when the family business went insolvent.'

Daniel sunk back into his chair. He had just been reminded of his own father's failure in family matters, and it pricked old as well as fresh wounds.

Fischer continued. 'Manor House is over one hundred years old, and in a severely dilapidated state.'

'Do we have to keep this one for ten years as well?' Alice asked.

No,' Fischer replied. 'This option is vastly different to option one, because it is worth a lot more than one million. You only have to keep this one for five years before it is assigned over to you.'

'Where is the catch?'

'The Manor House option requires you to spend a minimum of five hundred thousand Euros within the five-year period, and to appreciate the value by a minimum of ten percent by the end of that term.'

Daniel picked up his pen for the first time and started writing down the details.

'This option,' Fischer continued, 'allows you to purchase the old family Manor House, which is currently on the market. But there is a ceiling to what you can pay for this property.' He took a deep breath. 'Not a cent more than five million Euros.'

Letting out a gasp, Daniel gripped Alice's hand so hard she jumped.

'The denotable difference under this option,' Fischer resumed, 'is that there are more supplementary clauses.'

'What are they?' Daniel asked.

'We cover those in the next meeting,' Fischer replied.

'Why then and not now?' Daniel persisted.

34

'What if Manor House is not for sale?' Alice asked.

Fischer shook his head. 'It has stood empty for quite some time and been on the market for years. I would say there is no panic, but if you want Manor House, then follow up with the agents as soon as possible after the next meeting.'

There was silence in the room as the couple tried to digest everything they had just been told.

Fischer looked up at the couple opposite him. 'Have you understood everything so far?'

'A no brainer,' Daniel replied, and placed his pen back on the table.

He had only jotted down a few numbers and notes, but at this early stage his mind was already made up. Not even Fischer repeating the parameters of the second option was making any impression.

'So long as you do not exceed the ceiling price of five million, spend more than five hundred thousand on renovations and increased the property value by ten percent.'

'You mentioned assigning the houses,' Daniel queried. 'I thought we were inheriting a house?'

'The title deeds of either option will remain with this firm until you have satisfied all clauses and successfully reached either the five or ten-year stage, depending on which option you go for,' Fischer explained.

'Hold on.' Daniel raised his voice. 'What if we pay less than one or five million on either option?'

He had spotted what he would term, money left on the table.

'After the purchase price is agreed and the sale approved, most of the residual money from that allocated in the estate goes to a charity.'

'OK, explain.'

'It means you can buy a new house up to the value of one, or Manor House for five million or less. If the price of either property is less than the figures given, you receive a small bonus but most of the savings goes directly to a charity.'

Daniel's brain was working overtime. He had already decided on the old house and was trying to come to terms with why his uncle had stipulated the percentage figures.

He wrote down on his pad.

10% of 5 million = .5 million increase.

10% of say 4 million = .4 million increase.

He pushed the sheet in front of Alice.

'You see, the lower the price of the house, the less we have to increase its value. It's his way of making sure we bargain a good deal.'

Fischer was impressed. 'That is very astute Mister Somersby; I thought you may struggle to work that one out.'

Daniel gave him a cynical look in return, before turning back to Alice. 'The old owl has thrown some baited hooks our way Alice.' Then addressing Fischer, he asked, 'How much are they currently asking for Manor House?'

The Solicitor had been keeping a wary eye on him from over the top of his thin rimmed reading glasses.

'We believe it last sold for eight million.'

'Out of our league then,' Daniel huffed. 'So, does that just leave the one million option?'

'Not necessary Mister Somersby. I believe Manor House was auctioned off by the bank, had various tenants, but stood empty since the last family moved out.'

'From eight million down to five? I don't see that happening,' Daniel cursed. 'Damn Uncle Harry, why has he been so tight?'

The couple sat looking at Fischer, as if he held some sort of magic wand.

'Try out your negotiating skill on the property agents Mister Somersby. Go in hard, would be my advice.'

'That's not fair,' Daniel raised his voice, sounding more like a petulant child than a budding millionaire. 'Why put that sort of pressure on us?'

'We have our instructions and will score the value of the savings. The further you get below five million the more points go towards a final score. It will determine how much of the saving you get and will be part of the overall valuation as the final clauses play out.'

'Final clauses?' Daniel screwed up his face.

'Yes, there are clauses and letters, but some can only be revealed once you have secured the property and then others opened at various stages throughout the term of five or ten years, depending on your choice. There are even some that are triggered by associated events. And you will be scored along the way.'

'Scored?' Daniel looked confused.

'Yes,' Fischer replied. 'The men around this table will conduct regular audits and score your progress.'

'And how will that be evaluated? And how will that affect the outcome?'

'A complex spreadsheet,' Fischer replied. 'The results will be evaluated against a score in an envelope that can only be opened after the five or ten-year period. We have guessed that a good score may help you over the line should you have not reached one of the targets.'

Alice asked. 'Can we just have a peek to see where this is all heading?'

'No, it is kept under lock and key. As per instructions, only viewed by myself and an undisclosed person, whom your uncle appointed to assist me in adjudicating the process.'

The couple looked at one another and shrugged. They were at a loss as they tried to grasp the full complexity of what was being said.

'Who is this... undisclosed person he trusted so much?' Daniel asked.

'Confidential, I am afraid,' Fischer replied sharply. 'I have an address and that is all. We only communicate by email or by phone, and he disguises his voice. I have never met him or her. We refer to this person as X or the Undisclosed Person.' He took a gulp of tea. The five suits did the same.

Daniel shifted uneasily in his seat as he looked at each of the men in turn. 'Sounds like a fucking murder mystery. Constraints, clauses, final score and a undisclosed person called X… what a load of bullshit.' he muttered, loud enough for them all to hear.

Alice turned on him. 'Please… behave.'

Fischer ignored the outburst as he rearranged his folders.

'Manor House has six clauses attached Mister Somersby, and we will review them at the next meeting.'

'I am not surprised to hear of strings attached,' Daniel replied irritably. 'The old man was a shrewd old vulture. He wasn't going to give anything away that easily… and certainly not to me.'

Fischer smiled to himself, and thought of how interesting the next five or ten years might prove to be.

'What are the clauses?' Daniel persisted.

'As I have just said, the six clauses and selected letters will be dealt with at the next meeting, and then periodically over the next five or ten years,' Fischer reiterated.

Daniel sat forward, leaning over his elbows, and fixed him with a challenging stare.

'Why not now?'

'Your uncle's request Mister Somersby,' He said, meeting the challenge with a solid stare. 'Everything we do has been prescribed. We have a process to follow and unfortunately it will take some time.'

Fischer stood and excused himself, declaring the meeting adjourned until the following week. The young couple were led back to the lift by Harvey, who wished them well and said he was looking forward to seeing them again. Daniel looked at him and then at Alice in turn, and for once was at a loss for words.

Everything in their world had been moving along quite smoothly, with Aunt Wilma tucked up in her Austrian retreat, while they lived in a small apartment on the tenth floor of a modern tower block on the outskirts of Berlin. Having two respectable_salaries in a vibrant environment, with disposable cash that gave them everything they needed, while spending as they wished and enjoying city life to the full.

He spent his income on designer clothing, drinking out with friends and the odd bit of gambling. Nobody, not even Alice knew about the gambling. Alice saved half of her income for the homeless. She was committed to helping in the local soup kitchen and worked tirelessly raising funds, while he was out with the cycling group.

Daniel remained in deep contemplation. There was a lot to think about, and the terms of the will had left his mind reeling.

They pushed their bicycles from the solicitors to Tiergarten Park and found a bench, where they remained sitting without speaking for an hour. Heads swimming, hearts pounding and finding it hard to breathe, they snuggled into one another and drew comfort in this strange new world. That whatever happened, at least they would have each other.

Chapter 4
Cycling Club and Friends

The Somersby's had made a lot of friends since arriving in Berlin. In fact, they were extremely popular amongst most people in the cycling club and at their places of work. When they were not around, it left some feeling a little flat, as if an important cog were missing.

The cycling group gathered most weekends below the Brandenburg Gates in the centre of Berlin, before heading off on weekends of high-spirited adventure and fun. With newcomers finding themselves surrounded by a well organised crowd of mixed personalities who had two things in common, cycling and living life to the full.

Men enjoyed Daniel's reckless behaviour and laughed at his antics, while the women at times thought him amusing, although mostly a little outrageous. Alice joined in with the cycling crowd whenever she could, but not when it was her turn to help feed the homeless.

Colin and Debbie were their closest friends. Colin worked for the same firm of architects as Daniel and that was where their friendship hinged. While Alice and Debbie got to know one another at the Catholic school where they both taught various languages. Debbie preferred to spend time with Alice and often assisted at the soup kitchen, while the boys went off drinking or cycling with the group.

Colin found his friend entertaining while Debbie was continually telling him off for swearing, being cavalier, rude, and flaring at the slightest provocation. She preferred her husband's cool mannerism, never getting flustered or upset and always the perfect gentleman.

Debbie found out she was pregnant the same week the Somersby's announced the news of their own impending arrival. The babies were due within a week of one another, and it proved to be an ideal opportunity for some of the jokers in the group to poke fun at the couples.

'Had the foursome been together at the same wild party and spent too much intimate time in the jacuzzi?' And so the jokes went.

The cycling group numbers always varied, but one thing never changed. And that was a chant that echoed through the pack of bodies every time they cycled under a structure.

'Duck you suckers,' the leader would shout, as heads lowered in their own version of the Mexican wave, as they swept through underpasses and under bridge beams.

A custom that originated from a time when a lead cyclist, who was aware of a particularly low beam, stood on his pedals as he approached, and shouted back to his colleagues, 'duck you suckers.' So preoccupied with warning the others, he completely misjudged his own speed and was thrown to the ground after his helmet collided with the structure. It took a while for him to fully recovery, wore a neck brace for a month and was constantly needled by the rest of the group, who shouted the same chant every time they approached a low-level bridge.

'Duck you suckers' became a signature chant for the group and always amused newcomers when told of its origin.

The morning at the Solicitors office had meant that the couple had missed their weekend ride and picnic with the gang. So they met up with Colin and Debbie the following day, for a social ride around Tiergarten and a picnic on the banks of the Spree. Daniel had his own agenda as he casually shepherded them towards his uncle's old family home.

The couple had cycled past Manor House the previous evening after returning from the Solicitors, but it was late, and the light was fading. So, he thought he would incorporate a visit while with their friends, and after an hour of ambling along the riverbank, he drew up onto the verge.

Daniel had explained earlier that morning about the unexpected death of Aunt Wilma and the strangely worded will. Alice told them how they had been summoned to the high-rise offices in Berlin and been presented with the choice.

'That's the house,' Daniel said, pointing at the large stately building.

What they could see in the cold light of day left Alice feeling a little uneasy about Daniel's 'no brainer' comment as she felt a shiver race up her spine.

Colin nearly fell off his saddle laughing. 'You have to be joking mate… no way… it's more like a hotel than a home. Now I can understand why you called off yesterday,'

'I think my uncle wanted to help me get on the property ladder,' Daniel replied, then frowned. 'Or maybe he just wanted to punish me. I am not sure now that I can see it properly.' He laughed. 'Now that I can see the building in the clear light of day, it brings back all sorts of memories and not all of them good.'

'That's some building,' Colin remarked. 'But it looks like it has been standing empty for a while. A bit of a money trap and a front garden that looks more like a jungle than a lawn.'

Debbie lent across and gave Alice a hug. 'You must be so excited.'

'It feels like winning the lottery,' she replied.

Debbie shook her head in disbelief. 'I can't believe your uncle has left you that house?'

'We have to wait and see what else comes out of the will,' Daniel explained. 'As there is still another session or two with the Solicitors. We shall find out more about the bequest, with all sorts of terms and conditions that already have us totally bamboozled.'

Colin looked sceptical. 'Are you sure? This isn't one of your wind-up tales is it?'

'Our choice Colin. That monstrosity you see there or a brand-new house worth one million.'

'Holy smoke guys.' Colin sounded shocked. 'What an opportunity. A life changing one at that too. What a gift.'

'What the fuck, you only live once my friend,' Daniel crowed. 'One life and this is our one chance.'

'Will you please stop swearing,' Debbie scolded him.

It was water off a duck's back. He was brash, not afraid to say what he felt, and struggled to have a conversation without cursing. While it left Debbie feeling uncomfortable. Raised in a Catholic school and majoring in religious studies at university, it always left her feeling awkward. Given just one thing she could change about Daniel..., she thought. On the other hand, there were so many things to change it was not even worth thinking about.

Colin broke the awkward silence. 'Your fortunes have certainly taken a dramatic turn for the better.'

'You bet,' he replied. 'When the Solicitor went through the will it felt like a fucking A bomb going off in my head.'

Colin thought of the years he would still have to work and how his friends' good fortune had changed overnight. Even though the recent news of his friend getting the Junior Manager promotion had started a small crystal of envy forming, he now had a Mansion to boot. But, as Colin rationalised, he was a buddy, and buddies never got envious.

Colin and Debbie were at first surprised to hear the couple talk about a house and mystified as to how they could afford one. But as they stood looking at the large building, it explained some of their recent euphoric phone calls.

Both couples were keen to get out of the vertical sprawl. But there was only one problem, and it revolved around the cost of real estate in Berlin. They were prohibitive to most ordinary young people. Any house within a ten-mile radius of the city was owned by wealthy industrialists or handed down through generations of the same family. Well out of reach of the average first-time buyers.

Manor House sat atop a sloping bank five hundred yards from the Spree. Situated on the outskirts of the city, it was ideally located and would have been snapped up soon after coming onto the market. Except that it was deserted, looked forlorn and appeared to be in a state of utter neglect. A jungle of growth had started claiming the property and obscured most of the lower two floors from view. It gave the mansion a ghostly feel. Thick ivy crept over the building, threatening to envelop and overwhelm the building with its green tendrils, spreading like veins, encroaching over walls, windows, and roof.

It was obvious that Manor House had been neglected for many years.

Three stories of leaded windows framed by ornate sandstone lintels and pilasters overlooked a long sloping jungle of a garden. Walls not covered in the thick layer of ivy were pebble dashed and painted a dirty cream, patchy and peeling away in places where exposed brickwork broke through. Some windows were completely obscured by a thick layer of vine, while a few remained clear, or broken, and fronted what looked like thread-bare curtains hanging in various forms of decay.

A long row of attic room windows poked out from the pitched sloping roof. Their small gable ends dwarfed by the sheer expanse of slate tiles.

The neighbouring mansion on the upstream side extended to within fifty yards of Manor House, where someone had planted a row of dense conifers to screen the gable end of the derelict Mansion.

Downstream of the property, the former large family home had been renovated and converted into ten luxury apartments. It was something they thought could be done with Manor House once they had taken full ownership.

'Let us have a look around,' Daniel prompted.

44

'Do you think it wise?' Alice questioned. 'Should we not wait until we talk to the property agents?'

Debbie hung back as they all pushed their bicycles further into the overgrown garden. 'I will stay here and look after the bikes,' she called to them.

'I will stay with you,' Alice replied, and dropped back.

The property was covered in overgrown trees, bramble, and grass. It had obviously been neglected for years. Daniel took the lead and Colin followed, as they approached a well-worn path leading up one side of the property. The path passed close to the gable end wall.

'Looks like this is used as a short cut,' Daniel suggested.

Something moved in the undergrowth nearby and made them both jump back.

'What the fuck was that?' Daniel shouted.

Colin had already retreated ten yards down the path.

'I don't know, but it was something large. Maybe a wild boar.'

Daniel Laughed. 'What the fuck Colin, we are only ten miles out of the city centre. There are no wild animals here.'

A loud growl followed by a grunting sound, and something moved nearby. Daniel took off and ran past Colin, who remained frozen with fear.

'Wait for me,' Colin shouted after him. Then screamed when something shook a tree nearby.

He eventually got his legs moving and weaved his way back down the path, before breaking out into the open close to where Debbie was waiting.

'Where are the other two?' he shouted.

'What on earth is going on?' Debbie looked terrified.

'Let's get out of here Debs.' Colin looked around, however they were alone. 'Where are the others?' he repeated, as they scrambled through the clawing grass towards the towpath.

'Daniel came back in a hurry,' Debbie explained in-between breaths. 'He couldn't wait to get going and shouted at us to follow.'

Colin was furious. 'They didn't wait for you?'

'He told me to follow, but I couldn't leave you behind,' she replied.

Catching sight of Daniel and Alice waiting for them further down the path, Colin peddled hard, drew level, and dropped his bike on the ground.

'You could have at least stayed with Debbie, you bastard. Bad enough leaving me in that bush with some wild animal, then rushing off like you did and leaving us behind is unforgiveable.'

He took a wild swing at Daniel, who ducked.

'Stop that,' Debbie shouted.

Daniel made no move to retaliate and held up both hands in surrender. 'Sorry pal, but I had seen enough and just wanted to get back.'

'No, you hadn't,' Colin ranted. 'That wild animal scared you and you ran off.'

'What wild animal?' Alice asked.

Daniel looked nervously at each of them in turn. 'I think Colin is exaggerating Alice. Just some rustling in the bush.'

'Not just noises,' Colin retaliated. 'Something moved in the bush and growled at me.'

They looked at one another for a while as Colin dusted himself down.

'Friends?' Daniel approached him with both arms outstretched.

Colin gloated for a second before accepting, although he made a mental note to watch Daniel in the future. He was not entirely convinced his friend would always be there for him.

They cycled back along the towpath in silence for a while, before stopping close to a large field. Although Colin was still prickly, the atmosphere had returned to near normality as they spread their groundsheet under the dappled shade of a broad branched tree. The girls settled down while the boys went for a walk. Daniel was trying hard to make amends, and as they strolled through a field of wild grass and dandelions he bent over to pick a few flowers, to make up a small bunch for Debbie. A peace offering of sorts would help smooth things out, he thought.

'You are trespassing on my land,' a man shouted in a menacing tone.

The booming voice startled them and coming so soon after their experience at Manor House, made them both jump.

Standing a few hundred yards away they saw a man dressed in a waistcoat and cravat, with a large feather standing high in his alpine hat.

Daniel quickly recovered and shouted back. 'We are not doing any harm,'

'Come, let's go,' Colin urged, as he felt his hands starting to tremble.

The man stood his ground. 'This is private property, now put those flowers down and leave at once.' Then raising what Colin had first mistaken for a walking stick shot a round in the air.

'Daniel, the man has a shotgun, better get going,' Colin screamed.

'No Colin, there should be a law that says people can roam on open land, and if these rich buggers are so stuck up their own arses then they should be taught a lesson.'

Colin was not convinced that Daniel fully appreciated the danger they faced.

'Fuck off,' Daniel shouted back.

A second shot was fired in the air.

'He means business,' Colin urged. 'Let's go.'

They ran down a gentle slope before reaching the girls, who had by now got to their feet to see what all the commotion was about.

'Come girls,' Colin helped Debbie pack her bag. 'This is private land, and we are obviously not welcome.'

After having two strange experiences their day out was ruined, and besides, the girls were tired. So they decided to head for home.

'What about all this leftover food,' Daniel said, as he hoisted his backpack over his shoulder.

'I know just the place,' Alice replied. 'Follow me.'

They detoured a half mile off course and came to an underpass, where huddled up against the one wall were dozens of homeless people, who had set up makeshift cardboard homes and were obviously living rough.

'Who wants some food?' Alice shouted.

A couple of the tenants emerged, staggered towards them, and gratefully accepted the handouts as Debbie and Alice emptied the backpack.

'Now, this is where I get really annoyed,' Colin complained as they cycled back towards the city. 'There are dozens of homeless individuals sleeping rough and some guy who owns a large estate fires his gun at us for being on his property. The divide between the rich and the poor is driving me nuts.'

Daniel thought of becoming a homeowner with a couple of acres of land and decided to keep quiet. He was about to enter the dark world of being wealthy, with his own mansion, and was quietly looking forward to it.

'That old guy with the gun must have worked hard for that property Colin, while those smelly shits in the underpass need to get off their lazy arses and get a fucking job.'

Colin sensed, not for the first time that day that something had come between them, as a cold draft made him shiver. And when he glanced across at his friend, he saw an expression he had not seen before. Realising there was no longer that old carefree look of 'come what may' on Daniel's face, and it worried him. It concerned him that whatever the inheritance amounted to; his friend had already changed.

And he was not wrong.

Daniel was oblivious to the look Colin gave him. He was miles away as his thoughts drifted back to the previous day. When everything in their lives had taken such a dramatic U-turn.

Chapter 5
The Clauses

The week flew by. Every spare minute was taken up discussing the will and their inheritance options. Wildly speculating as to what was going to happen next, and before they knew it, they were once again back in the centre of Berlin, entering the oversized foyer with its row of turnstiles and lone security guard.

After being given a security pass, they travelled the twenty-two floors as they had done the previous Saturday. Entering the offices of JJ Fischer and Partners for the second time they knew what to expect and were punctual. There was an air of expectancy, and Daniel was champing at the bit to see what was coming up next.

Greeting them with the same charming smile, they felt secure as the receptionist ushered them down the plush corridor.

'The Somersbys,' Fischer greeted them as they appeared at the glass panelled door. The same five suits stood as if on cue. 'Please come in.'

They were directed to the two chairs they had sat on the previous Saturday.

Harvey was there, looking slightly more reserved but still greeted them with a friendly smile.

'Very nice to see you again,' Fischer smiled.

Settling into their seats, they accepted a cup of coffee and waited expectantly for the proceedings to start.

'We covered the first part of the bequest last Saturday,' the Solicitor began. 'Have you had time to reflect on the choice of house?'

'I want to hear the clauses first,' Daniel replied. 'Then we can decide.'

'That is quite in order Mister Somersby. Are we all ready?'

The couple nodded and Alice picked up a pen, ready to write down any questions she might have.

'Clause One, Part One states that you both ensure the purchase contract has no hidden clauses and you read all the documentation yourselves. I must warn you at this juncture that you cannot involve us, the executors of the will. You are of course at liberty to hire anyone you like, but so long as it is not this firm.'

'Why not your company?' Alice asked.

'Daniel's Uncle Harry considered it a conflict of interest in terms of what he wanted to achieve.'

'No problem,' Daniel replied confidently. 'I review contracts at work all the time and have a knack for getting through them quickly.'

Fischer nodded, as he hesitantly studied the young man over the top of his glasses, before returning to his notes.

'The second part of Clause One is a bit strange …'

Daniel interjected. 'This whole bloody process is strange.'

'As I was about to say,' Fischer continued. 'It is like all the other clauses I am about to go through. Bearing in mind that you are only privy to some of the information, Part Two of this first clause is to do with how you negotiate on price and manage the transaction.' He lifted a separate sheet from his folder. 'As an example, if the executors calculate you have not bargained hard enough, you will have to make up the difference out of your own savings.'

Daniel lent forward. 'You mean I may be out of pocket?'

'The assessment made by my team will be fair, I can assure you Mister Somersby. The legal team managing the estate will be interrogating the price to see how well you have bargained and that in turn will be subject to a strict audit. Your Uncle Harry would have wanted you to negotiate the best deal and avoid any, 'under the counter deals' with the agents. Whereby you pay too much on purpose and get a cash kickback.'

'Just hold on a minute,' Daniel was out of his chair. 'What are you suggesting?'

'Sit down,' Alice urged. 'Let Mister Fischer finish reading the will. I want to hear the remaining clauses.'

'I am suggesting nothing at all Mister Somersby. Your uncle obviously just wanted to know that you had secured the best possible deal.'

'This is like big brother,' Daniel protested.

'We are only following instructions Mister Somersby. Your uncle put a lot of effort into ensuring we have strict guidelines and a solid framework to work within. If you select Manor House, the legal team are obligated to monitor your progress and ensure you abide by all the clauses throughout the period, and I can guarantee you that it will be a fair process.'

Fischer was relieved to see Daniel settle back and return to fiddling with his pencil.

'The second clause states that money from the estate can only be used to purchase a property that you both intend living in as your permanent home. This must be for the duration of either the five- or ten-year option. If one of you leaves the house within the period, you break the terms of the will and the property will revert back to the estate. You will get your costs back, but the rest goes to a charity.'

They both shrugged and nodded.

'We plan on being together for the rest of our lives,' Alice said, as she placed her hand over her husbands. He smiled and blew her a kiss in return.

'The third, fourth and fifth clauses refers to the Manor House option only,' Fischer resumed. 'The third states that all renovations or alterations to the building must be paid for out of your own earnings and bonuses after tax. His rules stipulate that you cannot take out a loan, mortgage the property or borrow money. The funds must come solely from money you two have in savings or gained from earnest employment.'

'How will you know?' Daniel asked.

'These men you see in front of you will do unscheduled audits over the full term to make sure you are compliant. While annual reviews will be held in this office.'

Daniel's eyes moved from Fischer to the five suits opposite him. They studiously kept their heads lowered and studied the paperwork in front of them.

'The fourth clause states that you are not allowed to take in lodgers, students, rent rooms on Airbnb or any other internet site. You will not be permitted to have anyone other than direct family reside in the house for a continual period of more than a week.'

'We have no direct family,' Daniel conceded.

'I think he was referring to any children you may have,' Fischer explained.

Alice patted her belly, which made Daniel smile.

Fischer continued. 'The fifth clause comes in two parts. Part One states that if you ever find Francis, you must be gentle and treat him as a member of your family, look after him and be prepared to share your inheritance with him.'

Daniel's brow furrowed. 'What? In our house?'

'Only if you choose Manor House, the house on offer to you,' Fischer replied. 'Clause Five part one states that Francis has always been vulnerable and if he returns, you are to share any inheritance, including the house. And that extends to beyond the five-year period.'

'You mean until he finds somewhere else to live?'

'No, Mister Somersby. The will states that it has to be a permanent arrangement.'

'What if we decide to sell and he has returned?'

'You cannot sell with him in the house,' Fischer replied.

Daniel fell silent, and Alice noticed him starting to brood, while his face darkened.

'But be aware.' The Solicitor continued, as he looked sternly over the rim of his glasses. 'If Frederick ever returns, you are to contact the police and have him arrested and locked up. If he is ever found to have sheltered in Manor House, you will be evicted from the property and not a penny of inheritance will come your way.'

'Don't worry,' Daniel replied. 'I have seen what that idiot Frederick can be like. If he comes our way, I will personally kick his arse. I have been saving it for him ever since he beat me as a kid.'

Fischer gave him a wry smile before continuing. 'Clause Five, part two states that you are to be kind to anyone vulnerable or less fortunate than yourselves.'

'I don't understand why he included that clause. In any case, Alice helps the homeless most Saturdays in the local soup kitchen.'

'Very good Alice.' Fischer smiled at her. 'He would have been immensely proud of you.'

'Are we finished?' Daniel asked irritably.

'That is all the detail for now. As much as we are permitted to divulge at this juncture.' He indicated the stack of files on the table next to him. 'As you can see, there is a lot of back-up information that remains privy only to me, the executors around this table and one other, the person called X. Then there is Clause Six and further files and sealed letters that only I and X, the Undisclosed Person has access to.'

Daniel looked up at the five suits. They nodded in unison. Harvey looked so out of place that he hardly recognised his old biking pal. Daniel was clearly restless and irritable, but at the same time intrigued.

'What? Another clause?'

'Clause Six will most likely remain forever undisclosed,' Fischer replied with a sigh. 'It all depends on whether Francis ever returns.'

'What about the rest of his money?' Daniel was not going to be side-tracked.

'As I said earlier, he has divided it amongst a dozen charities.'

Daniel was incensed, 'Why charities when he has me? His nephew and only member of the family present.'

Fischer rounded on him in an irritable tone. 'I would suggest you are already receiving quite a substantial amount from his estate, Mister Somersby.'

'Whatever,' Daniel responded dismissively.

He needed time to go through the information. It was all in a pack Fischer slid carefully across the table towards him.

Although restricted to what they had just been told, the devil was always in the detail, he could clearly recall his uncle saying in a distant memory.

The couple were taken to an adjoining office by Harvey, where they were given access to a computer and the use of a phone.

'You have the rest of the day,' Harvey smiled at them. 'Up until five o'clock to make your decision. If you would like a drink or snack, just pick up the phone. Melissa on reception will get whatever you need.'

'Thank you, Harvey,' Alice replied gracefully.

Daniel stood gloating at his old cycling buddy. He was not thrilled to see him in what he had already regarded as the enemy camp.

Harvey noticed, and tried to console him. 'If it helps you in any way, I can arrange a cycle with you to Manor House and show you the state of the property from the path.' Then added. 'You would of course have to arrange a viewing of the inside of the house with the relevant agents.'

Daniel studied his old biking friend for a further few second before answering. 'Thanks, but will wait until we have a viewing.'

He was unsure of Harvey in his suit, but felt reassured that at least they had someone on the inside if needs be.

Clever old man, Daniel thought. He had been no fool after all. His bequest meant that if they went for the larger amount, they could not waste their earnings. They had to continue working and save enough to spend on renovations to gain the required increase in value, but they were also restricted as to when they could sell.

He fully understood his intentions, as strange as it may have appeared. Uncle Harry wanted him to be responsible and stop behaving like a spoiled brat, and besides, being as astute as he was, he would have had a sneaky suspicion that his nephew was putting a little money on a few side bets without anyone knowing. His hard-earned money wasted, if handed to him on a silver platter.

Daniel lacked a lot of emotional intelligence, but nobody could ever accuse him of not being self-aware. He knew exactly how badly he behaved, but it did not bother him.

The alternative option of purchasing a newly constructed home for the lower value was sorely tempting. Not being tied down with renovations or clauses. And the thought of Francis returning and living with him in the mansion threw him for a while, but that threat was quickly discounted as being far too remote.

Combined with the inability to sell the one million option for ten years and the slower release of equity, it was not an option he felt comfortable with. And it only equated to one fifth of the value of Manor House. There was also less potential to make a real profit with a new house. And that was what made him dismiss this option out of hand. While the five million deal made his head swim.

The more Alice thought of the old building, the more she insisted they should take a little more time before making a final decision. He however never once questioned his own judgment.

They had at least had a debate of sorts while sitting in the spare office.

'I want us to make a quick decision,' Daniel said, shifting restlessly in his chair. 'The longer we take to decide is time wasted.'

When Alice urged caution, he stressed, 'I want to get moving quickly. Fix it, live in it like a Lord, and retire in my thirties a multi-millionaire.'

'Sounds a little greedy my love. If we went for the one million Euro house, we could move in and have no restrictive clauses. Just wait ten years and then sell if we want.'

'Look Alice,' he added rather forcibly. 'We will only get one shot at something like this in our lifetime, and I am not going to let it pass us by.'

Manor House on the banks of the Spree was like a building he had always dreamed of owning, so he would roll up his sleeves, learn a few skills, and make a pot load of money.

He tried to console Alice when she voiced further doubts. 'It is not beyond us..., everything will be fine.'

'Don't forget I am pregnant, and limited with the amount I can do. Then busier than ever once the little one is born.'

'My darling, you need not worry, I will tackle this on my own. You just watch me.'

An hour later Daniel picked up the phone and spoke to Melissa on reception. 'Can you ask Fischer to meet us back in the boardroom. Tell him we have made up our minds.'

Alice looked at him in surprise and shook her head. 'Surely we need to discuss it a little further. Are you not rushing in?'

'Alice, can you compare one and five? I can, and you know what I get?' Alice remained silent, so he continued. 'The same old no brainer. Why waste the rest of the day stuck in this stuffy place, when it is such an obvious choice?'

Fischer and the five suits looked enquiringly at the couple as they walked into the boardroom and settle back into their chairs.

'You came to a quick conclusion.' Fischer looked at them with raised eyebrows. 'Are you sure you don't need more time? You *do* have the rest of the day.'

'Uncle Harry only gave us a day. And that suggests to me he already knew what my answer would be. Why waste any more time deciding on the obvious?'

'Yes, but the folder we gave you would have taken at least four hours to read. You have taken just a quarter of that...'

'You may have all day Mister Fischer, but I have a life to live. And to be quite honest, with five million in the bank in five years' time, I want to start enjoying our lives now.'

He stood abruptly, startling the suits around the table.

'Thank you all. We will be in touch.' He paused. 'Oh, and Harvey, will we see you on the next ride.'

Harvey smiled back at him. 'Unfortunately, no. I will not be permitted to cycle in the group any longer. It would be deemed to be a conflict of interest.'

'Really?' Alice exclaimed. 'You cannot be serious.'

Daniel was perplexed. 'Everything appears to be in conflict. What are you scared of?'

'There is a lot of information that we are not permitted to share with you,' Fischer replied. 'We are just doing the job of work as instructed. Now is there anything further you would like to discuss?'

'No thanks. Not unless there is more money.' Daniel tugged on Alice's arm. 'I think we are done here for now.'

Marching out and onto the sidewalk, Daniel let out a great whoop of joy.

Chapter 6
The Property Agents

Soon after arriving at work the following Monday, Daniel received a call from Alice.

'I have great news.'

'You sound excited,' he replied, as he glanced towards the meeting room where his team waited for his first weekly briefing.

'Well,' she paused, building to a climax, 'it's about Manor House.' He could detect the excitement bubbling out of her, and imagined her with a broad smile and nervous expression he knew so well. 'You did tell me to wait, but I spoke to the Agents and asked them if they would consider a lower offer. They in turn spoke to the current owners... and when they called back a few minutes ago said they were willing to negotiate a reduction. I can't believe it; the house may well be within our grasp.'

'That's just brilliant news,' he replied.

The Agents, who had all but given up on any prospect of a sale, had not even bothered to clean the 'for sale' sign that stood near the towpath. It was old, partially illegible, covered in a mouldy green film of moss, and about to topple over.

The couple had discussed how they would bargain. Which was obviously what they had been steered to do. They knew there was everything to lose if they failed. There were insufficient funds to pay the full asking price and if they failed to secure Manor

House, the only remaining option would be a brand new one million Euro house. And not forgetting that the legal team of suits handling the estate would be following up with their own audit and due diligence report on their negotiating skills.

At this stage it all had to do with the later part of the first clause in the will. How they negotiated on price and managed the transaction. If the executors calculated they had not bargained hard enough, the difference would have to made up by the couple from their own funds.

They discussed Clause One and guessed that Uncle Harry had wanted them to get totally engrossed in the sale and make certain for themselves there were no hidden clauses. Bargain the best deal, spend his hard-earned cash wisely, cross all the T's and dot all the I's. If they screwed up, then they would only have themselves to blame.

Daniel could hear a distant voice from beyond the grave.

'It is what some of the younger generation lack nowadays, taking responsibility for their own actions.'

The only bit of information Alice had gleaned from the agents head office when she made the initial enquiry was that the house had been vacant for many years, and besides bats, pigeon roosts and a few swallow nests in the eves, the house stood empty and would be ready for occupation once the contract was signed and electricity reconnected.

Priced on the internet at eight million, Alice had felt certain they could get it for less. At a discounted price well below the current eight that would surely impress the legal team. So she had made the follow up call to the Agents and said they were seriously interested, but would only take the next step if they dropped the price to five million.

The agent coughed and spluttered, but said he would talk to the current owners before getting back to her. Two hours later he called back to say that the owner would accept the lower offer.

She called Daniel and after a short while he answered. He was busy allocating his workload to the new team after checking out their capabilities.

'You are a genius,' he replied with a whoop.

And they had an appointment with the agents the following day.

Alice phoned Debbie and told her about the appointment.

'I am so happy for you,' her friend said excitedly.

'Thanks Debs, will you promise to still visit, even though we will be much further away?'

'Of course, Alice. I want our two little ones to grow up together. Which of course means I will always be close by your side.' She hesitated. 'But are you sure you are going to still want to mix with us commoners once you become Lady of Manor House?'

They both laughed and arranged for all four of them to meet up for a few drinks that evening after work.

The beer garden was busy, but they managed to find a table for four away from most of the noise. The smell of grilled sausages and roasted pork set their mouths watering.

'So, what do you guys think?' Daniel asked, after giving them an update.

'It is a hell of a commitment my friend,' Colin replied.

'It is,' Daniel said, pursing his lips and nodding. 'But I am up for it. There is nothing like a challenge to set me on fire.'

'You don't need a challenge.' Debbie chipped in. 'Everything sets you on fire.'

She could see his face flush and was right. Every shadow that crossed his path was a challenge, and he was far too quick to react.

'A house and a promotion all within weeks, congratulations,' Colin chipped in, keen to change the subject.

'Thanks,' Daniel replied, although his thoughts were elsewhere.

'I was up for that position as well,' Colin reminded him.

Daniel smiled and winked at his friend. 'Sorry old pal. But don't worry, I will always be there for you.'

Colin had seen how distracted the new Junior Manager had become lately, and doubted there would be much support coming his way, if any at all.

'How will you fit in all the cycling, weekends away and socialising now you have this new management role?' he asked.

'Easy,' Daniel replied self-confidently. He sneaked a quick look at Debbie and saw her watching him. He winked and blew her a kiss. 'I have to be on fire guys. Guns blazing while I do up the house. Working most evenings and the odd weekend, while leaving the rest of the time managing the office, being with the family, and playing out with you guys.'

'So long as it doesn't get in the way of our friendship,' Debbie clutched hold of Alice's arm. 'I don't know what I would do if we drifted apart.'

'That will never happen,' Daniel declared. 'I promise you.'

Debbie was more concerned about staying in touch with Alice than drifting away from him. But there was no way she was ever going to admit that.

When Alice searched the record of the deeds on the internet, she saw that the house had been bought and sold twice in quick succession, always selling for a lower price than that paid by the previous owner. Then the house had stood empty for a long period of time.

The most recent value of the house when it last sold was slightly over seven million, and it made the acceptance of their recent offer a genuine bargain.

'Do we need to be worried?' she asked when he arrived home.

'Some people just cannot hack it, can they?' he replied, turning to Alice with a self-confident smile.

'Tomorrow is our big day. We get to see the agents and arrange a viewing. I can't wait.' She said with a nervous chuckle.

There was nothing particularly funny about the situation, but there was a lot to be nervous about.

Chapter 7
The Agents

Waking up, it felt like they had hangovers. Not from having drunk too much, as Alice had not touched a drop since discovering she was pregnant. They were suffering from lack of sleep and over excitement.

The previous evening had been spent in a high-octane environment of excitement and anticipation. Arriving back from the beer garden, they showered and collapsed on their bed naked. Alice tried to settle, while he traced his finger over the growing presence of little Harry. To be aptly named after Uncle Harry in a deserved show of respect for the old man's generosity.

'What's that?' Thinking he could detect movement; he held his hand firmly on the bump. 'There,' he added, 'I felt him again.'

Alice laughed. 'It's all the excitement. He must be able to feel it.'

Daniel settled back and thought about his future. Watching his son grow up and playing football with him in the garden. Then as soon as the five-year term was up, they wouldn't have a worry in the world and could go cycling. Father and son together, riding side by side.

Getting up early the following morning, they ran through a quick schedule for the day while he demolished a bowl of corn flakes. He grabbed his backpack on the way out.

'I promise to be home before three.'

Alice had taken the day off. There was a lot to do in preparation for their visit to the agents, and the appointment was at four that afternoon.

Holding each other close they looked into one another's eyes and smiled before he turned and headed for the door.

'I love you,' she called after him.

'Love you more Alice,' he shouted back.

'Daniel!' she called out, louder than she meant to.

He paused in the foyer. 'What my darling?'

'I feel so excited, but nervous at the same time.'

She felt awkward and wished she had not raised it, but her mind had gone through so many emotional rollercoasters over the past month. Having suffered with serious bouts of morning sickness, she found the sudden changes unsettling. It was just all too much. Too many things were happening at once.

He retraced a few steps. 'Nervous?' he asked.

'Yes, nervous. I am obviously extremely excited about our sudden windfall, but extremely nervous that it may change us. We have such a lovely peaceful life, full of fun and days out with friends. I would just hate any of it to change... that's all.'

'Well, it won't,' he replied reassuringly. 'With little Harry on the way and our own house, we will have all the security we need and a great start in life.' He put his arms out. 'Now come here and stop worrying.'

He gave her a gentle hug and then raced for the lift as the doors slid open.

She stepped back into the apartment, looked around at the state of the room and sighed. Daniels clothes lay strewn all over the place. His iPad lay open on the couch, while she could hear his mobile phone ringing from somewhere amongst the debris. When she looked across the open plan living area it looked like a bomb had gone off.

The front door suddenly flung open.

'My phone and iPad,' he shouted in an urgent tone and scuttled back in. 'Have you seen them Alice? Bloody hell, I am already late for our departmental review meeting.'

He only managed to locate his phone by ringing it on Alice's mobile and following the sound. Then had to burrow deep into a heap of clothing he had worn over the previous week.

'Can you try and keep a little tidier. The apartment is looking like a rubbish tip.'

'Life is too short Alice. We just don't have enough time. Anyway, life is for living,' he added as he gathered up his electronic aids before racing back out again. 'See you at three,' he shouted as the lift doors slid closed. 'Love you'.

'Love you too,' she shouted at two stainless steel panels, waited a further few seconds to make sure he was well on his way before adding, 'you untidy lummox.'

The agent in the Central Berlin property sales office was surprised when Alice had initially made contact. They had not received any interest in the building for well over a year. Then when she had called and asked for a discount, the owners had apparently jumped at Five million. She got the distinct impression the current owners were desperate to get rid of the place... and quickly.

Then the salesman they met at the local branch was downright rude when the couple turned up on bicycles, wearing their old cycling kit and trainers. The sub-branch had obviously not been informed by Head Office of any details other than a short email and request for a viewing. Young Helmut had been expecting someone wealthy... an older man in a suit, with his wife on his arm... an expensive car parked outside, with an aid in attendance.

After objecting to having their bicycles chained to the shopfront railing, Helmut made them move them to a bike stand further down the street. When they returned, he looked them up and down and asked with a sneer.

'I take it you have seen the price of the house?'

66

Although they knew that first impressions were often made on appearance, they had not quite anticipated the reception they received.

Helmut coughed. He had been waiting patiently for an answer. 'Any idea how much it is on the market for?' He repeated.

'Five million, I guess?' Daniel replied, raising his eyebrows enquiringly.

Helmut laughed. Not a jovial sound, but a mocking chuckle that went straight to the red button in Daniel's head. Having some upstart mocking him was like tickling a hungry lion under the nose with a feather. His face turned red, then crimson as he looked from the agent to a smirking woman sat behind a nearby desk.

'Something amusing you?' Daniel asked with a tilt of his head, before turning to Alice, 'Should we try another estate agent? These clowns would be better off in a fucking circus.'

Undeterred, Alice turned back to the young man. 'Have you got a boss?'

Before he could answer, she saw a door with 'Manager' imprinted on a brass plaque. Not waiting for him to reply, she strode over and rapped on the solid door.

'Come in,' came a relaxed voice.

The elderly man sitting behind his desk smiled at her as she entered. Daniel followed, while Helmut did his best to keep up, suddenly appearing a little anxious while chewing on his lower lip.

The Manager took on a look of surprise. 'Can I help you?'

'Yes you can. I am Alice Somersby, and this is my husband Daniel. We have an appointment, arranged by your city center office, to discuss the possible purchase of Manor House.'

Looking past the couple and at Helmut, who remained standing on the threshold, he raised his eyebrows questioningly.

'They do Sir,' Helmut responded. 'The appointment has been scheduled for four this afternoon. They are a little early... I was going to let you know when they arrived.'

'Why was I not informed before?'

'You were out Sir and when you...'

'Can I help you then?' The Manager turned back to Alice.

He did not want it advertised that he had been out for most of the day shopping and looked rather uncertainly at the couple in front of him.

Alice took a step closer. 'Do you know of a Real Estate and Conveyancing firm in Berlin called JJ Fischer and Partners?'

'I have heard of them,' he replied confidently. 'Who hasn't?'

'Well, we are looking at buying this house.' She handed over a sales leaflet with a photo and description of the property downloaded from the internet. 'And Mister Fischer is in a position to elaborate on the extent of our funds. Your Agent here,' she turned to Helmut, 'appears to find it amusing that two young people such as us might be enquiring after such an expensive property.'

The Manager looked flustered. Caught during a peaceful time of his day. A time he normally spent catching up on local news, sipping on a cup of coffee whilst keeping an eye on the large wall clock and thinking of going home.

'Here is his number.' Alice passed over a business card. 'Can you call him?'

'And you are?'

'Interested in buying that house,' Daniel cut in, pointing at the sales leaflet. 'My wife has already introduced us. Everyone in this building appears to be either stupid, deaf…, or both.'

The Manager looked at the card and raised his eyebrows. The insult had gone straight over his head. Anybody with any clout in the estate agency business knew of JJ Fischer and Partners. This young couple even had one of their business cards, and it made him sit up and reach for his phone.

He punched the numbers, then leaned back in his tilting chair as he waited for an answer. Fidgeting nervously, he glanced up at Daniel, then at Alice and towards the doorway where Helmut remained leaning against the doorframe. He then looked back down and studied the card in front of him as light music and a recorded message told him he was now second in the queue. The sales leaflet he glanced at had a picture of Manor House and a price tag of eight million Euros.

Alice noticed the young salesman was still wearing an arrogant smirk, but his darting eyes gave away a sudden realisation that he may have just made a big mistake.

The Manager suddenly sat forward. 'Hello, Herr Fischer please?' He put the phone on speaker, so they could follow the conversation.

'Who may I say is calling?' asked the receptionist politely.

The couple immediately recognised her voice.

'Herr Khune,' the Manager replied confidently.

There was silence for a second, before the couple heard another familiar voice.

'Fischer here.'

'Good afternoon Herr Fischer, this is Herr Khune from Berlin Real Estates. I have a young couple with me called....'

'Who did you say you were?' Fischer asked.

'Herr Khune, from Berlin Real Estates.'

'Never heard of you or your company,' Fischer replied impatiently.

'You haven't? Well we have been trading for about twenty years, and I can assure you we are one of the top two hundred in the city.' A brief silence followed. 'As I was about to say Herr Fischer, I have a young couple with me...'

He looked up with a questioning look.

'Daniel Somersby,' Daniel reminded him impatiently.

'Daniel Somersby,' repeated Khune, 'and he wants to buy an expensive house... and has asked...'

'I know the couple and am aware they were going to see an agent today. What price is Manor House on the market for?'

'Eight million... it says so on the sales brochure...' he stuttered, then paused as Helmut passed him an email the receptionist had received earlier from their head office with the discounted price.

'Not the brochure price you fool,' Fischer barked over the phone. 'I want to know what price you are prepared to sell it to them for?'

'I was just getting to that Her Fischer. Our Head office has very generously discounted the price to five. I have it on an email right here in front of me.'

'What? You must be joking,' Fischer roared.

Herr Khune spluttered, saw a note on the bottom of the message from the Head Office Manager and smiled. 'I think we can safely say we can negotiate it down to four, Herr Fischer,' he hastily added in a rather subservient tone.

'They are important clients of mine,' Fischer growled. 'Treat them badly and I will have your head.'

'Yes, but of course, Herr Fischer.'

'Good day then.'

'I am sorry to have bothered you Herr Fischer, and nice to speak to you, maybe someday…'

But Fischer had hung up. There was nothing but a bleeping sound coming from the phone. Daniel looked at Alice with an impressive smirk, and thought of Fischer with renewed respect.

Khune slowly replaced the handset and stood up. He had been told by someone recently that nobody messed with JJ Fischer and Partners and he knew to tread carefully.

'Please have a seat.' He waved in the general direction of two chairs, before addressing the young man at the door. 'Helmut. Coffee, tea and biscuits for our guests, and snap to it man.'

Daniel excused himself and headed for the toilet. As he walked past the kitchen, he stuck his head into the room. Helmut looked up.

'Snap to it, dumb fuck,' Daniel growled.

Helmut looked back at the kettle and pretended not to hear. He had only recently moved jobs after an unsuccessful career elsewhere, and valued his new placement more than anything. Besides, the commission on this one sale alone would be equal to double his annual salary.

They arranged to view the house two days later, when they could both take time off work.

'So, you are both still working?' Khune enquired.

'Of course, yes,' Daniel confirmed. 'We are both fully employed, and after the child is born Alice will go straight back to work.'

Khune's gaze drifted over the small bump made more evident by the tight lycra cycling top. 'Congratulations Miss Somersby.' Then turning to Daniel. 'Herr Fischer has indicated you have sufficient funds to buy the house in question...' He looked down at the leaflet. 'I take it you are aware of the problems associated with the property.'

'We see it has been bought and sold a few times,' Daniel conceded. 'It used to be in the family many years ago.'

'Ah, so, you will be bringing it back into the family.' Khune replied with an ingratiating smile.

'Do you know why it exchanged so rapidly?' Alice asked.

'Tennant problems, I believe,' Khune replied.

'Well we will not have any tenants,' Alice said.

'No tenants,' Daniel repeated.

'Apparently there were unusual circumstances relating to Manor House. Very unusual,' Khune persisted.

The couple looked at each other and in unison raised their arms, and started swaying from side to side singing an old Tom Jones song. 'It's not unusual to be loved by anyone.' They stopped, laughed, and looked back at a bewildered Khune.

'Sorry, carry on, you were saying?' Alice urged.

'The unusual circumstances surrounding the house..., was due to a lodger, or tenant that would not vacate the property. There were also rumours of Manor House being haunted.'

'The house is empty,' Daniel replied. 'I can assure you. We have cycled past a few times now and have not seen a soul, and we do not believe in ghosts. So no, it is not a problem *we* will be facing.'

There was a momentary pause as Khune cleared his throat. 'May I ask how a young couple such as yourselves can afford this substantial property?'

'We are bringing it back into the family, as you have just indicated.' Daniels freckles darkened. 'And to be quite honest, it is none of your business.' Then added curtly. 'So now that you have been reassured by Fischer that we can afford the place, can we finalise arrangements for a viewing?'

Khune looked like he had been slapped across the face with a wet rag, but quickly recovered. 'Certainly Sir, any time to suit your good selves.'

An embarrassed looking Helmut returned with a tray of teacups and biscuits. He placed the tray on the table, doing his best to avoid looking in their direction. Then, as he turned to hand over a cup to Alice, Daniel moved his foot ever so slightly and caught his ankle. The young assistant lurched forward, crashed into the hat stand, and came to rest on the floor.

'Helmut, try and control yourself, you oaf.' Khune reprimanded the young man. 'Now get your diary, the Somersby's want to view the house in two days' time.'

Daniel stood up, ready to leave. 'Eight O'clock at the front gate, Helmut... and don't be late.'

They walked out, hand in hand, arms swaying and with a spring in their step, singing. 'It's not unusual to be loved by, da, da, da, da, da.'

Khune shuffled a few papers around on his desk before deciding to give Fischer a call back. He had never experienced anything as remotely unsettling as this last visit, and felt the need to make a follow up call.

'Herr Fischer, please excuse me for calling back. I know you are a busy man, but the young Somersby couple have just left, and I am extremely concerned about them. They appear quite confident in an area I take it they have no experience at all.' There was silence on the other end. 'Are you still there, Herr Fischer?'

'Yes, I am, however I am not in a position to intervene. I am acting on behalf of a deceased client and have clear instructions as to what I can or cannot say. And I am most certainly not in a position to direct these two young people as to what they can or cannot do.'

'But this house...'

He was cut short. 'Herr Khune, I have just told you, I am not in a position to interfere or discuss the business matters relating to these two people, other than to tell you they have access to sufficient funds in a trust account. If they want to buy the house, then so be it.' There was a pause. 'Just to be clear on a related matter. I, or my firm will not be conveyancing this transaction. The young couple you have just met will be handling their own affairs personally or through a third party. The way they decide to proceed will be entirely at their own discretion.'

'But why are you not handling it Herr Fischer? You are by far the most reputable legal conveyancing firm in the city. It makes no sense at all.'

'I have my instructions and that is that,' the Solicitor was clearly getting irritable. 'Now... if we are finished Herr Khune, I bid you farewell.'

The Agency Manager replaced his handset and sat staring at the wall for a long while. He hardly noticed the young sales assistant, as he came and went, clearing away teacups and saucers and then proceeding to mop the floor where some tea and sugar had spilled.

'How can I stop them buying the house?' he said quietly.

Helmut stopped mopping, realised his boss was talking to himself and crept silently out of the room. Taking one last glance back at his Manager, who sat with a strange expression of disbelief on his face, he closed the door.

Then again, thought Khune, the market has been dormant for a while, and the commission from this sale alone would put their subbranch back into profit. There would also be a sizable chunk of commission coming his way if the sale went through. Who was he to interfere, he reasoned? He had tried his best to warn them.

Then the image of the arrogant young red headed man with an obvious bad temper returned, and he smiled.

Their funeral, he concluded, as he looked through the small glass panel on the door and watched Helmut, who had moved across the office and was doing his best to chat up the young girl on the front desk.

He just could not believe anyone in their right mind would touch Manor House with a barge pole. The note appended to the bottom of the email from his head office had said 'Be prepared to drop the price to four million. Whatever you do, just get rid.'

Chapter 8
The Viewing

Helmut looked nervously around as he approached Manor House from where he had parked his small car. A bunch of keys jangled as they swung on a steel loop dangling from one hand. He clutched a folder in the crook of his other arm.

'Good morning Sir, Madam,' he greeted them respectfully.

Standing in a tight embrace, it was obvious they were a couple very much in love. Keeping each other warm as the cold morning air lifted off the Spree and drifted up to where they stood. The smell of log burning fires mingled with the mist and gave them the first taste of winter.

'Morning Helmut,' they echoed.

'Mister Khune will be joining us a little later. He was called off at the last minute on some urgent business and sends his apologies.'

'That's no problem Helmut, so long as we can view the house,' Alice replied.

'I am sure you will do a grand job,' Daniel added.

Helmut looked nervously at him, waiting for the punch line, but it never came. Alice had persuaded him to ease up on the salesman.

The young man certainly appeared to view them in a different light on this cold and frosty day. He smiled and nodded at every opportunity, pleased to be on an even footing.

Standing in front of the ornately cast steel gates they could see the curve of the drive as it wound its way around towards the front entrance. The anticipation of going in and seeing the interior of Manor House was generating a lot of excitement, as Daniel held Alice back and watched Helmut wrestle with the lock and chain.

Daniel suggested they walk around the grand entrance. There was access through the various shrubs and plants that formed the boundary, while Helmut insisted it was not the proper way to enter a stately home. Then the lock sprung open and fell to the ground.

'First one to the front door is Lord of the Manor,' Daniel shouted as the steel gates screeched on rusty hinges.

'You cheat,' Alice shouted. 'You forget, I am carrying our little one.'

He slowed and waited for her to catch up. He was full of energy, and as he looked back, he saw a fresh challenge wandering along the gravel path.

'Come on Helmut, we want to get there today. Why don't you race me to the front door?'

'If you like,' an embarrassed looking Helmut replied, as he loped off after him.

Alice doubled up with laughter as the two men ran down the circular drive. Daniel took a short cut through a rose garden and got there first, leaving red rose petals scattered over the weed filled beds of soil.

'What took you so long Helmut?' he jibed at the younger man.

'Sorry Mister Somersby, I didn't want to run through your garden.'

'My garden?' He turned to Alice as she calmly walked up to where they stood. 'Already Lord of Manor House, with my own garden.'

Turning, he ran back through the same garden and trampled a few more bushes as he went.

Alice shouted at him. 'Stop being a vandal. I want to look at the house, not mess around playing games.'

The broad sandstone stairway was framed by two robust looking pillars that guided them up to the front door. It was an impressive looking entrance by any standards.

Helmut had the brass handles firmly in his grip. It was a large double door, big enough to allow a small car through and snagged at first. Then emitted a loud screech on rusted hinges, before suddenly swinging easily open.

Daniel took hold of Alice and gently lifted her so that she was cradled in his arms. He was not that strong, but this was high adrenaline stuff and he was still riding that wave.

'Over the threshold my sweetest and into our new home.'

'Don't be silly, put me down. We haven't even looked around yet.'

Helmut in the meanwhile had walked into the entrance hall and drawn back the long blinds that covered the floor to ceiling windows. Dust devils danced in the sunlight as bright rays streamed in and lit up the room. It was a breath-taking sight.

'This is as big as our apartment,' Alice gasped, holding her arms outstretched.

They both laughed. There were doors either side, but the large ones in front of them were the ones they headed for. Daniel had flashbacks to when he was young. The house had appeared much larger then, but it had been a long time ago and his memory was vague.

Internal doors swung open easily, revealing the downstairs reception hall. A huge room dominated by a twin spiral staircase, with a large crystal chandelier hanging in the center. Sparsely furnished with white sheets covering each piece like ghostly shapes they would have looked perfect in a horror film.

Alice stood rooted to the spot as she took in the magnitude of the place. Hollywood produced films showing old stately manors with similar rooms and this would have given any one of them a run for their money. The couple had never in their wildest dreams ever thought they might be viewing such a large home, with the possibility that one day it might be theirs.

'According to local history,' Helmut started, 'they used to have regular balls in the house. This room was used as a reception room while a small orchestra played music in the Sitting Room. Then the hosts would make a grand entrance by slowly walking down the spiral stairways as groomsmen fussed around and cleared the way. Guests would stand around sipping champagne, while others danced.'

'How many guests would they have?' Alice asked.

'This inner entrance hall used to hold up to a hundred guests at a time, while maids served drinks and snacks from the kitchen on our right.

'Helmut, just to remind you that this used to be a relative's home. I have been here before and can remember those occasions.'

He had never been anywhere near the house when a function had taken place. His father had been barred from Manor House and he had not been there since Francis had gone missing. But he was not going to let Helmut know that.

The floor was covered with a mosaic of coloured square and triangular tiles while the walls were all wood panelled or painted white. Dark images remained where large pictures had once adorned the walls.

'Where would you like to start?' Helmut asked.

'Ground floor first,' Alice replied.

'There are two floors above us,' Helmut explained. 'Plus an extensive loft area where the staff used to sleep.'

'How did they get up there? 'she asked.

'There is an old sealed off doorway and stairwell to the rear of the kitchen which was used by the staff and for deliveries.'

'It was sealed off when I was here as a child,' Daniel added. 'I think it has been like that for a long time.'

Helmut pointed out a passage leading off to his right. 'We can look at this area first, if you like?'

'You lead the way,' Daniel replied. 'A quick tour to remind me of where everything is. Then we will most likely want to have a closer look on our own, once I have regained some of my bearings,'

They entered a passageway and came to the first set of doors to their right.

'Kitchen and Larder room,' Helmut indicated as he opened a double set of doors.

Alice was in awe as she looked around in amazement. 'The kitchen is so huge.'

'If you think this room is big, look at the size of the larder room.' Daniel's voice echoed out from the empty space, as he stood within the doorway of an adjacent room. 'Big enough to live in. I remember Francis and I playing in here as small boys.'

'Larder room?' Alice questioned.

'Pantry,' Helmut explained.

There were floor to ceiling shelving on two of the walls and a set of full-length cupboards on the third.

'I don't like the feel of this room,' Alice said, as she scuttled further into the kitchen. 'It smells of something rancid.'

'Maybe a dead mouse,' Daniel speculated.

'Close the door please Helmut, it gives me the creeps,' she urged and backed away. 'It feels like a fridge in there, I don't like it.'

A repetitive thumping could be heard from somewhere within the core of the building and made them all turn around.

'What was that?' Daniel asked.

Helmut reopened the door and peered in, but there was nothing there to indicate where the noise had come from.

'Old houses creak,' Daniel said, and closed the door as Helmut walked out. 'Come, we still have a lot to look at.'

They returned to the passageway, where Helmut opened a door to his left.

'The Dining room,' he announced.

The room stood bare, except for a large central chandelier that dominated the ceiling above where guests would have been served along a table with seating for thirty people or more.

Helmut continued to open doors to the left and right, revealing a second boot room, cloak room and a large panelled study. The library at the end of the corridor was the most impressive. Not because of its size, but notably because of the thousands of books still stacked along the oak panelled shelves. Daniel had vague memories of seeing the library, but he had been a young boy then and stared in amazement.

'Look at all those books. Almost as many as in our local library,' Alice stood looking around the room in astonishment.

'They were here when I last visited,' Daniel added. 'But when I was here, we were banned from the room and only sneaked a quick look inside when nobody was watching. I think they were books collected by my Grandfather after the war.'

Floor to ceiling oak panelling gave way to row upon row of shelves, with every book categorised and placed neatly in chronological order. It was a very impressive sight indeed.

'Look, there is even a sliding ladder that travels around the room so that you can get to wherever you want,' Alice said, clearly impressed.

'Not much to renovate in here other than to take out the books, varnish the oak panelling, and then replace them,' Daniel said with a smile.

They walked back through the Hall to investigate the only room on the opposite side of the ground floor. It was a large stately room, previously used as a lounge. A few pieces of furniture remained, covered in white sheeting.

'The sitting room,' Helmut announced, as Alice stood looking around in awe.

'Wow, this place is so big,' she turned to see why Daniel was so quiet. But he was nowhere to be seen.

'Where are you?' she called out.

Helmut had not seen him since they had stood looking up at the chandelier on their way through.

'Daniel,' she called again, then turned to Helmut. 'Where did he go?'

One of the white sheets moved and lifted as it came towards them. Helmut ran screaming from the room, while Alice walked up and gave it a kick.

'Ouch. What the fuck,' Daniel shouted, as he pulled the sheet from over his head and rubbed at his shin.

'Don't bloody scare me you fool. Do you want me to lose the baby?'

'Sorry Alice. Where is Helmut?'

'Guess?'

'Helmut,' Daniel called. 'You can come back…, the ghost has gone.'

They finished touring the ground floor, then moved up one level to the first floor. There was another library, much smaller than the one on the ground floor, billiard room, various small day rooms and three guest rooms.

The second floor had twelve bedrooms, interspersed with bathrooms and toilets. They only bothered to look in a few of them before climbing up to the loft area.

The air was musty and smelled of cooked cabbage. They could not quite identify the source of the odour but put it down to damp, and the house being shut up for years.

'The stairway from the second floor to the loft looks like it has been an addition,' Alice remarked.

'The rear internal stairway was sealed off by the original owners, who had these internal ones up to the loft area fitted,' Helmut replied.

'I remember they had a cook, his son and a cleaner who lived up here,' Daniel added. 'They used to get to their rooms via the same stairway as Uncle Harry and Auntie Wilma. Which, looking back was quite a strange concept.'

Helmut had been keeping a wary eye on Daniel. When they were back downstairs, he asked. 'Would you like to see anything else?'

Alice felt a shiver race down her spine and drew closer to Daniel. 'It feels spooky,' she whispered.

'Just not lived in,' he replied.

Alice felt a draft of cold air. 'Did we leave the front door open?'

Helmut checked, but it was still closed. 'Want to look again?' he repeated.

Daniel looked at Alice.

She gave him a weary shake of the head. 'I am shattered. And to be honest I have seen as much as I want to.'

'Me too,' Daniel replied, 'but I would like one more look at the kitchen.'

Trooping back into the spacious room, with its large coal burning stove, they stood waiting to see what had made Daniel want to return.

'I don't like the fact that there is no view of the outside garden or countryside from the kitchen,' he said as he paced the room. 'Whichever way you look it is obscured by timber fencing just meters from the windows. I don't recall it being like this when I was young.'

Alice walked from window to window. She got close to the glass and peered out at an angle, but all she could see was another section of timber fence.

'So, what do you think?' Helmut enquired.

'There are plenty of views to be had from the rest of the house, it's not a problem,' Daniel shrugged his shoulders. 'And don't forget the previous owners had servants who ran the kitchen. They were not bothered about the view the cook and maids had.' He turned to Alice. 'If it worries you, we can always look at removing the fence panels.'

'Makes sense,' she agreed, then shrieked.

Both men jumped at the shrill sound and looked at her. She stood pointing at the larder room. The door stood wide open.

'Helmut, you shut that door when we left the room, I saw you do it.'

Daniel walked across and swung the heavy door shut. It closed with a solid clunk.

'I couldn't have closed it properly,' Helmut replied uncertainly. 'Is there anything else you want to look at?'

'I tell you what,' Daniel smiled at the young salesman. 'If you play one game of hide and seek, we will call it a day.'

Helmut looked at him with a weary gaze of mild disbelief. He had never experienced anything like this. When at College they had covered every angle of the Estate Agency business, and this game had most certainly not been in his curriculum.

He emitted a false laugh. 'Very funny Mister Somersby.'

'Come on Daniel,' Alice urged, 'I want to go home.'

Daniel ignored her. 'No, I am not joking Helmut. Just one game and then we leave. Come Alice, we will go into the entrance hall and count to a hundred and then look for him.'

'I am tired and want to go,' she tugged at his arm.

Helmut looked at Daniel, who raised his eyebrows and nodded, indicating for him to go, while he steered Alice from the room.

'One, two, three.' He started to count out loud. When he got to twenty, he turned to her. 'Come, let's get out of here, but quietly now.'

He sniggered as they crept out and ran down the drive, to where their bicycles were chained to a lamp post.

'Was that necessary?' she asked.

He doubled over with laughter, while she looked at him in utter disbelief.

'What do you think of the house?' he asked once they had set off.

'Love it,' she replied. 'But if we go ahead, we will have to find Helmut first and move him out.'

'Of course, yes,' he sniggered. 'Uncle's fourth clause would put us in breach if Helmut were found to still be there. Remember, no lodgers allowed.'

It made Alice laugh, and her bicycle wobbled as she found the whole idea mildly amusing.

After a short while Daniel took his phone from his pocket and called Helmut's mobile. He tried a dozen times before it was finally answered.

'Helmut is that you?'

There was a muffled sound, as if Helmut were talking through a towel. This made him break out in fits of laughter again and he nearly fell off his bike.

He shouted into his phone. 'We have left the house Helmut. You can come out now, we were only having a bit of fun.'

There was no response, but as far as he was concerned, he had let Helmut know it was a hoax and it was up to him to leave whenever he wanted.

That evening they sat snuggled together on their couch looking at a computer screen. Where they were busy flicking through dozens of photos taken on their mobile phones.

'Shit, but the place is massive,' he said as they came to the last slide.

'And we have only seen some of the rooms,' she replied. 'It *is* fantastic.'

'A lot of work though,' he added as he scrolled through and pointed at some of the detail.

'Why didn't we consider the modern house then?' she asked. 'Brand new, with no work to be done, and no strange sounds or smells.'

'Ignore the smells Alice, and as for the choice? No contention and a no brainer.' he replied. 'Manor House will be worth twice its current value if we sell in five years' time. We could retire as multi-multimillionaires and live a life of pure luxury. Why have something for a fraction of that money and then still have to wait another five years before it is ours?'

Alice nodded and smiled. 'Do you think Helmut will hold it against us?' she asked.

'No, I think by now he would have realised we are a couple of fruit bats,' he replied with a smile.

After opening another beer, he turned up the music. 'Time to celebrate. I think we have just visited our new home.'

'Whoopee,' Alice shouted, as she gently danced around the sitting area, careful not to knock into furniture or fall over.

They had ordered a Thai takeout a half hour earlier, and after getting out trays, they started banging their chopsticks on an ornament that resembled a kettle drum. Then they heard the doorbell chime and a voice calling out. It was a voice carrying a lot of authority and sounded threatening.

'Is that the neighbours?' Alice called out over the loud music.

'No, but if it's that bloody delivery guy, he's getting far too demanding. It's high time I kicked his arse,' Daniel shouted back.

He took his time and had almost reached the door when he heard a second shout. This time he could clearly hear what was being said.

'It is the Police, open up or we will break down your door.'

He turned back to Alice and shouted. 'Turn down the music, I think the police are at the door.'

The following loud explosive sound made Daniel jump sideways as timber and pieces of their front door flew in every direction.

Chapter 9
Arrested

Their little party ended abruptly when confronted by two armed policemen carrying tasers, their laser beams resting tiny red dots on Daniel's shirt.

'Do not move, or we will fire,' shouted the larger of the two officers.

A third policeman stumbled in carrying a battering ram. He had obviously been the one who had just demolished their front door.

'What the fuck is going on?' Daniel shouted.

Alice fell back onto the couch, her eyes wide with fear. Daniel lost his bluster within seconds and raised his arms high in the air. He looked petrified.

The officer in charge pulled the plug on the music and looked at him. 'Are you Daniel Somersby?'

'I am, but what the hell is going on? You have just smashed our door in. Is it the neighbours? Were they complaining about the noise?'

'Mister Somersby, you are going to accompany us to the police station.' It was clearly an instruction, not a question.

The second officer walked up and took hold of his arm. Alice was advised to remain at the apartment and not go out. They left in a flurry, leaving her barely able to speak, in tears and trying to make sense of what had just happened.

As soon as her nerves settled, she picked up the phone and called Debbie.

Colin answered in a sleepy voice. 'Debbie's phone.' Then he saw who the call had come from. 'Sorry Alice..., didn't realise it was you..., are you OK?'

'I know it's late Colin, but I didn't know who else to call. Daniel has just been arrested.'

'Arrested?'

'It is a long story, but I am scared and wondered if you guys could pop across.'

'Debbie is in the kitchen making a hot chocolate. We'll get dressed and come straight across.'

They only lived in the adjacent tower block, so it was no more than fifteen minutes before the couple walked through the open doorway.

'Did you forget the key?' Colin asked with a gentle smile.

'Colin, this is serious. The police have bashed the door in and arrested Daniel.'

Debbie wrapped her arm round Alice and walked her to the couch. 'Make some coffee Colin, Alice is in a state of shock,' she commanded.

Alice suddenly felt a flood of relief and started crying, and in-between sobs told them the story. Colin and Debbie looked at one another and grimaced. They loved their friends but had warned Daniel on several occasions about taking things too far. Always playing annoying pranks on the cycle team when they were out on a ride.

The interrogation room was small and sparsely furnished with a basic table and four chairs. On a short ledge against the wall sat a recording device, while on the opposite wall a panel of two-way glass resembled a framed mirror. Daniel recognised the layout from various detective films he had watched over the years.

He remained on his own for what felt like hours. He walked around the room, tried the door, and shouted. Eventually three policemen came in. Two sat opposite him, while the third paced the room. He was obviously in charge and looked to be in a foul mood.

'I am allowed one phone call.' Daniel said, recalling what he had seen when a felon was arrested on television.

'You are not under arrest,' the officer replied. 'You can leave at any time you like.'

'Oh, well nice meeting you,' Daniel said and stood up. 'See you guys when my lawyer visits and claims damages for bashing my door in, then handcuffing and abducting me.'

'Sit down,' the officer replied sternly.

The authority in his voice made Daniel drop back onto his chair.

'This will either take a short while to clear up, or as long as you like, depending on how you cooperate. But we need some answers.'

Daniel flushed as he settled back into his chair. 'OK, but tell me what this is all about first?'

'Did you meet up with a Mister Cole this morning to view a house on the banks of the Spree?' the officer asked.

'Mister Cole!' Daniel shot back. 'Who the fuck is Mister Cole?'

'Firstly Mister Somersby, will you refrain from swearing. This is not a game, and if you persist, I will arrest you for contempt. Mister Cole is the estate agent. Do you recall meeting with Helmut Cole for a viewing today?'

'Sorry,' replied a slightly more subdued Daniel. 'I never knew his surname.'

'Then let me ask you once again. Did you meet up and view a house with Mister Helmut Cole today?'

'Yes, we did.'

'When you left the house, where was Mister Cole?'

'Hiding.'

88

'Hiding? Sorry, but can you elaborate.'

'Look, I played a silly joke on him and asked him to hide. You know..., hide and seek? Then we did a runner and left him wherever he was hiding.' He paused. 'Hang on, is Helmut laying charges because we left him in the house?'

'Mister Somersby, I don't think you understand the severity of the situation. Mister Cole was abducted, severely beaten, then gagged, and bound up in a dark room in the very same house you were viewing. He was found seven hours ago after a search party had been called in by his employer.'

'And you think I did it?'

'You were the last people to have been with him, and as far as we can ascertain, nobody else was present.'

The more senior of the men was called out and the remaining two settled back and fixed him with solid stares. Daniel rubbed his head. He was trying desperately to make sense of what was going on.

Looking around the room his attention focused in on the framed glass.

'I know what you are doing,' he shouted at the reflective pane. 'I watch a lot of crime movies on telly.'

He got up and strolled around the room. The officers made no move to stop him. He even thought of dropping his pants and mooning at the reflective window, but thought better of it.

But he would have been wasting his time doing anything. Nobody was at the window. They had gone to the front desk to have a chat with the Manager of the Estate Agency, Mister Khune, who had arrived to make a statement.

A half hour later the officer returned with a cup of hot coffee. He asked his colleagues to leave them alone.

'You're the good cop, aren't you?' Daniel said, once the door had been firmly closed.

'Excuse me?' asked the policeman.

'Good cop, bad cop. I know the routine. The other guys will come back in and kick the shit out of me, make me confess and you will stop them, and give me another cup of coffee.'

The policeman had been up all night and was clearly starting to get irritable. 'We aren't on television Mister Somersby, and this is not a game. My colleague has already told you.'

Then the door opened, and the other police officers returned. They were accompanied by Khune, who settled into the seat opposite him. The Estates Manager looked across with obvious concern.

'Mister Somersby, Helmut was found tied up inside the kitchen larder cupboard and gagged. He has suffered a severe blow to the head and been taken to hospital.' He paused, before asking. 'Tell me, what happened in that house?'

'Look, I have already told these goons here,' he pointed at the police officers opposite him, 'exactly what happened,'

The officers were not warming to Daniel and bristled. The older of the two was hoping he could throw the arrogant young man in a cell for the night, but from what he had just found out at the front desk it was unlikely.

Khune appeared to be taking over the interrogation. 'Tell me in your own time what you know Mister Somersby. Because Helmut has some serious injuries and we need to understand exactly what happened.'

After repeating what he had told the policeman earlier, Khune nodded. He had talked to Fischer just before arriving at the police station and was reassured that Daniel would not have harmed anyone. Yes, he was brash, annoying, loud, and constantly swore, but Fischer had gathered quite a few character references prior to the reading of the will, and Daniel's only redeeming characteristic was that he was not violent.

'Officer, I believe this young man. Now that Helmut has recovered somewhat, he described the attack and said he thought it to have been a much larger man. He also recalled seeing a beard and detected a strange body odour. He said our man here smelled quite fresh in comparison, and---'

90

'I did until these thugs made me sweat,' Daniel interjected.

'Please Mister Somersby, I am trying to give these officers reason to release you,' Khune said irritably, before turning back to the officers. 'He also has flashbacks of hearing a deep sounding voice..., more of a mechanical sound. He said it was not as high pitched and squeaky as this man's voice.'

'He said my voice was what?' Daniel was incensed.

'Shut up Somersby,' Khune snapped. 'We are trying to find out the facts, not listen to you carry on like a child.'

The Estates Manager no longer cared if the house was sold. He no longer cared about the loss of a sizable commission or even upsetting Fischer. He had endured more than enough stress for one day, and wanted nothing more than to go home and climb back into bed.

The door opened and a plain clothed man entered. He spoke quietly to the more senior of the officers before turning to Daniel.

'We apologise Mister Somersby for being a little heavy handed. We have just reviewed some CCTV footage which has enabled us to calculate what time you left Manor House. Helmut said in his statement that he looked at his phone just before he was attacked. If we compare the times, it appears he was set upon about the same time as you and your wife can be seen on CCTV, a good few miles away.'

Daniel was visibly relieved. 'Who attacked him then?' he asked.

'We don't know. It could have been someone who wandered into the grounds and found the front door open.'

Turning to Herr Khune, Daniel asked, 'Could you please apologise to him. It was a cruel trick to play I suppose.'

'You can go now Mister Somersby.' The Senior Officer gestured towards the door. 'But do not go far, you are not out of the woods just yet.'

Colin was waiting in the reception area, where an early ray of sunlight streamed in through the narrow windows.

91

'Come on, let us get you home,' he said. 'Then at least I can get to work.'

'How has Old Sniffer taken it?' Daniel asked.

'Don't even go there,' Colin replied with a shake of his head, as he took Daniel firmly by the arm.

When they arrived back at the apartment, a new door had already been fitted. Alice was calm but still unsettled, while Debbie hoovered up bits of splintered wood from the small reception area.

Daniel told them of his experience in what he referred to as the 'interrogation room' and how Herr Khune had come to his rescue after seeing Helmut in hospital.

'I think you have some apologising to do my mate,' Colin said.

'We did take things a bit far I suppose,' Daniel admitted with a grin.

'Not we,' Alice responded. 'You were the instigator. Now will you please stop being such an idiot?'

Still shaken from his experience, he surprised everyone by taking the criticism on the chin, and promised to visit Helmut in the morning and offer his personal apologies.

The question nobody had asked, was how an intruder knew to look for Helmut in the larder room. To add, Helmut's mobile phone had gone missing, and the young salesman swore that at no time had he received a call from anyone.

Khune had apparently arrived to join the viewing, knowing that he would most likely be too late. But when he saw Helmut's little car still parked down the road and the front gates open, he proceeded down the drive. The front door was closed and he assumed Helmut had taken a stroll along the Spree.

When the young man had still not returned to the office later that day, he called for some help. The police arrived and it was a while before one of the officers heard a tapping sound coming from somewhere near the kitchen.

If it had it not been for Khune's persistence, Helmut would have remained imprisoned, bound, and gagged in the larder room cupboard indefinitely. Helmut had only gained the search party's attention by kicking his heel against a steel pipe.

Chapter 10
The Purchase Agreement

When the purchase agreement arrived a few weeks later, the boxes of documents half-filled their small sitting room. They had been couriered to the apartment block by two men who had taken the best part of an hour to cart them up in the lift and stack them in their small lounge.

'Where do we start?' Alice asked.

'There are so many boxes,' Daniel complained. 'I thought it would come in two or three files at the most.'

He lifted the lid off one of the boxes. It was filled with old plans and smelled of mothballs.

'Just look at all this crap.'

'Nothing is *crap*…, and it all has to be gone through. Were you not at the same meeting as me when Fischer explained everything? Or were you just not listening?'

'Of course I was, but I never expected there to be this amount of stuff to go through.'

He phoned Fischer. The Solicitor was very polite but stern and referred him to clause one A of the will.

'Sorry Mister Somersby, but you have to deal with it yourself, and employ a firm of conveyancing solicitors. Bearing in mind there is no rush and no time constraints mentioned in the will. Take as long as you like, and spend a few thousand getting whatever help you need.'

'But the clock is ticking. The longer we leave it the later we cash in after five years.'

'That is entirely up to you Mister Somersby. We cannot influence you in any way. It is one of the requests your Uncle Harry was quite clear about.'

'How much do you think it would cost to get it done by a company like yours?' Daniel enquired.

'For a property like Manor House?' There was a slight pause before Fischer added. 'I believe the figure would be close to thirty thousand.'

'Sorry, did you just mention three with four zeros?'

'Maybe more, but then if you want my advice, check over the general information yourself and pass anything important over to an external body. That should bring the costs down considerably.'

'Whew, that's more like it.' Daniel sounded relieved. 'Well thanks Mister Fischer, better get moving, it would appear I have a bit of work to do.'

Placing his mobile phone on the side table, he started to pace the room, trying to decide on the most efficient approach. Eventually concluding it would be in their best interests if he took some time off work. It was short notice, but this was important and a priority if he was going to get the clock ticking.

The apartment was strewn with papers, files, and folders, as they divided the work into what they could do themselves and what needed to be scrutinised by a legal entity. They lived in a constant state of chaos and kept losing papers and folders amongst dirty laundry, empty pizza delivery boxes, and cycling gear strewn around from the last time they had been out for a ride.

Most of the folder titles meant nothing to them, but they did their best. Some papers slid behind cushions, under sofas, or found their way in amongst the general debris lying around the room. But by the end of the first week they had a system of sorts worked out and felt that they were at last getting somewhere.

All the documents they were going to review themselves were stacked at one end of the room. Those to be checked by a third party at the other end. A pile in their bedroom consisted of material they considered to be irrelevant. They had their system and it occupied all their spare time, including an extra few days off work to get the job done.

Old Sniffer's voice sounded brittle when Daniel called in.

'You have just been promoted Daniel. Who do you think is managing *your* office of architects?' There was a perceptible pause. '*Me.* That's who's doing your job, while *you* take another unscheduled week off work.'

Feeling exhausted, he mumbled an apology. He found Old Sniffer annoying. There were priorities in life and right now none of them related to anything at the office.

When Colin and Debbie called around, they found their friends had just finished stacking the last storage box against the entrance wall and were dusting themselves down. There were only a couple of folders remaining and then they were done.

Colin informed Daniel that he had been asked to stand in and manage the office. Old Sniffer had sounded tired and irritable, Colin explained. Apparently, the office had been under a lot of pressure of late.

'It's time you came back, I am not sure how much longer you can keep doing this.'

'Get off my back pal,' Daniel reared, then immediately put his arm on Colin's shoulder. 'Sorry, only tired, it's been a tough couple of weeks.'

Alice was just about to say something when Colin took his friend to one side.

'OK Daniel, but we are friends, not enemies. We used to talk all the time, now we don't hear from you from one day to the next. So, we thought we would come around and see if you guys were interested in getting out for a day. Maybe a cycle out to a beer garden. It may just be the sort of distraction you need.'

'That would be capital,' Daniel replied enthusiastically, 'and sorry again for my outburst. Getting away from all this rubbish would be like taking a breath of fresh air.' He spread his arms wide at the chaotic scene. 'Our lives have been taken over by boxes of smelly old paperwork.'

'Daniel are you alright?' Debbie asked.

'Yes, why?'

'You managed to complete a full sentence without swearing.' She turned to Alice, 'I wonder how long that will last?'

Alice shook her head and shrugged.

'Fuck off,' Daniel replied with a smile.

'Not that long then,' Debbie mumbled, as she moved closer to Alice.

The couple promised to get together that weekend with their friends and the biking crowd for a Sunday run, but for now they would remain focused on reviewing the last few folders of information.

They phoned around and received a very reasonable price from a small firm who quoted three thousand Euros to review the bundle as described.

The remaining documents were moved into the lounge where they started their own review. They selected a folder each and started the process.

'Going by these records, it looks like your uncle recovered the property from the bank and then sold it over twenty years ago,' Alice said as she scanned the list of previous owners.

'That makes sense, 'Daniel replied. 'It was around about the time when my naughty father lost the family fortune.' He flushed slightly and the tone in his voice changed. 'Fancy that being raised in front of all those people at the reading of the will.' Then added angrily. 'Bloody disgrace.'

'Calm down,' she replied, and opened a fresh document. 'What have we here? *Disclosure by Seller*?'

'Sounds interesting, let's have a look.'

Reaching for the folder, he settled back and started to scan the index and contents.

'Ahh, as we thought. The house close to the boundary planted some large evergreens when the owners complained to the local authorities about being able to see the run-down Manor.'

He looked down and saw a second item that looked like it might be a problem.

'There is a public right of way down the one side of the property,' he said with a surprised look. 'Between the Manor and the evergreens. That must have been the path Colin and I wandered up.'

Shivering, he recalled the growling sounds and being scared off by some strange animal. He made a mental note to get all the bush and vegetation cleared away from around the house as soon as possible.

'Interesting,' Alice added. 'But nothing there to cause us to change our minds. Neighbours and right of ways are normal. Anyway, I agree with having right of ways. Why shouldn't we all have the freedom to roam where we wish?'

'Not on my land,' he snapped back. 'Nobody roams on my land.'

Alice ignored him as she took hold of the document and flipped a page.

'The next item is a complaint regarding the footpath at the bottom of the garden.'

'The one we cycle on?'

'Yes, the last tenant complained that people were littering or picnicking on their lawn. The local authority suggested they stop cutting the grass and let it go wild, and it appears to have worked.

'Wild is hardly the word for it,' Daniel retorted. 'More like a fucking jungle.'

Alice ignored him; he was far too prickly, and she had no desire for an argument, but maintained her own view. 'I wouldn't object to anyone resting their bums in our garden.'

'No bums in my garden Alice,' he responded sternly, and took possession of the folder once again.

And the list continued. From bats in the loft that were protected, to objections regarding the conversion of the house on the opposite side into luxury apartments. Then one of them caught his eye.

'The Mansion has been vandalised a few times over the years.'

Alice shrugged. 'It's been empty for a while. Is there anything else?'

'No. That covers the main declaration,' he replied.

She reached across, took back the folder and ran an eye down the contents.

'You missed this one about the residents calling the police after they heard strange noises in the house.'

'You can't take any notice of strange noises Alice. Every house has a strange noise at some stage or other.'

'You have also missed this one about the police being called when the owner thought they saw someone in the kitchen. And another incident when their garden was vandalised.'

'All bullshit Alice,' he scoffed.

'What do you mean? These are things we need to investigate before deciding. We haven't gone through half the list of disclosures.'

'Alice, these were isolated incidents that happened years ago. Look at the comments next to most of them. The police could not find any intruders or culprits and blamed drunks and wayward children. The gardens a mess anyway.'

'But shouldn't we be worried then?'

'No. Most likely just an over jealous vagabond who hates the rich and has seen a large property standing empty. I am surprised it's not full of squatters. But not to worry, if there are any I will soon have them kicked out.' He paused and reached across for the folder. 'That covers it Alice. All done then?'

'Not yet,' she held onto the list. 'There are a few more. This one here mentions a lodger that occupied the property without consent.'

He shrugged. 'Aren't some people stupid allowing unwanted guests in their house. I would just kick them out.'

'We are not allowed lodgers,' she reaffirmed.

'No, we don't do lodgers,' he agreed with a chuckle, as he grabbed the folder and threw it back into the box. 'God, I'm tired. There is nothing more likely to make you drowsy than a pile of legal crap.'

'Are we done?' she asked, surprised. 'Shouldn't we go through the list more thoroughly and note any that concern us?'

'I don't think so,' he said, and took the Disclosure folder and placed it on top of the heap they would sign off themselves. 'Nothing there that is current or relevant to our situation. We can sign it off and be done.'

Early the following morning they dropped ten boxes of paperwork off with the small legal entity they had found on the internet. Then they went back to tidy the apartment and finish off. It was Friday and they wanted the deck cleared before the weekend. With the weather forecast showing clear skies and warm days they were eager to get out, enjoy the sunshine and be away from the lingering smell of old paper.

'Let's get ready for our cycle and picnic in the morning,' Daniel suggested.

'Only once we have finished what we have set out to do.'

'Alright, let's sign off the paperwork we kept and have it ready to return to Khune,' he acquiesced. 'Then when the boxes come back from the conveyancers, everything will be ready to go,'

They settled down at their dining room table and signed every page from the small heap they had decided to do themselves.

'Job done,' Daniel cried, as the clock struck five and the last document landed in the remaining box. 'Let's get down to the beer garden and celebrate.'

Booze was off limits for Alice, but she did not need to drink alcohol. She was flying high, full of adrenalin and looking forward to being out with their friends.

There was just one task left to do. They went into the city and purchased a gift voucher from a large clothing store and an expensive bottle of wine. Arriving minutes before their doors closed, the couple walked into the Estate Agents office. Helmut looked up when the doorbell chimed and nearly fell over in his bid to get away.

'A present to say sorry,' Alice called after him, holding out the gift.

'We didn't envisage you getting attacked,' Daniel followed up with a quick apology. 'No more tricks, I promise. Oh, and by the way, have they caught anyone yet?'

Helmut gracefully accepted the gift while fidgeting nervously. 'No but thank you... look I was being an arrogant twit when you first walked in and have learned a good lesson. From now on, everyone who enters that door is a potential millionaire. That is something they never taught us at college.' He smiled. 'The other thing they never taught us at college was how to play hide and seek during a house viewing.'

They all laughed.

'Well I don't think that will happen very often,' Alice replied. 'Care to join us in a couple of months for a meal... once we have settled in?'

Helmet looked noncommittal, but agreed anyway. 'That would be nice, thank you.'

The couple left the young man standing at the door staring after them. As they disappeared around the street corner he turned to the young girl on reception. 'You won't catch me going anywhere near that house. There is something very weird about them, and their Mansion.'

The following morning when they arrived on their bikes, Colin and Debbie were already on the pavement outside their apartment block. A few other members of the cycle gang were lounging around on the entrance stairs, catching the first of the warmth from the morning sun.

'Sorry everyone, we just had some last-minute things to take care of,' Daniel apologised.

'Lunch will be on us today. For being so late,' Alice added.

This met with shouts of approval as the group gathered up their bicycles and got ready for the ride.

Scowling at her, Daniel muttered, 'What did you do that for? Will cost us a bloody fortune. We weren't that late.'

'Where is Harvey?' one of the cyclists called.

'He has decided to join another group,' Daniel replied.

'I wonder why?' asked another. 'He really appeared to be enjoying his rides with us,'

The couple looked at each other and decided to keep quiet.

'Duck you suckers,' the lead cyclist shouted in traditional style as they sped under an overhead bridge.

Alice looked sideways and saw that the temporary homes made from cardboard boxes were missing.

'Where have they all gone?' she asked the leader of the group.

'Cleared out,' he replied. 'Moved somewhere else I guess.'

'The authorities need to be more empathetic. Always picking on the vulnerable.'

'Would you like to have them squatting near your apartment block Alice?' the leader responded. 'Bloody lazy, thieving layabouts, just waiting to rob someone,'

'They are not thieving layabouts,' she protested. 'They are vulnerable and homeless.'

'Look Alice, I know you do a lot of part time work in soup kitchens, but when they are squatting near your back door it becomes an altogether different issue.'

'That's a bit harsh,' she shouted against the wind.

'Come on Alice, you still haven't answered my question. Would you be happy if one of them came and squatted on our back doorstep?'

'No problem,' she replied and dropped back to cycle next to Debbie.

Chapter 11
Public Right of Way

JJ Fischer and Partners approved the purchase price after noting the substantial discount gained from the previous owner. It ticked all the conditional boxes and met with a big stamp of approval from the executors of the estate, JJ Fischer, and his undisclosed associate.

The Agency was happy to hand over the keys once a hefty deposit had been lodged, while the transfer of ownership documents moved rapidly along the conveyor of approvals. Manor House would be held in trust by JJ Fischer and Partners until the five-year period had expired. Then once it had been agreed that the couple had met all obligations the house would become theirs to do as they wished.

The couple waited patiently, while the electrics were checked over, and a plumber serviced the heating system. Winter was drawing in, and they would need a lot of warmth in the big building to get through the first cold spell.

'The electric bill will be a killer,' Daniel said, as a shiver passed over him.

'We will have to shut down certain rooms until we have double glazing installed,' Alice replied.

'Because of the expense, I will have to leave the loft room windows for the time being and wait until the roof is repaired,' he said. 'But it doesn't stop me decorating the loft area first before we shut it down.'

Every evening and most weekends they spent sweeping, dusting, and cleaning. They mostly concentrated their efforts on the lower floors, and tried to ignore the loft. They boarded up where windows were broken and they tore down old curtains. It was all superficial, as they had never really cleaned anything properly before. Although it looked good on the surface, thick dust still clung to every unseen nook and cranny.

Alice mopped her brow. 'This is going to be a full-time job.'

Daniel took the bucket and cloth from her. 'Take it easy, you don't want to overdo it in your state. Let's sit down for a while.'

Debbie had called around earlier, and the fact that Colin had decided to go cycling with the group had not gone unnoticed by Daniel. Once settled on a couple of fold-out chairs, Daniel started whining on about being abandoned by his best friend.

'You will have to make time,' Alice retorted when he complained. 'It is not Colin's fault, and in any case why should he spend every weekend helping you? Why shouldn't he be out with his friends having fun?'

'I thought he was *my* friend,' he whined.

'Manor House is not his inheritance,' she chided. 'He still lives on the twelfth floor of an apartment block, and will be saving for the rest of his life to pay off a normal mortgage. Never mind what we have been handed on a silver platter.'

Nevertheless he felt abandoned, and became morose, and used Alice's pregnancy as a good excuse to bury himself in work as they prepared for the big move.

They chose a large room which they assumed to have been previously used as a master bedroom for themselves, then employed contractors and a decorator to paint, lay carpets and hang some cheap curtains. The remaining house would have to wait for a while. They had already dug deep into their savings, and needed to take a measured approach as to how they were going to proceed with further spends.

The only other bit of work they commissioned, was for a fencing contractor to clear a swathe of what he referred to as the *jungle* along the full length of the public right-of-way, and erect a six-foot high wooden fence. It was to stretch from the road at the top of the slope down to the public footpath adjacent the Spree, and serve to stop anyone from drifting onto their land, channelling the public between the evergreens on their neighbour's boundary and the newly erected fence on their side.

Cycling out to survey progress on the fence erection, Alice pointed out how the ivy had covered most of the building and roof.

Daniel's eyes were drawn to one of the dormer windows. 'Is that a light in one of the windows?' he asked, shielding his face for a clearer view.

Alice scanned the row of dormers and said she thought the end window might be reflecting the setting sun.

'It's gone,' he conceded after a while. 'It must have been the sun.'

Settling on a nearby bench they talked about their move and what they still needed to do. A cold movement of air lifted off the spree and made Alice shiver.

She stood up. 'Come, I want to get back to the flat.'

He sprung to his feet and pointed at the house. 'Look, there it is again. I saw a flicker.'

Alice looked West. 'Well it can't be the sun.'

He swung around. She was right, the sun had disappeared a short while back, and the evening had already started drawing in.

He shivered. 'I am sure I saw a flicker of something.'

'The electricians checking the sockets may have done something with the lights,' she rationalised. 'They may even still be in there working late, to get it finished in time for our move.'

'There, there it is.' He raised his voice. 'I have just seen it again.'

Then he was distracted by the lonely figure of what looked like a delivery man, wandering down the right-of-way.

He bristled. 'Look, even the fucking Chinese takeaway man thinks he can walk on our land.'

'It's a public path, now calm down,' she scolded him.

The thin man dressed in black clothing appeared in no hurry, as he casually meandered down the path. He even stopped at one point close to the gable end of their house, but the remaining vegetation obscured their view, and they could not see what he was doing.

'Where could he be from?' Alice asked.

'There's a Chinese restaurant two blocks away,' Daniel growled. 'I feel the need to tell him to take another route.'

'I think you need some rest. All this excitement has been far too much for you. He has every right to be there.' She tugged at his arm. 'Come, I will race you back.'

She started peddling along the towpath.

'Wait Alice,' he shouted, but she had already made fifty yards and was rapidly gaining speed.

'Shit,' he cursed and peddled after her.

Two weeks later they received a call from Fischer. The Solicitor wanted to see the couple, but said it was not urgent and any time over the course of the following week would do.

They arrived at the tall office block the following Friday to find the five suits sitting, as usual, along the far side of the table. They smiled at the couple and as if on cue flipped open folders. Harvey kept his distance and although courteous, Daniel noticed something else. It was as if his old buddy wanted to blend in with the other suits and gain some distance from their previous relationship.

'Nice to see you both,' Fischer greeted in a business as usual tone. 'Thank you for coming in at such short notice. I thought it best to catch up before too much time passes by. To make sure we're still well acquainted with the ground rules.'

There was no response from Daniel, while Alice smiled politely.

'How are you getting on with everything?' he asked.

'Electrical checks almost complete and boiler serviced. We are almost ready to move in,' Daniel replied.

Fischer went through a page of preliminary notes. Alice showed an interest while Daniel sighed and yawned, while playing with an elastic band he had found in his folder.

Fischer opened a second folder. It looked identical to the ones placed in front of the suits. 'Let's start by having a recap and going over the clauses.'

He flicked a page and paused to look from Daniel to Alice and then back to Daniel, who openly yawned once again.

'You have chosen the old house with a higher value,' he stated matter of factually, before asking. 'Right choice?'

'Never had a doubt,' Daniel replied confidently.

'Good, and we were pleased to see you negotiated a substantial discount. Well done.'

'Alice did that,' Daniel conceded.

'Then well done to you Alice,' Fischer added.

'Thanks Mister Fischer,' Alice smiled. 'You did your bit as well. We could hear you on Khune's phone speaker.'

'Four million is a good price. The benefit is that you get a hundred thousand of the saving. Your reward for bargaining a good deal.'

While impressed, Daniel could not help thinking it was only a small amount compared to the overall saving.

'Thank you, Mister Fischer,' Alice smiled appreciatively.

He smiled approvingly at her, before turning his attention back to Daniel. 'You now have to wait five years, while spending half a million of your own money to increase the value of the property by ten percent.'

'We know that Mister Fischer,' Daniel replied irritably. 'We haven't moved in yet. Give us a break.'

'Apologies Mister Somersby. Please excuse me, but I am just trying to look after you, guide you where I can whilst still sticking to the rules.' He looked back at the list of Clauses. 'We are pleased to tell you that the savings you made, including the discount Alice negotiated,' he smiled at her, 'means that we can send a cheque for five hundred thousand Euros to a charity.'

All the suits looked at them with appraising looks of congratulations, smiled, and nodded their heads.

'So, we get a hundred and a charity gets five hundred.' Daniel whined. 'Hardly seems fair. Where does the rest go?'

'Back into the estate,' Fischer replied, and before anyone could say anything further, he continued. 'One of the undisclosed pieces of information we could not share with you up until now, is that you get to choose which charity the money goes to.'

'Oh great. Let's not forget the charity.' Daniel made no effort to hide his contempt.

'The homeless,' Alice said without hesitation.

It had always been a concern of hers that some people had no home while others had more than their fair share, and inheriting Manor House had started to prick her conscience.

Daniel stared at her and muttered quietly, 'Bloody homeless wasters again.'

'A good choice Alice,' Fischer smiled, before turning to the suits. 'Are we in agreement with the choice?'

They all wagged their heads. It made Fischer smile again.

'Good, that is part B of clause one dealt with and out of the way. Well done. One down already.'

'This is going to be slow five years,' Daniel said quietly to Alice and sighed.

The five suits eyed him with mild amusement, as Fischer continued. 'These gentlemen will be monitoring your progress over the next five years. Should any one of them leave the firm a replacement will be drafted in.' He paused. 'Now we note that you have chosen to deal with parts of the purchase contract yourselves and have only given over a small portion of the paperwork to an external law firm.'

'As you suggested,' Daniel replied. 'Saved us a load of money.'

'You did follow my advice, and *have* made a substantial savings, but we do not think it was wise of you to sign the Declaration by Seller documents yourselves. We think that by doing so you have made a big mistake.'

'Bloody hell, this *is* like big brother.' Daniel was almost out of his chair. 'Is there anything you don't know? Do you know which takeout we had last night? Did you approve of the starters we ordered?'

'Now, now, Mister Somersby.' Fischer tried to calm him. 'We are only acting under instruction and in your best interests.' He looked back at his notes as Daniel settled. 'To the second clause then..., I know you are only just about to move in, but just a reminder that you must both reside in the house for the full period. This clause will remain in play for five years.'

'Yes, we understand. We have to live there for five years,' Daniel sighed. 'You know what? We might even rent the house out once it is ours, or stay there for the rest of our lives.'

Five suits flipped through their files and nodded at the older man.

'Your choice Mister Somersby,' replied Fischer. 'An independent valuation will be done at the five-year stage to ensure you have met all your obligations. Once the terms have been signed off, the deeds currently held in trust will be passed over to your good selves. If you then choose to sell or rent the house out it will be entirely your choice. So long as Francis has not returned.' He waited a short while and when he got no response, continued. 'The third clause requires that you pay for all the renovations yourself. No loans or second mortgages allowed. Obviously, doing most of it yourself will ensure you have a better chance of keeping within your budget and not spending a lot more than the required half a million...'

'That's a hell of an ask,' Daniel interjected.

'You still have savings and I take it you are both still in work.'

'We are,' he replied.

'So, looking at your disposable income.' He ran his finger down a list of figures in front of him. 'Yes, looking at the figures and taking both your salaries into account, you can do it.' He looked at another line of calculations. 'Having two weeks holiday a year and eating out once a week should put you in a favourable position to save at least four hundred thousand over the next five-years. Oh, and course you have also just received a hundred thousand from the savings on the purchase price. That should be enough to see you through. Not to mention a good profit participation scheme at your work if your appraisals go well. Easily doable.'

'Big brother is watching us already Alice,' Daniel pulled a face.

'Only in your best interests,' Fischer reminded him.

'Hang on there. What if we get someone in, like a friend who is prepared to help us and not get paid?'

The five suits flipped to a page at the back of their files again and all nodded in unison.

'Allowed under the rules,' Fischer replied. 'You can pay any professional business you like, but nothing on credit.'

'Damnation,' Daniel thumped the tabletop.

'That was polite for you.' Alice pulled a face. 'Where did damnation come from?'

He ignored her gibe as a tray of tea was brought in. It allowed everyone a few minutes to settle back and relax, while Daniel fidgeted with his pencil and kept looking at his watch.

Once tea had been poured, Fischer continued. 'The fourth clause says you cannot have …'

'Lodgers.' Daniel completed the sentence. 'And if I ever find one in the house, he had better be able to swim, The Spree is not that far from the back door.'

Everyone ignored him. They had got used to his hot-headed flareups by now.

'The fifth and final clause.' Fischer started moving quickly through the remaining clauses. 'Part A states that if ever Francis returns and seeks sanctuary, you are to advise us and take him in. Frederick must never be allowed anywhere near the property, while Part B states you are to be kind to those less fortunate than yourself.'

Daniel rose to his feet. 'Alice already helps the homeless Mister Fischer, I told you the last time we were in. Now if you will excuse us...'

'We will see you in twelve months' time then,' Fischer said, as he stumbled to his feet, ready to shake their hands.

But Daniel was already halfway through the doorway and lifted a hand in farewell. 'See you guys,' he called over his shoulder as he tugged on Alice's hand.

Having the rest of the day off, they decided to cycle back to Manor House and see how work was progressing.

A swathe of bush had been cleared along the boundary and a six-foot wooden fence erected.

'Well, at least the fence will stop anyone from walking through our garden,' Alice said.

'The takeaway delivery chap can't just wander where he wants now, can he?' Daniel crowed.

'Will you stop being so obsessed and focus on what we need to do. You have only seen the poor man once before.'

'I will focus on his skinny little arse, and give it a kicking if I ever catch him loitering near our property Alice.'

They left their bikes at the bottom of the property and walked up the right of way. From within the walkway there was not much to see. The tall evergreens flanked the left, while the new fence to their right only allowed them a limited view of the top floors of their new home. That was up until they reached Manor House, where a section of the gable end wall was fully exposed and formed one side of the walkway.

'What idiot would build a house right up to a public right of way,' Daniel cursed.

Alice looked along the fifty feet of wall. 'Strange to think that our future kitchen is on the other side of this.' She tapped the wall. 'All private in there while the public wander by out here.'

'Just as well we have the fence. We couldn't have allowed strangers to roam into our garden where little Harry will be playing. Someone might abduct him.'

His hand brushed the plaster. He stopped and traced back over a steel door set neatly into the wall and painted the same colour as the rendering. 'Hey, what's this?'

Alice walked over and looked at the two-foot square of metal. 'Looks like some sort of cover. Must be where our electric meter is housed, but why so big?'

'Of course it's *big*, Alice,' he boasted. 'Bloody big meter for a bloody big house.'

Had he looked closer he would have noticed that the hinges were well oiled and recently used. While the keyhole was worn and surrounded by numerous shiny scratch marks.

Chapter 12
Creaking Floorboards and Baby Harry

After hiring a small truck and with the help of a junior colleague from work, Daniel moved the entire contents of their apartment across the city and into their new residence. Alice was eight months pregnant and although on leave from work, was in no fit state to assist.

Once the truck had been fully offloaded, their life's accumulation of belongings looked insignificant stacked, against the one wall in the kitchen. They placed the fridge against the opposite wall and their double bed in the reception room. The smell of paint from the recently decorated bedroom upstairs still clawed at the air like a chemical cloud.

'So, who owns this house?' Daniel's colleague enquired.

'We do,' Daniel replied. Then seeing the young man's expression, decided to elaborate. 'Don't look so shocked, it can be explained.'

'Did you rob a bank?'

'No, we didn't rob a bank…, or do anything else illegal. It's pretty simple really. My uncle died and left us enough in his will to buy this place.'

The young man who had sweated away all day, carrying boxes into lifts and straining his back while lifting the large double mattress, walked around the reception room. He took in the spiral staircase and the chandelier with an open mouth.

'Bloody hell, this is some place.'

'It's not all plain sailing,' Daniel explained. 'We have a lot to do before it is completely ours.'

The couple spent the first week camped in the reception room. It was uncomfortable for them both, but especially for Alice, who struggled to settle in her new environment. The room had an eerie low light that appeared from nowhere in particular, as it silhouetted the large chandelier and spiral stairway. It left Alice with a strange feeling of being overexposed.

Then, one night she woke in the early hours after being restless and not getting much sleep. Tired and thirsty, she reached for her mug of water, but it was nowhere to be found.

'Daniel,' she called across to him.

He did not stir. The past few weeks had taken it out of him, and he remained in a deep sleep.

Staggering to her feet, she headed for the kitchen. Finding it disorientating being in a strange house, her eyes soon adjusted to the dark and light zones, as she groped around in the unfamiliar surroundings. There was no need to turn on a light in the kitchen, as she could just about make out the large white fridge door with its shiny handle.

Something moved amongst the stack of boxes, grew in height, and then shrunk back again. A barely audible noise made her spin around, but it was too dark to see anything.

Fumbling around inside the fridge, she shoved aside a few provisions before finding some leftovers. The same noise caught her attention again, and she looked around. The Light from inside the fridge lit the room in an eerie glow and made her shiver. But besides the round dining room table, four chairs, and a stack of boxes, all was still.

As she turned back to the task of looking for food, the fridge light silhouetted the large profile of her bulging stomach stretching over her winter pyjamas.

The shadow shifted.

Alice rooted out a leftover ham sandwich and a can of soda before heading for their small table. It was a dark corner of the room, but she found a chair and as she settled, heard heavy breathing. Daniel had always snored and when she cocked her head towards the door, the familiar sound of his throaty rattle drifted through, and left her comforted by the thought that he was close by.

Resting both elbows on the table, she cradled her head and started to shiver. It had been a long day and she was desperate to get a few hours' sleep. Reaching for her can of soda, her hand brushed against something that made her jump. It was her water mug.

'I'm sure I took it to bed with me,' she mumbled and lifted the plastic cup.

Finding it empty, she popped the can of soda and took a swig. She belched and felt slightly better. Then took a bite of the ham sandwich and felt her stomach turn.

She groaned.

As she cradled her head in both hands, the shadow moved from behind the boxes and what appeared to be tendrils, slithered across the table and gently stroked a strand of her fallen hair.

A stale smell of unwashed clothing and body odour suddenly hit her and she retched. Racing towards the sink, she groped around in the dark, but it was not where she thought it was and had no choice but to throw up against a wall.

'Damn,' she cursed, and staggered back into the reception room, where she crawled back into bed, snuggled up to Daniel, and was soon fast sleep.

Waking in the morning to the rich aroma of freshly brewed coffee and the sound of boxes being moved around the kitchen, she coughed, and it brought Daniel scurrying through.

'I thought I heard you being sick in the night, how are you feeling?' he asked.

Seeing a small stain of vomit on her pyjamas, she recalled the previous night.

'Sorry about the mess in the kitchen. I woke up hungry and found a half-eaten ham sandwich and it bounced straight back up. I threw up against the wall where I thought the sink was. I lost orientation. I am sorry.'

He looked at her in confusion. 'Kitchens spotless Alice. You must have been dreaming.'

'Ham sandwich and can of soda on the table?' she enquired.

'You ate the sandwich, and everything was in the bin. Nice and tidy. Very impressive Alice. Especially in your state.'

She was about to question him, but he had already started heading back to move another box, and she concluded it must have been a dream. But when she looked down, the stain on her pyjamas was still there.

Feeling a cold draught of air, Daniel entered the larder and it made him shiver. He instinctively pulled at the cupboard doors on the far wall. Two opened, however two other appeared locked shut. Although they rattled, they remained firmly shut. He was looking for more storage space for his tools.

'Might as well use the shelves then,' he said to himself.

He glanced back at the cupboard doors for a second, scratched his head and then moved on to the task of emptying some of the boxes. The room smelt like a stale fridge and after placing a few tools on a shelf, packed them back in the box and decided to find somewhere more hospitable.

Two weeks later, Alice gave birth to Harry. He was premature and a grouchy little chap. Like father, like son, she concluded and smiled. But she soon became frustrated at not being able to pacify the child, as he kept her awake most nights. Debbie helped during weekends, but soon had her own baby boy they named Rodney, born a month after the arrival of Harry.

The two women shared a common interest and it drew them even closer than before, as the men started drifting apart. During weekends, Colin went cycling while Daniel relocated their bed to the decorated bedroom and continued to plan his approach to renovating Manor House.

'I could do with a bit of help,' Alice pleaded with him after washing, cooking, ironing, and taking care of Harry.

'We can't afford a full-time nanny,' He replied. 'It will drain funds from doing up the house, and put our project in jeopardy.'

They were seated in the kitchen at the small round table.

'I can't take it much longer. I am at my wits end. Harry will not settle at night and I desperately need some sleep.' She sounded tired. 'Maybe the sound of you snoring is keeping him awake.'

'Well let's move him into the kitchen,' he suggested.

'The kitchen?'

'Yes. We have a sound monitor, and regardless of where he is, we will hear him on the monitor. The kitchen has a large cast iron radiator and is by far the cosiest room.'

'I don't like it,' she protested.

'What do you mean Alice,' his patience was clearly wearing thin.

'I can feel a cold draught coming from the larder room. Every time we open the door, it lets a blast of freezing air out. And it stinks in there.'

'We keep the door closed then. No need for us to go in or to have the door open. The few things I put in there a while back I have taken out. It's empty.'

'What about getting Harry's room done sooner?' She sounded desperate.

'Too much work to do Alice, the kitchen is the solution.'

And it was. Harry settled and started sleeping through the night. Alice was thrilled and found a new lease of life as she started doing more around the house to help.

They put him to bed every night, placed the sound monitor next to his head and gently closed the door. Other than the regular feeding schedule, they did not see or hear him until they started making breakfast the following morning.

Then one night, Alice woke to hear him crying. Then as she crept downstairs, she heard a humming sound as the child appeared to settle and suck on his dummy. The kitchen door was slightly ajar, and as Alice approached, she thought she saw a shadow flit across the gap. She thrust the door open, tripped over a stack of metal pans and sent them clattering across the floor. It set Harry off again and it took a while before she could calm him down.

Daniel heard the commotion and came stumbling down the stairs. 'Are you alright,' he called.

'I could have sworn I saw something move just before I came in' she said. 'Then I knocked that box over, and... well you heard the rest.'

After making sure Harry was fast asleep, he guided her gently from the room, switched off the light, and quietly closed the door behind them.

'Come now, let Harry sleep,' he said, as they headed back upstairs to bed.

A dark form crept from the larder room and lifted a pair of large woollen gloves lying in the cot. Then Harry appeared to float above the cot and move around the room. He woke and drank from a bottle of warmed milk held to his mouth. The little face sucked away at the plastic teat while staring at--- nothing. The room was dark and with heavy snow forecast early the next morning, the sky outside had turned pitch black.

Manor House soon settled into a regular routine, as the family adapted to a new life with a baby, while at the same time they took stock of what was needed to be done over the following five years.

Daniel was finding it difficult at first to cope in his new role, managing an office full of architects, and meeting contractual deadlines. It was a whole new experience for him. He used to think that clients were awkward customers. Always changing their minds, wanting unrealistic outcomes on already tight schedules and budgets. But staff reporting to him were suddenly so much harder to understand than clients had ever been. They were so much more complex, and he started to wonder why anyone yearned for any form of managerial role. The days of sitting behind a computer and creating a design that wowed clients were gone. In its place was an endless number of 'people issues' that he had to deal with, and most of the problems landing on his desk appeared quite unresolvable.

One such day had him frustrated as two employees argued all morning over the space they shared. The one said the other was abusing his good nature and stacking files too far into his own storage space. Daniel tried his best to resolve the issue, but ended up having to separate them to different parts of the office.

That night as he cycled home, he spotted them both in a beer garden. Creeping closer to see what was going on, he saw them drinking together and having a wonderful time.

The following day they asked to be moved closer together. They said that they had missed being near to one another.

He started arriving home frustrated and annoyed that people he used to be friends with, and had worked alongside for years, were suddenly lazy and obstructive. Timewasters, he called them. While Alice reminded him of the higher salary and the need to man up to a more responsible role.

In the meanwhile, Colin was promoted and transferred to another office to manage a sub-branch on the outskirts of the city.

During the first six months, advanced planning on Manor House slowed and it served them well, because they needed the time to adjust to their good fortune, new surroundings, and various pressures.

Initially Daniel started arriving home and getting stuck in with the job of planning what they were going to do with the house. He knew it would be no easy task to increase the value of the house by ten percent, but he consoled himself with the fact that he had four and a half years left to complete the work.

Little Harry was moved to a freshly decorated room adjacent to theirs on the second floor. The contractors they had initially employed to give two rooms a 'lick and a promise' did exactly that, and Daniel suspected from the strong smell of paint they had used, it had been cheap emulsion. One of the reasons it delayed moving Harry from the kitchen, as they waited for the smells to dissipate.

It strengthened his resolve to learn the various trades and tackle the work himself. Besides reducing the cost by a substantial amount, he would be in control of materials and the finished product. He was after all an architect and already in the 'game', as he called it, and was full of confidence.

'What could be so hard?' he said during those first few months, while he planned and sourced the best materials.

All the while, Harry would not settle in his new room.

'He misses the kitchen' Alice suggested.

He was quite happy to lie in the kitchen all day. His little eyes darting around, always coming to rest on the larder door. As if he was waiting expectantly for someone to come out.

Then when they took him upstairs, he became restless and cried.

Renovating Manor House was eventually about to start, and as Daniel thought of the enormous task ahead of him, he remained undaunted and full of enthusiasm.

At roughly the same time, Alice had a baby carriage fitted to the back of her bicycle, but they had neglected their cycling friends. They decided to invite the group to Manor House for a Sunday meal. To try and rekindle some stretched bonds.

After taking everyone on 'a grand tour' of the building, they had beers and wine on the front terrace. The tour of the house had taken the best part of an hour, and their friends were impressed, to say the least.

But Alice overheard one of them say, 'I think the house feels spooky.'

'A hell of a task,' another said.

'Are we still going to see you?' asked the cycling group leader. 'If you intend doing up this place on your own, I can't see you cycling with us on weekends.'

'Watch us my friend,' Daniel replied. 'We will work magic and still have lots of fun time together.'

He did not sound over convincing, and as Colin had watched his old friend become more engrossed in his project and spending less time socialising, he knew Daniel was drifting away. The fact that they now worked in separate offices did nothing to improve their relationship.

He waited until they were on their own and approached him. 'Not having much free time old pal?'

'It's a lot harder than I initially thought,' Daniel admitted quietly.

'I suppose there are a few things I could help with when I have a free day,' Colin offered.

Alice overheard parts of the conversation. 'We can't expect you to spend your spare time working on our house when you have nothing to gain.'

'Thanks Colin,' Daniel replied. 'That would be a great help. You can come by every evening and weekend if you wish.'

Starting at the top of the house, he planned to work his way down. One drawback being the cost of getting a crane in to replace some of the roof and dormer windows, but it was an expense he would save for a later date. It was all about the internals for now. So, with that in mind, he strapped on his new tool belt and headed for a start on the loft rooms.

A quick learner and adept at learning new skills, Daniel had purchased all sorts of electrical appliances and tools, read the instruction manuals cover to cover, and followed tutorials on the internet. There were numerous experts giving advice and demonstrations on just about everything he needed to know, which bolstered his confidence no end.

He was full of enthusiasm, but the small leaded windows were covered in ivy and gave little light, while heavy snowfalls soon left him feeling oppressed and lonely in the darkened atmosphere.

All said and done, he accomplished little the first day. He stood for hours doing nothing. He had planned and programmed, drawn resource diagrams and histograms, printed off spend profiles and cash drawdown forecasts. While large charts and diagrams covered most of the walls in his study, he was suddenly nervous and hesitant. Nothing was more daunting than picking up a drill and drilling a hole in a wall. Or ripping off a false panel to find rats and rotten timber, or lifting a carpet to reveal wood rot, or finding an infestation of wood worms. It was beyond anything he had ever experienced before.

Then within months of starting, his friendship with Colin took another tumble.

His pal would call by after work, and start tidying up the debris left strewn around the rooms, but Daniel soon became irritable and complained about him getting under his feet. So Colin ended up sitting on the floor with a mug of tea and trying to make himself heard over the noise of a drill or wallpaper stripper. As a result, his visits become more infrequent as time slid by.

They seldom saw one another now that they worked in different branches, but when Colin overheard some of Daniels team talking amongst themselves at a group meeting, he grew concerned that his friend was taking advantage of their joint boss. Old Sniffer had developed an ongoing chest infection, which meant he was quite often off work himself. Daniel used this to his full advantage and when Old Sniffer was off, he ducked out to work on Manor House.

The following Saturday evening, Colin and Debbie called by with Rodney in his pushchair.

'Where is Harry?' Debbie enquired.

'In the nursery with our new part time childminder.'

'Very impressed,' replied Debbie. 'I thought Daniel was dead against you having one.'

'I had to work on him. I convinced him that I would be more productive freed up and could get back to work sooner. Why don't we take Rodney up to the nursery and I will introduce you to Olga? She is Russian and has limited conversation, but is incredibly good with children.'

The girls headed for the nursery, while Colin drifted upstairs to where Daniel was working, and offered to assist where he could. There were heaps of debris lying around and as he gathered up an armful of waste material, he heard a strange sound coming from somewhere down the corridor. He flicked the switch on the wall and the steamer Daniel was using spluttered and stopped working.

'What did you do that for?' Daniel bellowed when he saw Colin with his hand on the switch.

'I heard a noise coming from the other end of the corridor.'

'Bloody hell Colin, you can't stop me every time you hear a strange noise. I will never get done.'

'Just thought you needed to know, mate. That's all.'

'That is now the third time you have done the same thing. Kind of irritating, don't you think?'

'Listen,' Colin persisted. 'There it is again,'

Daniel heard it this time, climbed down the ladder, and walked the length of the corridor trying to isolate the strange sounds.

They came to a small room that had obviously served as a linen storage cupboard in the past. It was decked out with shelving, but otherwise quite empty. Daniel shone the beam of his torch around the space.

'Just empty shelves and lots of dust Colin. Must be rats in the cavity walls making the noise.' He had a good look around. 'I need to put a light in here, it will make a good storeroom.'

Then they both heard the strange sound again.

'It's an airlock in a water pipe,' Daniel speculated.

'Have you heard it before?'

'Sometimes in the kitchen.'

'What's that smell?' Colin asked.

Daniel stood shaking his head. 'Are you trying to waste my time pal? Why don't I stop doing renovation work and creep around listening for strange noises and sniffing the air?'

'Sorry mate, just trying to be helpful, but I'm getting on your nerves. I can see that, so I'll let you get on with it then,' he replied before going downstairs to join the girls.

Daniel muttered, climbed his ladder, and went back to steaming off wallpaper.

Working every spare hour, and if there wasn't one, he would find one, Daniel slogged on. Every now and then he would stick his head into the nursery and smile at Harry. He was a proud dad and promised he would spend a lot more time with the boy when he was a bit older. It was something his father had never done during their short period of life together and he vowed history was not going to repeat itself.

A few months later, Alice arrived back from work frustrated and tired. Olga was in a similar state of mind and annoyed at being kept late. Harry had been unsettled for most of the day and the minder was late leaving.

'He has been a good boy all day, but whenever I left him alone to sleep, he would start to cry.' Olga looked around anxiously. 'This house is very scary. I do not like being here alone.'

'Did you try leaving him to sleep in the kitchen?' Alice asked.

'The kitchen?' the Russian minder pulled a face. 'That is no place for a baby. Are you crazy?'

Alice pushed the pram into the kitchen and Harry immediately settled. She could hear a faint banging sound coming from the loft area. She turned to the minder. 'You shouldn't be afraid. Daniel is here to protect you.'

The girl looked confused. She was about to say something, but was already late. She muttered a few words in Russian, before rushing off to catch a bus home.

125

Knowing that Daniel was at last making good progress, Alice lifted Harry from his pram and decided to go and see how he was getting on.

'Daniel,' she called out. 'It's me, little Harry wants to see how you are doing.'

Little Harry was not old enough to convey any form of message other than to make it obvious he was happy or upset, but to Alice he was a puppet. She often spoke for him, using her baby voice and sounding quite ridiculous. 'Hello daddy,' she called. 'I have to have a bath now and want to say goodnight,' she continued, as she walked the length of the attic corridor, but all she found was mounds of rubbish.

The banging had ceased, so she called out again in a normal voice, more authoritative this time. 'Daniel, it's Alice here, Harry wants to say goodnight.'

There was still no response. Then a few seconds later she heard the faint sound of the entrance hall door on the ground floor being closed.

'Alice, where are you?' Daniels voice carried up the stairwell.

'I thought you were up here,' she shouted down. 'I could have sworn I heard you working.'

He met her halfway up the stairs. 'I had to pop out to the hardware shop and get a few things. I asked Olga to tell you.'

'Well, she never said a word about where you were and seemed eager to get away.'

'Maybe time for a change of sitters then Alice. We need someone we can rely on.'

'I will speak to Olga. The agency said she was exceptionally reliable.'

They had just started walking down the stairs together when Alice stopped on the second-floor landing and looked back up.

'I could have sworn I heard you banging up there when I came in.'

'I was at the hardware store Alice. I've just told you. You must have been hearing things. Do you want me to have a look around?'

126

She did not like the oppressive feel of the attic space, with little or no lighting and had no desire to go back up there.

'Some fresh air instead please, let's have a look at what we can do with the garden.'

'Do we have to Alice? I am just in the middle of wallpapering one of the rooms and it's a jungle out there.'

She turned to him. 'Have you taken another day off work?'

'I only took the afternoon off,' he retorted. 'Went to the hardware shop and here I am. There is a lot to do and it's not going to get done while I am work, will it?'

'I thought I heard you say the other night how busy you were with a new contract?'

'We are Alice. The optimum word is we, and as I am now the boss, the rest of the team need to pull their weight. No use the cart trying to push the mules. Anyway, there is a mountain of work here, and so little time.'

They walked around the front garden and stood looking back at the house as the sun cast it's dying rays over the building.

'The loft windows are so covered in ivy you can't see a thing out of them,' she said.

'We can't strip off the ivy and replace the windows until we get the crane in to do the roof,' he replied. 'I thought we agreed that. Anyway, you wanted to look at the garden, didn't you?'

'Yes, I did, but the roof is on year four of your schedule, can't we bring it forward?'

'We stick to the schedule Alice, and that way we stick to our budget. Is that not what we agreed?' He sighed. 'The garden?'

'I want to clear it and start again,' she said.

'Yours to do with as you wish. I have enough on my plate,' he replied, and turned back to the house.

Alice sighed in frustration. She had at least wished for some sort of discussion on the subject. Anyway, it was past Harry's normal bedtime and the cold evening air made her shiver.

As she went back indoors, he headed towards the end of the public right of way. Now that Alice had reminded him, he wanted to get some idea of where he could eventually gain access to erect the crane. Then he caught sight of the Chinese delivery man on his regular route down the road. The thin figure in black was carrying a large bag on his back. There had been numerous sightings of the man, but Daniel had never managed to confront him before.

'Hey, you,' he shouted.

Spinning around, the man took one look at him and disappeared down The Alley. This being the name Daniel had given the public right of way.

When Daniel reached the spot where he could see down the full length of the narrow walkway, the figure was closer than he would have expected, but moving off at speed. To his surprise he was no longer carrying the large bag on his back.

'Hey, come back here, I want to talk to you,' he shouted again, while looking around to see where he may have left the bag.

Alice prepared Harry for bed, while Daniel walked to the local Chinese restaurant to find out what was going on. They sounded surprised and knew nothing of any delivery man on foot. They used two scooters to do all their deliveries, and as it happened, no orders had been sent out so far that day. The shop had only just opened.

Arriving back at Manor House, he was frustrated and tetchy. And his mood took a further dive when Alice handed over a letter from JJ Fischer and Partners. They wanted a recap on the first year of progress.

Nothing had changed in the plush solicitor's offices. Fischer appeared the same. The five suits, including Harvey were the same somber looking individuals, never giving anything away, while remaining polite and cordial.

'We will be as brief as we can,' Fischer announced after the initial formalities.

Sitting back, Daniel cleaned out a bit of paint from under his fingernails with an old tooth pick he had found in his pocket, while Alice sat ready to take notes.

'My colleagues have been keeping an eye on you, and although you may be unaware of their presence, they are always around,' Fischer began.

'Fucking stalkers,' Daniel muttered, as he fixed them with a sideways stare. 'You know Harvey, I used to quite like you, but since all this started, I'm not so sure anymore.'

Harvey smiled at his old friend. 'Sorry, just doing my job. Complying with the terms and conditions... nothing more.'

'Yea, yea, yea, good on you pal,' Daniel muttered.

Fischer coughed and brought the meeting back on agenda. 'To start with, I want to review the five clauses.' He paused. 'We discussed the first clause the last time you were in and still maintain that you should have spent more time on going through all the documentation. As you are now aware, the public right of way runs adjacent to the external wall of your house. That is something you should have picked up pre-purchase and at least have been aware of the implications.'

'Not a problem,' Daniel shot back.

'We wonder what else you may have missed?' Fischer raised his eyebrows.

'Cut the drama Mister Fischer,' Daniel retorted. 'We don't see how anything else could affect us.'

The five suits looked at Daniel, and he sensed they were trying to tell him something. He decided he would dig out all the old documentation and scan them again. That was if he could find the time, or be bothered.

'We know that you both still live in the property and will have to continue doing so for the full five-year period.'

'Three of us live there now Mister Fischer. Aren't you forgetting little Harry?' Alice reminded him.

Fischer smiled at her in return and nodded.

'Got to watch that memory Mister Fischer,' Daniel jibed.

The Solicitor ignored him. 'Clause Three requires you to pay for repairs out of money earned.'

'I am back at work,' Alice told him.

'And I am still head of my department,' Daniel added.

'How are you coping?' Fischer asked.

'Busy,' Daniel replied sourly.

'I had a conversation with your boss the other day, and he is concerned you are being distracted. Taking a lot of time off work.'

'You spoke to Old Sniffer?'

'I spoke to the man in charge of your office. Though I don't recall him giving me that name.'

'No, he wouldn't, he doesn't know I call him that. But why speak to my boss?'

'All these checks are being done in accordance with the instructions given, I can assure you.'

Daniel looked at Alice then back at Fischer. 'What else have you got on me, big brother?'

'Just a reminder,' Fischer continued undaunted. 'You have to achieve an uplift of ten percent on the price you paid within the five-year period, and only then does the property transfer from being in trust and into your name.'

Moving from cleaning his nails to picking his teeth with the same thin splinter of wood, Daniel looked bored.

'Any lodgers?' Fischer asked. 'Clause Four is extremely specific.'

'No lodgers,' they chorused.

Fischer looked at them for a while before continuing. 'Then it is only Clause Five, and there have obviously been no sightings of Francis or you would have told us. And finally, a reminder that part two requires you to be kind to any vulnerable souls. Those less fortunate than yourselves.'

'You are not very nice to the Chinese guy,' Alice cast Daniel an accusatory look.

'Alice, who's bloody side are you on? That Chinese guy is not family, and insists on goading me by walking past our property.'

'We know about the Chinese man,' Fischer interjected. 'You are right, he is not family, but I do wish you would be more tolerant. Keep your emotions in check. That man has every right to walk on public land, and is someone we would classify as vulnerable.'

'Are we done?' Daniel asked, not in the least interested as to how Fischer knew about the Chinese man.

'Unless you have any questions, the only outstanding item is an update on progress.'

'You tell him Alice,' Daniel said, and leaned back in his leather padded chair. 'I have had enough of this.'

Alice lifted a progress report and passed a copy to everyone around the table.

'As you know, Daniel has drawn up plans, created histograms and schedules for completion. We have done a cost analysis and a spreadsheet that stretches over the full five-year period. You will find them all updated and enclosed.'

Pointing to the folders circulated, she started to read the narrative.

'Last month he started stripping out the penultimate loft room. The others are complete, except for a bit of detail, plastering and decorating. He has had plumbing and electrical issues, but confident he can maintain programme. And if you look at the updated schedule you will see it puts the completion of the loft about two months behind.'

'That is a lot of work for one man,' Fischer remarked. 'I'm not surprised you are behind.'

'Daniel's best friend Colin helps him when he can,' Alice added.

'And you feel confident you can make up the time, even with your friends help?' Fischer persisted.

Daniel was starting to become restless. Having only expected the meeting to take thirty minutes, they had already been there for the best part of two hours.

'Of course, we can.' Daniel was clearly irritated. 'We are well into the loft area and doing a great job. The windows and roof will be done at the end in accordance with my schedule.' He paused as he appraised the elderly Solicitor. 'Tell me Mister Fischer, do you get paid by the hour out of the estate, or are you just trying to waste my time?'

'On a schedule, according to hours set aside in the will and not a minute more. So, if you suspect we are lining our own pockets, forget it,' he added forcibly. 'That cannot happen. Your uncle was far too cunning to have allowed that loophole.'

'So why the cloak and dagger approach Mister Fischer?'

'We have our instructions and are unable to disclose certain information. He was quite specific about that. He appointed this Undisclosed Person to audit my every move, and if I step out of line, just once, the management of the whole estate goes to another entity. If you break any of the clauses, it would be a disaster and let me be clear about what that will mean Mister Somersby. You will have the house taken away and you will not inherit a bean.' He paused to let what he had just said sink in. 'I can tell you this much though, there is something about the house that previous tenants have not liked. And I am under the impression that there is something you are not telling me.'

Chapter 13
Year 2

It was obvious he was well behind schedule. Nobody could accuse him of being lazy. Alice had never seen anyone as determined, but he had not done anything remotely like this before, and was starting to feel overwhelmed by the sheer magnitude of the project.

After a year, he had fallen out with Colin, argued with Alice, and ended up working on his own. As it turned out, some of the loft rooms had been more difficult to renovate than others. The roof space had been butchered and altered by virtually every owner before them. The electrical wiring was a mess and pipes clattered with airlocks every time a tap on the ground floor was turned on.

'We don't have the funds to have plumbers and electricians crawling all over the house,' Daniel said one evening after he had come downstairs cursing.

'I know it's been getting you down,' Alice replied. 'Maybe I could get a second job.'

'No need, I have a plan,' he declared.

'Nice to see you positive. After a year on the project I was afraid you were starting to let it get the better of you.'

'No fucking way.'

'Now, that sounds like my old Daniel again,' she said with a grimace.

Harry had been sleeping on the couch and stirred.

'There is one thing you must promise me. Harry is at the stage where he will start picking up words, and I do not want you swearing. Is that understood?'

'No problem,' he replied, and lifted the little fellow into his arms. 'No swearing from daddy then.'

Harry looked at his father and smiled.

'So, what is your plan?' she asked.

'Which one?'

'The one that resolves the electrics and plumbing issues.'

'Oh yes..., that's easy. I will leave pipe conduits between all rooms and all floors for future plumbing and cables, then when we have enough money, it will just be a case of pulling everything through without destroying any of my handywork,' he crowed and gave Harry a hug.

'Clever boy,' she put her arms around them both. 'Now let us have a little family time.'

Family time was a treat in their household, and once Harry had eaten and put to bed, they snuggled up together in front of the television. It was a rare occasion, and at first, they struggled to find a channel that they both liked.

Then the phone rang halfway through a film. Daniel answered, and it was Colin. He had hardly seen his old friend over the past six months, other than at company meetings when the various branches got together.

'Hi Colin, long time no hear.'

There was an awkward silence as Alice tried to catch the tone of the call. She still saw Debbie a couple of times a week and understood that the men had drifted apart, and it upset her.

'You got another promotion?' Daniel reared. 'I never knew they were even advertising.' He looked across at Alice with raised eyebrows. 'You..., you have been promoted above Old Sniffers? Bloody hell Colin, that means you are now my boss's boss. How did that happen?'

His large freckles darkened, but soon calmed as his expression changed.

'Let me put you on speaker phone so that Alice can hear, then we can let you know straight away.'

'Can you hear me Alice?' Colin's voice carried clearly over the handset.

'Nice to hear from you Colin,' she replied, ignoring Daniels scowls. 'How is Debbie?'

'Good thanks. We were wondering if you could join us on a ride with the cycle group. Some of the gang have said how much they have missed having you two on our rides.'

Daniel nodded, and Alice nodded back. He had already forgotten about Colin's promotion and needed an excuse to put their fallout behind them. Besides, they were both feeling the isolation and missed having time away with friends.

'That's a yes from us, but what about our boys?'

'Debbie's mother is over for the weekend looking after Rodney and is more than happy looking after Harry as well.'

'Brilliant,' Alice replied with a smile.

She was desperate for a break from mothering, and needed to get away from dusting and cleaning the endless stream of fine particles that continuously rained down from the upper floors. Daniel was also looking forward to leaving the chaos far behind.

Although he was at last getting to the end of the loft renovations, the last room was proving to be a real stinker. The timber ceiling and floorboards had started crumbling, and when he pulled at a few beams, half the ceiling caved in. The floorboards were rotten, and he had to tread carefully for fear of falling through to the floor below. It all needed ripping out, and at times it felt to him as if he were going backwards.

'Where are we meeting?' Daniel enquired.

'At the gates for Seven O'clock. Are we on?'

'You bet; I can't wait,' he replied eagerly.

'I am so glad you called,' Alice chipped in. 'This is just the sort of tonic we need.'

'I thought I might pop over and help out a little this week as well. You know, make it easier for you guys to take some time off,' Colin added.

Although the experience from the last fallout was still raw, Daniel was getting desperate and welcomed any assistance.

'Bring Debbie and Rodney along,' Alice suggested.

'Wilco.'

'We'll see you during the week then,' they chorused.

They said their goodbyes as they turned to one another with a renewed sense of excitement, before Daniel's face darkened once again.

'Now I am fucking mad.'

'Daniel!'

'Sorry Alice, but you didn't hear what he said when he first called. Colin has been promoted and *he* is now my boss's boss.'

'I think you have been trying too hard to juggle your workload. Don't blame Colin, he used to be your friend and has just made the first move to restore that relationship. You've been under a lot of pressure lately. Just don't let this project get you down.' she said and took his hand.

'How can I Alice, when we are a year into our five-year period and there is still so much to do?'

'Don't forget Colin's offer. He can help with tidying up. He has been such a loyal friend.'

He hated it when she lavished praise on Colin. The so-called *loyal* friend who had just been promoted.

'Debbie and I can take care of the boys,' she added, 'then once they have gone to bed, we can help as well.'

'I'll take you upstairs for a progress tour before they get here,' he said, and took her hand.

They hugged and kissed before heading up to the loft. They were almost back to being themselves for the first time in a long while.

'Good grief, but this place is a mess,' she said, wading through knee deep heaps of stripped wallpaper, splintered timber, and piles of unused building material. 'How on earth do you know where you're up to?'

'I have been learning,' he replied defensively. 'I am, what they describe in the building trade as, new on the tools.'

Alice watched him strut around with his leather tool belt, hung over an old pair of worn out and weathered lederhosen's. They had aged more from years of partying at beer festivals than anything else.

'Come here sexy beast,' she said in a husky voice.

'This weekend Alice. I promise you. When I am not staring at mountains of work and stressed to hell.'

She hadn't really meant anything more than give him a bit of confidence, and was relieved to be turned down. All she wanted to do lately was get some sleep.

The following Monday evening Daniel gave their friends the same progress tour and a schedule of work he wanted completed by the end of the week.

'I still have to paint the walls,' he said, as they trooped from room to room. 'But, as you can see, it would help me if you guys could move all this rubbish into the junk room at the end of the corridor. Then I will find some way of getting it down to the ground floor without making a complete mess of the house.'

Colin looked at the newly plastered walls. It was clear that Daniel's skills at certain trades were on a learning curve, with the most recently renovated rooms finished to a much higher standard than the previous ones, but still a mess.

'I will have to redo some of the plastering on those early attempts,' Daniel admitted, when he saw Colin rub a hand over the rough surface.

The only bathroom on the top floor was showing signs of taking shape.

'Never done tiling before,' Daniel offered, as a form of explanation as to why the room had obviously stood unattended for a while.

Alice opened the door at the end of the corridor and investigated the once empty space, that was fast filling up with heaps of debris. A cold draft made her shiver.

'Is this what you have been calling the junk room?'

'Yes, but we can use it for whatever we want in the future,' he replied.

She surveyed the room from the doorway. 'I don't want to sound critical, but it's a hell of a mess.'

'That's why I call it a junk room. It's where you dump all the junk.'

Colin stood looking at the partially demolished ceiling and stripped floorboards in the adjacent room. 'Still a lot to do in here.'

'That's my nightmare room,' Daniel said in frustration, ushered Colin out, and quickly closed the door.

Alice, Colin, and Debbie spent every evening tidying out the rooms, while Daniel shut himself in his 'nightmare room'. They carted carpets, old light fittings, stripped wallpaper, and mounds of rotten debris to the junk room. The oldest wallpaper had pictures from various nursery rhymes.

Debbie stood looking at some of the scraps of paper. 'Children must have slept up here.'

'Looking at the crayon marks, it must have been a very naughty child,' Alice added.

'Bloody hell, children in the attic? Imagine being banished up here as a child?' Colin said, and shuddered.

'Not nice,' Alice conceded, as she tried to push the thought from her mind.

Debbie came hurrying back from the junk room and took hold of Alice's arm. 'There is something moving amongst the rubbish. I clearly heard it,' she said in a hushed voice.

'Rats in the roof space,' Daniel said, as he poked his head around the doorway.

They all stared at him, as he pulled a face, before ducking back into what looked like a dust filled rubbish hole.

By the Thursday night, Daniel had made little progress on the 'nightmare room'. Everything he took apart revealed further rot and dilapidation. He kept the door closed and the other three out, saying there was poor air quality, probably where the smell was coming from and he professed to have the only mask. He needed time to think this one carefully through before admitting defeat.

After thanking Colin and Debbie for their help, Alice found him sitting on the top stairway with his head lent on the banister. A streak of what looked like a tear had run down his dusty cheek. He quickly rubbed at his eyes, but looked defeated. While the other three had made real progress, he had gone backwards.

'I think I made a mistake Alice,' he suddenly blurted out.

'What do you mean?' she said, and settled on the step next to him.

'I am considering going back to Fischer and asking him if we can change our minds and go for the new house.'

'You mean give up everything you have done so far?'

He buried his head in his hands. 'Yes,'

There was a banging sound from somewhere in the loft and they both jumped.

'Rats,' Daniel muttered.

'Must be big rats,' Alice said, looking around.

'You should hear them sometimes. Scares the shit out of me. Just another reason to get out of here.'

'But you have almost finished the loft rooms, and after we helped this week you must be feeling better. I haven't looked in your so called 'nightmare room', but you must be finished by now.'

Daniel was not going to tell her the room was still a complete wreck. 'Almost done Alice.'

'There we go. You can finish things off next week, and you will feel much better.'

As they made their way back downstairs a dark form moved from the 'junk room', where a small mountain of debris had just collapsed. The form appeared to float across the stairwell to the far end of the narrow corridor. It hovered for a while as the couple descended from view. A door gently opened and closed and then another, as it moved steadily down the row of doors before opening Daniels 'Nightmare room', and it stood still for a while. Then as if it had never been there at all melted into the darkness, as the dust continued to settle and the couple made plans for an early night.

That Saturday morning, they dropped Harry off with Debbie's mother in the high rise, and cycled off to join the rest of the group waiting under the Brandenburg Gates.

They knew most of the current members of the bike group, who stood rubbing their arms to ward off the cold morning air. Colin introduced them to the newcomers, before they all headed off in the general direction of the Polish border and the river Oder.

Every subway they cycled through brought on the old chant of 'Duck you Suckers. Whooping and shouting with glee from the sheer exhilaration of being out in the fresh air and back with a social crowd, Daniel was in his element.

Then reaching Frankfurt on the Oder they stopped for a beer and meal in a beer garden, before following its course north to Szczecin in Poland. Pre-booked rooms were waiting for them in a guesthouse on the outskirts of the city.

Every room had been taken by the large group and the party began soon after they were seated around a long table in the dining room. Someone suggested that while they waited for their meal, they played a game of charades, and it proved to be hilariously funny as they vied to outwit one another.

Then they all went quiet when a couple stood up and walked around the room arm in arm, with their noses in the air. The girl

140

fluttered her eyelids and pouted her lips. But as hard as the group tried, they failed.

'Lord and Lady Somersby,' the man said at last when everyone had given up.

Not everyone knew them by their surname, so it took a few whispers before all eyes turned towards Daniel and Alice.

'That's not fair,' Daniel protested. 'I demand more respect from you commoners.'

It was funny, and everyone laughed, but it made the two realise that somehow they had become different in their friends' eyes. It made Daniel wish he had made more of an effort to join in with them over the past year. While Alice wished for the good old days to return and life to be normal once again.

On the journey back home, they turned towards Berlin at Stolzenhagen and cut across to the city. It had been a fun filled long weekend, but by the time they got back both were exhausted and had aching limbs.

Debbie's mother had done a great job of taking care of the two little boys and they arrived to find Harry and Rodney sat together in the middle of the lounge playing with a variety of toys. Harry heard his mother's voice and came tottering through to the entrance hall.

'Mummy, mummy, playing.'

At a year and a bit, his vocabulary was limited but advancing at a rapid pace.

'My little darling, we have missed you so much,' Alice told him, as she gave him a hug.

Debbie's mother stood watching them. 'He has been ever so good. Every time Rodney shouted or made a noise, Harry would put his finger to his lip and go ssshhh. He is so cute.'

'We have seen him do the same,' Alice admitted. 'I don't know where he gets it from.'

Arriving back at Manor House, they opened the blinds and the sun streamed in through the long floor to ceiling windows, lighting up the grand entrance hallway and reception room.

Alice sniffed the air. 'What is that smell?'

'I don't know. Smells like wet paint, plaster, and sawdust. I should know,' he replied.

They both shrugged and went their separate ways. Alice walked into the kitchen to heat up some instant food for Harry before taking him for a bath and bed. Daniel went up to the loft. He was cursing himself for not being able to totally relax on the ride. His mind had constantly drifted back to the work in hand. Or rather the enormity of the task and not for the first time questioning himself on whether he had made the right choice.

Struggling to find the temporary lights hung from the ceiling, he fumbled around until his frustration got the better of him and he pushed open the first door he came to. The smell was intense, and he tried to pry open one of the dormer windows, but the ivy covering the roof clawed at the wood and resisted every attempt. Nothing short of an electric cutter was going to free the frames.

He was about to leave the room when he stood on the extension cable, traced it back to a socket and flicked the switch. Stepping back, he stared at the walls. They had been freshly plastered. Slightly damp, but beautifully finished. He was torn between running downstairs or looking to see if anything else had changed.

The adjacent rooms were the same, but the real headbanger came when he opened his 'nightmare room'. The ceiling and walls had been fully reinstated, and flooring replaced. The plaster was still wet and when he touched it, he left a fresh finger imprint. He took a closer look at where the sockets were to be installed and could see ducting, ready for cabling to be pulled through.

Creeping into the bathroom, he found it beautifully tiled and ready for fixtures. Feeling clearly anxious he crept to the junk room and looked inside.

'Alice!' He shouted in a near hysterical voice.

There was silence. He ran back to the top of the stairs and shouted again.

'Please be quiet. Harry has just settled,' she hissed from the second-floor landing.

'I need you to come and have a look up here,' he persisted.

'I am tired, and Harry has just settled. Can't it wait?'

'No. Either I am going mad or the rats have skilled up and become very productive while we've been away.'

She reached the landing, where he took hold of her hand and marched her to a room.

'Look, all the walls have been freshly plastered.' Then took her hand, slightly more forcibly than he meant to, and hurried her to his 'nightmare room'.

'Look at this room, it is almost finished.'

'You did that. We left you to work on it all week while we tidied up the mess in the other rooms.'

'No Alice, it was a disaster area.' He paused. 'When I left here on Friday the room was a complete mess.'

'Really, I think the bike ride has taken it out of you.'

'I am telling you the truth…, and…, look at this, even ducting for future wiring had been installed. Just as I have done in the other rooms,' he protested.

'An early night. You will feel so much better after a good night's sleep,' she said and looped her arm into his.

'Well, if you don't believe me then come and look at this.' He tugged at her arm and led her to the junk room at the end of the corridor. 'Look, the whole room has been tidied. Everything you threw in here has been sorted into neat heaps. The stripped wallpaper folded in bales, the false panels placed neatly into heaps and even the old nails and screws have been put into an old ice cream tub.'

'Maybe Colin did that after Debbie and I left him to finish off on Thursday evening,' she said. 'He is very neat when he works you know.'

'Colin was not up here much longer than you. He could not have done all this in such a short space of time.'

Alice looked at him with concern. He looked highly agitated.

'Somebody is fucking with me Alice,' he said with a clenched jaw.

'How many times do I need to ask you to stop swearing? I am not going to talk to you until you promise me you will stop.'

She turned and walked back downstairs, to get a mug of Horlicks for them both. She was tired and had to be up early in the morning for an important meeting at work.

Daniel remained where he was and started to shake. He had not even got around to showing her the freshly tiled bathroom.

A week after returning from their cycling weekend, and while beavering away in the loft area, he heard the familiar voice of his friend Colin. He was talking to Alice as they approached the upstairs rooms.

'Wow,' Colin said when he saw the bathroom.

Daniel had just completed fitting the shower and handbasin.

'Just the toilet and then job done,' Daniel sounded more upbeat..

'You are so neat,' Colin praised. 'Honestly, I have never seen tiling like it before.'

Daniel got to his feet and puffed out his chest. 'Fucking pro bud, that's me. No dicking around in dust and muck when a professional is at work.'

'Daniel!' Alice shouted from the corridor. 'I heard that.'

'Sorry,' he called back and then grimaced. 'She is trying to stop me swearing. Fat fucking chance. Want a beer bud?'

Colin did his best not to encourage him. 'Listen mate, I was just dropping by with a few toys of Harry's. You left them behind last Sunday evening. I also wanted to remind you of that big bid we are putting in at the end of next week. It is imperative we win it.'

144

'I have it on my radar Colin..., time for a quick drink?'

'Sorry, need to get going. I have a busy day at work tomorrow and some prep work to finish off this evening.'

'Don't talk to me about work,' Daniel complained. 'I am so far behind I should really go in this Saturday morning. Old Sniffers been on my tail for a while now.'

Colin wanted to say more about the urgency of the bid and his friend's lack of attendance at work, but decided against it. He stood looking around the room awkwardly, before turning back to his friend.

'Shouldn't you be wearing a dust mask and safety glasses? And where are your gloves and hard hat?'

Daniel laughed. 'I am not at work now Colin. I leave all that shit at the office.'

'I am just saying. You have the responsibility of a wife and a little boy. You cannot afford to harm yourself. Health and safety should be the same as at work. You really need to take more precautions.' Colin pointed at the extension lead. 'Look, you don't even have a safety trip on the electrical plug.'

'Colin, I barely have time to sleep, let alone go out buying all that stuff. Anyway, it's an expense I can do without.'

Daniel walked Colin back down the stairway. 'Oh, by the way Colin, thanks for all the help. Great job on tidying up the junk room.'

'I didn't do that much my mate, just trying to help a friend, that's all.'

The following evening Daniel was about to place his bicycle in the garden shed when he saw the thin Chinese man duck down The Alley. He followed him to where he could take in the full length of the pathway, but was too late; the man had already disappeared. He had given up chasing him. The man was far too fast and after a while he started to feel like a dog chasing a car, and after all, it *was* public land.

Strolling down the path he looked back at the large building. A shiver went through him as he took in the full extent of their new home and the amount of work that still lay ahead. Lights flickered in the loft and he made a mental note to make sure they were turned off. Alice was in Harry's room wiping away condensation from the window and smiled when she saw him looking up at the building. He waved to her before walking around to the front entrance.

Alice had Harry wrapped in an oversized dressing gown as they stood waiting for him.

'Look Harry, daddy is home. He can help you with your new colouring-in book.'

Daniel gave her a hug and Harry a pat on the head before heading off to change.

'Alice,' he shouted back a minute later, 'I just need to finish painting one of the rooms? I promise to make some time for Harry tomorrow.'

The boy's lower lip jutted out and trembled as Alice led him through to the sitting room.

Arriving on the top landing, it was dark.

'I am sure I saw a light on,' he muttered to himself.

Then he found the newly installed switch and gave it a flick. He came to an abrupt standstill. An array of safety equipment lay spread out on his temporary worktable in the passageway. Everything Colin had mentioned, plus a few extras.

'Bloody hell Colin,' he said to himself. 'You *are* worried about me.'

When he called Colin on his mobile phone his friend sounded flustered. 'A bad day at the office,' he muttered. 'We lost one of our major contracts and it was down to my poor presentation. The one I was working on all of last week and then last night, before I fell asleep at my study desk.' He paused. 'Anyway, that is what I think happened. It is all my fault.'

'Colin, whoever says that needs sacking. Ignore them,' Daniel replied. 'Anyway, I was just calling to say thanks for bringing all this stuff around. I am well impressed.'

146

'Only a few toys bud, not really such a big deal. Anyway, I need to get going, I have another presentation to prepare for the morning and still plenty to do.'

'Thanks again bud,' Daniel replied with a smile.

That is what buddies are for, he thought. Always there for one another.

Two days later they had another visit, the second in as many weeks. But this time it was not his friend Colin but three somber looking suits from JJ Fischer and Partners. Alice had brought them upstairs and tapped on the open door.

Daniel nearly fell off his ladder when he saw them standing there in dark jackets and black ties.

'Jesus, but you gave me a fright. I thought the undertakers had arrived to cart me off.'

'We are doing one of our scheduled, unannounced audits Mister Somersby, I hope you will excuse us.' The more senior of the suits addressed him in an earnest tone, while the other two lifted note pads and took out pens.

'I have read the rules, go ahead, but excuse me if I continue with my work. As you can see it is a big house and I have a fucking lot of work to do.'

'Daniel!' Alice's raised voice carried down the passage.

The suits looked at one another.

'She doesn't like me swearing. She is right of course, just a bad habit of mine.'

The suits took an hour before reporting back.

'Mister Somersby, we have concluded our report,' said the senior suit as he looked down at a sheet of tick boxes and notes. 'I have to say we are extremely impressed.'

Smiling and sticking out his chest, he readjusted his tool belt. He was already proud of what had been achieved, but to get praise from them was more than he could have wished for.

'Thank you,' was all he could manage.

The senior suit took out his reading glasses and looked down at the check sheet.

'The one item that has really scored highly on our check list is how neatly you are working. In an impressively tidy and organised manner. Right down to the way all the rubbish has been carefully segregated and packed in the storeroom ready for disposal.

Secondly, the finish you achieved is to an extremely high standard.

Thirdly, you have all the safety and personal protective equipment one would expect to see on a building site.

Finally, we are most impressed with the staged approach. Working from one room to the next.'

The three men smiled at him as they slid expensive pens back into their tailored jacket pockets.

The lead auditor turned to him. 'Well done Mister Somersby. That concludes our audit. We hope we haven't delayed you longer than necessary.'

Totally taken aback, he stammered. 'What if the audit had failed?'

'You would have received what is referred to in the will as a yellow card,' the lead auditor said without hesitation.

'A yellow card?'

'Yes. What we can tell you, now that we have concluded the first such visit, is that if you receive three yellow cards you are out.'

'Out?'

'Yes, you are out of the house. It would no longer be yours. Taken back and sold in aid of a charitable cause.'

'But that's unfair,' he stammered. 'All the work I am doing, while you have a file of hidden rules that could mean us losing everything.'

'Mister Somersby, we will guide you as much as we can, but you need to work with us. And remember, we tread a very narrow path here, and have to be sure we stick to the terms of the will.'

The suits left, and Alice returned with a cup of tea to find him slumped down on the floor, against the newly tiled bathroom wall with his head in his hands.

'Well done. They read the results to me before they left, and what a glowing report. I am so proud of you.'

He slowly got to his feet and took hold of her hand. 'Can I show you something?'

'Yes,' she hesitated as she took in his expression. 'What's troubling you?'

He led her to his 'nightmare room' and opened the door. She looked around and then back at him.

'What are you showing me?'

'Look at the finished article Alice.'

'I had a sneak look in a here last week. I have seen it finished. Looks great, and beautifully decorated.'

'I didn't do it Alice.'

'Well I know Colin has helped out a bit, but you have done the lions share. Pat yourself on the back. You deserve most of the credit.'

'Come and look at this then.'

He took her hand and led her to the small linen room next door. It was mostly cleared out and been plastered and painted.

'Well done again. Do you want me to clap you on the back every time you make progress?'

'I haven't started on this room yet Alice… in fact, I was going to leave this room as it was.'

'What do you mean?'

'I haven't done a thing to this room.' He repeated in a slightly more hysterical tone. 'I haven't even been back to dust it down.'

Alice looked at him and then back at the ornate picture rail and linen cupboard doors stripped of paint and freshly varnished.

'You *are* incredibly talented. I have to admit that I was sceptical at first, but you are very skilled,' she replied with a laugh and started to walk out.

'Alice,' he called after her. 'I did not do this; it was not me.'

'Maybe Colin did it,' she called back.

Chapter 14
Second Floor

Harry at twenty-four months was all over the place. Alice had her hands full just trying to find him, let alone contain him in one room. There were so many hiding places in the large house, at times it took her a while to locate the little chap.

'Ah, there you are.' She said as he come out of the kitchen.

'Ssshhh mommy, don't talk,' he said.

'Harry, what is it with you and this ssshhh business?'

Harry put his finger to his lips and shook his head from side to side.

'Oh no little man, you are not telling me to keep quiet.' She picked him up and started up the stairs. 'Good grief, you are getting so heavy.'

'Where are we going mommy?'

'Daddy has finished the loft rooms and wants an official unveiling. We are going to have a party.'

'A party?' he wriggled out of her arms and ran up the next flight of stairs on his own, shouting 'Party, party, party.'

When she arrived on the loft landing, Daniel had a red ribbon pulled across the top of the stairs, while Harry waited eagerly by his side.

She took the pair of scissors Daniel handed her, and cut the ribbon. 'I declare the loft area officially finished.'

151

Harry clapped enthusiastically while Daniel poured two glasses of sparkling wine and a fizzy drink for Harry.

'I am really impressed, I never knew you were so skilled,' she praised, as he led her from one room to the next.

They had kept to an arrangement after a while. Whereby Alice did all the domestic chores and took care of Harry, while Daniel got on with the renovation work. Alice had rarely ventured back upstairs, not since the time Daniel had spooked her.

'All finished,' he said and raised a glass.

'An exceptionally talented daddy,' she said to Harry and cheered them both. 'Now if we can just get you to stop swearing, I might just have the perfect husband.'

'I can't get rid of that smell though,' he admitted.

'Not pleasant,' she agreed, sniffing the air.

'Can't understand it,' he replied.

'Smells like cooked vegetables, I don't like it. Come, let's go down, I have been slaving in the kitchen all afternoon, and Colin and Debbie are due in an hour.'

After their meal Daniel could not resist taking their friends upstairs to show off the finished product, and when they looked around, he was not disappointed by their response.

Debbie was impressed. 'Amazing. You are very clever.'

'Colin has helped a lot.' Daniel placed a hand on Colins shoulder. 'He has been a true buddy.'

Reaching for the bottle of sparkling wine left on the shelf earlier, he found the glasses, but the wine was gone. He walked from room to room and came back empty handed.

'I must have taken it downstairs,' he said with some resignation. 'Come on, let's have a drink in the lounge and catch up.' He looked at Colin. 'We haven't seen much of you lately.' Then drew his old friend aside. 'By the way, have you been doing a bit of work around here without me knowing?'

Colin looked perplexed. 'No, nothing other than what you know about. Why?'

'Forget I mentioned it then,' Daniel dismissed the issue, as they caught up with the girls.

He took a fresh bottle of sparkling wine from the fridge and remained convinced that someone was playing tricks on him. Although the missing bottle was minor, it added to his growing fear that something strange was going on in the house.

Settling into a regular routine of work at the office and then a quick change when he got home, he started renovating the twelve bedrooms spanning the second floor. After taking some advice he planned on turning them into four luxury en-suites with adjoining open plan bathrooms. Keeping a further three as single rooms, while converting the remaining room into a shared bathroom. It was an ambitious plan, but one he thought would add real value to the property.

Little Harry struggled to sleep through all the noise, as Daniel started knocking out walls and converting rooms into bathrooms.

'Harry wants to sleep in the kitchen,' Alice said, soon after he had started with the demolition work.

'The kitchen? Why there?'

'He likes it there. It's away from the noise and dust. And not forgetting he spent the first few months of his life in there. Or we could turn the larder room into a temporary bedroom until you have finished making all this noise.'

'It smells in there Alice.'

'I had a look in the hardware shop and there is a small air recycling kit we can buy.'

Harry walked in on the conversation. He looked exhausted. A reminder of his lack of sleep.

'Alright Alice,' Daniel conceded. 'Whatever makes him happy.'

It was difficult work, but Daniel was an architect and with the aid of 3D CAD it made his job a lot easier. Continuing through summer and into winter, going from sweltering hot days to freezing temperatures at night as snow lay thick outside, he slogged on. Single glazed windows, mostly free of ivy on the second floor, let in more light, but all the cold during winter.

Finding himself soon starting to fall further behind schedule, he blamed the cold weather. Then he took some advise, and stuck thick layers of newspaper on the glass panes to retain the heat. However, it had the adverse effect and made the rooms dark and oppressive.

Then within days of covering the windows he found the renovations moving along at a quicker pace. He had to acknowledge it was not the rooms being warmer or anything he had done; work was being completed while he was miles away at the office.

He did not tell Alice. She would have said he was going insane, but somebody was helping him.

At first, he thought it might be Colin coming in when he was not there. But he knew his friend was up to his neck in fresh bids. Then he thought maybe Colin had got workmen in without saying anything. He was not complaining. So long as Fischer never found out he would keep quiet. The pace of change was clearly accelerating, and he loved it.

Temporary lighting strung along the hallway on an extension cable made a big difference, but cast deep shadows where there were no bulbs.

'Is that you Alice?' he called out one evening.

He had seen a shadow pass by one of the lights near the stairwell. There was no response, so he called out again, but this time louder.

'Alice?'

'Do you need me?' she replied from downstairs.

'Were you up here a minute ago?'

'No, why?'

He looked around, feeling the hairs on his forearms rise.

'Nothing, I thought I saw you come up.' He realised how paranoid his voice was sounding and quickly changed the subject. 'Is dinner ready?'

Harry was growing up fast and at two and a half years of age had the run of the house. The second floor was child proofed and a metal gates barred him access to any area where there might be construction tools or materials.

Daniel had decided to take an afternoon off from the office and the continual grind of working on the house. Besides, he was rapidly recovering lost time on his schedule and desperately wanted some family time. Wanting above all else to spend a bit of time with his son.

The game Harry wanted to play consisted of his father pretending to try and catch him as he ducked and weaved from room to room, but tediously always ending in his temporary bedroom, the larder room.

Daniel sneaked up to the doorway and as he got close Harry stepped forward and put his finger to his lips.

'Ssshhh,' he said quietly and held up his other hand, telling his father to stop.

Alice had just arrived back from work and was standing in the kitchen. 'He always does that when he comes out of there. He has such funny little ways about him, don't you think?'

Walking into the larder room Daniel picked the boy up.

'Come on little man, let's get some fresh air.' He turned to Alice. 'Bring a blanket. There is time for a half hour on the terrace before the sun sets.'

A dull noise echoed down from above and Daniel cursed. 'Bloody airlocks again.'

'Mind your language please, Harry picks up on every word, and I certainly don't want him repeating any of your filth,' she said as they walked into the kitchen.

He turned to her. 'If you turn the tap down a bit it when running a bath, it won't airlock as much and I won't have to curse.'

155

'I am not running a bath…, what are you talking about?'

Holding Harry in one arm he scratched his head with his free hand. He struggled to understand the plumbing in this old building. He had made one or two minor changes to the pipes upstairs and added a few bathrooms, but he couldn't imagine it was anything he had done, and it was certainly starting to get the better of him.

They spread their blanket on the front lawn and were admiring the view as the sun tipped the horizon. Alice lifted two glasses and a bottle of wine out of a small cool bag, while Harry had his own little setup of plastic trays and bottles of fizzy pop laid out in front of him.

'Isn't this lovely,' she said.

Just as Daniel put the glass to his lips, he caught sight of the Chinese man disappearing down The Alley. He couldn't recall how many times he had seen him and no matter what tactic he used, the thin figure always appeared to have had advanced warning and manage to evade him. It was like bear baiting and over the months he had even lain in wait, but the wily man was extremely elusive. After a while Daniel wondered if he would ever find out what the thin man in black was up to.

Too much work and not enough play, he thought, before looking in the opposite direction.

What had brought the whole issue to a head, was on an occasion when Daniel was still obsessed with the delivery man and went into hiding, hoping to catch him or at least find out what he was up to.

So, one evening he had hidden in a skip standing outside the kitchen back door. The large steel container had stood there since soon after moving in, where it slowly filled with debris before being replaced by an empty one.

His head poked out from a few cardboard boxes he had saved for the occasion and placed strategically around the inside perimeter. He faced away from the house and could just see the upper end of The Alley.

In the deep shadows of the evening, a second pair of eyes had spotted the Chinese delivery man approaching from further up the road, wrestled him to the ground, and took the backpack. After adding a couple of bricks, the figure crept up to the house and hurled the pack into the skip.

When Daniel came around, it was dark, and Alice was calling his name. There was something sticky and wet on his head that had a strong smell of soy sauce and garlic, with an underlying odour of sour sweetness. A small heap of pork ribs in a sticky sauce had come to rest just in front of his face.

'What the fuck.' He had been startled, and for a while could not work out where he was.

Alice had been looking for him, heard him curse, and ran across to the skip. 'What are you doing in there you fool. I thought you were in the house working.'

There was blood on his forehead, right next to the sticky mess of soy sauce and a few grains of cooked rice.

'Fucking delivery man attacked me,' he replied.

Alice started to laugh. Then had to sit down for a while as she doubled over.

'What is daddy doing in the skip?' Harry asked.

'Trying to hide from doing work,' Alice replied, then doubled over again as Daniel climbed out.

He failed to understand how the delivery man had sneaked up on him, and tried to push the whole incident to the back of his mind. There was an awful lot to do in the house, and his obsession was proving to be a sap on his time and energy.

There had been takeout waste in the skip before and he had thought nothing of it, always the same striped cardboard cartons bearing the remains of various dishes. The downside of living near a takeout, he thought. People passing by the house often threw the odd small bit of trash away, but why anyone would want to throw away a backpack of bricks remained a mystery. Then Daniel put it down to someone playing a cruel joke on him. Possibly even the same Chinese character whom he had chased down The Alley. Maybe this was the man's way of getting his own back.

The gash on his head healed, but remained as a reminder to leave the delivery man well alone.

Most evenings after arriving back from work, he would have a quick change of clothing and get back into his scruffs.

And there it was, more progress made than he could recall the previous evening. Some nights he would leave a mark on the wall, and that remained, but the floor would have been swept or picture rail painted. Then one day he even came back to find the tiles in one of the new bathrooms grouted up.

He eventually raised it with Alice, but she had the same answer. 'You have been working too hard. Time for a break, or maybe even an evening at a festival.'

His lederhosen were starting to fall apart and would have been an impressive sight at any beer fest. That was, if he ever got to one, he thought.

She was getting worried about him, and chatted to Debbie as they served plates of food to the homeless that Saturday at the local shelter.

Her friend looked concerned. 'The men never get together anymore,' she complained. 'And of course, it doesn't help now that Colin is senior to Daniel. I think it would do them both the world of good to have some time out together. A bit of bonding time.'

'He will not relax,' Alice complained. 'He has become obsessed with the house and spends every spare minute talking about it or working on it. At least Harry has been relocated back into a fully refurbished bedroom down the corridor. It gave me the creeps to think of him in the larder room.'

'Daniel is certainly making progress then,' Debbie acknowledged.

'I sometimes think it's slowly driving him crazy. He says he sees shadows and even has some help from an invisible friend.'

'What?'

'Yes, he claims that someone is helping him during the day while he is at work. At first he thought it might have been Colin, or someone I had brought in.'

Debbie laughed. 'If you find out who it is, give them my address, I could certainly do with some help. Another pair of helping hands would be most welcome. As for Colin, his list of jobs at home is growing by the day.'

Alice drew closer to her friend and lowered her voice. 'You heard about the skip incident; I take it?'

Debbie looked at her for a while before she started to giggle. After a few minutes they were both still in tears. Alice had not laughed as much since buying the house.

Alice started getting the garden into shape. During the evenings, she would let Harry play with his toys in the dirt while she dug up flowerbeds and planted bulbs from her nursery.

However, when she took Daniel out to show him the progress, the plants had been pulled out and strewn around the lawn. Daniel calmed her and helped to replant them.

'Don't worry Alice, I will keep my eye out for whoever is doing this and when I catch them, they are in serious trouble.'

The suits conducted the following annual inspection and gave another glowing report. They looked at Daniel with renewed respect and signed off a second year.

As they descended the stairs, a thumping sound came from the loft.

'What was that?' one of the suits asked.

'Nothing,' Daniel replied. 'Just some unresolved plumbing issues.'

Harry was standing just inside the entrance hall, and when the suit looked at him, he placed his finger to his lips.

'Ssshhh, don't tell anyone.'

The suits looked at one another, then at Daniel, but there was no explanation, so they followed Alice out to see how she was progressing with the garden.

When they got close to the flowerbeds, they came to an abrupt halt, and Harvey sidled up to her.

'Alice, do you realise that these are protected cycads. They were reported stolen from the botanical gardens and include some rare specimens. It is all over this morning's news.'

Alice shuddered. 'They aren't the ones I planted. Who has done this?'

Meetings at JJ Fischer and Partners were starting to get on Daniel's nerves, and he resented the Solicitor and his five suits who sat interrogating them. Asking for progress reports and at the same time giving nothing away from their secret files in front of them. Their scripts were well hidden from view and at times he had no idea why certain questions were being asked.

The issue of the stolen plants from the botanical gardens had been settled, and with the assistance of Fischer all charges had been dropped. They considered the incident to most likely to have been carried out by a prankster. Someone envious of their inheritance.

They left the meeting and walked out into the sunlight.

Daniel turned to Alice. 'God, I would give anything to climb on my bike and have a good ride.'

'I don't even know if the bike group still exists,' she replied. 'Debbie never mentions them when we meet up and you haven't seen Colin sociably for a while. Anyway, the soup kitchen has asked me to stand in for a few more Saturdays a month. They are so busy.'

Daniel prickled. He resented the time Alice spent feeding the homeless and held a firm view that they should get a job and earn their own way in life. But he kept quiet. Every time the subject had been raised before, it had invariably ended in an argument.

'I see Colin at work, but we never discuss anything but business. It is better that way now that he is my boss.'

'I will give Debbie a call then,' she said.

'I miss my old cycling buddies,' Daniel reminisced. 'How about us getting reacquainted with the group and have a bit of time out? If they are free this weekend, we could hire a bike trailer for Harry and get away for a couple of days.'

Alice phoned Debbie and made plans to meet that Saturday morning. She was even prepared to forgo her shift at the soup kitchen to please Daniel on this occasion. Debbie said they were going to cycle across the border into Poland. A good cycle that required a certain level of fitness.

'Of course, we are fit,' he said after she had relayed the message. 'We have spent every day over the past two and a half years working on the house. I bet I can still whip Colin's arse on the straight.'

They set off from the Brandenburg Gates at nine. A tight group of cyclists and friends they had not spent enough time with of late.

Daniel drew level with Colin. 'The group has changed a bit.'

'It has, but remember how it used to change when you were riding all the time. You have just been away that long you are noticing the changes all that much more.'

Approaching a subway Daniel found the buggy a drag. It made no difference how hard he peddled, little Harry weighed down the carriage and it felt like he was dragging a sack of potatoes.

'Duck you suckers,' the lead cyclist shouted, and they flattened on their handlebars. The tradition had lived on, and Daniel felt a surge of joy and a longing for the good old days. He laughed and looked back at Harry, who beamed from his little carriage. The child loved the outing and the shout most of all. When Colin drew alongside pulling Rodney the young boys called out to one another, 'duck suckers', and giggled.

By the end of the day the Somersby's were cycling alone. They were saddle sore and exhausted. Their friends had gone on ahead after giving them some encouragement. Offering to have a cold beer waiting for them when they got to the guesthouse.

They never made the next day. Both were so exhausted they decided to quit the group and get a train back home. They were just not fit enough to continue.

'Can I get a puppy?' Harry asked.

The couple looked at one another, completely taken aback.

'Why a dog?' Daniel asked.

'I have no friends and want to play games. I can throw a ball for a puppy.'

Daniel sneaked a quick look at Alice and saw she was frowning.

'I know where this has come from,' she said. 'Rodney is not allowed to play with Harry anymore. They have even moved him from the same pre-school.'

'What the fuck...'

'Daniel!'

'Sorry Alice. What's going on? They used to play together all the time. Hell, they have been lifelong friends. Just wait until I speak to Colin,' he paused. 'I thought he was my best buddy, the bastard.'

'I don't need to remind you that Colin has a senior position in your company now. You cannot afford to lose your job as well as your best friend.'

'This is ridiculous Alice. It is our son we are talking about here.'

'Don't forget Manor House. Blow your job and there goes your inheritance.'

'I will get another job.'

'Think carefully about what you are saying. You do have a habit of rushing in.'

162

He brooded for a while, paced the floor, and then went back up to the first floor where he was now well ahead of schedule.

'I will see him at work tomorrow,' he shouted down.

Standing in Colin's office, three walls of glass allowed everyone to see in and Daniel knew he had to be careful. He could not afford to lose his temper in that open environment.

'We don't like the way Harry is behaving lately,' Colin responded, after receiving a venting of angry abuse.

Daniel's hands shook and his face turned red. 'What behaviour Colin? He is just a kid.'

'He keeps scaring Rodney with stories of a strange man. His best friend who lives in the pantry. A man who watches everyone through a gap in the door. Apparently when Harry tries to speak to him, this apparition of a thing puts a finger to his lips and tells him to hush.'

'That's bullshit Colin. He has done that silly thing ever since he could first walk.'

'That's not all. Harry claims the old man actually lives in your house.'

Pacing the office, Daniel was finding it hard to contain his temper. Holding back like he had never held back before. There was an office full of architects working nearby and when Daniel looked out, he could see furtive glances and hands covering mouths, as staff speculated as to what was going on.

'Your solution is to separate the two. Is that sensible Colin?'

'We can let them play together, but Rodney refuses to sleep at your house. He says that besides Harry's tales, there are strange noises and is scared at night. By the time Debbie picks him up he is usually exhausted.'

'What are you going to call your dog, Harry?'

'Doggie.'

'What about a proper dog name like Rover, Rocky or Duke?'

'No, I want to call him Doggie.'

'Let him name the dog,' Alice reprimanded Daniel. 'If he wants to call the animal Doggie, then let it be his choice,'

'OK, so long as I don't have to pick up dog crap, call him anything you like. Maybe we could train him to attack the Chinese delivery guy and chew his balls off.' He laughed and walked out of the kitchen, leaving Harry and Doggie to get acquainted and Alice fuming.

She stood with her hands on her hips staring after him. She had been drying a small pot and if she had not been in full control, would have thrown it at him.

Harry placed the dog basket and bowl in a corner of the kitchen, out of the general thoroughfare, while Alice phoned the dog breeder and ordered a puppy.

The little three-year-old ran out into the yard and Doggie followed, nipping at his heals. The Alsatian pup was playful and an intelligent animal. It lifted Alice's spirits to see the two of them romping around the garden. When Harry fell over Doggie would dive on him. Harry would get to his feet, then shriek in delight as the pup bowled him over once again.

That evening Doggie was exhausted and lay in his bed, while Harry sat in the dining room with his parents. Ground rules had been established and Harry's pet was not allowed the complete run of the house.

'Animals should have their place,' Daniel commanded.

'He is my friend Daddy. Can't he sleep in my bedroom?'

Alice looked at Daniel, who repeated his objection as he stood up to leave the room.

Harry helped Alice with clearing up, while Daniel went back up to the first floor where he was making a start on stripping out the small first-floor library. The boy carted a stack of dinner plates through to the kitchen, before settling at the small table next to where Doggie had passed out. His ginger hair fell over his face as he started colouring in a book he had been given at pre-school. Alice noticed that so long as Doggie was close by, he was content.

She left him for a while and took a fresh cup of tea up to Daniel. When she returned, Doggie was out of his basket and staring at the larder room. The hairs on the back of his neck were bristling.

'I though Doggie was sleeping?'

'He was, but the old man woke him up.'

'What old man, my little pumpkin?'

Alice had heard the same thing from Harry ever since he had first learned to talk.

'My friend in there.' He pointed at the larder room door.

As she had always done when asked, she went and had a look inside, as she had done so often before and found nothing there. The room was empty.

'Nobody there today my little storyteller. How come I have never seen him?'

'The old man only comes to the door when you are not here'

'Does he scare you?'

'No, but why does he always stare at me?'

'Now Harry, I have told you before, it is not nice to scare your mommy. There is no old man in there. Why don't we go in together and you can see for yourself?'

She opened the door to the large room that had stood empty since they had moved Harry up to his bedroom on the second floor. The space was fitted out with rows of shelving and tall standing internal cupboards that had gathered a thin layer of dust. A strange, but familiar smell made Alice shiver.

Harry started to shake. 'It's cold mummy, can we go out? I don't like it in here anymore.'

She took his hand and walked out, closing the door gently behind her.

'Happy now Harry?'

'But he comes from there mommy, then always holds his finger to his mouth like this and says ssshhh. Like you show me when you want me to be quiet.'

Alice and Daniel had discussed Harry's repeated sightings of the mystery figure. There had always been an old man in the larder, holding his finger to his mouth.

They had searched the room after arriving home. Opening all the cupboard doors that were not jammed shut, and looking under each shelf. Although they found nothing, there persisted the same lingering smell, regardless of how much air spray they poured into the space.

'No Ghosts Alice,' he said as they emerged. 'The boy has a vivid imagination, that's all.'

Soon after dinner the following week, and while Alice was making a cup of Horlicks, Doggie started to growl.

'Stop that nonsense,' she chided, then turned to see the pup standing with its tail rigid and teeth bared.

The larder cupboard door rattled, followed by the sound of wood scraping on concrete and Doggie barked.

'Who is there?' she called out.

About to take hold of the handle, she drew back and called for Daniel.

When he looked inside the room it was empty.

'This is getting a bit much Alice. First Harry, and now you.'

She had no answer, but quickly finished tidying up and followed Daniel back upstairs. The kitchen was starting to give her the creeps.

Chapter 15
Harry's 3rd Birthday

The child's birthday party was going off with a bang. Little children ran everywhere, while parents gathered in the sitting room and socialised. A few older children assisted Olga and kept an eye on the youngsters. Making sure they did not stray too far, as parts of the house were still a building site.

'Happy Birthday to you, Happy Birthday to you, Happy Birthday dear Harry, Happy Birthday to you,' they sang as the boy sat at the head of the table, ready to blow out the three little candles on his cake.

'Hip, Hip, Hooray,' they all chorused.

Harry blew and waves of ginger hair fell over his little freckled face. He looked around, proud to have blown them all out with a single breath.

'Now make a wish,' Alice shouted over the din created by fifteen excited little children, all eager to get a slice of cake.

'I wish my old friend in the kitchen could have some cake,' he replied.

Everyone clapped, while Daniel drew close to Alice. 'His imaginary friend in the kitchen again,' he whispered.

'I wish he wouldn't keep talking about him. It gives me goose bumps,' she replied.

Debbie was handing out paper plates nearby and overheard them.

'Still seeing ghosts then. Anything we should know about?' she asked with raised eyebrows.

'Come on Debbie,' Daniel said in frustration. 'We have been through this so many times before.'

'But you have to admit it. You must think something is going on. Be honest.'

'No Debbie, no more talk of bloody ghosts,' Daniel said in a harsh tone.

A sudden hush fell over the adults nearby, and he flushed with embarrassment.

'Ghost busters,' he shouted, and pulled his jersey over his head.

The children shrieked and ran off in all directions, while cake landed on the floor and the party erupted into chaos.

Alice stood shaking her head, wondering when Daniel might start to take things seriously. Hoping that one day he might grow up.

Colin approached her. 'It is our Rodney's third birthday soon, why don't you come over to our apartment for a little celebration?'

'That would be lovely, thanks Colin,' she replied.

'We would invite more children,' he added, 'but our place is a little cramped.'

Arriving back from chasing the children, Daniel approached his old friend. 'Hey bud, we don't see much of you lately.'

'We are still in the same apartment. Out cycling with the same group every weekend and going to the beer garden on Fridays.' He looked at Daniel with an expression verging on pity. 'We are always there for you guys. You just seem so busy lately.'

Harry's birthday party was a huge success, but by late afternoon they were exhausted, and relieved when the last of the guests had departed.

Returning to the lounge, they wanted nothing more than to put their feet up for a while before tackling the mess. Doggie was still chasing Harry around the large sitting room. Both were high on sugar and had excess energy. Olga, trailing after them, saw Daniel's glare, and shepherded the two out into the garden.

Then, just as they started to enjoy the peace and quiet, a sudden noise startled them.

'I thought everyone had left,' Daniel said, as he reluctantly got up and went to investigate.

Thinking that one of the guests may have popped back for a coat or umbrella, he went first to the boot room off the entrance.

'Hello, is anyone still here?'

Turning back, he heard a different sound and it came from the kitchen.

'Anyone there?' Alice called from the sitting room.

'No, most likely just a plate settling in the sink,' he called back. 'I have never seen such a mess.'

She wandered through and settled at the small kitchen table.

'I am exhausted. Can you sort it?'

'Might as well get this all done now that I am here,' he muttered, and started the laborious job of rinsing and stacking the dishwasher.

He failed to notice that one of the plates had the remnants of a Chinese meal still painted on the surface. A smear of wasabi, a few strands of ginger and the odd soy-soaked grain of rice.

'Not much food left.' He surveyed the remains. 'Even the candles on the cake are gone.'

'The result of not giving out goodie bags,' she replied. 'Some child has obviously wanted something to remember the party by.'

Harry walked in with chocolate cake still smeared across his mouth, while Doggie collapsed on the cold slate floor. Olga made an exit with a quick farewell, as the boy stood surveying the remains, before starting to fill a plate with biscuits and sweats.

Alice reached for the plate. 'Oh no little man, it might be your birthday, but you have had enough sugar to last you a month.'

Harry moved a step away from her. 'It is for my friend.'

Daniel turned to Alice with a concerned look. They were starting to get worried about the boy. He mixed well at his pre-school, had plenty of friends, and they had just seen how well he had interacted with all his little party guests. So, they saw no reason why he should invent an imaginary friend.

Clearing the kitchen took a while, and as they were about to retire back to the sitting room, Alice saw a flickering light reflect in one of the kitchen windows. She recalled leaving a table and chairs outside for the smokers to use. But this wasn't a smouldering cigarette butt, it was a raging fire.

Daniel dialled the fire services. 'We have a container on fire,' he shouted hysterically. 'It could spread to the house if the winds come up.'

The fire was soon brought under control.

'Most likely a careless smoker,' a fireman said before leaving.

Steaming remains revealed melted and charred remnants of their garden chairs and umbrella.

Daniel looked on in frustration. 'Who would do that?'

'It looked like the man from the kitchen,' Harry said, as he arrived and surveyed the burned-out embers.

'You saw someone do this?' Daniel asked.

Harry shrugged and walked off.

Taking Harry to a child psychologist had been a debatable issue. Having discussed it at length they both soon agreed that it would be for the best.

The specialist said that being an only child might be the reason he was inventing imaginary friends. Offering a few other explanations, the only sound advice he could give was for them to try for another child. Harry would then have a sibling to focus on.

'Another little one?' Alice prompted.

'No.'

'Just one?'

'Can't afford it.'

'When we can?'

'Possibly one day.'

'When the house is finished, and the five years is up?'

'Not a bad idea,' Daniel said as he turned to her with a smile.

He had not smiled for a while and she felt a welling up of emotion. 'Now, why don't you do that more often. Reminds me of the person I first met.'

Walking out of the medical centre where Harry had been assessed, they headed for the tram stop.

'What do you think of Harry's obsession and the psychologist's verdict?' Alice questioned.

'Bullshit,' Daniel replied. 'It has all become too much. All the bloody time, my friend this, my friend that. Every time he opens his mouth it's the same old rubbish.'

They looked at their little boy ten yards ahead, wobbling along on his bicycle, while small trainer wheels bounced over pebbles.

'He looks normal enough,' Alice conceded.

The child was well out of hearing range, but he turned, and gave them a reassuring smile. They relaxed a little. Yes, he looked normal enough, thought Daniel.

'Are you racing, my darling,' Alice called.

'I am racing to get home to see my friend,' he shouted back.

Three years of change had impacted on all their lives, and everything was not quite what it used to be.

Three fifth of the allocated time to complete had slipped by as they continued to work feverishly on getting the house into shape. The amount of work still outstanding was mind boggling and their funds were draining away at an alarming rate.

When the third annual meeting with Fischer took place, Daniel felt full of himself as the suits heaped praise on his attention to detail and the finish achieved.

'You appear to be ahead of schedule and the finish is to an exceedingly high standard,' Fischer praised.

'We have run out of money, and it is slowing me down,' Daniel complained.

'You are not keeping to your schedule.' Fischer wagged his pen at him. 'That is your problem. Your own spends profile linked to the acceleration of work way exceeds your income.'

Daniel prickled. He absorbed praise, but rejected any notion that he may be at fault.

'I know what I am doing Mister Fischer, and don't forget, I am the architect and have been in the building game since graduating. I know what needs to be done.'

'Just a comment.' Fischer held up both hands in surrender. 'Not criticism.'

Fed up with sitting in on these annual interrogations he shifted restlessly. 'Are we finished?'

'Just about,' Fischer continued undaunted. 'The only issue I want to raise revolves around clause four.'

'I can assure you there are no tenants in our house.' Daniel was quick to respond. 'We are aware of the implications of clause four and wouldn't do anything to put ourselves at risk. Why do you ask?'

The lead suit answered. 'During our recent inspection and whilst on the second floor, we became aware of a noise coming from upstairs. Somewhere at loft level..., can you explain that please?'

Daniel looked at Alice. He had been out at work and she had taken the suits on the last tour.

'I don't understand,' she replied. 'It was most likely Harry or the childminder moving around in the boy's bedroom.'

'Both Harry and the childminder were in the garden having a picnic, if you recall,' the suit pointed out.

'Then there must be some other explanation,' she protested. 'Because we do not have any lodgers, it is as simple as that.'

'When we went outside,' the suit resumed, 'we spoke with your son and he told us that a man lives in the room next to the kitchen. He told us that the same man set your rubbish skip on fire and sometimes makes a mess of the garden which makes you angry.'

'A mess of the garden? What has that got to do with us inheriting the house?' Daniel was clearly at the limit of his patience.

Alice gave an exasperated sigh. 'Every time I plant something in the garden, it gets dug up. You know about the botanical plants, because Harvey was visiting at the time. But it did not stop there. Plants dug up and lawn sprayed with poison has left large brown patches of dead grass.'

Fischer hesitated, before continuing in a gentler tone. 'Do you suspect Harry is having some sort of difficulties?'

'He is only behaving like any normal three-year-old would,' Daniel replied defensively 'He lives in a fantasy world. Anyway, this is all bullshit. There is only the three of us living in the house.' He looked around in frustration. 'Would you like to bring in a search party?'

'That will not be necessary,' Fischer replied. 'I know that renting out a room would bring in the extra income you desperately need and we are just looking after your interests. The terms of the will are quite specific. It would be a tragedy if you lost the house for the sake of a lodger.'

Having endured enough humiliation, Daniel reared at the men sitting opposite him. 'I will only say this once more. Just so that you hear this loud and clear.' He raised his voice. 'We have nobody living in our house. There is nobody there but us... and certainly no lodgers.'

Fischer could see he was getting angry. 'Should we draw this meeting to an end?'

'Bloody right. I am fed up with this interrogation.' Daniel stood and pulled at Alice's hand. 'Come on, were off.' Then looking around the table he muttered. 'See you lot at the next inspection..., whenever that may be.'

Once they were out on the street he turned to Alice. 'Can you please keep Harry away from them in future.'

'It is not my fault. Stop being such a grouch.' She pulled at his hand and turned to look him in the face. 'Ease up on me. I have had enough of your foul temper... and while I am at it, your swearing is getting on my nerves.' She dragged out the next three words. 'Cut... it... out.'

Pulling his hand free he strode off in the general direction of their house. Alice found a bench under a broad beech tree and composed herself before following.

Walking back into Manor House, Alice thought she saw something move in the kitchen.

'Doggie, come here boy,' she called.

Doggie came into the house through the dog flap. He stood panting at his food bowl. Daniel came wandering in a minute later.

'I thought I would take him for a quick walk. Clear my head after the meeting.' He looked at her. 'Sorry Alice, I know I lost it at the Solicitors and took it out on you, but this house is starting to wear me down.'

'All right. Just take it a bit easier on me. I am not your punch bag.'

They had a cuddle before he went back to the library. Alice looked suspiciously at the larder room door. She was not sure why, but then it moved ever so slightly again.

'Daniel!' she called.

There was no response, so she went looking for him, and found him balancing precariously on the ladder in the library, replacing the last of the five thousand books.

She decided it was not the best time to mention anything that may upset him. It had taken him a week to remove all the books and stack them in the boot room. Then a month sanding, rubbing down and varnishing the panels. This was the final stage and he was in high spirits.

'Looks good, a very, very professional job.'

'Thanks Alice,' he climbed down and took her hand. 'Sorry for being such an arse. I am just getting fed up with the solicitors, that's all.'

'I think you need a break,' she suggested.

Looking around the room, she noticed that he had replaced the books in random order. Not categorised A to Z as they had been before. However, there was no way she was going to mention it, and thought it well within her capabilities one cold and wet weekend to do it herself.

'A break? Where?' he asked.

'I don't know, what about arranging something with our friends. We haven't seen them for a while, and since you fell out with Colin it has upset the relationship I have with Debbie.'

'I didn't fall out with Colin.' His voice rose an octave. 'He was being a prick and accused Harry of upsetting his precious little Rodney.'

'Well, we should be adult, get over it and move on.'

'We saw them just last month at Harry's birthday party and then a few weeks later when we went to their apartment for Rodney's party. I see him at least once a week at work. Do you want us to live in their pockets?'

'We used to live in each other's pockets before this house came along. We used to have so much fun together. But look at us now?'

'As long as we don't get into any arguments over Harry's ghost sightings, then yes, let's give it a go.'

'That reminds me,' The words were out before she could stop herself. 'When I got home, I thought I saw the larder door move, and not for the first time either.'

'Not you as well Alice.' He rubbed his eyes wearily. 'Do you honestly think we have a ghost in the house?'

She saw the anger surface and quickly changed the subject. 'Which room next Captain Marvelous?'

'Boot room. Now that the books are back in the library, then the lounge. That is the big one before the kitchen, roof and finally the windows.'

'I will get hold of our old pals and arrange something then.'

'Yes, you are right,' he said with some resignation. 'I could do with a break.'

They had a great couple of days away with their friends. Alice had arranged a walking holiday and they enjoyed some beautiful scenery and challenging inclines as they fought their way up steep hills. Reaching the summit, they were rewarded with stunning views of mountains and beautiful valleys that stretched far below.

Both boys played together and kept up with the pace, while Alice kept a close eye on Harry. She had warned him not to say a word to Rodney about the house or any imaginary friends.

When they arrived back home the house was peaceful and quiet. There were no sounds, no shadows, or smells. The garden was as they had left it and the rubbish skip had been replaced.

Alice walked through to the Library, where she wanted to review a few work-related documents for an early meeting the following day. She settled at the large wooden desk. It was the only bit of furniture in the whole room. A piece they had found at an auction and purchased at a very reasonable price. Due to its size, not many houses could have accommodated it.

Looking up at the floor to ceiling shelves of books she started to wonder who had collected them. They mostly related to case law and legal matters regarding property development.

Interesting, she thought. These are exactly the type of books we should have been reading. Maybe there is something here that would help us with our current situation.

Then a sudden realisation hit her.

'Daniel,' she called out, then regretted doing so.

Passing by, he appeared at the door.

'Nothing,' she lied. 'Just wanting to know if you could take Harry to school in the morning. I have an early start.'

He stood looking at her for a while. 'Of course, I can drop Harry off. Are you alright? You look like you have just seen a ghost.'

'I am fine thanks,' she replied.

He went back to the kitchen and she looked up at the five thousand books surrounding her.

They had been neatly rearranged. Back in alphabetical order. A to Z.

Chapter 16
Year 4

The final six months was fast approaching, and they were once again summoned to the offices of JJ Fischer and partners.

Two of the suits had been replaced with younger versions. Their old cycling companion Harvey was still present but appeared tense and shifted restlessly in his chair.

They now had an equal balance of male and female, old and young.

'Very politically correct,' Alice said, after picking out the changes. 'I am impressed.'

Fischer grimaced. He had thought the changes would go unnoticed. He was of the old school and had initially put up quite strong resistance to correcting the balance. Harvey appeared to have aged considerably since they had last seen him.

'Still cycling Harvey?' Daniel asked.

'Not anymore. We have just had our second child. With the demands at work and spending time with the kids, I just don't have much energy left come the end of the week.'

'Welcome to my world Harvey,' Daniel smiled.

Alice prodded him in the ribs. 'You should be spending more time with Harry.'

Looking uncomfortably at her and then at how pale and tired his old cycling partner appeared, he was not so sure. That is how I would look if I spent more time with Harry, he thought to himself.

Fischer appeared to be in an agitated mood as he sat facing the couple. He was not his usual collected self.

'How are you getting on?' he asked. 'You have a little over six months remaining and ten percent to gain on the purchase price.'

Daniel was exhausted. He had been up until midnight most nights. Cutting, drilling, sanding, and painting. It was a never ending, thankless task, and when he finished one job, another waited.

'Ground floor nearly complete,' he answered curtly. He was not going to be bullied. 'Your suits are up to speed. It is only a week since they last invaded our house.'

Fischer ignored the jibe. 'Sounds good, what problems are you encountering?'

'None. Just an endless amount of work, not enough money and wasting time coming here. Why do you ask?'

'We have undisclosed notes in the will that requires us to ask certain questions,' Fischer explained. 'We have to keep a close eye on your performance as well as your wellbeing.'

'So, what's the problem?' Daniel pressed.

Fischer shifted uncomfortably in his seat before flipping through a few pages in front of him. He found the section he was searching for before looking up at Daniel.

'Have you experienced any paranormal activity in the property?'

Daniel looked surprised by the question, but at the same time perplexed.

'No, why do you ask?'

'With only six months left I need to check on a few things, such as the fire in the skip, the plants being dug up and the noises. Do you not find it strange that so many unexplained things have happened since moving in?'

'Not in today's world,' Daniel said dismissively. 'With all the vagrants living rough, I am surprised it is not more prevalent.'

Alice rounded on him. 'It's not *their* problem they are on the street.'

He ignored her, while Fischer produced a second sheet of paper from a folder.

'I have a recent valuation carried out by one of my team.'

'We were about to have one done ourselves,' Alice said in surprise.

Fischer passed a folder across. 'No need, you can have a copy of ours.'

Daniel looked at Alice and then back to Fischer. 'I don't recall anyone doing a valuation,'

'It was actually me,' Harvey spoke up. 'When I popped in for a visit a few weeks ago.'

Daniel was half out of his chair. 'What?'

'It was a request made in his will,' Fischer intervened.' One of those that could not be revealed before.'

After four and a half years Daniel was starting to feel defeated. He had always suspected this to be a poisoned chalice, but could not believe anyone would have subjected him to such cruelty.

Fischer spoke in a low voice. 'Do you recall the document we challenged you on after the purchase? It was called 'Disclosure by Seller'?'

'Yes.'

'Well, if you had read all the way through the entire document and put two and two together, you would have guessed that Manor House had either an unwelcome guest, or a ghost.'

'That's bullshit,' Daniel flared.

'Language.' Alice thumped his arm.

'OK, well let's put it this way,' Daniel rephrased his response. 'I don't believe in ghosts and I would know if someone else lived in our house.'

'That's all I need to hear. Harvey couldn't see any signs of a stranger in your house and he discounted the idea of you having any enemies. I just needed to ask you directly.'

Alice shifted uneasily in her chair. She had started to believe that the house was haunted, but was not going to raise it in front of this lot, and especially not at this juncture.

When the couple got home, they dropped their few bags of shopping on the kitchen table.

Daniel turned to Alice. 'What was that all about?'

'I don't know,' she replied, frustrated and tired. 'But I don't like it. Maybe we should get an independent valuer in to see how we are progressing. Old Fischer's valuation was on the low side and he is clearly trying to warn us.'

'Good idea. But let's get another month or two under our belts first. At least we should have the house looking a little more presentable by then.'

Alice went to put the kettle on. 'Ouch,' she yelped.

Looking up, he saw her holding her hand under the cold-water tap. 'What's up?'

'Bloody Kettle was roasting hot. As if it had just this very minute boiled.'

'Language Alice,' he quipped.

'Not funny Daniel.'

'Where is Harry?'

'Still at school..., come on Daniel, you don't even know when he is at school. You need to become more involved in the boy's life.'

'All right Alice, calm down.' He got up and had a look at her hand. 'I have some burn cream in my tool bag.'

He went to the boot room where he had started piling all his equipment. With most of the ground floor renovated, all his tools were either stacked in the boot room or laid out on the shelves in the larder room.

'Not in the boot room,' he called back and headed for the larder room.

He found the tool bag and retrieved the lotion.

181

'Here Alice, spread this cream over the burn. It should take away some of the sting.'

She rubbed the lotion over the palm of her hand.

'Will you please close that door, there is that smell coming from the room again.'

'Not again,' he replied. 'You'd think we had a bloody restaurant in there.'

Continuing to work hard at their day jobs they spent most evenings sanding and painting, then weekends walking around reclamation yards looking for artefacts they could use in the house. Railings, door furniture and even old kitchen units recently ripped out of a nearby home. Anything that would be cheap, in keeping, and add value to the property.

Alice had given up on the garden after the vandal had returned. Daniel blamed the Chinese man and had a camera installed. But the grainy images from the camera went further than exonerating the man in black. It cleared the Chinese man altogether. The figure they watched hack out plants was more thickset and arrived and left in a small river craft, crossing from one side of the Spree to the other.

Then the vandalism stopped.

'The camera has scared him off,' Daniel proclaimed. 'I should have done that years ago.'

Chapter 17
Strange Happenings

Only the roof, windows and rendering remained to be completed. The ivy had by now spread and claimed most of the upper building.

'This is going to be the most expensive part of the project Alice, and we are fresh out of funds.'

'We have another two months. Stop worrying.'

'I think it's time to get the valuer in without old Fischer knowing. We have already spent just over four hundred thousand on the place and it's looking good. If the private valuation shows us having reached anywhere near the ten percent gain and I get that big bonus I have been promised for the past year, then there's not much more we need to do but spend it on upgrades. At least then we can take our foot off the gas.'

They had been sitting in the kitchen, having their first real discussion regarding the selling of the property since moving in. Harry was outside playing in the garden. He was quite an independent child. A lonely little chap, keeping himself amused, while Doggie remained a playful companion, never leaving the boys side.

'Who do we get to do the valuation?' she asked.

'Let's get Khune and an independent estate agency, and see how they compare?'

Khune came back with a very disappointing valuation. They were two hundred thousand off the mark. The property market had suffered a slight downturn and that was not helping matters much.

'It is mostly to do with the loft windows and the roof,' they were told. 'It's not showing off the property to its best potential. And of course, the garden looks a mess and gives the whole place a shabby appearance.'

'Is that all?' Alice asked.

'The Disclosure by Seller document,' Khune went on to explain, 'will weigh heavily against attracting a good bidder. The declaration that says a team of paranormal investigators was called in by the last tenants is not going to go down well with most potential home seekers.'

'How did you miss that?' Alice turned on Daniel.

'Don't blame me. We both had a look at the documents together.'

'You never mentioned that part though,' she fixed him with a steely look.

'Alice, don't you dare...'

Khune intervened. 'It would also appear that you failed to read about an exorcist who was called in by one of the previous tenants. If you recall, I did try and warn you.'

Alice was fuming. 'Did you know that Daniel?'

'It makes no difference Alice; I don't believe in that sort of thing.'

Alice sat staring him, at a complete loss for words.

Khune coughed. 'I have provided you with your valuation as you asked. Now will you excuse me.'

He barely waited for them to reply, before he was out of the house and up the drive.

Daniel walked out and looked up at the roof. 'Time to get that sorted,' he said, more to himself than Alice.

The following day the second valuer came back. The feedback left them devastated. It was worse than Khune's.

'Can't you put in more hours at work Alice?' Daniel asked.

'I already do five days a week and feed the homeless every weekend. What more do you want me to do?'

'Give up the soup kitchen and get a paid second job instead.'

'No chance,' she replied. 'Who would feed those poor people on the street then?'

Early the following morning the couple did their calculations and realised they were totally reliant on Daniels bonus. It was time to engage a roofing and glazing contractor.

'It's cutting it fine,' he said.

'You appear anxious, what's bothering you so much?'

'I can't wait to get out of this house,' he complained. 'Just look out of the window.'

They stood on the second floor looking toward the Spree. At first, she saw nothing strange. Then she saw the familiar figure of the Chinese delivery man with a backpack slung over his shoulder. She followed Daniel's gaze back to where Harry was wandering around in circles with Doggie by his side. Neither the boy nor the dog could have seen the stranger over the fence.

In all the years they had lived there, Daniel had failed to catch up with the strange man.

'What is Harry looking for?' he asked.

'He says he is gathering wildflowers so that he can give them to his friend,' she replied.

'Who? Rodney?'

'No, you know he never sees him anymore, just as you don't see Colin.'

'He has Doggie.'

'No, those flowers are for his imaginary friend.'

'Oh, my fuck,' Daniel groaned. 'I can't take any more.'

Alice looked at him and saw the strain. He was no longer the placid, playful, couldn't care less man she had married. Then she saw his gaze fix on the Chinese man as he wandered back down The Alley, and saw his face flush. Alice wanted him to release all his pent-up frustrations, and for the first time ever, urged him on.

'Confront your demons Daniel. Get hold of him and find out what he is up to, and then have a serious chat with Harry. If it helps at all, that's the best advice I can give.'

Daniel wasted no time and bounded down the stairs.

By the time he arrived at the top of The Alley he was just in time to see the thin man straighten and walk away without the bag. It had always been the same patch of alley where the mysterious bag had disappeared. But when he looked around, the man in black had vanished.

He searched the area central to the gable end of their house and noticed a few fresh marks around the steel hatch. The one they had initially taken for an electric meter box. He tried to pry it open, but it was locked shut.

Not to be outwitted, he returned with a crowbar and levered at the steel door, but all he managed to do was mangle the metal and scratch the surface.

When he returned to where Alice now sat weeding the garden, he was frustrated and annoyed. 'One day he will be too slow, and that's when I get to hear what he has been up to for all this time.'

Harry arrived with his bunch of wildflowers, artfully arranged with a long stem of grass binding them all together.

'Where are you going Harry?' Alice asked.

'To get a vase,' he replied.

'He should be playing with Rodney. Not messing around with a bunch of flowers,' Daniel objected.

'You're right, but Colin and Debbie feel quite strongly about the ghost stories Harry keeps going on about,' she reminded him.

'They can go to hell. I don't want to see them again.'

186

'It makes no difference. If you hadn't noticed, we don't see much of any of our friends anyway,' she replied.

Walking back into the house, he stopped and cocked his head to one side. Then slowly crept into the kitchen, and stealthily headed towards the kitchen sink where he paused and whispered back to Alice.

'Listen,' he looked at her with his eyes raised. 'Can you hear that noise?'

'What noise?'

'Water running somewhere in the house. I can hear it running through the pipes under the sink.'

Alice was at her wits end and had a strong urge to get out of the house. Her nerves were in tatters.

'I am going out for a while,' she said in exasperation. 'I need to get some shopping done and buy Harry a new jersey. The poor kid has hardly any clothes. When he leaves for school in the morning, he looks half frozen.'

Daniel picked up a few spanners and a hacksaw. 'I will sort this out,' he muttered under his breath.

He found the valve at the back of the kitchen sink and closed it. Then altered the pipework so that there were only two feeds remaining. One to the kitchen and one to their bathroom. The other ten outlets he sealed with blanking plates.

Feeling as if he had achieved some sort of result, he smiled to himself and whispered, 'That should be that.'

It was getting dark as he went around turning on a few lights, and was returning to the kitchen when a loud popping sound came from the fuse box, and all the lights went out.

'What the hell is going on,' he cursed.

A loud thump echoed from somewhere above him. He stopped and listened. Then it came again, echoing through the larder cupboard.

'Get out of my house,' he shouted in a rant of madness. 'And stay out.'

Three loud thumps echoed from above and Daniel took off. The hairs on the back of his neck stood up like bristles, as he charged out of the front entrance. The safest place he could think of was in the garden. Whatever was in the house could not get him out there. And when he looked around, Doggie was standing by his side whimpering.

'A fat lot of good you are,' he said, scowled at the shivering dog.

Chapter 18
Under Attack

Daniel never let on just how scared he was. He was supposed to be the man of the house and at that moment in time he felt more like a mouse. And, although the little creatures had hardly featured in his life, he was about to get acquainted.

He had never been particularly fond of them, but the following evening, soon after Alice had returned from work, she opened the outside shed door to get at her garden implements and was confronted by dozens of large brown river rats. She slammed the door shut and waited for Daniel to return from work.

He looked at her in horror. 'Where did they come from?'

'They weren't there yesterday. I was in and out of the shed a few times all week, but always kept the door shut.'

It was getting dark, so they decided to check again in the morning, hoping that the pack of rats had moved on by then.

Opening the door, the following morning, he peered in, and quickly shut it again.

'Bloody hell, the place is still teaming with them, it's a plague.'

Alice was searching on her phone and picked out the first rat catcher she came across.

He arrived a few hours later.

'Can't understand it,' the man said after turning up with all sorts of nets and traps. 'I have never seen them do that before.'

He caught as many as he could, and placed them in a wire basket.

'Twenty rats,' he said holding up the cage.

'Are you sure you have them all?' Daniel asked, as he stood warily eyeing the fury little creatures.

'Might be one or two left, it's a big shed full of stuff,' the man looked confident. 'But don't worry, I have set a trap and you can check it in the morning.'

Then later that evening, soon after retiring to bed, Alice returned to the kitchen for a glass of milk. Harry had been restless all week and wanted a drink by his bedside.

The full moon lit up the kitchen and guided her to the fridge. She poured a drink for Harry and then saw the remnants of a chocolate bar which she stuffed into her mouth, before closing the door and heading back towards the stairs.

Something caught her eye and made her look back. And as she did so, she could have sworn something moved near the larder room. She turned on the light and saw the door standing slightly ajar. Inside was the normal clutter of Daniels tools and equipment, but other than the usual lingering unsavoury smell, nothing looked to be out of place.

She decided to keep her experience to herself. Daniel was under enough stress and his tolerance levels were at rock bottom. Running an office full of architects, and then juggling time to work on the house was no easy task. Let alone being burdened with ghostly encounters in the larder room.

The following afternoon, after getting home, Alice planted a few cuttings before standing and admiring the results of her hard labour. It was starting to take shape. She had demonstrated a flare for landscaping she never even knew existed. Even the lawn was starting to recover.

Harry was throwing a Frisbee for Doggie, who chased after the plastic disc and caught it in the air. She took little notice of the pair, as they drifted from one end of the garden to the other.

Then the boy wandered over just as she was preparing to pack up for the evening. 'Doggie has run off with the frisbee,' he complained.

'Well, that's strange, because he's never done that before. Maybe he's tired.'

Alice placed the garden implements outside the shed door for Daniel to pack away later. After the rat experience, there was no way on earth she could be enticed to go back in there. Especially as the rat catcher had muttered that there may still be a few running around.

'Alice, will you call Harry in, it's getting late,' Daniel called, as he set the table for dinner.

'He is looking for Doggie,' she sounded concerned. 'It's very strange, he has never gone off like this before.'

Daniel walked around the estate, and was about to call out, when he saw the garden tools lying outside the shed. 'Better put these away,' he muttered and gathered them up.

As he warily entered the dimly lit space, he kept his eyes on the ground, looking for any rogue rats. Then his head thumped on something heavy and wet hanging from a timber beam. Jumping back, he wiped at his face, puzzled to feel his hands sticky wet. He ducked out of the shed just as Harry arrived.

'There is blood all over your head Daddy. Have you cut yourself?'

Not sure what he had encountered he looked at his hands in the half light, then back to the darkened interior.

'Harry, go back indoors,' he ordered, and gave him an urgent shove towards the house, as he followed him in.

He walked back out again a half hour later with two policemen.

'Our Alsatian dog went missing this afternoon and I have just found a sack hanging from the shed beam with something heavy inside, and it is dripping blood. I think it's our dog.' he told the officers.

They cut down the sack as Daniel watched. It hit the ground with a plop, and he heaved, as he thought of Doggie trust up inside, then darted out and took a gulp of fresh air.

'Better have a look at this,' the officer called, as he dragged the sack out and emptied the contents.

Ashen and trembling, Daniel turned to look at what they had found.

'Four dead rabbits with their throats cut. Have you any idea what is going on?' the officer enquired.

Daniel stared at the carcasses. 'Thank God it's not Doggie.' He took a deep breath. 'But why would anyone play a prank like this on us?'

The policemen shrugged, as he added a few notes to a small pad he took from his pocket. 'Better to have the shed locked Sir,' he replied.

A sudden noise made them spin around to see Doggie come bounding out of the hedge, and head straight into the house.

'Is that your dog?' the officer asked.

'It is, thank God,' Daniel replied.

The following evening Daniel's mobile phone rang. He was busy pulling together a schedule of the windows he needed to replace. He ignored it at first. Then after a few more rings it went dead. Two minutes later it rung again. He thought he had better see who it was.

'Hello?'

'Get out of my house,' a muffled voice commanded.

'What..., who's calling?' his temper flared.

'Get out,' the voice repeated.

Looking down at the screen, he saw a picture of Helmut and his mobile number displayed on the screen.

'Helmut is that you?' he shouted.

The phone went dead.

'Who was that?' Alice asked when she came in to see what he was shouting at.

'That fucking numb nuts Helmut. Wait until I get hold of him,' he cursed, still holding his phone.

'Helmut who?'

'The estate agent we dealt with nearly five years ago.'

'What did he say?' Alice pressed.

'Get out of his house?'

'Are you sure? Why would he say that?'

'Maybe he is just getting us back for what we did to him all those years ago.'

'I doubt it,' she replied.

When Daniel spoke to Khune the following day, he was told that Helmut had emigrated to Australia. Khune explained patiently what they had already been told at the time. Helmut's phone had gone missing the night he was attacked in the larder room, and the device was never found. He reminded them of the prank played on his agent and how Helmut had been found bound and gagged. He pulled no punches, and said he still held them responsible.

Settling in the sitting room the following evening with a hot cup of tea, Daniel decided to take an evening off from doing up the house. He would have a bit of 'me' time as he called it. His nerves were still in tatters and the film he was about to watch was a good distraction. Alice and Harry had gone to the cinema to see one of Harry's favourites. The latest Harry Potter film had just been released.

Hearing a noise, he assumed they must have changed their minds and returned. Doggie was fast asleep by his side, so he called out.

'I wasn't expecting you back for hours, couldn't you get in?'

There was no reply, so he hit the pause button, got wearily to his feet, and stretched his legs. Having just dumped his dinner tray, he thought that maybe a plate had settled in the sink. He was tired and reluctant to return, and slunk back into his chair.

Then a sudden banging on his front door made him jump. Doggie was on all fours and barking. Thinking that Alice might have forgotten to take a key, he ran through to let her in. As he turned the handle, the door pressed open and a black clad figure came stumbling in.

It was the Chinese delivery man he had been chasing all these years. Savagely beaten, with blood still running from several cuts on his head and one eye dark and swollen.

Daniel dragged him into the entrance hall and laid him out on the carpet, loosened his collar, and used a cushion to prop up the man's head. His one eye was swollen closed.

'Please, no police or ambulance,' the man croaked.

'You need help bud, you're a fucking mess,' Daniel said, as he examined the cuts and bruises.

Soon realising that the injuries were mostly superficial and that nothing was broken, he pried him for information.

'What happened to you?'

'I thought it was you chasing me and beating me,' the man said, as his one good eye roamed the room. 'But you are here. Who do such a thing to me?' the thin man wailed.

Filling a bowl with warm water, Daniel retrieved his first aid kit from the larder room, and started gently cleaning and dressing the cuts and abrasions. The first aid course he had attended at work, and not paid too much attention to, was coming in handy.

'You need that eye seen to, but otherwise you got off lightly,' Daniel said at last, as he surveyed his handywork.

After giving him a glass of water and box of pain relief tablets, Daniel wrapped a towel around his head, then held the man gently in his arms as he helped him to his feet.

'Thank you, Mister Dan,' the Chinese man managed a crooked smile. 'I thought you bad for chasing me, but you are very kind man.'

Something stirred in Daniels soul, and he looked the thin man in the face. 'If you find out who did this, you tell me, and I will bust his fucking nuts,' he said angrily, as he led the fragile figure from the house.

Watching the man stumble towards the shadows, a sudden realisation hit him, and he called out. 'How do you know my name? And what are you always doing here?'

But the man was gone.

What with all the sounds and flitting shadows, the mysterious phone call and now the injured Chinese man, he was not sure what to expect next. Recalling the earlier noises, he crept through the hall and peered into the kitchen.

Reeling back, he saw a dishevelled looking figure standing near the entrance to the larder room, with something in his hand. Daniel took a step back and nearly fell over Doggie, as he searched his pockets for his mobile phone. Then recalled having left it on the floor in the entrance hall when he had attended the injured Chinese man.

'What are you doing in my house?' Daniel shouted at the deranged figure.

Lanky grey hair hung over ashen skin, and the figure started to sway from side to side, causing the curtain of hair to part slightly. The eyes that bore into Daniels made him take another step back.

'What the fuck are you doing in my kitchen. I saw what you did to the Chinese man and I warn you, I will fight back.'

The figure started to raise a hand holding something metallic and shiny.

'If that's a knife or gun, put it down now,' Daniel screamed.

Then as his knees started to tremble, he decided to get moving, and dashed back to the entrance hall. Retrieving his phone, while keeping an eye on the kitchen door, he dialed the police.

'I need help. There is a dangerous burglar in my kitchen, and he has something in his hand. He could be carrying a gun or a knife,' he shouted hysterically before giving his address.

Two armed policemen arrived within minutes, and found Daniel standing in the entrance hall. He took them directly to the kitchen, where they had a good look around. While he explained in detail what he had seen, the two policemen probed around the room, looking in cupboards and behind doors.

One of the men turned to Daniel. 'We were here a few days ago looking at a sack of dead rabbits. Have you any idea who may be causing you a problem?'

Shrugging, he recalled the same officer attending earlier in the week, when Doggie had gone missing. He was about to answer, when he saw them staring at his blood covered shirt.

'Oh shit,' he muttered, 'it's from the man that was attacked outside our house. I helped him.'

'When was that?' the older of the two asked. 'Was it called in?'

'A Chinese man… knocked on the door… he was attacked, and I helped him.'

'Did you call the police?' the same elderly policeman repeated.

'No. He said not to call the police.'

The officers looked at one another sceptically. The one made a note in his little book and then beckoned Daniel forward. 'Show us where you saw this man with the knife?'

'It could be the same person who attacked the Chinese man,' Daniel suggested.

'You said the attack on the Chinese man took place outside, but you saw the man with the knife inside?'

'Maybe he is following me around and sneaks into the house?' Daniel replied unconvincingly.

'Show us around Sir,' the second officer muttered, then hesitated, and took a close look at Daniel. 'Have we met before?'

Daniel shook his head. 'Never seen you before.'

The officer hesitated a while longer as he studied Daniel's face. 'A good few years back if I recall. I am sure it was you we interrogated after a property salesman was assaulted in this house.'

'That was a long time ago,' Daniel replied dismissively. 'Now can you look for this man before he escapes?'

They had been busy that evening, and this was the last thing they needed just as their shift was coming to an end. The officers searched the house, but could not find any sign of forced entry or anyone sheltering in any of the rooms.

They returned to the ground floor.

'You have a big place here and we have done our best, but there is no sign of any intruders.'

'But he was standing right here in the kitchen with a knife in his hand. Elderly, with long grey hair and a stooped back.'

The older of the two policemen turned to his colleague. 'This sounds familiar. We had the same problem at this house around twenty years ago. In fact, on two separate occasions.'

'So, I am not seeing things then?'

'Sir, we found nothing then, and we cannot see any signs of an intruder now. If I may suggest, keep your doors locked and we will send a patrol car past every evening over the course of the next week.'

The two officers left, and Daniel went back to the sitting room where he finished his cup of tea. Ten minutes later he heard another noise. It was a door opening. He got up and walked briskly through towards the entrance hallway.

'I can't say how glad I am to see you Alice. You will never guess...' he stopped as he passed by the kitchen door.

Thinking Alice had returned, he was shocked to see it was the grey-haired man he had seen earlier, standing quite still, and staring at him through long strands of greasy grey hair.

He was not going to be intimidated in his own home, and with his heart thumping, his mind raced through various options. If he ran, the intruder might chase him. But if he could wrestle him to the ground it could save Alice and Harry when they arrived back. He had seen the injuries inflicted on the Chinese chap, and he was not going to take any chances.

Then when Doggie trotted through and licked the stranger's hand, he decided it was time to confront him.

'What are you doing in my house?' he commanded, trying his best to sound confident.

Tilting his head to one side, the grey-haired figure took a small pad from his pocket and tapped on a keyboard. Daniel recognised the pad as the item he had earlier mistaken for a knife.

A second later a message transmitted from the very same box.

'I want my water turned back on.'

Daniel stood transfixed, as the man's fingers darted across the keyboard and a second message followed.

'And don't phone the police. If the lawyers find out you have a lodger, all will be lost. You would have defaulted on one of Harry's clauses, and loose the house.'

'How do you know about...' Daniel stopped mid-sentence. 'I must be going mad..., I'm talking to a fucking ghost.'

The man watched him closely, before dragging two chairs into the Larder room and indicating that Daniel should follow and sit down. Daniel was transfixed, semi paralysed with fear, and obeyed. It was just as well, as his legs were about to buckle anyway.

The grey-haired man typed. 'No ghost. I live in this house. I am real flesh and blood... and this is *our* house.'

'How did you get in here?' Daniel's voice squeaked. 'No, this is bullshit, there is no way you could have got in without me knowing.'

It was obvious to him that this man had a speech impediment. So, he formed the words with his lips so there could be no mistaking what he had to say next.

'This is *not our house*. It has nothing to do with you. This is *my* house.'

198

The stranger typed. 'I live in the attic; my room is in the very top of this house, and am not deaf, I just can't speak.'

Daniel stared at him in disbelief. 'No, I have refurbished all the attic rooms, you can't be up there.'

'How many attic rooms do you have?' asked the man.

'Fuck you,' Daniel shouted. 'And stop playing games with me. Get out.'

The stranger shook his head as he typed.

'I can assure you of one thing; this is not a game. This is also my house and you cannot sell. I want you to finish all the renovations, but you cannot sell it. And if you do, I will tell Fischer you have a lodger.'

'How do you know about Fischer and his legacy?'

He watched and waited as the man kept one eye on him while typing on the keyboard.

'I live here. You talk about all your personal matters and I am not stupid. There are other means of finding out, but mostly I watch you through the gap in the door and know everything that goes on.'

'Bloody right, we do talk openly. It is *my* house and we have every right to say whatever we like in *my* house.' Then the realisation hit. 'What the fuck, you've been spying on us all this time?'

The grey-haired man pulled the long strands of hair back over his ears and smiled. He displayed an array of discoloured teeth, framed by an ashen face and red rimmed eyes. Daniel could feel the anger rise and he flushed.

'You have absolutely no right to be in this building.' He paused and stared at the man before adding. 'And I certainly don't believe you live here.'

The tapping of fingers on the keyboard sounded loud in the confined space.

'I will show you my room if you don't believe me...., follow.'

Having kept his phone handy ever since the police had been called, he turned it on.

The man quickly typed another message.

'Do not call the police.'

'I am calling my wife, you prick,' Daniel snarled. 'If anything happens to me, she will know all about you and call the police.'

Her phone went to message service.

'Alice, I guess you're still in the cinema, but when you get out and pick up this message, please be careful. If you have not heard from me since this call and twenty minutes have elapsed, call the police. A madman has broken in and I am trying to keep things calm and find out what he wants.'

The stranger stood watching him. Eyes just visible through his hair, as he took in Daniels every move, before typing.

'I will not harm you.'

'You had better not even try. I did Karate when I was a kid, and will kick your arse if you even try and get smart with me.'

Picking up a large knife from a rack in the kitchen, Daniel returned to follow the stranger, who stretched an arm between two cupboards and pulled on a thin lever. One of the cupboards came away from the wall and swung gently open, revealing a low doorway.

Ducking, Daniel followed the figure down a short passageway and into a small room. A steel door on the side wall caught his attention. The man pointed at the hatch, then at his mouth and made out to be eating.

'You get your food from there?' Daniel enquired, and the man nodded.

A dim light bulb hung from cables near to what looked like a narrow stairway.

He was suddenly overcome with claustrophobia and shouted. 'I want answers, and do not lie to me, or you get this blade in your belly.'

The computer voice appeared to boom in the confines and made Daniel jump.

'I have a delivery man who brings food every day…, and don't shout, I am not deaf.'

'You mean that thin Chinese man?'

He smiled at Daniel, squinted his eyes, and nodded.

'Stop fucking with me old man,' Daniel growled. 'This is bizarre, but I am starting to put two and two together now. Something about all of this is starting to make some sort of weird sense…, although I am struggling to understand how this has been going on for all these years and I never found out.'

He drew nearer, wanting to punch the intruder, but shouted instead.

'The rats in the shed, damage to the garden, and then kidnapping Doggie. Oh, and what did that poor Chinese man do? Fail to deliver your meal on time? So, you beat him up? Who else is in on this?'

He was starting to sound hysterical and raised the knife in a threatening manner. Grey hair dropped and masked the strangers face as he typed. He was slower in the half light, and Daniel waited until he was finished.

'Why would I beat up my only friend? And believe me, I hate rats. As far as the garden Alice has been working so hard on, well, think about who stopped that brute from vandalising it.'

'Alright, so show me which room you have in my house, and make it snappy. I am about to throw up.'

'*Our* house,' the stranger corrected, before turning his back on him and heading for the narrow stairway.

Waiting for the stranger to gain some elevation before following, Daniel recognised the smell and recoiled. It was the same odour that had permeated through the larder and loft space since their first viewing.

Eventually coming to a small landing, he saw a doorway to his left and a bedroom with a single bed, side table and chair to the right. Against the back wall stood an amazing array of computers and hard drives. Small blue and red lights flickered on the front panels. He was almost at a loss for words.

'Have I just left my world and stepped into a parallel universe?'

The stranger went to a computer keyboard and typed, and the message was relayed to a speaker nearby.

'Welcome to my world Daniel. Oh, and by the way, my name is Frank.' He extended his hand.

'Do all your computers speak?' Daniel asked.

Frank was a lot faster on the large keypad.

'Marvellous technology, don't you think? Designed and built by myself.' He stood and extended his hand once again, waiting for Daniel to reciprocate. 'The portable one,' he added by typing with his free hand, pointing towards the devise he had used earlier, 'is new. Still getting used to it. I need it when my friend delivers food.'

His hand was still extended, but wavered when Daniel shook a finger back at him.

'I am not shaking your fucking hand, you idiot. I want nothing to do with you, and the sooner you get out of my house the better.'

The larger speaker made him jump.

'*Our* house. I can live with sharing it with your lovely family, but you cannot sell this house. Where would I be if you did that?'

Shutting his eyes, Daniel slapped his head with both hands, but when he opened his eyes again Frank was still there.

'How come I never found this room?' Daniel said with some resignation.

The artificial voice boomed back.

'The passageway has a concealed door between my living space and the linen room next door. It is not obvious from the other side. I live a solitary life. I do not need company.'

Daniel looked at the window. 'You can't even see out. There is so much ivy on the window, there's no light coming in. How do you live like this?'

'I do not want to see the outside world and cannot go out. I suffer from a condition they told me about when I was a young boy. They said I was afraid of open spaces.'

'Agoraphobia?'

'Yes.'

When Daniel sniffed the air, he noted the same musty smell. Then he recognised something.

'Those were the candles on Harry's birthday cake when he turned three. What are they doing here?'

'A memento. And by the way, the cake was delicious.'

'And that missing bottle of sparkling wine when we celebrated finishing the loft?'

'Gone,' boomed the speaker. 'Very tasty.'

Although feeling lightheaded, he was not about to give up. Not just yet anyway.

'And the work done on the house when I was away at the office?'

The man gave a nervous grin. 'Just a bit of help. You were struggling, threatening to move out and I wanted to help you finish.'

'Where is your bathroom?'

Frank beckoned him to follow. Leading him to the second door and opened it. A tap, a wash bowl and a small table with a kettle stood against one wall. A curtain concealed a small toilet. On the opposite side was a meagre supply of coffee, tea and odds and ends.

'Is this all you have?'

Frank nodded.

'You have washed and bathed up here all this time?'

Looking around at the cramped space, it dawned on him then just where he was.

'The small room I used as a junk room is on the other side of this wall, isn't it?' He tapped the wall.

Frank eased past him and levered a handle and suddenly they were looking into the room next door.

'The linen room,' the handheld computer boomed.

'So, this is how you got into the upper floors. I don't believe it.'

'Up until a little while ago I had no need to venture out. My assistance on the renovations had come to an end and other than to collect my food from the hatch, my life settled back into the way it had been before you arrived. Oh, I think one of the last things I did was sneak into the library and rearrange all your books when you were off cycling. Then when you tampered with my water supply, I had no option other than to go through your kitchen and use the cloakroom.'

He thought back to all the times he had heard water running through the valve and his recent crude attempt to sort it by isolating most of the house.

'I needed my water back and after a while had no option but to confront you. I can do most small bits of handywork, but reconnecting my room to the valve under your kitchen sink was a step too far.'

'And the delivery guy supplied you with food through the hatch?'

'Whatever I ordered on the internet. That was how we communicated,' Frank typed. 'He also took my trash away a couple of times a week.' He hesitated. 'Well, sometimes he forgot and left it downstairs.'

'So, that's what the smell was.'

Frank grimaced. 'I relied on him, and he seldom let me down, but he was attacked on occasion and couldn't always make it.'

'What about all this stuff you have here?' Daniel asked, pointing at the array of electronic equipment.

'He brought me whatever I wanted.'

'That was your only contact with the outside world, the Chinese guy on the internet?'

'Until you used a crowbar on the hatch and bent the metal. From then on it wouldn't open. Ming had to use one of your kitchen windows at midnight.'

'Who the fuck is Ming?' Daniel flared.

'Delivery man. Chinese man. My friend.' the computer boomed back. 'The man you treated after being attacked tonight.'

'It's starting to make sense now, but why threaten me on the phone?'

'I do not have a phone Daniel, only a computer. Anyway, what use would a phone be? I cannot speak.'

'You told me to get out.'

'Why would I do that when I am doing everything I can to help and keep you here?'

Daniel stood rubbing his face. There was a lot to take in, and he was feeling confused and tired. He wanted nothing more than to get out in the open and take a breath of fresh air. He had been living in the Mansion for close to five years with a lodger in the attic, and could not understand how he had not discovered him.

Brought back to reality by the tapping on the keyboard, the computer voice boomed.

'Daniel, just to remind you of the time.'

'What about the time?'

'You told Alice to phone the police if you did not get back to her in twenty minutes. It is almost twenty minutes since you called her.'

'Oh shit,' he wailed, saw he had no signal and then repeated 'Oh shit', as he careered down the stairs and stumbled from the larder room into the kitchen. Then just as he started to press redial, he tripped over Doggie and fell. His head snapped back and connected with the edge of the table nearby.

His last recollection was of Doggie licking his face before his vision blurred and he passed out.

Chapter 19
Hallucinations

Slowly opening his eyes, he quickly closed them again. The light hurt, and he was in a lot of pain.

'Are you alright my darling?' he heard Alice's familiar voice.

Although she sounded a million miles away, he could hear everything she said.

'I think so,' he responded hesitantly. 'Where am I?'

'In hospital. You had a nasty accident and have serious concussion. Not to mention ten stiches across your forehead.'

He tried to sit up. His vision blurred, but he could see enough to know that Harry was not there.

'Where's Harry?'

'At home. Now relax, you have to rest.'

'He can't be at home Alice.'

He tried to pull himself up again. Then could not recall why he was worried about Harry being home alone, and slunk back down again.

'Now, now Daniel, you have had a bad knock to the head. Harry will be fine.'

Alice grimaced as the nurse administered an injection, and Daniel settled back into his pillows as the sedative took hold.

'We will see how he is later,' the nurse said sympathetically. 'The specialist is on his way and will have a look at his head. Now it's time you got some rest yourself. You have been here for hours.'

'Thank you, nurse. I need to get home to our son. He will have been on his own since getting back from school.'

'Time to go then,' the nurse said, as she ushered Alice out of the ward.

'I will call back tomorrow morning,' Alice called over her shoulder, 'I am sure he will be a lot better by then.'

The ambulance dropped Daniel off two days later. His headwound had started to heal, but he was withdrawn and morose. His memory of the fall was still a haze and when he tried to recall the events leading up to his accident, it made things worse.

Alice settled the wheelchair in a sunny spot of the lounge and brought him a cup of tea.

'I know you have just come out of hospital, but I need to clear up a few things that have been worrying me.'

He nodded, then instantly regretted doing so.

'When we were on our way back from the cinema, I saw I had a message from you, asking to call the police. Something about a strange man in the house. I called the police and they said they had already been to the house and after searching had found nobody there. Then when we got home, the ambulance medics were attending you. They told me they had received a call from a man with a foreign accent.'

'I don't remember anything just before or after the fall,' he replied hazily.

She shook her head. 'No, I don't suppose you do. That is quite a bump you had.' She paused. 'So, I wonder who made the call?'

Daniel sagged back and shrugged. 'Not me Alice. I only vaguely recall the police coming around earlier.'

'Umm,' she looked at him, trying to make eye contact, but was unsuccessful. 'That leads me to my second question. I received an incident report from the police after getting home, and it mentions a man being attacked. Then when I walked through the entrance there was blood on a cushion and all over the shirt you had been wearing. What happened?'

His eyes glazed over, as he struggled to recall some of the detail. 'Alice, it was the delivery man. He was badly injured.'

She spoke gently, but with a firm voice. 'Did you eventually do it? Did your temper get the better of you, catch him and beat him up?'

He shook his head as she drew in a deep breath.

'Because I know how you can flare, and you were forever chasing that poor man. Please, tell me the truth?'

His head thumped and he struggled to focus, but he was very aware of how bad this looked. 'Someone beat him up and I treated him. That is all Alice. Now please, I feel like death warmed up.'

'Alright,' she relented, 'but this conversation is not over.' She got up. 'No more work on the house until you are one hundred percent better.'

He looked at her, before turning back to stare at the distant wall. He had done a lot of that since the accident. Looking vacantly across the room, or patting Doggie when he was nearby, and not saying very much.

Harry was on his iPad nearby playing a game. Daniel could hear some strange sounds coming from the console.

'What game are you playing?' he asked.

'The flickering light,' the boy replied.

Trying to make conversation, and feeling guilty about not having spent more time with Harry, he asked. 'What is the game about?'

'Halloween, spooks and spirits. It is such good fun.'

Daniel slumped back in his chair and gave Doggie another pat on the head.

A week later and Daniel was up and about. Not back to full form, but strong enough to think about returning to work and getting back to renovating the house. After all, time was against him, and the clock was ticking.

He turned to Alice. 'I heard from work today. They have promoted Colin to General Manager, and Old Sniffer has been moved into my office,' he complained.

'You have been off for weeks, what do you expect? Somebody has to manage the business,' she replied.

'But why Old Sniffer and my best mate?'

'Your best mate that you have not seen for a while?'

'I need to go back', he complained. 'I can't afford to lose my job, especially since we are so reliant on both incomes and a big bonus to finish the house.'

'Stop. Get back to work, but stop being so obsessed with this house.'

'I want out of here,' he shouted at her. 'This place is haunted, and there is no way I am going to spend a minute longer in this building than I have to.'

'Haunted? Stop being ridiculous,' she chided him.

Harry had been colouring in a picture book nearby and tugged on his father's shirt sleeve. 'Did you see my friend Dad?'

He was not sure what to say.

'Harry, this friend of yours, describe him to me please?' Alice asked.

'He is very friendly. Sometimes he just smiles at me and other times he uses his hands to talk. He helps with my homework, and has been my friend forever.'

'Uses his hands like what Harry?' she asked.

'Like the people on TV do when they are talking to a deaf person.'

Alice looked terrified.

'What does he look like? Describe him,' Daniel asked.

'He is old and has long grey hair.'

Staring at the boy, Daniel started to shake.

'Harry, tell me again, have you've seen him in this house?' she asked.

'I always told you when I saw him. But you used to say he was my imaginary friend, so I stopped telling you about him.'

Slowly getting to his feet, Daniel instructed them to stay put. 'I will have a look around.'

Recollections of what had happened before his fall came flooding back, and he trembled. He was going to have a good look around, and get to the bottom of whatever was going on.

Returning to the kitchen, he came to an abrupt halt. The stranger he recalled, and the one Harry had just described, stood by the larder door with Doggie by his side. His long grey hair and stooped shoulders brought on an instant panic attack.

'Alice, phone the police, we have an intruder,' he shouted.

Frank's small computer transmitted a message. 'Don't forget the terms of Harry's bequest.'

Frank had obviously been prepared for some sort of reaction and stood his ground. And it had the desired effect.

Daniel ran back into the siting room.

'Don't call the police,' was all he could muster as he struggled to regain his breath.

'Are you alright?' Alice asked, as she put her phone back on the table. 'What's going on?'

'Just, just out of breath, that's all.'

'What on earth is going on? Is someone in the kitchen?'

He straightened, looked at her and muttered. 'We have a lodger Alice. A bloody lodger.'

'This is surreal, I don't believe it,' she saw him smile. 'If this is a prank, it's taking it too far. Are you trying to scare me?'

'Alice, this is not a prank. Believe me, this is about as real as it gets. I am smiling, because this confirms it was not a ghost I kept dreaming about when I was recovering in hospital, but a real person. I have been thinking I had gone out of my mind since my fall, but he is real.'

'Please tell me this is a joke.' Alice said, looking around anxiously.

'No Alice, we have a real problem on our hands. I have to get rid of this man, whoever he is.'

She crept towards the kitchen. Daniel was right behind her. Then when she let out a shriek and jumped back she knocked him over.

Harry walked in to see what all the fuss was about.

'Harry, please go to your room and stay there,' she shouted. 'Now.'

Harry waved to the old man. 'Hello Frank.'

Alice watched in horror as the old man returned a wave and smiled.

'Harry, do you know him?' She was starting to sound hysterical.

'Alice, we need to be careful what we do,' Daniel shouted, as he struggled to his feet.

Frank had become agitated with all the commotion, and his small computer went clattering across the floor. He tried to communicate with them in sign language.

'What is he saying?' Daniel asked.

'Something about 'don't do it,' she guessed.

'Get me a pen and paper,' he urged her.

'You don't need paper,' Harry interjected. 'I can understand him. He taught me how to do sign language a long time ago.'

'He what?' Daniel turned to Alice. 'What the fuck is going on here?'

'Language,' she scolded him. 'Harry can hear you.'

'To hell with swearing, Alice,' he replied hysterically. 'Harry has been talking to him for all these years and we haven't known a thing about it...is this for real?'

'Stop being such an idiot, this man is real enough, look at him.'

Frank spoke to Harry in sign language.

'He wants his water supply reconnected,' Harry translated. 'He says that he will not come back down again if you turn it on.'

Frank tapped on the side of the doorframe and then signed Harry again.

'Oh, Dad,' Harry translated. 'He just wants to remind you about repairing his food hatch. The one you damaged with a crowbar.'

Alice turned to look at Daniel, but he had already slunk out of the room.

Chapter 20
Alice in Frank Land

Daniel returned to the dining room carrying a heap of files balanced precariously in both arms. He had spent a long time explaining to Alice what he had seen when Frank had taken him into the loft just before his accident, and needed to check the old house plans. He dumped the files on the table.

'These are all the old records of the house they gave us before we purchased the place.' Then added. 'We never really looked at them too closely, as there was so much to go through.'

'Maybe *we* should have taken more of an interest in *all* the information we were given. You kept throwing them back saying it was just a lot of boring old rubbish,' she replied.

He ignored her accusatory tone. 'What are we going to do?' he asked her.

'I don't know. *You* are the man of the house and should be advising *me*.'

'Call the police?' he suggested.

'How will that effect our standing with the terms of the will?' she asked.

'Frank knows all about the terms Alice. He even threatened to tell Fischer we had a lodger.'

'That's risky. There are so many clauses and not forgetting the ones we haven't seen. I think at this late stage of the process we have to think extremely hard before saying a word.' She hesitated, and then screwed up her face. 'How does he know about Fischer and the will?'

'Never mind Alice, but we have to tread carefully. We keep quiet for now,' he suggested. 'Humour him and find out what he wants before we decide. We can't go rushing into this and risk losing the house with only months to go.'

'Good idea. Wow, you not rushing in. This *is* refreshing.'

Daniel had the bit firmly between his teeth by now. 'He looks harmless enough, and it gives us time to work out our best options.'

Soon after their encounter with Frank, Daniel found the water supply pipe and altered it, fitting a T piece to allow water back up to the whole of the loft area, then went to the expense of replacing the hatch cover on the gable side of the house. It was expensive, but he reluctantly paid for it to be done immediately.

'I don't want to encourage him,' He told Alice. 'I don't want him coming back down here again.'

The old plans recorded every dimension of every room and when Daniel measured the loft corridor it all started to make sense.

'We never made the connection with the number of windows seen from the outside and the number on the inside,' he explained to Alice. 'If we had counted them, we would have realised there was one less on the inside.'

Brooding over the plans, he sat tapping his pencil on the desk surface as his face took on a ruddy colour Alice knew all too well.

'I want him out. He could harm little Harry,' he ranted. 'The crazy old bastard has to go.'

Alice sat looking him. Daniel had not slept in days and appeared to be on the verge of a breakdown.

'I want you to take a break,' she suggested.

'I am not taking a fucking break,' he shouted back.

'You need to relax,' boomed a speaker from behind them.

They both spun around to see Frank holding his small computer in his hand. He was standing at the entrance to the Larder room with one hand covering his eyes.

'You have your water back, and your takeaway hatch is fixed, now get the fuck back upstairs and out of my fucking space,' Daniel shouted, shaking his fist at the stooped-over figure.

Frank stood his ground, turned to face the wall, and typed frantically.

'Are the fence panels still obscuring views from the kitchen windows?'

'What?' Daniel asked.

The computer blared back. 'I cannot see outside space, it will drive me crazy. I have agoraphobia.'

'The fence is still there. It's safe to come in,' Alice replied.

'Don't go encouraging him,' Daniel shouted. 'I want him out of my fucking house.'

Frank ignored him and approached the kitchen table. He pulled a chair out and sat down. 'Daniel, I am not sure if anyone has told you this before, but you swear too much. It is not particularly good for you.'

Daniel stood staring at the man, and for once was at a complete loss for words.

'Frank is right, you should calm down and relax a little, and, as for the swearing...'

'Alice... stop... who's side... I cannot believe it. Firstly, I have some ragtag drifter telling me how to behave, and then my wife who has only just met him, supporting him... in my own house. I don't bloody believe it,' he shrilled.

'Our house,' Frank responded.

'Daniel,' chided Alice, 'I support the homeless, and this man is obviously without a home. Give him a break, will you?'

'I will break his fucking neck,' he raged.

'Daniel, *stop*,' she shouted sternly.

Just then Harry walked in. He had just returned from school.

'Why are you shouting Dad? Oh, Hello Frank,' he greeted the man.

'Good day Harry, did you have a nice day?' boomed the computer. 'How did the spelling exam go?'

'Good thanks Frank,' he replied. 'Thanks for helping with my homework, it really helped.'

Harry collected a cold drink from the fridge and two packets of crisps from a cupboard and threw one across to Frank, before heading up to his bedroom. Frank sat patting Doggie, who licked his hand in return.

Daniel's mouth dropped open and he started stuttering. 'What, what the fuck. Am I going mad?'

At risk of sounding completely hysterical, he held both hands in the air, mouth moving, but not saying a word, while Frank and Alice stared at him. Spinning around, he stormed out and headed for the study. He was ready to place an order with the crane company and double-glazing contractor. When that was complete, the house would be ready for the five-year deadline. Ready to be evaluated and become theirs to sell and get out.

Alice was not quite sure what to do, but she saw something in the man that made her hesitate. He had been kind to Doggie and appeared to have Harry's confidence, so she poured two cups of tea and served up a generous helping of Daniels favourite, caramel and cream pie.

She was used to dealing with people who were down on their good fortunes and found the old man quite good company, as he regaled her with tales of how he had lived in the same room for as long as he could recall. His friend, the thin Chinese man had brought him everything he had needed, and his computer gave him instant access to the rest of the world. He told how he had looked after Harry when they had first moved into the kitchen, and fed Doggie when they were out.

He told Alice about how his friend had been attacked and how Daniel had treated the man's wounds on the kitchen floor.

'I think I owe Daniel an apology,' Alice said.

His speaker boomed. 'Don't Alice. He needs to learn a few lessons. Let him stew for a while.'

She laughed, before becoming serious again. 'How come you stayed here?'

She had got used to him typing by now, and the computer delivering the message. After a while it was as if Frank was speaking without it.

'The house was vacant years back and then when the new tenants arrived and had part of the building renovated, I saw an opportunity. Each night I would sneak in under the cover of darkness, use their tools and timber and make my own space in the house. You understand, it had to be a big house with many rooms, a place where I could live for the rest of my life and not be discovered. It was during that time I found I had a knack for handywork.'

'How old were you when you first arrived?' she asked.

'Fourteen.'

'Fourteen? That is young to be on the run from your family.'

'They treated me like an animal. My father could never accept my condition, and used to belt me if I refused to go out. He never had any time for me and was always busy with work. My brother was different, but he turned on them. They never allowed anyone to ever see me, and I was obviously an embarrassment to them,' he added, before looking down at the floor.

'That sounds terrible,' she commiserated.

'You don't know what it is like being rejected and hated by your parents, bullied by your brother, and then threatened with wide open spaces.'

Alice was taken aback as the man suddenly became highly agitated, and rocked from side to side. She moved her chair slightly, ready for a quick escape. Frank heard the scraping of the chair on the floor, and quickly typed, as his straggly hair swung across his face.

'Sorry Alice. Sorry about the outburst. I have just had such a lonely life, and you are a very caring person. A generous woman as well. I should have not behaved like that. That was wrong of me.'

Alice settled back.

'How far back can you remember?' she asked. 'Surely you couldn't have just sat around in your room all that time.'

'No, I went to university. My Chinese friend Ming discovered that a degree in Information Technology was taught in a basement lecture room. No windows.'

He smiled at Alice to reaffirm the choice of venue.

'Then the people renting the house got into financial difficulty and the bank sold it on. Tenants came and went. I think I might have scared a few off. I am not sure.'

Alice sniggered at the thought and recalled all the reports of paranormal activity in the Sellers pack.

'What did you do when we moved in?' she asked.

'Watched and waited. I wanted your family to stay and did whatever I could do to help. I am sure Daniel must have suspected something after a while, because of the amount of work I was getting through when you were both out of the house. It helped me a lot on the second floor, when Daniel covered the windows with paper.'

After returning to the room Daniel stood leaning on the back of one of the chairs. 'Right, old man, time to go back upstairs to your quarters. This is my house and your room's in the loft.'

'Daniel, you need to hear his story, and I want to find out more about him.'

'No Alice, I don't want to hear his sorry tale. He needs to go upstairs and out of my space.'

Frank sat watching Daniel rant, before typing.

'Thank you for not swearing, I do hate it.'

'Fuck off,' Daniel barked and stalked off.

Alice gave an apologetic smile, and ushered Frank from the kitchen and into the larder room.

'Don't worry Frank, I deal with homeless people a lot and will make sure you are well taken care of.'

Frank pulled the lever, revealing the narrow corridor leading to the stairway and his upstairs space. She peered in and could see the dimly lit corridor. He stopped and turned back as he reached for the door.

'Goodnight Alice, you are such a kind woman. Please give my regards to Harry in the morning, he is a good child.'

'Thank you Frank. We can continue having a chat another day, I am finding it interesting,' she replied.

'You are a very generous person Alice,' the computer boomed, as he swung the cupboard closed. 'I think we will be incredibly good friends.'

She remained standing in the doorway for a while. Trying to adjust to the recent strange turn of events. Then turned to find Daniel watching her from a few meters away. He wore an expression she had never seen before.

'Incredibly good friends! What the fuck?'

The following morning, they both readied themselves for work in silence. Little was said while they ate their breakfast, other than to remind Harry to pick up his schoolbag from the dining room table.

Standing on the front drive, Alice could see Daniel was in a pensive mood.

'I will collect you from school this afternoon Harry,' he said and ruffled the boy's hair.

Alice looked at him and frowned. 'Why not let him walk home, like he has done over the past year?'

'What,' Daniels voice raised a pitch and his freckles darkened. 'With that old pervert in our house? You must be off your bloody rocker.'

'This is nothing new. Frank has been here the entire period we have lived here. Helping to look after Harry, when as a baby he slept in the larder room. Living side by side with us all this time, and we have come to no harm. Oh, and by the way, he is not old, he is in his early thirties. About the same age as you.'

'Oh great,' Daniel said, as he slung his backpack over his shoulder. 'Maybe we could have a joint birthday party and invite all our friends. Maybe we could all squeeze into the larder room and celebrate together... over my dead body.'

'A bit harsh,' she replied calmly. 'He is such a nice man.'

'He looks like an old goat,' Daniel raged.

Trying his best to hold his temper and not swear. He was aware of how it upset Alice, and was trying his best to control himself. Especially since Harry was standing close by.

'I don't want Harry to be alone with him. In any case he will be gone soon. This situation we are in is just ridiculous.'

'I asked him directly, and he said he would never hurt a hair on Harry's head,' Alice said defensively. 'He said he would like you to understand that.'

'Oh, so it's Frank calling the shots now?' he sneered as he kicked at the gravel drive, before turning to Harry. 'See you at the school gate my boy, and don't be late.'

Alice walked Harry to school and then went on to work. She was worried about Daniel, and would have a serious word with him that evening. In fact, she was extremely worried about his erratic behaviour of late.

That night, just as Daniel was about to turn off the light, he turned to her. 'Sorry about my outbursts this morning. Let's start afresh tomorrow.'

'Thank you,' she replied, 'but please don't be too harsh on our guest.'

He muttered something inaudible in response.

'What was that?' she asked, suddenly aware of his tone.

'That bastard is not going to get away with this,' he replied, quite clearly this time.

Chapter 21
Who is Their Lodger?

Daniel was in no mood to discuss the matter any further in the morning, and the following evening buried himself once again in paperwork. He was checking the quotes received for a crane hire.

When Alice caught up with him, she insisted he explain himself.

'What did you mean, when you said Frank was not going to get away with this?'

He dithered before drawing her aside. 'Outside, where walls have no ears.' He marched her out onto the front drive. 'That is not Frank living in the loft.'

'What do you mean? Does it really matter what his name is, he is vulnerable, isn't he? Besides, I have grown fond of him.'

'Well, change your mind Alice, become un-fond of him. Because if you don't, he will bring the whole bequest crashing down around our heads, and leave us with nothing but trouble.'

She looked at him. 'You mean if Fischer finds out he is lodging with us?'

'Not entirely Alice. It's not the lodger thing, it's because it's who Frank is, and that will be our undoing.'

She was becoming frustrated with his cat and mouse game. 'If he is vulnerable, and not paying rent, then he is not a lodger. Isn't that right?' she smiled. 'Clause five, part two, states that we are to be kind to anyone vulnerable and less fortunate than yourselves.'

'No Alice, that is not alright. Remember Clause five part one?'

'Yes.'

'Well the chap you have become so fond of is actually Frederick.'

She looked at him for a long time before shaking her head.

'No, it can't be. From what I have heard Frederick was evil. That man in there is gentle and mild. Even when you provoked him he took it all in his stride.'

'That is Frederick Alice, and to prove it I saw the scar on his arm. I had my suspicions when I first met him but couldn't prove it. I see the evil in him, and he is a past master at manipulation. That is why he has managed to wrap you around his little finger so easily.'

'I don't believe it, and bearing in mind you said that Francis also had a scar on his arm. You could be wrong, and it may even be Francis.'

Daniel remained persistent. 'I am telling you it's not Francis. I can see the old evil Frederick lurking in his eyes. Calculating and scheming and a devil in disguise.'

'If you are right, what do we do?'

'Don't let him think we know, and watch our backs. I will get rid of him when I can... and make a good job of it. Nobody will miss the bastard anyway.'

Alice was at a loss as they walked back into the house. She tried her best to relax, but every time she looked at her husband, she had her doubts. Doubts about who she had married, doubts about Daniels sanity, and at a complete loss as what she should do. If Frank turned out to be Frederick, he was certainly not as evil as they had all made out. Besides, she was a good judge of character and this man was kind, vulnerable and in need of some compassion.

Daniel pulled her to one side in the entrance hall. 'So, mums the word Alice. Don't let him know we have discovered his identity. Not until I have found the right time to test him by using his real name,' he whispered.

'Promise me you won't harm him Daniel. I will never forgive you if you do,' she hissed.

'Trust me Alice.'

She nodded. 'OK, if you say so.'

The outer gate bell rang, and Alice looked on her mobile phone to see who was there.

'It's the Suits,' she called.

'Tell them to fuck off, I'm busy,' Daniel shouted back.

'Hello, can I help you?' she called over the intercom.

'Can we please come in. We have an unannounced audit to do, and it shouldn't take long. Apologies if it's inconvenient, but we will be quick.'

The last unannounced audit had been before they knew about Frank. She had no choice but to let them in, while Harry raced into the larder room and up the three flights of stairs to warn Frank. Once done, he ran back down again to indicate that their lodger was cooperating.

The suits walked around the house and when they came across Daniel in the study, they complimented him on the finish he had achieved. He was in no mood to make conversation, and gave them a surly nod, before turning back to shuffle through a heap of quotes.

They covered the house floor to ceiling and saw nothing of concern. Another audit without a yellow card and the couple breathed a sigh of relief.

Daniel watched them walk up the curved drive before turning to Alice. 'Time to get the crane in,' he declared, 'and then get the hell out of this house.'

Alice had grown to love the house and tried her best to change Daniels mind, but he was resolute. He was not going to live with a lodger in the attic. And most certainly not if it was Frederick. Then it dawned on him that if it was Francis, the will stated he had to share the estate, and the rest of his inheritance with the man. Neither option was appealing, but Alice was proving to be a bit of a thorn in his side.

'I am growing fond of the place,' she replied.

'Too much of a risk Alice.'

'Why not explain it all to Fischer?' she persisted.

'We risk losing everything we have worked so hard for.' He shook his head. 'Let's just get the valuation and transfer of ownership out of the way. Once that is done, we sell and pocket millions.'

'What about poor Frank?'

'Poor Frank will just have to look after himself.' He was starting to get irritable with Alice's persistence. 'And good fucking riddance to poor Frank or Frederick, or whoever the poor fucker is.'

'I do wish you would stop swearing, Harry will be repeating those filthy words at school,' she pleaded.

Ignoring her, he settled back in the study and started to look through a spreadsheet of their finances. He concluded that they were now totally reliant on his big annual bonus.

Fischer called a couple of weeks later and asked them to attend an exceptional meeting.

Debbie said she would pick up Harry when she collected Rodney after school and then stay with them at Manor House until the couple returned.

Colin was visiting Daniel's branch and had Old Sniffer trailing after him, and complaining about Daniels lack of commitment and poor attendance. The old man was getting exasperated with the amount of time Daniel kept taking off work.

'This will be the last time I have to visit the Solicitors,' Daniel explained, when Colin confronted him.

'Can I remind you that you are up for promotion and a large bonus,' Colin did his best to remain calm. 'Do I also need to remind you that your team of architects have given you their undying support, and are most likely the only reason you have been so successful? And nothing personal, but apparently you have had the support of our chairman, and when he approached me I gave a glowing account of your efforts to build the branch.'

Daniel swaggered out of Colin's office. His promotion would place him on the Board of Directors, and he would take no prisoners. When one of the team looked up, he told them to get on with what they were doing, and stop wasting time.

The same suits lined the one side of the table. A few had been exchanged, while the original ones appeared to have aged more than the five years that had passed.

Life was tough, Daniel thought.

Formalities out of the way, they focused in on financial forecasts and the five year-end results. During this entire period Fischer had sat silently observing, and had allowed his lead Solicitor to take charge of proceedings.

As they were drawing to the end of the review, the Solicitor turned to Fischer. 'I believe you want to deliver the next bit of news.'

'Thank you,' the elderly man replied, and turned to address the couple. 'I called you in... because there has been a change to the terms.'

Sitting up, with a concerned look on his face, Daniel asked. 'A change?'

'Yes,' Fischer replied. 'I received a rare message from the Undisclosed Person, and an extension of six months to the five-year term has been granted.'

Daniel looked perplexed, but also relieved. 'Why would he do that?'

'Your recent accident has denied you time at a critical stage, and whoever this person is, thinks it's only fair to give you an extension of time.'

Alice was ecstatic. 'That is wonderful news, we were about to start packing our bags.'

'No need Alice. So long as your husband gets his bonus and the contractors doing the roof and glazing don't let you down, I think you will be home and dry. But we can go through all of that in a short while.'

Fischer called for a refreshment break and when they reconvened, he focused in on Clause five.

'I take it you have not seen any sign of Francis over all this time?'

'No,' Daniel shook his head. 'Nothing at all.'

He sneaked a furtive glance at Alice, but she had a deadpan expression and appeared to be cooperating. No mention was made of Frederick, but he was suspicious as to why that clause had been raised.

The remaining time at JJ Fischer's was taken up with focusing in on a few remaining issues, such as the timing of his bonus and the completion of the roof. It was going to be touch and go, but Daniel was tired and impatient and soon became restless.

Fischer suggested they get together if they required any further assistance. 'You don't want to fall at the final hurdle,' he said encouragingly.

After yawning, Daniel stretched and thanked him. He was eager to get back and check on Harry, even though Debbie was looking after him.

They arrived home to find Harry and Frank playing cards and having a cup of tea in the larder room. Daniel stood in the doorway and pointed, while looking back at Alice.

'Does that strike you as being particularly healthy for a five-year-old boy?' he asked. 'To be sitting in a cupboard with a dirty old man. Come on Alice, how many times do we have to argue about this? And where the hell are Debbie and Rodney?'

'Dad, will you please not interrupt. Frank is teaching me a new card game and I need to concentrate,' Harry said irritably.

Taking hold of Alice's arm, Daniel led her back into the kitchen.

'This is dangerous. I know what Frederick is capable of and if you think it's safe to have our son in there with him, then you are out of your mind.'

'He is harmless, and I enjoy his company. I never see you anymore and he has some stimulating topics to discuss. Have you noticed how well Harry's vocabulary has come on? And according to his last school report, he is doing exceptionally well in class? 'A well turned out boy' was the comment on his report. That's all Franks doing. Oh, and by the way, he takes care of Doggie when we are all out of the house.'

'But where is Debbie and Rodney?' was all Daniel could muster.

Alice saw an unread message on her phone, which she had kept on silent during the meeting.

'Debbie has left a message saying that Rodney started throwing up and they had to rush off to the doctor. She locked Harry in, and said he should be safe until we got back.'

'Fat lot of good your friend is,' Daniel muttered.

Venturing outside to check on the tower crane erection, he was surprised to see that it was already fully installed and ready for use.

The foreman from the crane company came striding over shaking his head. 'I am worried about these foundation Sir. I am not sure how my team were talked into even proceeding with this erection. It doesn't look right.'

Daniel had the answer, but kept quiet. He had mild misgivings about what he had done, and a tinge of guilt about parting with the thin brown packet of cash to get the job done cheaply.

'Too costly,' Daniel replied. 'The layer of gravel I had tipped should do fine.'

The foreman shrugged his shoulders. Daniel had spent his life in a construction related trade, and understood that the thin dusting of gravel was grossly insufficient to do the job. But the building industry was going through a serious recession and tower cranes were twenty to the dozen.

The foreman however was not that easily fobbed off, and threatened to have the crane removed. In the end Daniel had to sign a disclaimer, or face the threat of having the crane taken away, with costs.

He was in a foul mood when he arrived back in the entrance hall, and snatched at a pile of recently delivered mail.

'What is this one?' he muttered to himself, frustrated at being threatened by the foreman.

The letter was from the 'Association for the Homeless' and addressed to Alice. He tore it open.

Dear Miss Somersby,

We already appreciate all the work you do for us, and as you are aware, we still have a long way to go before all those sleeping rough have a roof over their heads and at least one meal a day. We would appreciate a small donation to be set up on the attached direct debit form and---

Not bothering to read any further, and fed up with just about everything that came his way of late, he took out a pen and wrote 'FUCK OFF' across the front page. Then he placed the original letter in the prepaid return envelope and placed it back on the table, where other mail was waiting to go.

Alice was with Frank, huddled in the larder room, and in deep discussion over steaming mugs of soup. A platter of crusty brown bread and cheese lay between them. This was Daniels favourite lunchtime treat, and when he saw the cheese board, his mouth watered. But he was having nothing to do with the lodger and stormed off to make his own sandwich.

'What did your family do?' he could hear Alice ask.

'They never found out where I went, and they never looked awfully hard either.' He could hear Franks message clearly from the minicomputer speaker. 'I suppose, for them it was a bit of a blessing once I had disappeared.'

'How did you get money to live your life?' Alice had so many questions to ask.

Although out of sight, Daniel had his head cocked to one side listening in.

'Just because I was deaf didn't mean I was stupid. I used my IT skills to hack into various sites, where I could syphon off a little money. Not a lot, but just what I needed to survive.'

Daniels attention focused and his mind whirred. This could be handy, he thought.

'How did you arrange for your food to be delivered?'

'A Chinese man I had known for most of my life. He was an absolute wiz on computers. Not as good as me, but good all the same. So, I devised a plan. I gave him a new identity and paid for his lodgings, while he looked after my interests from outside the house. If I wanted something, I would email him, and he would drop it off.'

'Through the hatch?' she asked.

'Yes, through the hatch. Your husband did a great job of trying to catch him. It became a joke between me and Ming. I had a small remote camera placed on the fence you erected, and it gave us an advantage when Daniel was on the war path. Some of the images made me crease with laughter.'

Daniel let out a low growl.

Doggie had been resting at Franks feet and when he heard the growl, he barked. Alice put her hand down and patted him.

'Doggie likes the delivery man, while Daniel has always hated him,' she added. 'The camera was a good idea.'

'The camera shows the stranger attacking Ming and it was not Daniel. I saw the whole thing,' Frank added.

Daniel returned to the larder room. 'You see Alice, it wasn't me. I told you at the time and you wouldn't believe me.'

'Calm down. Frank told me soon after we first met, but I never let on that I knew.'

He had heard enough and was tired of Frank, the Chinese man, and how he had been made to look a fool. He stormed off.

Harry had walked in a minute earlier, in time to hear the end of the tale and see his father stride out. He smiled and told Alice he had been aware of the camera and had partaken in the cat and mouse game, sometimes warning Frank when his father became suspicious.

'Don't for God's sake tell him that, he is already threatening bad things,' she warned, before turning back to Frank. 'What did you do when the house was vacant?'

'I used to come down to the larder room at night. The wooden fence in front of the kitchen windows was my idea and erected by Ming. Otherwise I waited for the sun to set and found I could walk around the house, just so long as the curtains were drawn.'

The little meeting eventually came to an end, and Frank went back upstairs, while Alice ushered Harry into the study to complete his homework.

The following week, Daniel arrived at work early and was sat at his large desk, wondering why his promotion had been delayed.

Old Sniffer put his head around the door. 'Have you a minute?'

'Sure,' Daniel replied.

'My office... now?'

'On my way,' Daniel replied, and leapt up, as he felt a whole swirl of emotions.

This was supposed to be his promotion and bonus day, but he read into his bosses' tone and braced himself. By his own admission, his performance and attendance had slipped recently, and he had rather hoped his boss had not noticed.

'Come in,' Old Sniffer commanded, as he held the door open and then closed it firmly behind them.

A large balding man sat at one end of a small informal meeting table holding a rolled-up piece of paper in one hand.

'Can I introduce you to the Group Chairman, Mister Warren.'

Warren made no sign of getting up or extending his free hand, as he started to tap the paper scroll on the table. Daniel was unsure as to what to do and stood waiting expectantly, with a forced smile. He had a vague recollection of having seen the same man before, although it had been a much slimmer and younger figure he recalled.

The balding man unfolded the sheet of paper and held it out. 'Do you recognise this?'

Daniel took a closer look, and his heart skipped a beat. It was the letter he had returned to the 'Association for the Homeless'.

'A joke,' he replied weakly, not knowing what else to say.

'Not a joke,' Warren replied. 'You did not know I was the president of the association, did you? In fact, if you had taken the time to read the letter in full, you would have seen my name at the end of the letter and a reference to this company. Would you have not?'

'I suppose so,' Daniel muttered.

'You do not recall who I am, do you?'

'I'm trying,' Daniel's mind whirled.

'Let me make it easy for you. Your father's friend. A yachting holiday together. Just the three of us. You, the petulant child. It would appear you have not changed very much.'

Daniel started making the connection, however it was too late and the damage was already done. Warren excused himself and left the office without once looking back at Daniel, who stood staring after him.

'Sorry, no promotion and definitely no bonus,' Old Sniffer reaffirmed with a shrug.

'What? I worked my butt off for that bonus,' Daniel protested.

'You should be more careful,' Old Sniffer replied. 'Always read everything carefully, and never overreact.'

Arriving home, he decided not to say a word about his meeting with Warren to Alice. She was already behaving strangely, and he was not prepared for an argument. They were back on speaking terms, but only just. If she found out about the charity letter he had sent back, it may well be the last straw. Most of all, he was most certainly not going to let Frank find out. The sneering old, or not so old bastard, he thought, was not going to have the upper hand.

A small team of workers had already started work on the roof and windows. A heap of Ivy had been stripped off and lay in a heap in the garden.

When he viewed the house from the Spree, he noticed Frank had covered his end window space with a sheet of timber from the inside. He now knew exactly where to look for the lodger's accommodation and it all made perfect sense. One more window than the number of rooms he had renovated and the one they had once seen a flickering light in.

'How did I ever miss it,' he cursed.

That evening, they had their first bit of family time together for what felt like years. A lovely meal and then a game of cards on the kitchen table. Doggie had wolfed down his usual heap of leftovers and was sprawled out on his bed.

Retiring to the lounge, Daniel ignored the plate of food Alice took into the larder for Frank, and played a game with Harry on his console connected to the television.

Alice wandered back, picked up the remote and changed channels.

'What did you do that for Alice? I was winning that game,' Daniel whined.

'Frank has just warned me about a weather alert,' she replied.

The weather warning got his immediate attention and he put the games console to one side.

'Look at that,' Alice said, as she squeezed onto the couch between the two boys. 'They're forecasting a storm. Coming from the Alps and heading straight towards Berlin. And would you believe it, they have called it Storm Frederick. What a coincidence?'

'Why Frederick?' Harry asked, looking at his mother.

'They go through the alphabet and alternate between genders. The next one could be called Gail.'

'Let's hope it veers off somewhere else,' Daniel added sourly. 'I have a crane hanging over our house and a Frederick of our own to contend with.'

That night, as they lay trying their best to sleep, the wind intensified, and shortly after midnight reached force nine strength. Manor House started to creak and groan.

Then Daniel heard a loud metal wrenching screech and the ground vibrate. He ran up to the loft area and found it all intact. There was no damage. Nothing was visible from any of the windows. Although most of the ivy had been removed from the panes, it was still impossible to see much through the dirt and the driving rain.

'Phew,' he said quietly, 'that could have been the crane.'

A half hour later he realised it had been the crane. It had toppled sideways and smashed into the neighbour's house, destroying the west wing and half of their roof. The neighbours had called the police, who banged loudly on Daniel's front door to make themselves heard over the sound of driving rain and roaring wind.

'You had better have a look Sir,' the officer shouted.

Alice pulled on her waterproofs and followed.

Their neighbours were a family of four, besides themselves with fear and sat huddled together in the only room that was still dry. Water poured into the rest of building from a large gaping hole left by the toppled crane.

'You had better come into our house,' Alice suggested.

They had met briefly when out doing the garden, but rarely spoke. Besides, Daniel was always in the house working, or at the office in Berlin and did not have much free time to socialise.

The family packed a few belongings, and dragged their bags around the wooden fence and down Manor House drive. Alice held the doors wide open and welcomed them in. She apologised once again, and said they could stay as long as they liked.

'I'd say it's an insurance job,' Frank said in sign language after hearing the bad news.

Alice had taken a crash course in sign language and was incredibly good at making herself understood. The silent form of communication helped, because the neighbours now shared their kitchen. It allowed them to converse in the larder room without being overheard.

Frank, Harry, and Alice had set up a table and chairs in the larder room, where they met most days for a cup of tea and a chat. Daniel had not dared alter the room after being threatened by both Frank and Alice.

'If you do anything to my little world, I will bring yours down on top of your head,' Frank had said when Daniel approached his space with toolbox in hand. 'Crane damage is nothing compared to what I can do,' he had then added for good measure.

Alice had translated for Daniel and Frank smiled when he saw her version of 'on top of your head'

'I am quite certain he would have taken out insurance,' Alice said the following morning, as she continued to discuss the dramatic turn of events with Frank.

'From what you have just told me, the damage is considerable and will cost a fortune to put right,' Frank replied.

Alice peeped through the keyhole and when she saw the coast was clear, she crept out and found Daniel in the study looking through the crane hire documents.

'Have you got insurance?' she asked.

'I thought it would be automatic. They gave me a bundle of papers and I presumed it would be in here somewhere,' he replied, shuffling through the heap.

'How many times do I have to ask you to read documents before signing them,' she berated him.

'Who's put you up to this Alice?' He stood up shaking a threatening finger at her, 'Are you here because that fucking attic monster asked the question?'

Alice hesitated a moment too long and Daniel stormed out. He met the neighbours coming in through the front door and barged them out of the way. The thin Chinese man was just about to enter The Alley and when he saw Daniel a smile started to form, but quickly disappeared when he saw how angry Mister Dan looked.

'Come here you bastard,' Daniel shrieked. 'Feeding my bloody attic rat all these years. I know everything about you, you little shit. Now come here so that I can kick that skinny little arse of yours.'

The man took off and Daniel gave chase, but had only covered a few yards before collapsing.

Hearing the Chinese man shout for help, the neighbours rushed out.

'Master of house collapsed,' shouted the thin man. 'Quick, you must get ambulance,' he urged the dazed looking group.

Alice came out when she heard the commotion, and found Daniel sprawled on the ground, the neighbours crowding around, while Doggie licked his head.

She called for an ambulance and once the medics had checked his vital signs, they turned to Alice with grim faces.

'He is in an awfully bad way; we need to rush him straight into hospital.'

The waiting room was quiet, as Alice and Harry sat patiently waiting for news. When the doctor eventually appeared, his theatre clothes were covered in blood.

'He is stable for now, but this is going to be touch and go. We can see that he has suffered recent trauma to the head and this fall has caused a blood clot. The rate of bleeding is causing us a lot of concern, and I think you had better prepare yourselves for the worst.'

Chapter 22
Frank to the Rescue

Arriving home, mother and son found the neighbours occupying the hall. Having already commandeered three bedrooms on the first floor, their occupation of the house appeared to be spreading.

There was an awkward silence as Alice and Harry walked into the reception hall, where the family were sat around a makeshift table eating a roast dinner. As far as they were concerned, her husband was the cause of all their woes and thought his fall to be possibly some form of cruel justice come his way.

But they never voiced their opinions. They smiled politely after listening to the latest update, and got on with their meal.

Colin and Debbie arrived on hearing the news, and Alice took her friends into the kitchen for a catch up. Harry and Rodney went to the newly established games room to play on the Play Station.

'I don't know what to do with the neighbours Colin. They are refusing to leave, demanding money, and are with us until their house is repaired. While I have Daniel desperately ill in hospital.'

The couple had seen the neighbours when they had arrived, and grimaced.

The larder door opened a crack.

'Excuse me Alice, can we have a chat?' The message boomed from a speaker.

Colin leapt out of his chair and grabbed a steak knife, while Debbie screamed.

'Who the hell it that,' Debbie shouted.

'Quiet Debbie, we don't want the neighbours, or anyone else to know about him,' Alice cautioned.

The couple looked at one another.

'Does Daniel know about him?' Colin asked.

'Of course, he does. Its Frank, he lives in the attic.'

Colin and Debbie looked at one another in confusion.

'Are you sure you are alright Alice?' Colin asked..

'I know this all looks very odd, but I have a lot going on right now and don't have time to explain.'

Colin gave Alice a peck on the cheek. 'I will pop in and see Daniel first thing in morning on my way to work.'

Alice whispered back. 'Please do not say a word to anyone.'

After being consoled by Alice that Frank was not dangerous, Debbie got up and followed Colin, who was busy weaving his way between piles of furniture and boisterous children. Then they had to avoid the adults, who were busy unpacking a large delivery box of camping gear. They had talked about getting away over weekends to give both families a bit of breathing space.

Alice turned back to the larder room, to find out what Frank wanted and have a word with him.

'Don't ever do that to me again,' she scolded him in sign language.

'Sorry,' he signed back.

'And get rid of that bloody computer. I have taken a crash course in sign language so that I don't have to listen to that damn noise. Do you want the neighbours to hear you?'

Alice was still angry as she slipped into the dimly lit room, shutting the door firmly behind her. She was not going to risk the neighbours finding out about him.

'How is he?' Frank signed.

'Bad, but he is strong. Before leaving hospital, I saw the Head of Neurology. He said Daniel has turned a corner and is out of danger.'

She struggled with sign language for neurology, but he understood.

'That's encouraging news Alice. I have sorted the insurance by the way.'

'What do you mean, sorted? How?'

'I hacked into the crane company's system and back-dated a fully comprehensive schedule. You are covered for any third-party damage.'

'Even from a storm?'

'Everything,' He signed back with a smug look on his face.

She looked at him in amazement. 'You have done that for us?'

'Yes, to save our house. If you had to pay out, we would have to sell this place to cover the costs and end up being homeless. I had a look at the claim the neighbours submitted, and it is just over three million Euros. Plus of course a few debatable incidental losses.'

'How do you know?'

'I read all their mail. Everything they send, I intercept. They are using your WIFI.' He smiled at her. 'We have to save our house Alice.'

That evening when she went to visit Daniel he was sitting up. He was still heavily sedated, but alert enough to ask what was happening at home.

'Alice, I have to tell you, I am terrified we may have to pay out for the damages from the crane accident. I am so sorry.'

'No we won't. We are insured,' she replied.

'How come? When I looked through all the paperwork, there was nothing there.'

'You wouldn't have found anything. Because it was *never* there. But don't worry, Frank has sorted it out.'

Daniel looked around before whispering. 'You mean Frank did something to make sure we were covered?'

'He did. He saved our bacon. Otherwise we would be over three million out of pocket and on the street.'

Two weeks later Daniel was discharged.

Alice wheeled him past the lodging family who had by now taken over most of the house. They asked him how he was, but it was a polite conversation. They still held him responsible for all their woes. They were packing up for a full week's camping in the mountains and Alice sighed with relief. At least they would be out from under Daniels feet during his initial recovery period.

'Can I see Frank please?' Daniel asked as they passed by the kitchen.

Alice looked up at a small camera set just above the larder room door, clicked a remote pad, and ten minutes later Frank could be heard moving around in the adjacent room.

'How did you do that?' Daniel asked.

'I had Ming help me,' She explained. 'We installed the camera so that we could have privacy in our kitchen without Frank opening the door. I can control the camera and turn it off when we are in and the neighbours are not around. Camera off, and Frank knows not to disturb us.'

'Will you help me communicate with Frank?' Daniel asked. 'I can't do sign language.'

Frank was seated at the small table and rose when Daniel entered. He smiled and communicated through Alice. 'He says he is pleased to see you making a speedy recovery. He was genuinely concerned about you.'

'Thanks Frank,' Daniel replied uneasily. 'But we have business to discuss. Oh, and by the way, thank you for sorting the crane insurance.'

Frank smiled as his fingers went to work.

Alice turned to Daniel. 'He says he will do anything to help. He wants to be your friend.'

Looking at the long grey hair and hunched figure, Daniel felt a tinge of compassion for the man. He noted that under the straggly hair was a face not much older than his own, and the scar on his arm was less prominent in the half light. He wrestled with the idea that this might just be Francis. Because if it was Frederick, he must have gone through a transformation of sorts, as he recalled the young bully he had known as a child.

He turned back to Alice and ask her to translate. 'I need some money to finish the house. Can he do the same little trick he did with the insurance, but this time make it turn into cash?'

Alice hesitated at first and then when Daniel prompted her, she started to translate, then stopped. 'You know he can lip read as well as hear you?' she said halfway through.

'That will make it much quicker.' He turned to Frank. 'Can you hear me?' Frank nodded. 'I want money. Use your magic on the computer and get me two hundred thousand Euros.'

Frank looked flustered at first and then angry. His hands and fingers moved at speed, almost out of control.

'Slow down Frank,' Alice reprimanded him, then turned to Daniel. 'Frank says he is finding you disrespectful and doesn't like your attitude. He says he is not a crook and will not be your slave to be commanded around like a puppet.' She paused, 'And I agree. Unless you change your attitude, we are done here.'

She stood up to leave, and for the first time ever, saw Daniel start to simper. 'Sorry Frank, sorry Alice, I am a prick and I know it, but we are desperate.'

'What do you need money for anyway?' she asked. 'You were expecting a promotion and a big bonus from work.'

Frank's hands went to work. 'He lost his promotion and had his bonus taken off him. I thought he would have told you?'

Alice looked horrified. Daniel had no idea what Frank had just signed as she turned on him.

'Why didn't you tell me you lost your promotion and bonus?'

He reeled back. 'How do you know?'

'Frank just told me.'

Turning to Frank, he asked. 'How do you know?'

'I know everything,' Frank signed back to Alice.

When she relayed what Frank had just signed, Daniel stormed out of the room, slamming the door as he went.

He paced the kitchen for a while, before returning to the larder room.

'OK, I am not being very honest, I acknowledge, but I need some money to make sure I get the value on the house.' He paused as a realisation hit him. 'Frank, you are desperate to stay here, am I not correct?' Frank nodded. 'Then help me get the house value up and I promise to find a way for you to keep your room.'

'How would you do that?' Alice translated his response.

'Reinforce your access and make it easier for you to get provisions in the future, regardless of who lives here.' He paused. 'Look Frank, you managed to deceive us for years, living under the same roof as us and nobody knew. So, by making some further improvements you could live here forever without ever being discovered. Even if we are thrown out, you could stay on.'

Frank swept his grey hair aside and smiled. It was the first real look Daniel had of his long-lost cousin and realised how much younger he looked.

'Thank you Daniel. Maybe we can be friends from now on.'

'You have certainly changed cousin,' Daniel said and watched carefully for some sort of reaction.

Frank nodded and smiled. Alice was overjoyed.

'You have changed so much Frederick, I can't believe it.'

There was still no reaction.

'Or Francis?' Daniel added.

Frank gave nothing away. Both names had drawn the same neutral reaction.

'Then let's leave you as Frank,' Daniel conceded. 'But if Fischer finds out Frederick has been lodging in the house, it could be the end of us all.'

There was still no reaction from Frank other than a smile. So, he decided not to mention anything again, as it might upset their new relationship, and at this moment in time, he needed this man's full cooperation. He had quickly come to the realisation that although Frank was deaf, he was incredibly clever.

He did not understand why, but he had a sudden urge to help this poor soul. The only relative he had, and one that had gone through what would appear to have been an unbelievable transformation.

The charitable urge surged like a wave and then receded just as quickly. It would have been far too out of character for Daniel. He was selfish, self-obsessed and had his own agenda. His current target was to make a lot of money, but had to admit he was struggling to make it over the finishing line on his own.

He extended his hand. 'Friends..., Frank?'

Frank looked overjoyed and sprung to his feet.

'Yes Daniel, I only have Ming as a friend, and I would like to be friends with you,' Alice translated.

Daniel could see the emotion in the man's eyes. The tears were real enough, and they looked like tears of joy. Alice saw the change come over her husband and hoped above all else that this was a new start for the man she had loved and supported through thick and thin.

'So, what can we do to get more funds to improve this house?' Daniel pressed.

'Give me a day and let's see what I can come back with.' Frank waited until Alice had translated, before turning to her. 'Please don't let him pressure me Alice, this may take some time.'

They parted, with Frank returning up the hidden stairway and Daniel and Alice going off to find Harry.

'I am so proud of you,' Alice crooned, and gave him a hug. 'You handled that so well.'

'Thanks Alice, but we have to be extremely cautious. Fischer is watching us closely, and if he finds out we have Frederick lodging, or if it is too transparent that we have suddenly come into heaps of money it would be the end of our dream.'

Alice looked at her husband and decided it best to break the news sooner than later.

'Fischer has been on the phone. He said we are allowing the neighbours to lodge and Clause Four says we cannot have lodgers.'

'Oh shit,' Daniel wailed. 'I never thought of that.'

Chapter 23
Daniels Gets Some Help

Daniel waited patiently for Frank to return, and by the end of the third day he was getting desperate. No matter how hard he banged on the concealed passageway door, there was no response. He flicked the CCTV switch, but still no Frank.

The lodging neighbours were due back soon and he had been avoiding any contact with Fischer and the suits, who had been demanding an urgent meeting regarding the damage to the neighbour's property.

He looked at Alice in desperation. 'Frank said a day. Its nearly three and I still haven't heard a peep.'

Alice waited until Daniel was out of the room and stripped the adhesive tape covering the CCTV camera and held up a hand-written message.

It read; *Daniel needs to talk - urgent.*

An hour later there came the familiar tapping on the larder room door. They made sure Harry was seated at the kitchen table doing his homework while acting as lookout, before slipping into the dimly lit room. Frank was sitting at the table waiting for them. He had piles of paperwork laid out and was tapping a pen on the table.

'Thanks for coming down Frank. How are you?' Alice asked.

'You *have* been busy,' Daniel said, eyeing the paperwork.

Frank used his computer to relay his message. There was a lot to get through and he was not going to waste any time.

'Sorry for taking so long, but it became complicated. So let's get the ball rolling.'

He swept the strands of long grey hair back from his face and Daniel could clearly see a change in him. There was a sparkle in his eyes.

'You're enjoying this aren't you?' Daniel made the question sound more like a statement.

'Haven't had so much fun since helping you decorate the rooms,' Frank replied.

Daniel's face fell. 'What?'

'Who do you think was helping you Daniel? And I did tell you when you first came up to my room, but you have had so many falls you must have forgotten. The quality of finish was quite impressive, would you agree?'

Alice looked at Daniel. 'I thought you were going mad at first, and then you stopped mentioning it.'

'Sorry,' Frank apologised. 'but I had no way of letting you know and was afraid if you found me you would throw me out.'

'What about all the safety gear?'

'Via the internet and delivered by Ming. But let's get back to the issue in hand?' He patted the pile of paper.

They both nodded and settled back as he shifted the sheets into a dozen heaps.

'I have lots of documents for you to sign, but first will go through my proposal, and if you agree we can get the ball rolling.' He paused. 'Firstly, we set up a building company and register me as the Financial Director. You and Alice will be appointed silent partners.'

'How does that help?' Daniel asked.

'Be patient. If you don't like my idea, we scrap it and start again, but listen to me first.' Daniel nodded and sat back. 'Your unfortunate neighbours are currently discussing the reconstruction on their house with the insurers and loss adjusters.

The loss adjusters have specified they get at least three quotes and give the work to the contractor with the lowest price.' He paused. 'So, we intercept their tender process and make sure our newly formed company is registered on the tender list.'

Looking at Frank with renewed interest, Daniel asked. 'You can do that?'

'Yes, and then I can intercept the submissions on the internet and make sure that ours is the lowest.'

'You what?' Daniel was impressed.

'Recall how I got insurance cover for the damages the crane caused,' he smiled. 'Well, I have free access to all parties from my server and have a method whereby I divert mail to my inbox, alter it, and then send it on.' Alice was looking confused. 'Alice, it's like catching the postman before he delivers post next door, taking the letters off him, altering the contents then dropping them in their post box.'

Daniel was all smiles. 'So, we check the competitors and make sure we have a better quote.'

'In essence, yes.' Frank gave one of his rare grins. 'We fabricate our quote to be slightly below the lower of the other two. Not forgetting it is a design and build reconstruct, and we will nominate WASP as the Project Managers. Then we subcontract the work back out while your company actually manages the project.'

'I am impressed,' Daniel said, with a smile. 'So, we hijack the whole process, and once Wasp are involved it gives us a cover and puts us firmly in control.'

Daniel was on his feet and pacing the room.

'And that will give you a legitimate reason to visit site as often as you need,' added Frank.

'We have a lot of money to make,' Daniel reminded him.

'Don't worry about the detail, I will hide some clauses in our contract which will increase the price once we get going. Then you, as the architect, working for the Project Management Company can approve additional costs as we go. The insurers rarely look at the fine print and tend to always go for the lowest price... anyway, leave that detail with me, that's my responsibility.

The practicalities of getting the building work completed are yours. I cannot venture out, so it will be up to you.'

'No problem,' Daniel agreed confidently. 'I am involved with contractors daily and can Project Manage packages of work without having to be on site all of the time. But we will need a front man.'

'I have just the man, or a front man, as you call him.'

'Who's that?' Daniel cocked his head.

'My Chinese friend who has looked after me for the past eighteen years. Ming'

Daniel glared at Frank. 'No, not him, I hate the bastard.'

'He was only doing his best to look after me. You did not need to become so obsessed and chase him. Anyway, after you treated his injuries from the beating, he likes you. I think you will get on well.'

'And the money paid from the insurers?' Alice enquired.

'Paid to WASP. Meanwhile, having regained some credibility from the Chairman for bringing in the work, Daniel can negotiate a small bonus, while authorising stage payments to our Construction Company as the work progresses. After paying the sub-contractors, we claim a few extras, authorised by Daniel of course, and that should make up for any shortfall in his reduced bonus payment.'

There was complete silence around the table. Frank slid a heap of freshly printed documents across the table. 'Can you sign these, so that I can get to work.'

Daniel nestled them in the crook of his arm. 'I want to read them first. Make sure the process is flawless.'

Frank's serious expression slowly morphed into a smile.

'What's so funny?' Daniel asked.

'You,' Frank chided. 'How you have changed from the man who read nothing,' he pointed at the pile of documents. 'To this.'

'Well you learn lessons in life, don't you. I've had my arse well and truly burnt in the past, and it is not going to happen again.'

248

'Not to put a damper on anything guys and I don't want to spoil this blossoming romance,' Alice had been sitting quietly by. 'But Fischer called and is chasing a meeting regarding the crane incident, but more worryingly, to say we may have breached the terms of the will by having lodgers in the house.'

'Me?' Frank asked with a look of shock.

'No, the neighbours. They are deemed to be lodgers.'

'I had almost forgotten,' Daniel said in frustration.

'Read clause five again Alice,' Frank replied in sign language. 'Read the part about being kind to the less fortunate. In addition, ask him to confer with the Undisclosed Person. I think that will put it to bed.'

'What did he say Alice?'

'To stop swearing or he will stop helping you,' she lied.

'Are you kidding me?' he looked from her to Frank.

'Well, in part,' she laughed, 'but he did say that we have a get-out in clause five part two. These people from next door are vulnerable and we are taking care of them. Leave it with me and I will talk to Fischer.'

Frank stood up and turned towards the stairway. He signed Alice to say that he had a lot of work still to do and time was of the essence. Daniel gathered up the paperwork left on the table and headed for the library, where he would carefully read each page. He had already picked a few holes in the process that would require changing, and needed to concentrate.

'So,' Alice said from the library doorway, 'has your opinion of Frank changed?' There was no response. 'Because I think he's saved your bacon. Without him we would have sunk.'

'Once I have what I need out of him,' Daniel hissed in a venomous tone, 'he will have to go. I am not having him around, possibly blackmailing us in the future. Once we have all of this behind us his days are numbered.'

She took a step closer. 'What do you mean?'

'I will have to drug and dump him in a forest hundreds of miles away, or something like that. A place where he can remain lost forever.'

Alice was horrified, 'Don't be stupid, that won't work. Do you think I would allow you to do that to our friend, or possibly your only relative?'

'Oh, our friend now?'

'Yes, our friend, and if I ever find out you have harmed even a single hair on him, you will never hear the end of it.'

Chapter 24
Frank Gets a New Room

Daniel had taken another day off work, while waiting for Frank to set up their business. The phone rang. Alice had only just returned from work and was passing by.

'An emergency?' she said in a heightened voice.

There followed a minute's silence. Daniel had heard the word emergency and came rushing through to where Alice stood with the phone to her ear.

'No, we haven't read the paper in weeks, let alone this morning.' There was a pause. 'OK, we will be there in an hour, I just need to find someone to take care of Harry.'

'Who was that?' Daniel asked.

'Fischer.'

'What does that old goat want? Another bloody meeting?'

'Daniel…, listen to me, this is important. The papers are indicating an imminent crash on markets and apparently property has already been badly hit.'

'Shit.'

'Yes, shit, and we are up the bloody creek if it's true.'

'I have never heard you swear so much Alice, quite impressive.'

'Will you please take this seriously. Fischer says that most properties have been seriously devalued, and if that's the case, we're doomed.'

Fischer had summoned the five suits to the meeting, and when the Somersby's arrived ten minutes early they were all waiting patiently in the boardroom. As they settled down with a cup of tea the couple took in the somber mood.

'Mister Somersby, we have a number of problems,' Fischer started. 'Firstly, the crane incident has not been fully resolved, and although you mailed me an update, there are several issues still concerning us. Then secondly, there is still a slight shortfall in your income now that you are not getting a bonus. Then again, with the six-month extension, we think you may have just scraped through. But those two issues can wait.'

Well if those can wait, Daniel thought, whatever comes next must be serious.

'With the property market crashing, we have had to complete a fresh assessment, and unfortunately if we had to value your house in the current market, it would be worth no more than four million Euros.'

There was complete silence in the room, bar the sound of Daniel, fidgeting and tapping his pen on the table. 'Does that mean we don't get the house? Is that what you're telling us?'

'According to the terms of the will you have to achieve a ten percent gain on the purchase price, and the new valuation would leave you four hundred thousand off that figure. The difference is just too big to bridge within the remaining time.'

Daniel looked horrified. 'So, all of this has been for nothing? Five years of my life, and all my hard work wasted.'

Fischer picked up a separate document. 'There is a possible lifeline. It is a detail that only I and the Undisclosed Person has access to. An interesting statement which we have taken to a reputable firm of probate Solicitors for a second opinion.'

'What's in the statement?' Daniel mumbled, as he emerged from his trancelike state.

'I can only tell you that it relates to exceptional and extraordinary conditions surrounding a fluctuating market, and the valuation of the property.'

'Which means what?' Daniel was starting to get tetchy. 'Surely you haven't brought us in for an emergency meeting just to give us bad news and then tell us it's not actually an emergency.'

'What I have learned from an initial meeting with the probate firm,' Fischer continued patiently, 'is that if we get approval, it means we can take a slightly different approach at the end of the extended five-year period.'

'And that is?' Daniel prompted.

'You would have to vacate the house for at least a week while we completed a forensic examination and place a value on the refurbishments you have completed. We would have to look behind the walls as it were. Then regardless of what the market is doing, we can make an assessment.'

Daniel suddenly sat up. 'Behind the walls?'

'Figuratively speaking that is. Of course, we will not start tearing down walls, or any other part of the house. We just take a detailed look at the workmanship and quality of materials used and put a value to the renovations and improvements you have made.'

After settling back, Alice asked. 'When will you have an answer back from the Probate Solicitors?'

'In two days', Fischer replied. 'The Chairman of the firm has assured me that he will be thorough, and if in any doubt seek guidance from a high court judge.'

Harvey had been sitting quietly watching his old cycling friend and noted how tired he looked. Five years of all work and no relaxation had taken its toll.

Two days later Fischer called with the result they had been praying for. A forensic examination would be allowed. And for the first time since walking out of the Solicitors office they both looked visibly relieved, as they slumped back on their couch.

'Now we really have to get Frank out,' Daniel said. 'If they do a detailed examination of the house and find he is living here, we are doomed.'

'You cannot move him. I can talk to him, but he finds it difficult even being in the kitchen. Let alone moving around in open spaces,' she replied sternly.

'Maybe we could drug him?' Daniel suggested.

'Stop being a fool. Where would we take him?'

A noise came from the larder room and Daniel spun around as the door flung open. The small computer had its volume turned up and Franks message came through loud and clear.

'I am not going anywhere. I am not leaving this house, and if you try, I will contact Fischer and tell him I have been lodging here all along. I will also tell him about the crane insurance and the Project Management fiddle going on next door.'

'You see Alice, I told you he would blackmail us at the first opportunity,' Daniel shouted, and stormed out.

Frank climbed back up the three flights of stairs and locked himself in his room.

Undeterred by Frank's threat and once he had calmed down, Daniel climbed the stairs and knocked on the loft room door. Frank opened it. He was as friendly and helpful as ever, and pointed at a plan rolled out on his desk.

'I got a copy of the neighbours planned extension from your offices and have been studying it,' he said.

'You hacked into my work server and stole that?' Daniel asked.

'You really need to upgrade your security, it's not particularly good,' Frank's computer relayed as he pointed at the plans. 'I also managed to get them electronically transferred onto CAD, so you can 3D them and sort out any issues where the roof structure extends into the new west wing.'

'New west wing?' Daniel queried.

'Yes, your neighbours have lodged a planning application to extend the west wing at their own cost while the repairs are being done.'

Daniel traced his finger over the network of roof beams. It was all new to him. The architect who had done the work had not yet shown him the detail.

'Interesting design,' Franks computer made him jump.

'I see we have not utilised any of the roof space in the extension.' He noted out loud. 'They have the same loft area as this house but none of it is to be converted.' Then he took a closer look. 'And the rooms on this new west wing extension are huge.'

'The first time you have seen these, I take it?' Frank asked.

Ignoring the underlying insinuation, he scratched at his scalp. 'Maybe they are planning on sub-dividing the rooms later,' he speculated. 'What I can see from the photos, is that most of the damage occurred on the west side of the building and they are taking advantage of the rebuild.'

Frank rummaged through another heap of paper and handed it to Daniel, who nodded.

'Ah, that's interesting. This is part of their panning application for the extension to the west wing. They have stated that they have no immediate plans to utilise the extension and it will remain vacant until needed. It also explains that the rooms must be of a certain size. This is to allow the house to be converted into a guesthouse at a much later date.'

Impressed, but outraged that Frank was one step ahead of him, Daniel was fuming. Most of all he was still feeling anxious about having Frank, alias Frederick living in his house. Threatening to undo everything by not vacating during the full inspection. Due at some stage within the following three months.

When Daniel spoke to the neighbours in the sitting room, they gave him the answer he was hoping for.

'We have no intention of doing anything with the west wing. It is surplus to requirements and an investment for the future when we eventually sell. We will leave it boarded off for a few years.'

A week later Franks new Construction Company was awarded the rebuild contract.

As Daniel studied the CAD image of the west wing, he realised it was better than he had first thought, and his newly hatched plan was going to work well. But he had to deceive Frank, Alice, Ming, and the neighbours first. It was not going to be easy, but here, right in front of him was the answer to all his prayers.

Visiting Frank in the loft, on the pretense of looking at the plans again, he took some measurements with his electronic tape. Then pretended to be on his phone but had the video recorder on and slowly turned around, doing his best to record every detail.

'Could we decorate your room Frank?' he asked.

'Why?' Frank frowned. 'I did it about four years ago when you were working on this floor. When I used to nip through and do work for you. If you recall, I even tidied up all your old rubbish.'

'That is precisely the reason I want to help you with your room. It would make me feel like I have done something for you, in return.'

'Thanks, I will help, if you like.'

On the way out, Daniel shut the Loft door and started measuring everything on his way down the three flights of stairs. Then he did the same with the larder room and kitchen.

Returning to Franks room he rapped on the door and stuck his head into the room. 'Sorry Frank, but I failed to tell you that I have a lot of deliveries coming into the kitchen over the following three months. A new kitchen for us and furnishings for next door, so stay up here please.

Frank nodded, smiled, and gave a thumbs up.

Two months later Daniel was having his regular morning meeting with Ming in the portable cabin he had kindly allowed the sub-contractors to place in his garden. Although at first, he had made a big fuss over it being there. He wanted to avoid appearing too eager.

A substantial platform of rock and sleepers had a new tower crane standing on firmer ground, where it could reach the entire roof of not only theirs, but the neighbour's house as well. There would be a big saving on the insurance invoice, and the loss adjusters agreed to give Daniel a sizable discount for using their land.

'Progress please Ming?' Daniel demanded.

Ming was smart and had adapted quickly to his new role. 'Damaged roof removed, and mostly replaced Mister Dan.'

Mister Dan was what he liked to call him. Daniel couldn't have cared less what he was called, so long as he got the job done.

'New loft room built and being fitted out,' Frank continued, as he traced the line on the progress chart.

He had told Ming that the room was going to be for Frank to use during the inspection, but he was not to say a word as it may upset him. He went into detail regarding the upcoming audit and how the move was in Franks best interests.

The joiners employed were East European and spoke little English. They followed the plans without questioning the detail.

'What about the inner wall Ming?'

He was referring to a false wall that contained an identical secret stairwell. Identical to the one in Manor House.

'Four feet wide and complete Mister Dan. Nobody would know it's there.'

He knew that by taking four feet off the width off the oversized rooms on the west wing it would be hardly noticeable.

'The larder room and new kitchen?'

'Larder room built, and new kitchen to be fitted out at the same time as the one in your house Mister Dan. After neighbours have done final inspection.'

Daniel was taking the opportunity and was going to replace his entire refurbished kitchen with a new one as well. Knowing that Ming had never seen the inside of Frank's room, he knew there would be no questions asked as he duplicated the shelving, cupboards, washroom and every other bit of detail he extracted from the video and measurements taken.

Once the shell of the extension was complete, Ming took the neighbours on a tour. As per instructions from Daniel, he did not let on about the hidden stairwell or attic room. They were thrilled with their investment and praised the finishes, but were restless and wanted their house back.

'Two weeks and soon finished,' Ming reassured them.

He also confirmed that once done, the new extension would be sealed off and secured for future use.

Work on repairs to the neighbour's property, as well as upgrading Manor House was almost complete. Daniel convinced Frank to paint his own room, while Daniel splashed out on a new carpet. The colour of the carpet and paint on the walls was an identical match to that in the new west wing next door.

Frank's window was replaced while he sat waiting in the adjacent linen storage room. He returned to find misted panes and a new ceiling fan installed, with a much higher output.

The false window in the neighbour's new attic room was identical to Frank's new window. With one exception. It was not on the external roof and had been installed in a false panel within the roof space. The builders questioned the idea and Ming asked Daniel if he was serious about this part of the design. Daniel reassured Ming that it was all part of the bigger picture, and he was to keep his mouth shut.

Nearing completion, the foreign workers were keen to move on. They had been attacked on several occasions. The perpetrator always accosting them as they left the property soon after dark. They were vicious attacks, and left one man with a broken arm.

'Who is doing this?' Daniel asked.

'Bad man,' Ming replied. 'He the same bad man that beat me in dark.'

Ming urged Daniel to make sure he had all materials on order, as the workers wanted to get finished and be away. Daniel told him he was willing to donate the cupboards from his larder room and install them next door. It would help speed things up.

Once both kitchens had been finished it was impossible to tell them apart.

'You very clever man Mister Dan,' Ming said, as he surveyed the completed extension. 'Kitchen the same as your house now. And a surprise for neighbours one day.'

Three months since starting on the rebuild, and Daniel was ready to implement the final part of his plan. Fischer was about to conduct their forensic inspection and he had to make his move. Careful not to purchase anything on the internet or pay by card, he paid cash only.

When the parcel arrived at his business address, he looked furtively around, made sure nobody was watching and took the package into his office, where he locked the door.

He found it amazing what could be bought on the open market. The box of tablets had no labels, only a hand-written note attached. 'No more than one tablet per day to fully sedate your patient. Keep patient on drip throughout. Continuous sedation period to last no longer than two days.'

Daniel looked at the six bags of saline drip and threw them in the bin. 'No need for those,' he mumbled.

He gathered his briefcase and headed for the lift, talking to himself. 'Come on Frank my old buddy, time for a change of address,' he said to himself, and dropped the tablets into his pocket as headed for home.

Chapter 25
Goodbye Frank

Reconstruction and extensions to the house next door were complete, and bar a good cleaning and dust down, ready for the owners to move back in.

After arranging and paying for a weekend of luxury river cruising with the neighbours, the time had arrived for their trip. This being in appreciation for their patience and understanding while their house was being repaired.

The minibus arrived, and the couple and their two children climbed eagerly on board. Daniel, Alice, and Harry followed with bags of snacks for the road trip. Ming had a house key and was looking after Doggie while they were away.

The driver loaded four cases into the luggage hold.

'All aboard and ready for two days of fun,' Daniel said, and raised a bottle of beer, as they all laughed and drunk a toast.

'To the most understanding and patient neighbours in the world,' Alice added.

The neighbours laughed. They had ended up with a totally refurbished and extended house. Alice sighed with relief. The family had been a nightmare and a blight on their lives, and she couldn't wait to see the back of them.

The driver settled into his seat and as he was about to set off Daniels phone rang.

'Hold it there please, I have an emergency,' Daniel shouted.

The bus went quiet as his brow screwed up in obvious concern.

'What is it?' Alice urged.

He lowered his phone and grimaced. 'Unfortunately, it's my work Alice. We had a deadline of next wednesday for a submission on a massive project, and the client now says he wants it this Monday. I am going to have to stay behind and go into the office.' He looked around the bus, 'Sorry folks.'

'But this has been planned for a while,' Alice complained. 'You can't leave me to do all the entertaining.'

'Don't worry about us,' the neighbours shouted from the back of the minibus. 'We are quite looking forward to having a good time, with or without you.'

Daniel walked away as quickly as he could, before Alice had time to interrogate him further. He waved at them as they drove by and shrugged his shoulders. He had to do what he had to do. Life was tough at times and he had made some difficult decisions.

He put his phone back to his ear. 'OK Ming, just a few things to do and then you can have tonight off.'

'Why did you ask me to phone you, Mister Dan? And what about Doggie?' Ming asked.

'I want you to help me move the neighbour's belongings back into their house today. So that when they return it's all done. Tomorrow morning, you go and visit friends and be back after lunch. And don't worry about the dog in the morning. I will be taking him for a walk.'

'What about Frank, Mister Dan?'

'I will look after Frank. Don't you worry about him. But be back tomorrow afternoon to help me move his furniture across to his temporary room.

'I keep Franks room a secret Mister Dan,' Ming reassured him.

'Good man,' Daniel replied.

Ming lingered on the call. There was something clearly concerning him. 'Where does Frank go while we move his room, and how you get him across to new room?'

'I am working on the detail Ming, leave it with me.'

'Ah, you very clever Mister Dan,' Ming replied.

He did not even know if Ming had friends to visit that night. The thin Chinese man had certainly not mentioned anyone.

When they had finished carting all the neighbour's boxes and belongings across to their renovated house, Daniel bade the thin Chinese man farewell, before running up the internal stairway and banging on Franks door.

'Hello Daniel, I thought you were going away,' Frank signed after opening the door.

Having taken a crash course in sign language, Daniel was quite proficient.

'I had a last-minute call. Things to do at the office.' He smiled at Frank. 'Before I go, can we review the completed as-built plan I have in the larder cupboard? I meant to bring it up, but forgot.'

When they arrived at the foot of the stairway, Frank found to his horror that the revolving cupboard had been replaced with a normal door.

'Where is my cupboard?'

'Being renovated Frank,' Daniel lied. 'I have taken all the cupboards out to clean them. They will be back soon.'

Daniel lifted two plastic bottles of ice-tea that stood on the table next to a rolled-up plan.

'I know you like these Frank. Lets drink a toast to how well we have done.' He handed Frank the bottle that had a small pen mark on the lid. 'Down the hatch my friend.'

Frank followed his example of drinking the contents in one go.

Five minutes later he started to feel tired and was soon flat on the floor, snoring loudly. Daniel dragged him out of the front door and placed him next to the rose bushes, where a pair of clippers and cuttings lay. He pulled out his mobile phone and called for an ambulance.

'I have a man working in my garden and he has just collapsed. I am worried that he may have suffered a heart attack.'

The wailing siren arrived within minutes, and Daniel sat in the back with the patient as they headed for the nearest hospital. A paramedic checked Franks vital signs, and by the time they had him checked in at the emergency ward nobody could explain what was wrong with him.

'I will be back tomorrow morning to check on how he is doing.' Daniel told the orderly. 'Don't forget to hook him up to a saline drip, he looks dehydrated,' he added and dashed out to a cab he had pre-ordered.

The following morning, he went to visit Frank in hospital, and found him stirring. He was starting to come around. Daniel popped the second tablet from his box into a glass of water and sat holding Frank's head up until he had drunk it all. The long grey hair had been washed by a nurse and collected around his face, hiding his red rimmed eyes.

Daniel stared at the scar on his arm.

'Cousin Frederick, how the table has turned,' he murmured under his breath, before checking that they had the saline drip still working.

Moving all of Frank's personal belongings was easy. Ming had arrived to help soon after mid-day, and they spent a lot of time making sure his new room replicated the old one in every conceivable way. Daniel had taken detailed photographs and printed them on A3 paper, enlarged, so that he could compare the two and check for any variances. By the time the work was done he was exhausted and after seeing Ming off, collapsed on the sitting room couch.

He had told Ming not to come back until the following week, when Frank would need his food delivering.

The whole of the following day was spent checking over everything he had done. He checked that the CCTV camera in Frank's new room was connected to their kitchen, so that he would see them moving around in their own kitchen from his new location. He paced the bedroom and looked at it from every conceivable angle. The windows were frosted out like his old room and a vent allowed fresh air to flow in. The bedroom in the neighbour's loft faced north, not south, so that the food hatch was on the same side of the stairwell as before.

Smiling and rubbing his hands, he walked from the west wing side door and called a cab.

Getting Frank discharged was not that easy. The ward sister put up a good fight, but Daniel won and soon had his lodger in the back of a taxi.

When they arrived back at Manor House, Ming was standing in the entrance looking concerned. 'Where have you been Mister Dan, and where has Frank been in taxi?'

Daniel was flustered. The thin man was supposed to have taken the rest of the extended weekend off. 'What are you doing here Ming?'

'I am worried Mister Dan. I came back with a small cake for Frank.'

Daniel's mind raced. 'I took Frank for a check-up at the hospital today. I needed to know he is well. Now help me get our friend into his new room. He is still a bit sedated from the tests.'

Both men had Frank, one on each arm, as they half carried him between the narrow gap in the evergreen hedge and through the west wing extension side door. The drugs kept him in a stupor and although his eyes opened and he looked around, he was oblivious to what was going on.

Once back outside, Daniel held a brief meeting with Ming. 'See that metal hatch on the neighbour's house?'

'Yes Mister Dan. The same as your house.'

'Good man,' Daniel patted him on his thin shoulder. 'Remember, from now on, that is where you put Franks food and deliveries. But be careful, if the neighbours find out he is living there, they will call the police and if the inspectors know about him, they won't allow him back into our house. He will have

264

nowhere to live.' He patted him once again. 'I am going to give you a good bonus for all the work you have done, and then payments to deliver food to Frank. Just remember, it will cause a big problem if anyone, including Alice, sees you delivering the food or finds out Frank has moved.'

'All right Mister Dan, if you say so,' replied the thin Chinese man, before scuttling off.

The minibus returned with everyone looking tired and ready for a night on dry land. The neighbours had come to the realisation that sea sickness was not confined to the sea, and they had spent most of the time leaning over the side of the river cruiser retching and begging to be allowed back onto dry land.

They went straight into their refurbished home, after Daniel had told them all their belongings were back in their own house. They shouted farewells and promised to keep in touch. Alice waved back and wished them well. She hoped to never lay eyes on them again.

Daniel was waiting at the entrance to the neighbour's house with their keys and wished them luck in their newly refurbished home. He told them that the west wing side door was jammed shut and he would attend to it, but as they were not planning on using the extension, he couldn't see it being a problem. The whole extension was now sealed off from their main building.

Alice turned to Daniel as he walked back into Manor House. 'The house is ours at last. No more neighbours taking over the ground floor.'

Harry moped around for a while. He had got on well with the neighbour's boys and felt lonely. 'Have you seen Frank?' he asked his father.

'Frank asked not to be disturbed,' Daniel replied.

The following morning after leaving Manor House, Daniel ducked through the evergreens, unlocked the side door, and emerged in the neighbours West Wing. He was on his way to work, but wanted to clear up a few issues with Frank first.

'How are you?' he asked, as he walked into the loft room.

'Tired. I feel as if I have been drugged. My brain is fuzzy, and I am confused,' he signed. 'Feels strange being in this room. Somehow disorientating, but at least I can't see out.'

'Business as usual then,' Daniel replied.

'Have you fixed the side hatch?' Frank asked. 'I will need to be able to get deliveries from Ming.'

'Replaced a long time ago, if you recall. It even has a brand-new coat of paint on the inside. Just for you.'

'Thank you, I forgot. You are kind.'

'I just wanted to pop around to make something clear, and give you this mobile phone.'

'I have never used one before, I only use emails to message Ming.'

'Plug it in to charge and it has my phone number in the memory. Not hard for a techno whiz like you Frank. I have your email address and mobile phone number, so we can keep in touch as much as you like. But no calling anyone else, even in an emergency, is that clear?'

Frank nodded. 'So, what happens next?'

'The house is ready for inspection, so you are to stay up in your room and be quiet. They will take about a month to fully inspect the property, so please, no noise. I have arranged with Ming to deliver anything you need, and ask that from now on you both communicate through me. Send me an email or call on that phone, and we will deliver whatever you need.'

'How do I get my food from the hatch?'

'You can go down to the hatch, but be quick and return to your room.'

'That's fine,' Frank smiled. 'I appreciate you taking care of me. You are a kind man. Are Alice and Harry well?'

'Oh, great. Which reminds me, when the inspection is over, I only want you coming down to the kitchen when we are out.'

'OK?'

'You can see our kitchen in your monitor right now Frank, but my mobile phone can turn it on or off. I can't have you watching us in our own home, now can I?'

'Quite right Daniel.'

'New rules state that you can only come down when we are not in the room, and you will know that when I turn the camera on. We need our privacy, is that clear?'

'Quite clear,' Frank replied.

'Good, because I will call you on your new mobile phone when I go downstairs and turn the camera on. Just so you can see how it works.'

He raced down the stairs, out the side door and back into his own kitchen next door, where he activated the camera.

'I am downstairs in the kitchen Frank, can see me?' Daniel said, while looking at the camera.

Frank responded using his computer voice. 'I can see you. I am even waving back. Hello Daniel.'

'Alright Frank. Remember, we have an agreement. I will only turn the Camera on when we are out of the room, or I want to communicate with you, and only then can you come down. If by some chance the kitchen is occupied, you do not come down, ever.'

'Got it,' Frank replied, 'but when can I talk to Alice and Harry.'

'When the inspection is over Frank. We have to be careful.'

He ended the call and smiled to himself as he muttered. 'When we have sold the house you can talk to them as much as you like.'

Chapter 26
Goodbye Daniel

Alice approached Daniel a few days after arriving back from the river cruise. 'I haven't seen Frank for a while. Have you seen him?'

The Solicitors and building inspectors were ready to conduct their forensic valuation of the house, and the Somersby's were packing in readiness for their move to a hotel.

'I told him to lie low,' he replied after a long pause.

Alice looked unconvinced. 'Strange, I thought he would have at least come down and said something after I got back.'

'I told you Alice, he is lying low,' Daniel repeated, as he lifted their two cases off the bed and made for the stairs.

Fischer had booked them into a city centre hotel while they conducted their valuation. All expenses paid.

Alice was concerned about Frank's well-being and worried that he may need something. 'If the suits are at the house all day and the hatch jams, how will Frank get food?'

'I have asked Ming to keep an eye on him. Now will you please stop fretting.'

Daniel stood guard in the kitchen as she fussed around. He was not letting her get anywhere near the larder room.

'If you want to wave to him, I will turn on the monitor,' he said as he activated the app on his phone.

Alice waved at the camera, and much to her delight saw Frank wave back on Daniels phone.

'Hello Frank, Alice here, can you see me?'

Frank had balanced the phone on a table so he could use both hands to sign back. 'Yes Alice, I can hear you. Did you have a nice time?'

'Very nice thanks Frank. Is my lovely husband looking after you?'

'Your husband has been marvelous Alice. You are a lucky girl.'

Alice said her goodbyes and gave Daniel a hug.

'You can be so sweet when you want to be,' she added with a kiss on the cheek.

Frank had little to do now that the building work was complete and the excitement of the move was over. However, it was not long before his new mobile phone pinged. It was a message from a different number to the one Daniel had preset in the directory.

'Daniel here. Has the insurance company released the last payment for the building work?'

There was a short delay as Frank checked his computer, then messaged back.

'Yes, arrived in the company's bank account this morning. I was going to let you know.'

'Can you transfer it into my new account? Number attached. I have bills to pay,' the message read.

'No problem will do it now,' Frank replied.

Arriving at work the following day, Daniel found a large note on his desk.

Dear Daniel,

Old Sniffer has taken early retirement and I have been drafted in to cover until a suitable replacement has been found. Considering you no longer answer emails and your mobile diverts directly to voicemail, I have resorted to leaving notes on your desk.

Please see me in the boardroom as soon as you read this.

It was signed by his old friend Colin.

Daniel strode down the corridor and greeted his team of architects. Most returned blank looks or ignored him. One of them said 'Hi', before sniggering.

When he got to the board room it was obvious the large man behind the desk, whom he now knew to be the chairman, was not in any frame of mind for casual banter. Colin sat at a side table, looking nervous.

'Sit.' Warren commanded.

Daniel sat.

'You were once an aspiring young man. Apparently very annoying but aspiring.'

Daniel smiled at him. This could be the promotion he had been promised a while back, he thought. He glanced across at Colin who failed to make eye contact.

'I try my hardest,' he replied.

'I have watched you for most of your life young man,' Warren added.

'You have?' Daniel looked perplexed. 'But I have only worked here for eleven years.'

'Your father, Mister Fischer and I are old friends. You don't remember me, do you?'

Daniel studied the robust looking man for a while and then a very distant memory of a much thinner man, obviously younger and more athletic looking returned. He could recall a friend of his fathers with a yacht.

'I think I do now. In fact I had a vague memory of you and my father being friends the last time we met.' Daniel replied hesitantly. 'It was sailing weekends with my father, wasn't it?'

'At last ... got there in the end, didn't you?'

Daniel felt pleased to have made the connection and gave Colin a smug look.

'How else do you think you got this job?' the heavy-set man continued. 'There are plenty of architects out there with a lot more ambition and who are a lot less annoying than you. And I can see you never once tried to find out what WASP stood for.'

'Is it important?' Daniel asked.

'Not really, now that we are in this situation, but I thought it right to explain that WASP stands for Warren and Somersby Projects.'

'My Uncle Harry and you?'

'That's right, and I have to say you are a disappointment and not proved worthy of your last promotion.'

'I worked hard for my promotion,' Daniel rallied. 'Ask Colin, he is my friend.'

'Daniel...,' Colin said defensively, 'this has not been any of my doing. I supported you for a lot of years, but members of your staff have brought forward numerous complaints. I am sorry.'

'You may have worked hard for a short spell,' Warren resumed, 'but since your first promotion, your interests have been divided between fixing up your house and working here.'

'Work life balance,' Daniel put forward the modern concept most companies were promoting.

'Not a balance when it is ninety percent home and ten percent work.' The large man cleared his throat and straightened in his chair. 'Look, I don't quite know how to break this to you gently, so I am going to be straight with you.'

'I like straight talk,' Daniel replied.

'You're fired,' Warren said, and sat back in his chair.

Daniel reeled back and shook his head. He could not believe it. He thought he had been doing so well. Then the familiar figure of the company security guard entered, and Colin left.

'Bob will escort you off the property. I wish you well wherever your life takes you. Goodbye,' Warren concluded.

With that, the large man walked out as the security guard took hold of Daniel's arm and led him back to his desk. Where he had the opportunity to collect anything personal he wished to take with him.

As he passed rows of his subordinates, he saw smirks and smiles. There was not a friendly face or an ounce of sympathy in sight.

He arrived back at the hotel to find Alice pacing the reception. She had walked out to get some fresh air and was surprised to see her husband back so early, but also relieved. Because there was something bothering her.

'Wait until I see a lawyer,' he said before she had time to speak.

'Why aren't you at work?' she asked.

'You aren't at work either,' he shot back.

'Because I have a week's leave. Unlike you, I have mine signed off by my boss.'

'I can't take any more leave Alice.'

'Why?'

'Because I no longer have a job,' he blurted out. 'The Chairman has just fired me.'

Alice turned and followed him as he marched into the elevator.

'Where is Frank?' she asked.

'I told you. He is lying low and out of the way until Fischer has finished his inspection, and we put the house on the market.'

'Then why is his loft area cleared out?' She pulled at his arm. 'There is nothing left in his room.'

'You went into his room?'

'Yes, because I was worried about him. I went back to the house this afternoon for one last look around, before the Fischer crowd arrived.' Alice took a step closer and looked him in the eye. 'Now tell me. Where is he?'

'He must have left. You know, moved out,' he replied unconvincingly.

'What have you done to him?'

'Nothing Alice, he must have decided enough is enough. Anyway, let's get into our room and sort this out.'

Alice slammed the door behind her as she followed him in and pulled at his arm. 'You killed him, haven't you?'

'What?' Daniel took a step backwards.

'You have threatened to kill him at least half a dozen times, and you know what I think?'

'Is that really what you think?' He looked at her angrily.

'You have eventually flipped and done it,' she said, close to hysteria.

'That is bullshit Alice, I would never harm him.'

'Then, where is he?' she screamed.

'I can't tell you,' he said bluntly.

'Ah, so suddenly you know, but can't tell me.'

He remained silent. He was worried about letting this conversation get out of hand, but she was not letting up.

'I am giving you exactly thirty seconds to tell me or I am going to fetch my bag, collect Harry from school, and leave you.'

'You cannot leave me Alice, remember clause two says that we both have to reside in the house.'

'In your own words, fuck clause two. I will pick up Harry on my way.'

She turned and walked into their bedroom, where a bag was already packed. She had made up her mind earlier in the day and not much was going to make her change it.

Two weeks after conducting a thorough examination of Manor House, Fischer left a fresh voicemail on Daniels phone, asking for him and Alice to attend a meeting at their offices.

'Is Alice not joining us?' Fischer asked when Daniel arrived alone.

'She is away on business,' he replied curtly.

'That is not what we heard,' Fischer shot back. 'We believe she has walked out on you.'

Daniel sat on his side of the table facing Fischer and the top of five suit heads. They were all preoccupied with a pile of paperwork in front of them.

'Are you saying I have breached clause two because Alice has left me?' he asked after a long period of silence.

'Not exactly Mister Somersby. Under normal conditions, and with only weeks to go, I would call for a ruling from the Undisclosed Person, but am struggling to make contact.'

Sitting up, he cocked his head to one side. 'You mentioned normal conditions. Is there something I don't know about?'

Fischer picked up a sheet of paper and looked at it.

'We received this email from a man who claims you abducted someone and took him to your house. It is difficult to understand, because everything he told us in this message is a little hard to comprehend.'

'Are you telling me you believe some nutter?' Daniel's face contorted and turned red.

'We will get to the truth in time. Currently we have only received an email. Besides the accusation of abduction, he claims to be the son of your Uncle Harry.'

'So, this person waits on the side-line,' Daniel was beside himself with rage and ranted. 'While I have bust a gut doing up the house. He waits and then claims to be Francis when all the work has been completed. Surely that is not grounds to throw me out. Anyway, this person, whoever he is, will have to verify his claim. It certainly does not give you grounds to evict me.'

'Maybe not now, but it has caused a lot of consternation in the office and we are currently reviewing all the relevant clauses and requests in the will. We are also trying to locate this man who claims to be Francis.'

'That is pure bullshit,' Daniel erupted and stood up.

'We do not know what it is, but from the information we received, we have had no option other than hand the matter over to the police.'

'You what?'

'It is a serious issue, and unfortunately we have no other choice in the matter.'

Two police officers were waiting in the reception area and cautioned Daniel as he walked out of the boardroom.

'Mister Somersby, we would like you to accompany us down to the station. We believe you may be able to help us with a report we received saying that someone fitting your description abducted a man from a hospital bedroom and took him away in a taxi.'

This was the second time in two days he had been escorted out of a building. First at work and now here, and he was starting to tremble with outright indignation and the humiliation of it all.

Chapter 27
Daniel and the Soup Kitchen

Special investigators questioned Daniel for two hours and got nowhere. While they had him under interrogation a search party carried out a forensic search of Manor House, and found nothing suspicious. No sign of anyone living in the small loft room Alice had told them about and certainly no corpse. There was no sign of Frank anywhere.

When they studied CCTV footage taken from the hospital reception area, they could clearly see someone supporting a man who looked to be under the influence as they walked from the entrance. The images were grainy, but while being questioned in an adjoining room, Alice confirmed one of them was Daniel. Then the ambulance records of them arriving two days earlier removed all doubt.

Alice held a meeting with Fischer and explained in detail about their lodger and the hidden room in their house, but refrained from naming him as Frank or speculating as to whether he may be one of the missing cousins. She said that the man had recently vacated the loft and moved out.

'Do you know the man?' asked the policeman for the umpteenth time.

'No, he was a tramp who wandered into my garden.' Daniel followed his well-rehearsed script. 'I gave him some work and shortly afterwards found him collapsed near the rose garden. I thought I was doing the charitable thing by taking him to hospital.'

'Your wife says he was a lodger in your house and that you had threatened to kill him.'

'That's bullshit,' Daniel shot back.

'But then why remove him from hospital the following day?'

'He asked me to take him away. So I took him back to my house, gave him some clothes and a meal. He then left the property.'

There was nothing further the police could do. They could not charge him with anything and there was certainly no corpse. And after a night in a cell they released him under caution and told him not to go far.

When he arrived back at Manor House a security guard stood at the entrance barring the way.

'This is my house,' Daniel protested.

The guard stood his ground and repeated that he was only doing what he was paid to do and acting under orders.

'Who's orders? Who do you work for?' Daniel shouted in frustration.

'He works for me.' A voice he knew all too well came from behind him.

'Fischer.' Daniel said as he spun around. 'What the hell is going on?'

'I have all your personal possessions packed in a suitcase and box, ready for you to take with you. Unfortunately things have got out of hand, and you have been evicted from the house.'

Transfixed, Daniel was exhausted and at a complete loss.

Fischer handed over an envelope containing cash and a debit card. 'That should get you some food and accommodation. There is sufficient on the card to see you through until you resettle.'

Daniel took the envelope and walked to where his personal belongings stood in a heap at the front gate. As he reached down to pick up a bag, his phone pinged. Looking at the screen he could see he had a message. It was a text from Frank using his new mobile phone.

'Hello. I was wondering how the inspection is going?'

'Sorry Frank, busy now,' he messaged back. *'Stay put and be quiet. I will see you soon.'*

The reply came within seconds. *'Thanks Daniel, you are my best friend.'*

Daniel felt a wave of anxiety sweep over him as he tried to understand who had contacted Fischer, the police, and why he had been evicted from his own home. Leaving him confused and short of breath, his head started to spin as he staggered towards the nearest stable object he could find and clung to it.

When he regained focus and his vision cleared, his arms were wrapped around a lamppost and he was using it as support. A man was standing nearby. He thought he recognised him, but was unsure.

'What's going on?' he said as he steadied himself.

'It is me, Ming, Mister Dan,' said the man.

'Do I know you?' Daniel mumbled through what felt like clouds of fog. Standing by the gated entrance to Manor House, he looked down the drive. 'Big house.'

The Chinese man smiled. 'Are you confused Mister Dan?'

'Do I know you?' he repeated. 'What did you say your name was?'

'Ming, Mister Dan. I hear you have nowhere to stay so I came to see if I can help. You no longer live in big house.'

'Mister Dan? Ming? Which one is me, and what big house?'

'You carry case Mister Dan,' Ming replied with a smile. 'I go back and get box. You wait here.'

'Where are we going Mister Dan?' Daniel asked.

'Me Ming, you Mister Dan,' the Chinese man corrected. 'Now, I get you some accommodation,' he added, and darted off to get the remaining box.

He returned balancing the box and a toiletry bag in his arms.

'Follow me Mister Dan. I live rough for many years and know a good place.'

'Wouldn't it be easier to get a taxi to wherever we are going?' Daniel asked.

'No need Mister Dan. Only around corner.'

A couple of miles and what felt like hours later, on the outskirts of the city, they came to an underpass.

'This is good spot Mister Dan. Big soup kitchen on that corner over there.' He pointed at an old building with a few disheveled looking individuals standing around the entrance.

'Thanks Ming. I was hoping for something a little better though.'

'You have sleeping bag Mister Dan?'

'Nothing but a case of clothes, that box and a bit of cash.'

'Don't worry then Mister Dan, I will sort you out with everything you need.' He looked around at some men huddled up against the concrete wall. 'I will introduce you, they friends of mine.'

Their names slipped into oblivion soon after Ming had introduced them. They appeared friendly, but were dirty and smelly. Daniel held his breath when he got close. When they smiled at him, he saw blackened teeth and red eyes shining through straggly masses of unkempt hair.

'Look, they are very kind. They give you a special place in the middle of them, so you stay warm,' Ming said, as he dumped the box in a clearing they had made amongst their cardboard homes. 'I go and buy you sleeping bag now.'

There was little option other than to cooperate, as they tugged at him and dragged his box and bag to a spot between their cardboard homes. At least it was away from the freezing air that whistled through the underpass. When he looked sideways, several of the homeless had started rummaging through his box and were busy distributing clothing and toiletries amongst themselves. His phone slipped into a pocket, and before he had time to react, someone removed the credit card and money Fischer had given him.

Minutes later they were all back in their makeshift homes, or huddled under blankets against the underpass wall.

That night after gathering, they resembled a waddle of emperor penguins as they shuffled towards the soup kitchen. Daniel was hungry and tired and gratefully received his ration of vegetable soup and a thick chunk of bread, then settled down in the canteen amongst his new-found friends and ate his first meal on the streets.

One day was very much like another and if someone had told him it was Thursday, he would have shrugged and agreed. It hardly mattered, so long as he could keep warm and there was a plate of hot food in the soup kitchen each evening.

The weeks rolled together, one following the other, and soon turned into months. The difference being summer was fast approaching and he could feel the air warming.

The only constant in his life was Ming, who would call in every other day to see how he was doing. And after suffering with a cold, he had woken to find a small bag of antibiotics and a packet of throat lozenges tucked in by his side. The thin man had recovered his mobile phone, but the battery was dead and although the soup kitchen had a charging point, he did not see the need.

Ming arrived out of breath one morning and scrambled over to where Daniel sheltered.

'Wake up Mister Dan, wake up.'

He shook Daniels blanket until the fiery head of red hair emerged and stared at him.

'What do you want Ming? I am tired.'

'Men looking for you Mister Dan. Two of them roaming around asking for you, and another one follows them. I see them before at your house long time ago and they are hunting everywhere for you. The one following them is bad man.'

Daniel looked wildly from side to side, but besides the bulges of his comrades under blankets, there was nobody else in sight.

'Thanks Ming, I will keep a lookout,' he replied before crawling back under his dirty blanket.

Warmer weather also brought out the cyclists, who raced past in groups. This was not unusual. He had got used to them streaming through the underpass and knew to pull his legs in and hold on tight.

'Duck you suckers.' The shout came one such morning as the cyclists following the leader shouted and laughed.

It stirred something in Daniel. But his memory was foggy, and his brain felt numb. Even though he was starting to have flashbacks of his previous life, whatever returned, quickly slid back into a dark recess.

When he tried to walk more than a few yards he grew tired and needed to rest. His joints ached, and the lice were a constant annoyance. Six months of sleeping rough was not only uncomfortable but turning out to be seriously bad for his health.

One day, he heaved himself out of his cardboard makeshift shelter and started shuffling towards the city centre on his own. Ming dropped by and found Daniel's box empty. He raced off in the direction given and soon caught up.

'Where are you going Mister Dan?'

'The soup kitchen keeps running out of food. The boys complain every night and I am tired of listening to their griping. I want to see what's going on myself.'

'But I bring you your food when you need it Mister Dan.'

'I share it out Ming, but the soup kitchens have to be more organised.'

'I am very worried about men looking for you Mister Dan, please be careful.'

Ming appeared to be in a rush. 'Sorry Mister Dan, I must go, I take some food to Frank. I just come to see if you need anything.'

As Ming disappeared around a corner, Daniel arrived at a large center he had not visited before. The queue was half-way around the block and the few seats inside the basement room were crammed full of men and woman of all ages. When he eventually got to the food counter there was nothing left.

'Why have you run out?' he asked.

'We have collection boxes and bags where people can donate food, but the results are always the same.' The weary young girl answered, as she scraped away at an empty tray. 'There is just not enough food for the number of people who come in.'

Daniel started roaming the streets, and found the same scene at every soup kitchen. The demand was always higher than the amount of food available.

His memory had started returning in larger chunks by now. But he was stuck in a rut and had carved out a new way of life that he would find difficult to leave behind. He recalled having a son called Harry and now had clear visions of Alice. He also recalled having let them down. And then there was a man called Frank, whom he had very mixed emotional memories of. Most of them bad.

He often spoke to Ming about his former life and what he had left behind, and Ming spent hours telling stories of how he had looked after his best friend Frank for a very long time. He told him that Frank was still holed up in the Neighbours house, knew he was there but asked Ming not to tell anyone. Not even Alice. He found it more peaceful and had sworn Ming to secrecy.

After plucking up some courage, Daniel asked. 'Do they know where I am and do they ask about me?'

Ming looked at the ground. 'Sorry Mister Dan, I keep away from them all. I say nothing about you to Frank and never hear anything from him. He knows you are here though, and that I see you.'

'And?' he stared at the thin face.

'He still very cross with you Mister Dan.'

Then one day, as they entered a soup kitchen together, Daniel reeled back at the sight of someone behind the counter.

'What wrong Mister Dan?' Ming asked.

'Look who's serving the mash,' Daniel whispered.

Ming scanned the row of helpers before his gaze rested on a familiar face, as she served one large ladle of potato after another.

'It's Alice,' Ming said in a low voice.

'We must leave,' Daniel said in an urgent tone.

'No, be brave and get your food or you starve. Frank says she still very cross with you, but you look like shit and nobody will recognise you.'

Daniel joined the queue and shuffled forward. The young girl standing next to Alice dumped a spoon of peas on his plate and Alice served a ladle full of mash on the side. She glanced up at him and smiled, but there was no sign of recognition.

'There you are Sir, hope that keeps your belly full for the night. God bless you.'

Then he was shoved by the man behind, and moved off to join Ming on a wooden bench.

Alice left at the end of serving time and Daniel watched her go. As she went, he felt a sadness creep over him that he had never experienced before.

Weeks dragged by, and as always, he sat waiting for Ming to arrive and keep him company. They covered a variety of topics, but mostly drifted back to the same old subjects. How difficult it was for these poor people to get out of the hole they were in, and how much he missed his former life.

Then a week went by without him seeing his Chinese friend and he started to get agitated.

'Where are you Ming?' he called from his box. Surely Ming had not abandoned him, he thought.

Then he saw a person who looked like Ming silhouetted against the backdrop of light close to the underpass entrance. He appeared to be watching someone Daniel had not noticed in the poor light, as the figure slowly approach the mishmash of temporary homes. The figure carefully lifting blankets or box lids before moving on to the next shape. Slowly drawing closer to where he sat. Recalling the warning from Ming about men out looking for him, he slid under his blanket and held it so that he could peer out without being seen.

Suddenly the silhouette moved and ran at the person searching nearby. But he was no match for the brute of a man, who swatted him aside with a backhanded blow, sending him reeling towards where Daniel lay. Landing with a thump as he fell on solid ground, Daniel could now clearly see it was Ming. Distracted, he was too late to escape the blows that rained down on him from the brutish figure, and all he could do was try his best to shield himself from further harm.

A small group of the more agile community gathered and rushed forward, joining in the brawl. Then as the brute slid from the fight and made a bid to escape, Daniel saw what he thought to be a scar on his arm and wondered if it could be Frederick.

Weeks later, after moving to a new location and as both men recovered from their injuries, they spoke about the attack.

'He follows me for days, but I outwit him,' Ming said. 'But I think he a determined man. That is why I stay away that week. I know he was following me.'

'It's Frank,' Daniel said. 'He has it in for me because of what I did to him.'

Ming looked confused. 'Not Frank, he too scared to come out of house, and why attack me, his friend?'

'What about the other two men you warned me about?'

'They still look for you, but I send them in wrong direction. We need to find a bed in shelter for you. Safer there.'

284

That night they went to the local shelter and soup kitchen. Beds were in high demand and it was out of food. The queue of restless souls stretched around the block.

Walking to a shelter on the other side of the city, they received a similar response when they enquired at the front desk. There was a shortage of beds, and donations.

Feeling dejected and angry, they strolled back to the underpass and shared out the remains from the bag of food Ming had brought with him the previous night.

The following morning, Daniel woke to the familiar sound of threats and scuffles. When he inched his eyes over the top of his cardboard shelter, he saw a dozen uniformed men dragging his colleagues off to a waiting vehicle. Then they had hold of him, but he was too weak to resist and got pushed into the back of the van with the rest.

An air vent in the roof gave them fresh air as the vehicle set off at speed. After hours of travelling on tarmac, they made a few turns, bounced down what could only have been a dirt road, and crunched to a standstill.

Spilling out of the van, it was impossible to make out where they were, other than in the middle of a densely wooded forest. There were no familiar landmarks and they wandered around for a while before settling down under a tree.

Wrapping themselves in the few blankets they had managed to bring along, they soon blended in with the low brush and bramble. Summer had started settling in, but the air was a lot cooler than in Berlin.

Daniel deduced they must have been taken to higher ground, and possibly into the foothills of a local mountain range. After searching his small bag of possessions, he realised that his mobile phone, which he had never used, was missing.

A full day passed by and they were starting to get hungry and restless. As Daniel got to his feet and stretched his aching back, he saw a couple cycling towards them. He put his hand out.

'Food please?' he called.

The young girl was riding with a much older man and drew up hesitantly. She looked for reassurance from her cycling partner.

'Can I give them our sandwiches please dad?'

'Of course, you can, we are close to town and can get some food there,' the older man replied.

'Where are you going?' Daniel asked.

'We are heading for Dresden, but stopping for the night nearby in Bad Schandau,' replied the man.

'Thank you,' Daniel said appreciatively. 'You are truly kind.'

The rest of the homeless stood around and gratefully received a small piece of sandwich, but it was not nearly enough for them all. A few wandered off when one of them discovered a large cave nearby. The word spread and the remaining men joined them.

Daniel guessed their location from what the young girl had said. He had cycled a lot of the river Elbe. All the way from Dresden to Hamburg. It had taken a week of following the course of the river, and although it had been a while since he was in Bad Schandau, he guessed they would be somewhere close by. From the direction the cyclists were heading, somewhere due east.

The rest of the homeless were not for moving out of the large cave, and although Daniel tried, he eventually gave up. He decided to go on his own and get some food and see what shelter was on offer.

Surprised to see the tall church spire so close, he headed toward it and found the town nestled on the banks of the river. The towering hills closed in on the Elbe in places and the sight brought back memories of having been there with Alice.

It had been a driving holiday soon after arriving in Berlin. A magical time, sitting in wine bars and watching the sun set. The memories from the past brought tears to his eyes, and when he wiped them away, they left dirty smudges down both cheeks.

Suddenly lonely and tired, he wanted his life back, but knew there would be no welcome from Alice. He had to change first, reverse his past mistakes, and ask forgiveness. Deciding there and then that he would start right here in this little town, where he and Alice had their first romantic holiday.

Ming arrived at the underpass and was shocked to see all the cardboard homes being loaded into the back of a truck, along with other debris that had accumulated in the area.

'Where are the people?' he asked a man in a yellow jacket.

'Gone, and good riddance,' the man growled, before striding off.

Chapter 28

Waste Not

From his vantage point at the end of the narrow road, Daniel could observe all the comings and goings at the rear of the small town's main store. He had been there for a week and slowly worked through the schedule they had of disposing food to waste. When he sneaked up after dark, he saw that most of the goods being disposed of were a day out of date.

Every evening, soon after the store had closed its doors for the day, large clear plastic bags of unsold bread were removed by one of the stores staff. It was always the same man. Some days he removed two bags and on other days just one, but Daniel calculated there must have been at least twenty loaves to a bag. Enough to feed an army of homeless people, he reckoned. He watched them being fed into a hatch, that dropped into a large underground waste container, and groaned.

Food that had reached it's sell by date, was placed in wheeled dumpsters at the rear of the shop and removed by a collection service later that night. The truck collecting the dumpsters also loaded general waste from other bins as it went, churning it all into a product that would only satisfy the appetite of worms and maggots.

Sneaking a shopping trolley away from a store, he managed to get some of the food before it was disposed of. Quickly developing a knack for darting in and out of the dumpster when nobody was looking, he filled his trolly. The man with the bread was easier, and when asked, handed the bags over willingly, relieved at not having to carry them all the way to the hatch.

Carting heavy bags back and forth to the cave was tiring, and took most of each evening. He did not mind and started to get a sense of achievement, being rewarded with smiles of appreciation from the ragtag crowd that formed his little community in the cave.

He spent the remainder of his time begging on the street corners. Saving up enough to purchase an old delivery bicycle. The basket on the front was small, but it made his trips so much quicker and easier to carry larger loads.

Venturing further afield he came to other small towns where out of date food was being thrown away every evening. He was alarmed at the volume of waste, and calculated this to be only a small sample of something he imagined to be going on across the world. Just the tip of the iceberg, he thought.

Internet Bars were fast becoming a thing of the past, but Daniel managed to find one when he reached Dresden, and logged into his personal email account. There were hundreds of messages and he was taken aback at how many were from Alice.

Initial messages appeared to have started a few months after his departure. She spoke of the past and wished him well.

Some were sent on days when she had obviously been feeling less nostalgic, saying that she was content with life and realised how much stress Daniel had added to her life. Harry had asked after him, but then as time went by, there was less mention of his name.

He found it strange that no mention had been made of Frank, and considering the trouble it had caused between them both, it left him feeling there was something she knew but was not saying.

She went on to explain how her fortunes had changed, allowing her to give up her job, stay in Manor House and work full time for the soup kitchen. She had asked Debbie to help and the two of them now managed one of the local kitchens. Alice worked full time and Debbie on a part time basis. Colin appeared to be spending time with Harvey. They were up to something, which they claimed to be a private matter. Debbie was none the wiser.

Colin had been promoted once again and now oversaw the European Division, which covered ten large offices spread across the continent. The family were even considering moving out into the country, where they could now afford to purchase a detached house.

Reading all the news made him nostalgic. He missed his family and was full of regrets, but he had something to prove first. He would get in touch when the time was right. For now, there were a hundred ideas buzzing around his head, and any attempt at a reunion would have to wait.

Daniel logged into his second email account. The one he had reserved for dealing with Frank.

To his surprise there had been no new messages or conversations since shortly after he was evicted. He reread the last exchange.

'Hello Daniel, sent you a message on the phone. You told me to stay put and be quiet and would see me soon. Please get back to me, you are still my best friend.'

Feeling a welling up of emotions he reread the short exchange, wondering why Frank had not tried to contact him since. Then recalled Ming telling him how cross he had been, he felt a welling of guilt.

He sent a short message.

'Where are you Frank?'

A short while later, just as he was about to log off, a bubble appeared, and he knew that someone had read his message and was typing a reply. It came a second later.

I want nothing to do with you.

Daniel scratched his head. A young girl next to him jumped when something fell out of his hair and crawled onto her keyboard.

He tried again.

Frank, I am so sorry I moved you. If I had my time over, I would have behaved differently.

He grimaced at the thought of having Frank living in his house forever. But this was not the time to tell him that.

Go away Daniel. If you send another message, I will put a block on your e- mail account.

Frank, I know who you are and am prepared to keep it a secret. I will also forgive you for attacking Ming and myself. It was not called for.

I don't know what you are talking about.

Frank, I don't swear any more. Would you believe it?

Well, if pigs could fly, came the response.

At least he's not blocked me, Daniel thought.

Frank please be patient with me, I have been living rough for eight months myself and now understand what it is like to be homeless. I have an idea how we could help people who are stranded. I am busy working with them and need some help.

It was an exaggeration. He had some great ideas, but feeding a dozen of his homeless buddies in a cave near Bad Schandau was hardly working with the homeless. It however got the right response and he smiled, as a message pinged straight back.

What do you want?

There is a ton of food being thrown away by shops because it is out of date and I need you to set up a charity for me so that I can get the food diverted to those who can't afford it.

There was no response and Daniel panicked, thinking he had pushed Frank too hard?

Frank, I have limited time on this computer. I am in an internet bar with little cash, so, will you do a few things for me?

Holding his breath, he startled the young girl next to him when he let out a whoop of joy, which quickly turned into a grimace as he read the response.

Why should I? Since you ran off with the last insurance payment, I had to work my magic to pay those sub-contractors.

I don't know what you are talking about Frank. Can you help me now though?

Go ahead, came the late reply.

Name us both as trustees of a new charity. The benefit is for the homeless and name the charity 'Waste Not' Then register the company.

Get back to me tomorrow…

Daniel could see that his time was up, but at least Frank was cooperating. The missing insurance payment was something he would investigate when his life returned to normal, he thought.

That evening he walked the streets of Dresden looking down back roads and side alleys. Then on the outskirts of the city he found exactly what he was looking for. A large window with an old sign above the door advertising Turkish food. Below it read a message, 'Eat as much as you like'.

When he peered in through the dirty window, he saw a crude cafeteria style layout with rows of tables and benches.

No wonder it failed, he thought.

He wrote down the name and address printed on a small sign above the door.

When he logged on the following day, he was delighted to hear that the charity was registered, and a certificate was being emailed across to him.

He sent Frank the address of the Turkish restaurant.

I need to know if I can rent the place.

What for?

For my charity. The one you have just registered.

Call me tomorrow.

The link disconnected and Daniel sat back. There was a lot to do and he would need to get moving.

First, he had to get cleaned up. He was still sleeping rough and looked a mess. The soup kitchens and shelters in Dresden were hopelessly inadequate. They continually ran out of food and the showers were beyond repair, while sleeping arrangements drove people back onto the streets instead of the other way around.

He begged all day and by early evening had enough to buy a thirty-minute slot back in the internet bar.

Frank, I need some money.

I had a feeling that this was where our conversation would end. Goodbye.

Daniel frantically typed.

Do not cut me off. I just need enough to pay for a minibus taxi to collect my homeless friends. They are stuck in a cave miles from here and I need them to help me set up the charity shop.

There was no response and his heart sank. Then he caught his breath as a message arrived.

I have rented the shop under the name of the charity. The chap who owns it will see you there tomorrow morning at eight. I have also set up a float of five thousand Euros. Bank details attached.

Daniel wrote down the number of the account Frank had given him.

The Visa card is being sent to the Turkish shop address.

Thank you, Frank. You will not regret doing this… I promise.

There was no response. He waited until his allotted time had run out just in case Frank wanted to say more, but he had obviously signed off.

After finding a massage parlour down a back alley he paid them cash up front to attend to his friends. The group of women were told that they had to wash, shave, and clean the men. That was all.

He hired a hotel room for the night and once he had showered and washed his hair he looked like a different person. He had lost a lot of weight and although he kept his unruly head of hair and beard, he could see under it all his face was sallow and drawn.

When the group of homeless trooped into the parlour the woman in charge took one look at the dozen men and swore.

'Gloves on girls, they're filthy and covered in bugs.'

Although clean and dressed in fresh clothing, nothing could disguise the fact that these men had been out of circulation for a while. They stood around like sheep, and when Daniel told them to move, they crept forward in a group. When he told them to line up, they formed a ragged row and stood waiting. He knew then that he had his work cut out and settled into the task.

He met a stranger the following morning who handed over keys to the restaurant, and once alone, he walked around the interior. It had obviously lain empty for quite some time and was a mess. Dirt had accumulated in every corner and all surfaces were layered in dust. The ceiling hung where boards had come loose, and long strands of cobwebs joined to give the place an eerie feeling of neglect. The kitchen was no better, but fortunately most of the stainless-steel cooking ovens and hobs were still in place, albeit crusted in grease and grime.

Daniel shepherded the men he had previously named the 'dirty dozen' across the city as they made their way to the run-down area of small apartments and takeaway outlets. To where his rented premises stood. They shuffled down the pavement in two rows of six, like convicts in shackles and as Daniel watched them, it strengthened his resolve to tackle the issue head on.

He purchased brooms, buckets and cleaning cloths from a local trading store, who dropped them off at the property. With electricity and water reconnected, he put the men to work.

Once they had cleaned a table and two chairs, he set himself up with a laptop and called the men forward one at a time. He wanted to find out from each of them what their previous occupation and circumstances had been prior to landing up on the street.

When he was done, he listed two carpenters, a bricklayer, a bookkeeper, six general factory workers, a cook, and a doctor. None of them were felons on the run and when he asked Frank to run a search, none appeared to have a criminal record. The only black mark against one of his team was a minor issue the medical council had with the doctor.

He was surprised to find he had a doctor in his team. He was not particularly old, and once properly clothed looked quite respectable. He was a doctor who had been struck off, but a man with a medical qualification all the same. Daniel made a note to do some digging when he got the chance.

He purchased a camera and once he had an internet connection, sent Frank a video of the inside of the building with all the men working at getting it into shape. He then added a photo of the men before they had been spruced up and a snap of them afterwards.

When he studied the picture, he smiled. They looked like a motley bunch, but there was something different about them now. If Daniel was correct, it was the look of hope.

A response arrived soon after he had sent the photos.

I was about to cut you out of my will on seeing the amount you squandered.

Ha Ha, Daniel typed. *I didn't realise you had a sense of humour.*

A message bounced straight back.

I don't.

He sat the bookkeeper in front of the computer and gave him clear instructions.

'I want you to add up the value of all the items we bring in from the dumpsters. Then I want you to go on the internet and find out what it costs to empty one of them. Remember it is food waste they are getting rid of and may be subject to an additional disposal levy.'

He set the doctor up in one of the back rooms with all the literature he could find regarding e coli and other forms of bacteria normally found in decaying food. The man protested, saying he was not a scientist, but after a while settled back and started his research.

After listing all the laboratory equipment the doctor asked for, Daniel sent a copy to Frank.

Can you advance me another ten thousand please? List of Lab testing equipment attached, and it does not come cheap.

What are you doing?? Are we into drugs?

I am going to revolutionise the food waste sector. Trust me.

The response was immediate.

That I would never do.

What? Go into the food waste sector?

No..., trust you, came the quick response.

The money was transferred into his account that evening, and the following day he purchased all the equipment, along with stainless steel tables, cutlery, and a long list of consumables.

The joiners made up shelves and refurbished the existing tables and chairs. It was a hive of activity, and soon after starting they had to place newspaper over the large windowpanes, to ward off the scores of people gathering on the pavement to stare in. However, it did not stop enquiring looks from passers-by when they erected a large sign above the front entrance. Nobody could understand why a new business venture would be called 'WASTE NOT'.

There were strict rules in 'WASTE NOT'. No booze or drugs and swearing was outlawed.

He threatened everyone during an initial briefing.

'If I find any of you taking drugs or drinking, then be prepared to be thrown out, and definitely no swearing. Arguing with customers will not be tolerated, and remember, if you want to stay a member of this exclusive club of misfits, then behave.'

The bookkeeper came back with the results of a week's investigatory work. Looking through the figures it was not difficult to extrapolate the numbers into something of a national or even an international problem. Thousands of kilograms of food were being thrown away every day by stores and large outlets, and that was just in one country. A country that already had a proud record of recycling and reducing waste.

Disposing of food waste appeared more expensive than manufacturing or producing the food in the first place. The only winners were the waste carriers and pig farmers, who were making a fine living out of this steady increase in disposing of food still perfectly fit for human consumption.

The bookkeeper was instructed to write up a report, including the cost of the waste, as well as the cost of disposal.

Walking through the laboratory at the back of the restaurant Daniel spoke with the Doctor turned Scientist, who was hard at work. Pipettes of food samples stood in racks and a large chart displayed his findings.

'Still not found a single sign of bacteria Dan,' the man said as he peered at him over his wire framed glasses.

His lanky hair had been cut short and Daniel barely recognised him.

'Keep going Doc, I need to be one hundred percent sure of my facts before we go big.' He paused and picked up a plastic container of yogurt, checking the date. 'You have done a one-day test, now test up to three days and see if we get anything different.'

The Doctor went back to work and wrote down another result.

When Daniel turned to walk back into the main restaurant, he was almost bowled over by one of the general workers.

'Dan, you had better come quick. I think we have a problem.'

Chapter 29
Big Business

After rushing through to the main dining room and not knowing what to expect, he arrived to find every chair occupied by various shapes and sizes. It appeared that the city's homeless had turned up for a meal---en masse.

'How did they know about us?' he asked.

'Word must have got out,' replied the general worker nervously. 'They look like a real hungry mob as well. I think we need to feed them, or we may just have a riot on our hands.'

The chef had finished cleaning the kitchen and the new microwaves and fridges had been installed. He was ready to start serving meals but had no raw ingredients. The only stock was in fridges and freezer in the doctor's laboratory, collected from dumpsters the previous night, ready to be tested, but all a day or two past their use-by date.

'Should we give them some of this?' the chef asked.

'No' Daniel shook his head. 'We don't want to poison the poor souls. That would be rather counterproductive to what we are trying to achieve here, wouldn't you say?'

The chef nodded, and Daniel went to the room he had converted to an office.

Frank, I need some more money. Urgently.

A message came straight back.

This is becoming a little tedious. Do you realise that our relationship already hangs on a very tenuous thread of trust? And that thread, I hate to say, is getting close to snapping.

Daniel drew in a deep breath and typed.

I have a restaurant full of homeless who thought we were open and have come for a meal. I cannot turn them away, can I?

Then a thought occurred to him.

Hang on a second, I will be right back.

He returned, uploaded a photo, and posted it.

I see your problem. Two thousand Euros and that is it. I want to start seeing a return on my investment. And while we are on about commitment, why have you not tried to contact Ming? He has been out of his mind worrying about you.

Daniel grimaced.

Two weeks later, after checking and then rechecking that everything was in order, Daniel sent a message and photo to every city news editor from a list the bookkeeper had made. Then stood waiting for the press to arrive. It had not been what he would have called a stampede at first, but then one of the local tabloids saw it as an opportunity and a newsworthy story. Something that had once hit the front pages and then become old news, as the debate strayed into a political argument between various governmental departments.

But here was something tangible they could write about and clearly demonstrate how wasteful society had become.

They published a short article that barely made the middle pages.

Then from out of the blue, a film crew from a television channel arrived, and the word spread amongst local journalists.

Germany was just ending a year of reportedly having the fasted growing world economy, and the story of people sleeping rough on the streets was in direct contrast and bound to gain some interest.

Explaining in detail the cost of the waste and cost of disposal, a well disguised Daniel showed them the lab results, as the camera zoomed in on the doctor hard at work. Then he walked the crew through the food hall, where dozens of dishevelled people sat eating plates of food, while discounted stock filled the shelves in the adjacent shop. It was an impressive display and they wanted to take a photograph of him for their cover story, but he refused.

After an hour, the reporters thanked him and left.

That evening Daniel sat glued to the television channel. He watched the early news and then the late edition, but nothing appeared. He felt deflated by the time he went to bed, where he shared a room with the twelve men at the rear of the restaurant. The men he was so determined not to let down.

Sending an email to Frank, he sat back and waited. Surely there was something he could do.

Four hours later and he had still not heard back. He started to get worried.

A week later and Daniel was besides himself with worry. The owner, or agent of the building was threatening to evict them because of the sleeping arrangements at the rear of the building. While the stores in Dresden had guards in place to stop their dumpsters being raided.

There was also the continual rattle on the door from the homeless wanting a meal.

Just as he was about to start explaining to the twelve anxious men that his plan had gone awry, his phone rang. His new mobile had not rung since he had purchased it, so at first, he wasn't sure where the noise was coming from.

'Hello?' he answered hesitantly.

'Frank here.'

'How did you get my number? And why didn't you get back to me when I emailed you? I am just about to call it a day.'

'Is that the way you greet an old friend? You may be surprised, but getting hold of your number was not that easy. It took a while.'

'What is going on Frank, you aren't using your voice computer and why haven't you been answering your emails?'

'I *am* using my voice box. Technology has moved on a bit and it sounds like a real voice now. And I have had a bit of trouble with my email account. Call me on this mobile from now on. My mail account could have been hacked and has a virus.'

'Your last mail said our relationship hung on a tenuous thread, and then you haven't exactly been falling over yourself getting back. I have been going out of my mind,' Daniel added irritably. He had hardly slept all week. 'Alright, so why the call?'

'I was scanning the newspapers and saw your article in one of the less circulated tabloids. So, what do I call you? Dan, or Daniel? Wow, a reborn Daniel.'

'Frank, have you gone to all this trouble just to tell me that? And why are you being so abrasive?'

'I thought you would be pleased to hear from me. After the way you treated me and then all the help I gave, the very least you could do is be civil.'

'Alright, I will be civil, why the call?'

'Well, I phoned to say that I hacked in and kept watch on the local television company mentioned in the newspaper report. Would you believe that their system is not that secure?'

'And.'

'And they decided not to run with your story on television.'

'Oh no,' Daniel muttered in frustration. 'I was really relying on them.'

'Very impressive. A whole sentence without a swear word, I cannot believe it. But don't worry, they have changed their minds. Oh, and by the way, I like what you are doing. Do you need any help?'

'Why would they change their minds?' he asked. 'And yes, I am desperate for help.'

'Thought as much. I sent an anonymous email on an official looking letterhead saying that the subject was going to be discussed at National level by the Government.'

'Is the Government really going to take it up?'

'No, they have other things on their minds right now. But I bet they will as soon as the channel runs the story.'

Daniel sat watching every news report, and finally at mid-day, shortly before the weather report, they showed an edited version of the tour of Waste Not.

Two hours later the full uncut version appeared soon after the headlines, and then reporters started queuing up for further information.

A day later and a row of dumpsters stood outside their front entrance. The local store managers who knocked on their door said there would be daily deliveries from then on.

The following week Daniel started his campaign aimed at more supermarket stores. He targeted the larger chains first, and on the back of his television interview got to see some of the leading marketing and management teams. He always turned up in disguise.

'I will pay you thirty percent of the shelf price for stock that is a day from expiry,' his message was repeated. 'You save on the disposal costs and you get good press coverage. The only expense you incur is the cost of transporting the goods to my outlets. Still cheaper than disposal and think of all the publicity.'

'You have more than one outlet?' asked one of the managers of a large chain.

'I will have six by the end of next month,' he replied. 'By the end of six months I will have one in every major city. And a year from now I plan on having outlets in most cities.'

'That is some undertaking. Where do you get your funding from?'

'I cannot reveal that, suffice to say I have the backing of a very clever and generous man.'

The six-month projection had been optimistic, but six months later he had thirty outlets in half that number of cities. Frank supported him throughout, reviewing his business plans and turnover forecasts. The charity was now well established, and an on-line advert soon got donations pouring in. The food he had delivered from stores was used to feed the poor, while profits were diverted to set up shelters for the homeless.

The year passed, and Dan as he was known, had a hundred kitchens, outlet shops and shelters spread across central Europe. He was starting to receive a lot of media coverage, but declined interviews, fast developing a knack for always being one step ahead of flashing cameras.

The income was staggering, and he struggled at first to manage the large flow of cash. Amongst those out of work were numerous shop owners and accountants who had fallen on tough times and they taught him, guided him, and worked for the charity as it grew. All the while, Frank remained as the self-nominated Financial Director with the final say.

They kept on touch via mobile phone and spoke on average once a week.

Racing from one town to the next was taking its toll, and after a year he decided to purchase a small plane. To be flown by an ex commercial pilot who had been caught drinking on the job and was out of work. No longer in need of the press, he declined interviews. Business was booming, and the charity had more than enough to cope with.

Calls between Daniel and Frank had become sporadic. Daniel was busy, and when he enquired, Frank assured him that he was taking good care of the finances and there was no need to worry.

He missed Alice and Harry more than ever. When he thought of what he had lost, he berated himself. With the belief that when the time was right, he would get back in touch with them.

Working seven days a week while attending meetings and flying from one town or city to another, he found he was gaining weight and going to flab. So, he turned to the one form of exercise and relaxation he was well acquainted with.

Being based in Dresden, it gave him easy access to numerous cycle routes, short or long. Depending on time constraints, he chose an appropriate route. Weekdays were taken up managing what had become a multi-million Euro business, while weekends he went cycling.

The bank manager sent a message to Daniel, inviting him to a meeting, and reminded him of the exceptionally large amount of cash that was now sitting dormant in a low interest account.

'If we invest this amount in stock, we could get you a higher return. I suggest you talk to one of our brokers,' the Manager informed Daniel.

'No,' he replied, 'I want to use some of the money to help people with special needs. People who suffer from debilitating illnesses such as agoraphobia. I also intend investing in a hostel chain like the YMCA, but for people of all ages who have hit on hard times and need somewhere for the night. I will talk to my Financial Advisor and get him to start spending the money.'

The Bank Manager raised his eyebrows and asked if there was anything else, he could do. Daniel said he would be in touch.

He had a few ideas, but with money to spend, it was time to get some media exposure and raise the charities' profile. He would then announce his new expansion programme, and went about getting more media coverage.

The press was soon all over the story and clambering for more information.

Distracted by events, Daniel sent Frank an email by mistake.

Hi Frank, that is some good publicity we got.

A minute later, a reply bounced back. At the same time Daniel realised he had used the email address Frank had said was hacked.

Long-time no hear, are you still talking about publicity? After all this time?

Daniel quickly deleted the message and put a block on any further emails coming from that address.

Coaching the 'dirty dozen' into fitness for a charity cycle was a challenge. In his first public display of raising the profile of his charity to a new level, he invited in the press. It was a rare chance for the media to interview the elusive philanthropist.

Arriving in their droves, they clamoured to get a photograph of the man. The man who had appeared recently on the cover of Time magazine. A dark silhouette of a person nobody had yet actually managed to identify. This would be the first opportunity to possibly get a picture.

Then they were disappointed when Dan turned up sporting a cycle helmet, wraparound sunglasses, and a wild beard. There was not much one could see.

Daniel and the 'dirty dozen' were heading to Berlin and then on to Hamburg on their sponsored bicycles. This was a big event and supported by most of the supermarket chains and various charities who were eager to get some exposure. On the back of each rider's vest was their charity address where they could deposit a donation, while the media followed in a fleet of vans, cars, and motor bikes.

One government minister who had been interviewed, spoke about restarting a fresh campaign to reduce food waste and take better care of the homeless.

Utterly exhausted, the cycling group reached Berlin and settled into one of their own shelters. Where they were served meals alongside street people they supported. Daniel continued to maintain his disguise, even when in the confines of his own establishments.

Staff who worked at the first center told him about a shortage of beds.

'We are managing to feed everyone, but we need more beds if all the people sleeping rough are to be accommodated,' the Hostel Manager informed him.

More beds Daniel messaged Frank on his phone.

'Another fifty will be delivered this week,' Daniel reported back to the Manager. 'I have instructed my Financial Director to get on with it.'

Early one morning as they readied for another day's ride, Daniel told the rest of the group he wanted to escape the press for a while and sneak off. He had something very private to do and would see them later that evening.

For most of the 'dirty dozen', they were back in their home city of Berlin, however none of them had friends or family to visit.

Setting off, Daniel stopped off at every subway and tapped on numerous sleeping bodies, but nobody had seen Ming. Some knew of him, while others returned vacant looks.

He called in at the tower block where Colin and Debbie had lived. A stranger who opened the door told him that the couple had moved a while ago and there was no forwarding address.

Cycling along the banks of the Spree and through underpasses, there were cardboard homes still very much in evidence, and it strengthened his resolve to do more.

His stomach was in a knot as he approached Manor House. It all looked so familiar, but also very strange. So much time had been invested and so much lost.

Sitting on a bench near the water's edge he contemplated his next move. He wanted to see Alice and Harry, but the timing had to be perfect. Then to his surprise he saw Ming wandering down The Alley. He wore his usual attire of black clothing, with his signature backpack slung over one shoulder.

'Ming,' he shouted.

The thin figure turned to start off in the opposite direction, but then stopped when he thought he recognised the voice.

'Ming, it's me, Mister Dan.'

Ming slowed in his bid to escape and turned. Daniel removed his glasses and helmet and it made Ming smile, showing off his familiar crooked teeth.

'Mister Dan, where have you been. I look everywhere for you, but you vanished. Then Frank said he not heard from you for long while. You look very hairy.'

'Ming, I don't have a lot of time, I have been busy. Are you still taking care of Frank?'

'Yes, Mister Dan, I still feed him every day.' He tapped the backpack.

Daniel laughed, and Ming looked at him with renewed interest. Mister Dan had certainly changed. He was not the angry looking young man who used to chase him down The Alley.

'Where you been Mister Dan?' He took a step back. 'You look very different now. The last time I saw you was in underpass with my friends who live in boxes. Then one morning I went to see you, but you were gone. Everybody was gone.' He spread both hands wide. 'I looked everywhere, for a long time. But no Mister Dan.'

'Do you recall being beaten up at the underpass Ming?'

'Sometimes a man who looks like that bad man in the underpass chases me. But I am fast, and Frank looks after me.'

Now convinced it was Frederick who had attacked him, it made the man in the house Francis, but until he knew for certain he was not saying a word. He doubted Frank would double as both protector and perpetrator.

'Do you see him?' Daniel asked.

'No, never see Frank, just phone call and drop off food. He very good friend,' Ming added with a smile.

'Umm, let us hope so,' Daniel replied, 'I think we all have to try and be positive. Not forgetting that someone might be deceiving us.'

'You make very good Chinese proverb Mister Dan.'

Daniel was distracted. 'Help me for a while here, will you please Ming?' he handed over his bicycle.

Leaving Ming holding his bike, he walked up The Alley to a point where he could see the entrance to Manor House. The sun lit up the whole front garden and the roses were in full bloom. It was a beautiful sight and lifted his spirits.

Then a young boy aged about eight years of age, with wavy ginger hair emerged from the front door and ran across the lawn. He was followed by an aging Alsatian dog.

'Come on Doggie, fetch the ball,' the boy called.

Chapter 30
Back in Berlin

The urge to run forward and hold his son was overpoweringly strong. All sorts of emotions welled up as he sagged back against the fence. But the timing was wrong, and he did not want to meet up after all this time in this way. Not without carefully planning the reunion first.

Ming drifted up, handed him his bicycle, and excused himself. He said Frank would be waiting for his food.

'Send Frank my regards Ming. Tell him we are doing a great job and I will come and visit him as soon as I can.'

'Frank and I agree not to talk about you Mister Dan. He sometimes gets very cross.'

Daniel scratched at the scar on his head and wondered why.

Walking back down The Alley, he stopped to look at the gap in the neighbour's evergreen hedge where Ming was delivering food to Frank's hatch. As he stood there, a ball came flying over the fence behind him and came to rest close to his feet. He turned to see a small head of ginger hair peering over at him.

'I can climb this fence if I want,' the boy said, 'but I might get into trouble. Could you throw the ball back please Sir?'

Doing as he was told; he took his time. He had not seen Harry for close to two years and noticed the changes. He could not see how tall he was, but his face was more mature. Older than his seven years of age. Not trusting himself to say anything, he threw the ball back. The boys head dropped, but his voice carried through the fence.

'Thanks Mister.'

Ming returned and repeated to Daniel what Frank had told him. Alice had moved out of the house two years previously, but a couple of months later moved back in and was still there.

'I will see you again soon Ming,' he said as he gathered his thoughts. 'I have a few things to attend to and then will be back.'

In a complete daze, he cycled back towards the city centre. It was time, he thought. To get cleaned up and make proper arrangements to see Harry. He would also use the opportunity to see Alice. He still owed her an explanation and a big apology. He thought it an ideal time to make an appearance.

It was now or never.

He would let the cycle team continue without him and meet them back in Dresden. He checked his mobile phone, had a signal, and called one of the 'dirty dozen'.

'You guys carry on without me pal, I have a few personal things to sort through here in Berlin. Take it easy and see you when I catch up,' he said and pocketed his phone.

Daniel was an emotional mess and his head buzzed as he tried to focus on the path ahead, where an underpass took him below a large motorway. He took the downhill slope at a steady speed, and as he reached the structure a voice called out from behind and he stood on his pedals to look back, to see who it was?

'Duck you suckers,' rung through the air and he could hardly believe his eyes, as he looked back to see his old cycle group leader, mouth open, shouting the old chant, while a pack of cyclists followed close behind. He wiped his eyes and tried to focus. He could see Colin, Debbie, Alice, and Harvey amongst a host of others he knew well.

Then he saw himself and froze.

'What...,' he started to shout, but the low concrete beam hit the top of his helmet and threw him off his saddle.

There was nobody around to see his spectacular double summersault. Catapulted from his saddle, he landed amongst a heap of cardboard and litter. His bicycle wobbled slightly, but continued in a straight line for a while before veering off and disappearing down a bank.

Hours later he regained consciousness and slowly took in his surroundings. Difficult to see at first, but as his eyes adjusted, he could make out the familiar landscape of the littered underpass and he felt at home. His head hurt and he could barely move his neck, but he was on familiar turf. Large areas of exposed skin on his arms and legs were scraped and bleeding, but he was not in too bad a shape, considering the way he felt.

Pulling himself from the heap of cardboard boxes, he sagged against a pile of old blankets. He was at a loss as to why or where he was, or how had he come to be injured. He recalled seeing a group of cyclists, but his head spun. Then he took a deep breath, before muttering 'This is my home, this is where I fucking live.' He felt better after having rationalised his situation, and calmed down.

A group of teenagers came drifting through the underpass. They did not see him at first, then one of them suddenly turned and snarled. 'Get a job and stop littering the street you dirty piece of shit.'

'Fuck off,' Daniel shouted back.

Recoiling, he held his arms up to protect his face. In his distant memory he could recall similar bouts of abuse, where punches were thrown. But the boys moved on, shouting something back at him he couldn't quite understand.

That evening a straggle of homeless people started arriving. Shuffling into the underpass and settling down alongside him. They started spreading blankets and opening old cardboard boxes.

'You are in my space,' one old man growled, 'move yourself.'

Daniel shifted sideways and then after being moved a few more times, found a vacant spot and settled in for the night. He could not work out why these people were being so abrasive. They used to be his friends.

Early the following morning he followed the crowd, as they emerged from under blankets and boxes and headed into the city. They were going to a new charity food kitchen and were eager to get there before the queue got too long.

'Good food,' said the same old man who had growled at him the previous night.

Latching onto the stooped old figure, Daniel followed. They soon arrived at a place that looked strangely familiar, and although he could not understand the connection, the smell was overpoweringly strong. Freshly baked bread, fried sausages and eggs lay in heaps on silver trays, as a group of people in aprons rushed around behind the counter replenishing any empty ones.

He saw a sign above the counter and slowly read out loud. 'Waste Not.'

'That's us, nothing goes to waste in or world,' a young girl said from behind the counter.

'Strange name for a soup kitchen,' Daniel muttered, as an elderly woman with an apron came around and took his arm.

'Good grief my man, you are covered in blood. You look a mess.'

She took him to the accommodation block and got two young men to assist in cleaning him up. Daniel complained that he was hungry and wanted food.

'You look like the boss who runs this place,' said the one youngster, after Daniel had stepped out of the shower.

He dumped his dirty clothes in a bag. He was dressed in a fresh set given to him by the same young man.

'Better get all these cuts and scrapes bandaged over before they get infected,' said the other.

'Isn't that odd,' persisted the first young man, standing back and taking a second look. 'He was only here yesterday on a charity ride.'

'What was his name?' Daniel asked.

'Dan,' they chorused.

'Well, I am Daniel, so it's not me then is it?'

'Come on now,' interrupted the second assistant. 'Let us get you plastered up and back to the food counter before it runs out.'

'Have you any beds,' Daniel enquired.

'Unfortunately, we are short of beds. We were told there were dozens on order, but not seen anything yet. So, it's back to the subway for a while, I'm afraid.'

A week later most of the tabloids were still running stories relating to the missing tycoon, although the articles had shrunk and had started slipping further towards the middle pages with each passing day. An edition discarded a few days earlier blew into the underpass and stuck against Daniels blanket, where he sheltered from the icy dawn wind.

Mystery man Dan from Waste Not still missing, appeared as an article headline. Below, in smaller print, the story continued. *The police are not at present suspecting foul play but have yet to rule out the possibility of a kidnapping or even...*

He saw the headline, but was finding it difficult to stay awake, let alone focus on the fine print, and his head felt like it was going to burst.

'Duck you suckers,' echoed through the underpass and Daniel stirred. Where had he heard that before? He felt slightly better, and the old man next to him turned when he saw him awake.

'Wondered if you would ever wake up properly. Been on and off for a week, you have, while I have been steering you to the food hall and then to the toilet and feeding you like a baby.'

Chapter 31
Who am I?

Feeling better, now that his head had stopped pounding, Daniel dragged himself to the edge of the underpass to get some fresh air, and with a musty old blanket wrapped around his shoulders he settled against the wall. The draft through the underpass was bitterly cold and when he looked around, he realised he was the only person without a cardboard box. It was starting to snow, and he shivered.

After a few taps on a nearby box, the lid lifted a few inches and a balaclava appeared.

'Where do I get a box?' he asked the balaclava head.

'Down the road, behind us and in a back alley. Next to the furniture store,' the voice said before the lid dropped back down again.

Wandering in the general direction given, he soon spotted the store and in the back street stood a stack of folded boxes. He chose a sturdy looking one with Siemens written on the side. It was difficult to drag between pedestrians and he struggled against a strong gusting breeze. Eventually he made it back to the underpass, and within minutes his new home was erected.

Climbing in was a challenge and after a few attempts he decided to just tumble in over the edge. It hurt the cut on his head, but at least he was out of the biting wind.

Weeks drifted by, as Harvey and Colin gathered more and more clues that pointed them in the general direction of the underpass. Red hair, bad temper and the general height of their old friend were good clues. They followed the information given and eventually arrived at an underpass crowded with cardboard boxes.

Approaching the nearest one, Colin tapped on the lid.

'What?' a gruff voice echoed from within.

'We are looking for a man with red hair, swears a lot and knows the phrase 'duck you suckers.'

The lid dropped back down, and they tried the next box. After three more attempts they got lucky.

'I only know him as Mister Siemens,' said the homeless man as he tumbled out of his own temporary home and walked up to a nearby box.

He lifted the lid and shouted. 'Hoy, Mister Siemens, someone looking for you.'

The form inside lifted a few inches and they could see an eye peering out from under a blanket. It blinked. Then a dirty hand came up from within the box and rubbed the eye. The eye opened and closed a few times and looked from side to side, as the two men came into focus. Then as they watched the old threadbare blanket slip sideways, a matt of unkempt red hair appeared.

'What the fuck do you want?' came the voice from within.

'Is that you Daniel?' Colin asked.

'No, it's Mister Siemens,' said the homeless man standing nearby.

Harvey turned to him. 'Thank you, we will handle this from here,' and gave him a handful of coins.

'Cold air is getting into my house, now fuck off,' the voice resounded from within the box.

Harvey smiled at Colin, who nodded back. 'It's him alright.'

Colin took a step closer. 'It's your friends Colin and Harvey.'

'Please put the fucking roof back on my house. All the warm air is escaping. You fucking idiots.'

Harvey looked at Colin. 'It's definitely him. What a mess.'

Colin lent over the box. 'You are coming with us mate.'

The red-headed figure instinctively cowering into a ball, as two hands lifted to cover his head. 'Please do not hurt me again,' he whimpered.

'It's Colin here. We are your old friends and here to help you.'

'Who the fuck is Colin?' the muffled voice asked.

Harvey moved closer. 'Your old friends, Colin and Harvey. We have come to take you with us.'

'But I have nowhere to go,' the voice wailed. 'Leave me alone. It's fucking cold out there.'

The blanket dropped further, revealing his blue shivering lips, as two grubby hands pulled the worn blanket tight around his body.

'We have a thick woollen coat for you, and a car waiting around the corner,' Colin said.

'You took some finding,' Harvey added. 'We have been looking for you for months.'

'They keep moving us on. I am happy here,' Daniel complained.

They gently removed the box by lifting it over his head. The smell caught in their nostrils and Colin gagged. 'You are going to need some cleaning up my old friend,' he said with one hand over his nose.

Stooped over, with a dirty blanket pulled up around his neck, the mop of unruly red hair looked around desperately for an anchor. His gaze settled back on his Siemens home, and he hobbled over and threw himself back inside.

Both men ran up and saw the crumpled-up figure of their old friend lying motionless in the base of the box. A stream of blood started pooling around his head.

'Harvey, quick, get him out of the box and into the recovery position,' Colin shouted, as he called for help.

Harvey took Daniel in his arms. 'He is still breathing, and the gash on his head is just an old wound opened up. Be quick, the smell is getting to me.'

Two paramedics arrived and started checking his vital signs, while a third fitted a neck brace.

'He appears to be alright,' said the more senior of the two.

'Where am I?' Daniel looked around. Then his gaze fell on his old friends. 'Colin, Harvey, what are you doing here?' Then he looked at the blanket in his arms. 'What am I doing here? Phew, I stink.'

'You can say that again,' the medic replied.

Colin was on his phone. 'Hi Debs. Yes, we found him at last, but I am afraid it will be a while before we can let anyone see him. He is in a bit of a state right now.'

'How did I get here? Daniel asked. The last thing I can remember was cycling from Manor House.'

Both men sat with him while he was being examined.

'Appears to be a minor headwound,' the medic concluded. 'I would advise you getting him to see a doctor within the next few hours and checked for concussion, but he needs cleaning up first.'

'I think he had concussion long before this recent fall,' Harvey told the medic. 'When we first got to him, he had no idea who we were. The knock on the head may have done him some good.'

'Maybe he needed that knock a long time ago,' Colin added, and both men laughed.

'Have you seen Alice?' Daniel asked. 'When I had to leave home, it broke my heart.'

'That was two and a half years ago,' Harvey replied.

'That long?' Then he looked down at his ragged clothing and his dirt encrusted hands. 'How did I get to be here, and into such a mess?'

'Sounds like he is suffering from some sort of intermittent memory loss,' the medic said, as he repacked his bags.

'Yes,' Colin agreed, 'he appeared confused when we first saw us and didn't recognise us. Now he knows who we are but can't recall how he got here.'

Colin noticed tears had started to slide down Daniels cheeks, leaving fresh lines through the grime.

'If I have been gone two years, how did you find me?' Daniel asked.

'We were out on a cycle a week ago and heading for an underpass, when a cardboard box blew across our path. The leader shouted the old 'Duck you Suckers' cry as he pulled up. That was when a homeless man approached us and told us about you.'

'But nobody knows my name; how did you know it was me?'

'Apparently, after a few cans of lager you would shout 'duck you suckers' every time a large group of bikers cycled near to where you were sheltering.'

'That makes sense,' Daniel muttered. 'I missed the old days Colin.'

Harvey turned to Colin. 'He's not swearing anymore. Since banging his head in the box, he hasn't sworn once.'

'I don't like swearing,' Daniel replied, 'it's not necessary.'

Colin put his arm out. 'Come my old friend, time to go,' he turned to Harvey. 'Whatever's going on with him has me flummoxed. How many more bumps on the head before he becomes completely normal?'

Harvey smiled back and slowly shook his head. As Daniel staggered to his feet, Colin came forward with a fleece lined coat and put it around his shoulders. They could not believe how thin their old pal was.

'I am not sure I can leave my friends,' Daniel said, as he looked around at a dozen heads poking out from under blankets.

'I thought you would be eager to get away?' Harvey said.

Daniel looked confused. 'I feel a closeness to them. It sounds strange, I know, but they are my friends.'

'You can come back and help them later, but our priority right now is to get you back to the car and cleaned up.'

'You have a car?'

'Not mine exactly,' Colin replied, 'but we can explain later.'

Harvey walked around the curious figures in the underpass and handed out packets of sandwiches and crisps.

When they got to the side street, Daniel saw a large black limo parked on the verge. The driver was holding the back door open and it made Daniel pull back.

'This way, the car is for you.' Harvey urged him on. 'We are taking you to a hotel, where you can get cleaned up, get a proper night's sleep and a meal.'

They lifted him gently onto the back seat and then before he had chance to escape, slid in on either side.

'This is the best abduction I have ever heard of,' Daniel said with a smile.

Colin laughed. 'You have never been abducted as far as we know, but yes, if you were, this is about as good as it gets.'

The Royal Hotel lived up to its name. Colin had pre-checked into the room, so they walked straight to the lift. A young couple got in on the second floor, made it obvious that something smelled, and quickly ducked out just as the doors started to slide closed.

They shared a three-bedroom suite on the top floor, with a sitting area overlooking the newly developed quarters.

'Guys, I am feeling very strange, so if you forgive me, I need to wash, eat and sleep. Then you can ask me anything you like after that. Maybe I am dreaming after all.'

Colin walked over to him and gave him a pinch on the arm.

'Ouch, what was that for?'

'Two reasons. The first to show you that this is not a dream and the second to verify what we suspect. You don't swear anymore.'

'Swearing is bad Colin, it destroys the soul and leaves you feeling angry.'

Colin took a step back. 'Bloody hell Daniel, but you stink. When did you last have a wash?'

'You need a shower,' added Harvey. 'Then we get you presentable before the doctor arrives.' He opened a door to a large bedroom. 'This is yours. It has an en-suite and a fresh set of clothing in the wardrobe when you are finished.'

'And don't worry old mate,' Colin called from the sitting room. 'We will be in the lounge making sure you stay in here, and don't disappear again.'

Both men had been watching television when Daniel appeared in the doorway, drying himself with an oversized towel. They looked at his emancipated figure and laughed.

'We are most certainly going to have to feed you up. You are all skin and bone,' Harvey laughed.

'Get a dressing gown on,' Colin added in a gentle tone. 'There's a hairdresser on the way up and then a doctor to check you out.'

'I need food, not a hairdresser. And the last time I had an out of the body experience was when I was left a fortune, but that did not end well, so excuse me for looking a bit anxious.'

'Nothing to worry about mate,' Colin tried to reassure him.

'Care to tell me what is going on then?' Daniel looked suspiciously at his friends. 'My memory is so erratic. Right now I am finding it hard to distinguish fact from fiction.'

'All in good time, my friend,' Harvey replied.

There was a sharp rap on the door, and a young woman entered and cut at his unruly growth of hair.

The doctor arrived soon after and gave him a thorough checking over. He said that besides a few abrasions on his head and the need to gain some weight, he was in reasonably good condition. He did however advise a visit to the dentist. There were one or two teeth on the brink of collapse.

Before leaving, the doctor dropped a newspaper on the table he had picked up at reception.

Daniel scanned the headlines before flipping through the pages, then hesitated on page eight.

'That's me,' he blurted out.

His friends gathered around.

'It certainly looks like you, but hard to tell with that helmet and glasses,' Harvey agreed.

Colin read the headlines over his shoulder and laughed 'It says multi-millionaire of 'WASTE NOT', a food and shelter charity for the homeless goes missing in Berlin. Nice try mate.'

'I am telling you it is me,' Daniel repeated.

Harvey took the paper from him and read the full article, before looking up at his old friend.

'Have you been living a double life?'

Taking back the paper, Daniel read the full story. Then reread it a second time, before going silent.

The doorbell rang.

A late-night delivery of food kept them all quiet, and by the time Daniel had finished his second helping he started to feel the effects of being in a warm environment. His eyelids fluttered, and started to close.

'I need sleep,' he said, turning to his friends.

'One of us will be in the lounge at all times,' Colin replied.

Daniel was about to ask them what they were doing in a hotel, when Harvey added. 'And you will find out in the morning why you are here.'

As Daniel closed the door to his room, they both dived for the newspaper and read the article.

Colin looked at Harvey in disbelief, 'Surely it can't be him.'

Harvey shrugged. 'How do we find out?'

They phoned the charity called 'WASTE NOT' and got put on hold for a while, before a sleepy voice answered. They asked for photographs and hit a blank. Then managed to get hold of one of the senior partners, who had the strange title of 'dirty dozen number four'. It was almost midnight, and he sounded just as tired and irritable as the first person they had spoken to.

'All I can tell you is what the newspapers have been reporting. That the CEO of 'WASTE NOT' has been missing for a few weeks now. It has not received a lot of press, as the police are treating his disappearance as a possible kidnapping.'

'Have you a photo?' Colin asked.

'Why?' number four asked.

'Because we believe your Dan could be our friend Daniel, and we have him safe in a hotel room. It looks like he had a bad accident and has been living rough.'

'You're not holding him for ransom, are you?' number four asked.

Colin laughed. 'No, if by any chance he is your man, you can have him back as soon as he has seen his solicitor.'

'Give me an email address,' replied number four, 'and I will send a photo across.'

Harvey did as he was asked, then turned to Colin. 'I don't know what the hell is going on, but now that we have him, we keep him close.'

Chapter 32
Fischer

The same limo picked them up shortly after breakfast. Much to their annoyance, the man called number four at Waste Not had failed to send a photo. Every time either Colin or Harvey tried to get to speak to anyone senior, they were put on hold for a while before being disconnected.

They dragged Daniel around outlets and fitted him out with new designer clothing. He complained that his eyesight had deteriorated, so they had a pair of glasses made up while he waited. The tailored suit he wore fitted him like a glove, and with his hair styled he looked like an executive businessman. When he emerged from the large limo with two chaperones, people stopped to stare, and wondered who he was.

The reception area had not changed and the young lady behind the front desk smiled politely at them as they entered.

'Mister Fischer is waiting in the boardroom, but our other guests are waiting in the meeting room on your left, if you would like to take Mister Somersby through,' she said.

When they opened the meeting room door, Daniel's heart stopped beating for a second. Alice and Harry were waiting for him.

Alice sprung to her feet and approached, unsure at first. Harry hung back and waited until his parents had embraced.

Daniel wiped away a tear as he turned to the boy. 'I have missed you my son, and there is so much I want to apologise for, but I don't quite know where to start.'

The family were given an hour together before Colin and Harvey returned. Alice excused herself and said she was not needed at the meeting with Fischer, and Colin was taking her and Harry home. She said they would be waiting for him back at the house when he returned.

Daniel followed Harvey down the long corridor and as they went, he thought back to the first time he had entered the building, after receiving the exciting news. He had Alice by his side on that occasion, and he felt his stomach do a flip.

Fischer rose as they walked in and so did the four suits who sat alongside him.

'Mister Somersby, I am pleased to see you, and if I may say so, you are looking very smart.' He gave Harvey an appreciative smile. 'Thank you for bringing him in.'

Harvey took a seat next to the other suits, and Daniel did his best to recall if any of them had been replaced since the last time he had been in the boardroom. The time before his world had been torn apart.

Walking around the table to each one in turn, he shook their hands. He was not quite sure why he did, but it felt good. He then went towards Fischer, who looked hesitant at first.

'I am pleased to see you again. Could you please call me Daniel, it will make me feel a lot more comfortable?'

'Nice to see you... Daniel,' Fischer replied with a look of surprise. 'Would you care to take a seat?'

There was a small folder placed in front of each person and although he was sorely tempted to open his and have a look, he refrained.

Everyone was settled and looking expectantly at Fischer, who turned towards Daniel. 'A lot has happened over the past seven years. Some of it good and some of it bad.' He paused. 'Harvey has briefed me and told me your memory is sketchy, and am not surprised after what you have been through.'

Smiling at the older man Daniel nodded. 'My memory of my life up until I was evicted from Manor House is fine, but since then there are a few voids and you bringing me here is not making it any clearer.'

Harvey smiled at him. 'You recall standing outside your house after being told to leave, and you recall coming with us to the hotel to get cleaned up yesterday.'

'I recall a lot more than that Harvey.' Daniel sounded less vague. 'But I can't understand how I was in such a mess and what I was doing under that subway with all the homeless. Oh, and I recall cyclists shouting duck you suckers,' he added.

Fischer looked around the table with his eyebrows raised.

'A cycling chant,' Harvey explained. 'Not relevant Mister Fischer.'

The elderly Solicitor turned back to Daniel. 'You were gone for over two years. That is quite a big chunk of your life. I wonder what you were doing during all that time?'

Daniel shrugged. 'I started a charity to help the homeless.'

'Harvey mentioned something earlier, but we are still trying to verify the detail,' Fischer explained, as he looked at the folder in front of him. 'I must apologise for the stress and tension we put you through, but it all relates back to the terms and conditions laid out in your uncle's will.'

A shiver crawled up Daniels spine at the mention of the will.

'But finally,' Fischer continued, 'we are in a position to reveal the full contents of his will, and be open with you about everything contained therein. It will explain a lot.'

'I am sorry you have been placed in this difficult position.'

'Thank you Daniel, but it is not for you to apologise, we had a job of work to do. Let me start at the beginning, and please, stop me at any point and throw questions my way. I will hopefully deliver your uncle's message in the way he would have wanted you to receive it.'

Daniel smiled and settled back.

'Firstly, we are aware that you were under the impression that your forebearer was wealthy, but not a millionaire. I believe you looked it up on the Forbes rich list. Did you not?'

'I did,' Daniel replied. 'I was so greedy, and now know how bad that must have appeared.'

The suits all smiled, while Fischer continued, 'Well he wasn't worth anything near tens of millions.'

'I always thought that sounded a lot,' Daniel conceded.

Fischer paused for a short while, before delivering the jaw dropping news. 'He was in fact worth over a hundred million.'

'Wow,' Daniel muttered in amazement, 'I can't believe it. How come he was not on the rich list then?'

'His fortune was listed, but under your Aunt Wilma's maiden name.'

'Greedy of me to look in the first place,' Daniel squirmed.

'We all make mistakes.' Fischer hesitated. 'Now for the reason he constructed a will with so many unusual terms.' He cleared his throat. 'His biggest concern being that you were ill equipped to inherit a large amount of money. He wanted you to mature, but more than that, he wanted to test you.'

'He certainly did that,' Daniel conceded.

'Let me read you a page that we were not permitted to share with you at the time.' Fischer opened his folder and lifted a sheet of paper from the top. 'There are number of these to get through, and knowing what you have been through I can stop at any time. This is going to take a couple of days.'

Dear Daniel,

If we are at the stage of reading this, I presume you have been through the mill and hopefully popped out the other side a better person. I am truly sorry for any inconvenience or hurt I may have caused, but I had several concerns.

Firstly, as you are aware, you may not be the only heir to my fortune, and not my only remaining relative. After initially searching for Francis, the detectives we hired kept coming up empty handed.

But I held a firm belief that he lived, and I soon found out that although he was, he had no desire to ever be found.

I passed the work on to Fischer when I became terminally ill and about to die. It became extremely important that if Francis ever wanted to reveal himself, he would be taken care of. I asked Fischer to look after him if he returned to Manor House, and that is why I put a sixth clause in my terms. Which I hope will one day be unlocked.

I needed to know that you would have the compassion to take care of him if you found him or if he ever came back to the family home.

God save us if that Frederick ever surfaces, but if he does, please protect Francis, and take good care of yourself. Frederick is pure evil.

Yours Truly

A short period of silence followed before Daniel asked. 'But why all those clauses?'

'Mostly red herrings,' Fischer conceded. 'He wanted you to focus and show commitment, and he thought the only way he could get you to do that was to make the terms complicated. He wanted to see what you were made of and whether you were capable of handling his empire.'

'I see, but there must be a lot more to it than that.'

'There is, and you will realise his fears the further we progress with the letters.'

'Did they ever find any clues as to where my cousins went?'

'No, and we resigned ourselves to the fact that they may never be found.'

'The terms directed me to that house, didn't they? Uncle Harry knew I couldn't have resisted the higher value and quicker return.'

'He did. It was just one of his tests. He wanted you to take on Manor House for many reasons. Mainly to test you, but also to safeguard Francis if he ever returned.'

327

'What a fool I have been.'

'How were you to know Daniel? Don't berate yourself. The house was part of the estate when you purchased it. With the title deeds altered to show it selling a few times and then rented to people he knew he could trust, but unfortunately nobody ever stayed that long. Then it stood empty for a long while. He thought if he could tie you up to a long-term stay, it would allow time for Francis to return home, and the only way he could do that was to stipulate the five-year period. Much longer and he knew you would decline.'

'The house was owned by Uncle Harry all along then?'

'Yes, most of the time, other than when it was repossessed by the bank and rented after your uncle moved out. The story about it being sold many times was fabricated for your benefit. The truth being that nobody would stay in the house for long.'

'The documents referred to previous owners buying and selling in quick succession, and mentions ghosts.'

'Fabricated Daniel. Although tenants did not stay long, and the police were called out several times due to some strange unexplained happenings. It gave him the idea to incorporate some of the reference to ghosts to see if you would be put off.'

Daniel sighed. 'I signed those without even questioning the detail. What a fool.'

After the morning coffee break, Fischer read the second letter from the recently opened file.

Dear Daniel,

I am sorry to have put you through the 'ringer', as I imagined you calling it, but there was a lot about you that reminded me of my brother, your father, and it troubled me.

Daniel shrugged and smiled.

I recall you coming to work for me in my Head Office the year before you went off to New York. You were unaware of it at the time, but my terminal illness had been diagnosed and although the cancer was not an aggressive type, my health was destined to slowly fall into decline.

Your parents had been tragically killed and I had lost two sons. I wanted an heir and wanted to keep my wealth in our family.

During that summer school break we placed you with our legal team, to look at purchase contracts and make sure there were no hidden clauses.

'This is going to be embarrassing,' Daniel sighed.

The feedback I got from my Office Manager was quite disturbing.

You were disruptive, swore continually, and never took notes. You had no real interest in looking at the detail and the few contracts you handed over for final signature would have cost the company a lot of money if they had not been rechecked by one of the other team members.

Then when you turned seventeen and attending the academy in New York, I offered to buy you a car.

'Oh no, I know what he is going to say,' Daniel cringed.

The choice was either a cheap new car or an expensive vintage. You chose the vintage, had it checked over and sold it the following week, so you could use the money to travel away with your friends and have a boozy holiday.

You were, to put it bluntly, greedy, lazy, and carefree with my money. If you did not get a quick result, you lost interest.

All I could see was a younger version of your father and it made me nervous, while I needed an heir that could handle large sums of money. At the time I had little faith in your ability to do that.

Then I grew concerned for your future, but there was a lifeline.

During the early stages of building my conglomerate of businesses, I acquired a firm of Architects owned by an exceptionally good friend of mine, a chap called Warren. We renamed the firm WASP.

Daniel could clearly recall Warren sacking him and cringed.

Fischer adjusted his reading glasses and continued.

I new you would take the bait and move from New York. It was an attractive offer and I knew you would have liked to be closer to Wilma. Warren said he would keep an eye on you and would try his best to guide you.

'It's starting to make sense now,' he conceded, still reeling from the revelation.

Then, I put in the last two clauses.

The first. In the event you ever came across my son, your cousin Francis, I needed to know that you would be there for him if he was ever found. I needed to know that you would care for him and be on guard against that devil Frederick returning. Although we have long concluded that that evil young man may have disappeared for good.

The second, was that you had the ability to responsibly manage my vast wealth.

Fischer finished, and placed the letter on the top of the file.

Daniel was at a crossroad, he needed to find out more about the implications of having Frank in his house for the entire period they had lived there. He was now convinced that the man who had resided in Manor House was Francis. Francis had agoraphobia and never left the house as a child, and that fitted with what he knew about Frank. Then there was the man who had attacked him in the underpass and if that was Frederick it all made sense.

He looked up at Fischer.

'You never found any clues, did you?' Then paused before asking. 'You referred to someone during one of the early meetings with us as the Undisclosed Person. Someone who you had to refer to at times. Who was that person?'

'Ah, so your memory isn't as bad as it appears, and contrary to what I was thinking at the time, you were paying attention,' Fischer smiled. 'Yes, there is still the issue of what is referred to as the Undisclosed Person and a number of unopened files.'

'Who is he…, or she?' Daniel asked.

'We still don't know,' Fischer conceded. 'Although as we unlock more and more files, we suspect your uncle is leading us somewhere, and we will only know as events unfold.'

'How do you contact this mysterious person?'

Fischer shrugged. 'Mister X we called him... or her. A postal address was initially used. Then along with advances in technology the address got superseded, and an email address became our only form of communication.'

'And no sightings of either Francis or Frederick since they went missing?' Daniel pressed.

'It would appear so.' Fischer sighed. 'One of the leads we followed for years kept going around in circles. There had been sighting of him near a local college. Then when we got close to where he had been seen he disappeared. It was like chasing shadows. According to the detectives we hired, they thought he may even have changed his name.'

'What to?' Daniel asked.

'One name kept cropping up,' Fischer paused, as if he was reluctant to say the name.

'Yes?' Daniel was on the edge of his seat.

'Frank,' Fischer replied.

Chapter 33

Is This Really Me?

Although Daniel was not shocked at hearing the name, the implications took a while to sinking in. He said nothing about the man called Frank who had been living in their house for all those years, and departed with a promise to return the following day. To hear the next stage of the will.

He sat back in the big limo with Colin, who had returned after seeing Alice home. Harvey had stayed behind for a debrief with Fischer. Apparently there was a lot of work to be done by the team, and they were going to be working late.

Daniel was quiet, deep in thought and barely said a word to his old friend. He wanted to find out exactly who Frank was, but would need to be careful.

Alice stood waiting in the living room, and before Daniel had a chance to say anything, she said, 'I know that you moved Frank next door.'

'Ming said he never told you. How do you know?'

Alice shrugged. 'I found out a couple of months after you left. One day I was tidying up the study and came across plans of the extension. They were the layout drawings for the new west wing extension next door. What caught my eye was a few notes you had attached and then when I searched the filing cabinet, I found photographs of Frank's room and the house next door. It all started to make sense. So, I kept a close eye on The Alley and followed your Chinese friend one day, as he sneaked through the evergreen hedge with a backpack. I found the hatch later that day and after a few more checks on the drawings, realised what you had done. It appeared the neighbours were unaware of his existence and it allowed me time to think. I was so angry with you at the time, and glad you never returned, or I'm not sure what would have happened.'

'And did you ever try and contact him?'

'No, I thought it better to leave him where he was. I presumed he knew I was here and obviously did not want to make contact. Maybe he thought I was involved in what you did and was angry with me as well.'

'I will have to see him and make my peace,' Daniel said.

She picked up her handbag and headed for the door. 'I have to collect Harry from football practice. Please be understanding with Frank, he may not want to talk to you.'

Slipping down The Alley, Daniel crept through the gap in the tall evergreens and approached the side door. Where he knew a spare key had been hidden away for emergencies.

Once inside, he opened the hidden panel leading to the stairs and attic room. There was the familiar smell of Chinese food, the same odour that used to permeate through their upper floor when they had first moved into Manor House.

Arriving on the top floor landing, he took a deep breath and knocked on the door. He waited a minute and then knocked again. He thought Frank might be sleeping, so he gently levered the handle and opened the door a few inches.

What he saw inside made him reel back in shock.

The room was completely empty. Not a single piece of furniture remained. Even the heavy curtains had been removed, and he found himself panicking as he ran back down the stairs, not caring that the neighbours might hear him, as he slammed the side door shut and raced back to Manor House.

Frank had somehow returned to his old room, he speculated, as he hurried through the kitchen and into the larder cupboard. But after arriving out of breath and his head spinning on the top floor of their own house, he found Frank's old room as empty as he had left it.

Running into the study, he logged onto his desktop and sent an email.

Daniel here Frank, where are you?

The message remained undelivered and after trying a further three times he gave up.

He sat staring at his computer screen for a long time, and by the time Alice and Harry returned, he was feeling anxious and more confused than ever.

'What did he say?' asked Alice after a while.

'He is not there. I even looked back in his old room and that is still empty. He is not answering his e -mails, which I now recall him telling me was hacked, and my mobile phone with his number went missing when I was sleeping rough. So, I have no other means of contacting him.'

Arriving back at the solicitor's office the following morning, after having spent a fretful night worrying about Frank, he decided to keep quiet about their former lodger.

Continuing from where they had left off, Fischer produced a file that nobody had seen before.

'This file was only unlocked on reaching the five-year stage and I thought you should hear what it said.'

'This is getting complicated,' Daniel grimaced.

'Your uncle was most likely one of the most astute businessmen I have ever come across, but also a stickler for detail. People used to say he overcomplicated everything by getting into fine detail. As you can see, he went to a lot of trouble to make sure a process was followed for his wealth to be distributed. With you being the major benefactor, it became even more complicated... as you have already discovered. So, let me explain a few things I could not fully divulge during the early stages.

All these documents were left with instructions as to when they could be opened. Some were opened and read at the reading of the will, while others remained sealed, only to be opened at key times or when certain events took place.

On the anniversary of you both having held the house for five years, one such folder was due to be unlocked. However, when you failed to achieve the required growth in value, a judge who specialises in this sort of probate, ruled that we could not default purely because of exceptional market forces.' He looked at Daniel. 'Then Alice left the house within weeks of reaching the full period and defaulted on clause two. Which meant neither of you had claim to the property.

When we opened the sealed letter on the anniversary, it exonerated you, but by then you had already vanished.'

'Evicted,' Daniel reminded him gently.

'Well yes, I am afraid we were only complying with the rules and had no option. We spent a lot of time looking for you, but you were extremely difficult to track down. Both Colin and Harvey searched everywhere, and after a while they followed a Chinese man whom they suspected of being in contact with you. Unfortunately, you were one step ahead and then when Harvey was attacked one night, they had to be extra vigilant.

Let me read you something before we go much further.'

To the executors of my estate

At this juncture, I presume that by the very fact you have opened the folder, Daniel has met his obligations.

I am extremely impressed he has made the journey, and would like to congratulate him. If the experience has caused some pain I apologise. Further, if the strain of abiding by all the clauses lain down have caused a problem with the couple and even if they have become estranged, I still want them to have achieved their goal. I am hopeful that this will bring them back together again.

Failing Francis turning up, Daniel will be the sole owner of the Manor and estate. Should Francis ever be found, the clause six file will be opened, and instructions followed.

My final wish is that they remain in Manor House for as long as possible. It is theirs.

Please acknowledge that you accept the contents of this letter by notifying the Undisclosed Person.

Yours truly

'So, the house was ours after all, I can't believe it. But who is this undisclosed person?' Daniel asked.

'We may never know,' Fischer replied. 'But whoever he is accepted the proposal from the unlocked folder, and that is the reason Alice could return to Manor House, while we searched desperately to find out what had become of you.'

'How many more unlocked folders are there?' Daniel asked.

'Just the two I told you about,' Fischer replied.

'And what events trigger their opening?'

'The one follows a review of your ability to manage his fortune responsibility and I am afraid the other may never be opened. That is the one titled Clause 6.'

'Why may it never be opened?'

'It can only be opened if Francis is found.'

He sat quietly for a while, as he thought about what had been revealed over the course of the past two days.

'Francis never spoke, and suffered from agoraphobia as far as I can recall,' Daniel said after a while.

'He did,' Fischer confirmed. 'Said to be caused by repetitive beatings from Frederick. Why do you ask?'

Daniel felt his head going. This was all a bit much, and he needed some time to think. He stood up and staggered towards the door.

'I am sorry, please forgive me, but I am feeling a bit light-headed.'

Fischer stood, 'Do you want to take a break?'

'Yes, I need to follow up on something. I have so many questions and am still suffering from slight memory loss. I barely know where to start.'

'There is no rush, take your time.'

'Just to be clear,' Daniel said, deep in thought. 'You need to know that I can manage uncle's fortune responsibly. Is that correct?'

'We need to have irrefutable proof. It will provide the evidence we need that you are competent enough to manage the estate.'

'Can I have an office with access to WIFI please? I want to check on something.'

'First office on the left,' Harvey directed him. 'The one you and Alice used the first time you were here. Take as long as you like.'

He left the room and walked into the sanctity of the plush office of leather and wall to ceiling bookcases. He logged on to his email address and saw dozens of unread messages. He read the most recent one.

Dan, if you read this, call us straight back. We are devastated at losing you and worried. Someone is asking for a photo. Bill.

He knew straight away who Bill was. He was dirty dozen number four. Opening the second message, he saw it was from a family begging for money.

Then he saw amongst the latest messages, one from Frank.

Daniel, are you trying to get hold of me?

He typed *Yes* in response and waited five minutes before a message came back.

You have been off my radar for a while. What have you been up to? You keep disappearing. I thought we had something going there with the charity.

Daniel became frustrated after a few minutes and followed up.

Frank, I am tired of this game, tell me who you are, Francis or Frederick?

You know who I am. Where have you been, I could not get hold of you?

Are you Francis or Frederick? Please tell me, I need to know.

There was no response, and in frustration he was about to reach for the delete button when an answer popped up on the screen.

Frank

Just as he was trying to console himself, a fresh email with the title 'Waste Not' pinged up on his screen. It was another message from Bill, alias dirty dozen number four.

He sent a short message in return, divulging a bit of detail that only he and Bill knew of and asked that he urgently send as much information, press cuttings and other documents across. He needed to verify his identity after recalling the article in the paper the doctor had left behind in the Royal Hotel.

Seconds later, a flood of folders arrived. There were several documents in each.

Opening the first, it was a newspaper article from a local paper in Dresden. It had a report about how a man sleeping rough had opened a food hall to feed homeless people. The man called Dan had negotiated a deal with various supermarket chains for food that was about to reach the sell-by date.

A wall of photographs showed crowds of people filling shopping baskets and trolleys. A sign on the wall limited shoppers to two of any one item or they paid full price.

The camera had zoomed in on the man called Dan, and he recognised himself in disguise. He also recognised the article from the time it had been circulated soon after opening the Turkish restaurant in Dresden.

There was still a chunk of his past missing and he was not happy. Something had happened to his life of which he had no recollection at all. He kept having dreams of living in a cardboard box, and then when he read the press reports, small sparks ignited, but then died. He started having flashbacks and made notes. There were still large blank periods in his life and try as he may, he could not recall all the time he was away.

He read a more recently dated attachment. Published roughly a month before, an article featured the charity that had by now grown into a large organisation. Listed as one of the fastest growing in Europe. He skipped a few paragraphs and read on. How the man named Dan had opened scores of outlets and within eighteen months had a charity worth tens of million. The reporter wrote about Dan's follow up venture with sleeping accommodation for the street people.

He could recall reading that article, so there was nothing new there.

Starting to read the most recent folder of attachments, the first was a news report. The photograph showed a picture of Dan in Berlin, and how the mystery man was completing a charity ride from Dresden to Hamburg with a dozen former street sleepers in a bid to raise the profile of his charity.

Not a single photograph showed a clear image of the man's face. Peak caps, woollen hats, large sunglasses and turned up collars always obscured the man's identity.

From then on, the tone of reports changed to one of mystery as the man called Dan had disappeared somewhere between Berlin and Hamburg. Nobody had seen him, and it was feared that he may have been kidnapped.

Daniel recalled seeing Harry over the fence and passing his ball back. He could recall cycling away from Manor House and feeling quite distressed. This was followed by a solid blank spell, that lasted until Colin and Harvey had found him in a box.

He sat transfixed and was only woken from his trance like state when the phone rang. Fischer wanted to know if he was alright.

After printing off all the photographs and news articles, he returned to the meeting room looking calmer.

He stuck the photos up on the glass panel with blue tack and stood back. 'Does anyone recognise this man?'

'That's you,' Harvey said without hesitation.

'Then, if that's me, then this is also me,' he said as he passed everyone a printed sheet of the newspaper cuttings. 'Does everyone agree?'

Fischer and the five suits studied the photographs and read the stories.

'Where did you get these from?' one of the suits asked ten minutes later.

'From Bill at Waste Not.'

'Who is Bill?' Fischer asked.

'While we are questioning names,' Daniel started. 'You mentioned the name Frank and I have to tell you, I know a Frank.'

'And the relevance?' Fischer asked.

'It's who you said Francis might have changed his name to.'

'Frank is a common name,' Fischer suggested.

'Like the Frank who lived in Manor House for the entire period we were there?'

'What?' Fischer sat forward, as did the other five suits.

'I don't know what to say about him, I thought him to be a weird stranger living in our loft. We only discovered him half-way through the project, and then when I suspected he might be Frederick, decided to keep him away from you, although I would have said he behaved more like Francis. I was afraid of losing the house because of breaching clause five. Then, when you were about to do a final valuation of the property, I had to get him moved, or you might have discovered him.'

'We always suspected something strange going on in the house,' Fischer said, 'and that incident where you were accused of removing a man from hospital? Was that Frank? And if so, why didn't you tell us at the time?'

'Clause five,' Daniel shrugged. 'I was scared we would be in breach of a Clause Five. Whether Frederick or Francis, I wasn't going to chance it.'

'Where did this man called Frank live?' Harvey asked. 'We never came across him during our audits.'

'He had a hidden room in the loft with private access. The one the police searched, but I had already moved him to another house by then,' replied Daniel with a sigh. 'Colin knew, but he was

340

sworn to secrecy, and I am afraid Alice never mentioned it to you either.'

Fischer held up one of the A4 sheets.

'Let's just get back to the newspaper stories for the time being.'

Daniel scratched his head and felt the scar from the accident.

'I think I lost my memory more than once. It is all I can think of.' He paused. 'Wait a minute, Ming will know. I remember seeing him when I went back to the house. The time I saw Harry in the garden.'

'Who is Ming?' Fischer asked.

'The Chinese delivery man,' he replied.

Everyone looked at one another in confusion.

Harvey was flicking through some notes in his file and when he found the page he was looking for, held it up.

'Ming was the son of the cook. Remember the letter Uncle Harry left in the will. He mentioned Ming being chased around the garden by Frederick on a powered mower. He was also the chap who kept hanging around Manor House whenever we turned up. We even ended up following him after becoming suspicious that he knew where Daniel was.'

There was a loud murmur as numerous conversations broke out. Fischer brought the meeting back to order.

'If you are Dan in this newspaper article as you claim, then we need to let a few people know. The story when it broke made national news and it was the topic of many a conversation at board meetings. Rags to riches was the way I heard someone describe the man behind the charity.'

Harvey had been searching on his laptop and came back with news that made everyone sit up and take a second look at Daniel.

'Charity formed about seven months after you went missing from...'

'You mean evicted,' Daniel cut in.

Harvey ignored him and continued. 'Manor House. Then there is that first photo when Dan appears in Dresden and the rest is history.'

Daniel was about to say something, when Harvey held up a hand while staring at his computer screen.

'This next bit of information is unbelievable, but true. The charity was registered as a trust and has a total net worth of a hundred million and is growing fast.'

Everyone around the table looked to be in shock.

'You have no recollection of it?' Fischer asked.

'Of course, I do,' Daniel replied, 'but with my memory being in such a poor state I wanted to gather all the facts together first.'

'If it is you Daniel, it will mean you have more than met the criteria to unlock the folder. The one that reviews your capability to manage the rest of the estate, including assets locked away for Francis if he is ever found,' Fischer reaffirmed.

Daniel returned to Manor House after the meeting was adjourned. Harry came down the stairs, apprehensive at first and then ran into his father's arms. Doggie was getting old and ambled up and licked his hand.

Going into minute detail, he explained everything that had gone on at the Solicitors.

Alice looked visibly relieved. 'Daniel, you are so different. It is like being with a stranger.'

'I have had time to think about a lot of things and realise how terrible I would have been to live with.'

She stood staring at him for a while with raised eyebrows, then asked. 'Where is Frank?'

'Alice, I don't know. He is not next door and obviously you know he is no longer here. I will find Ming as soon as I can. He will know.'

'Thank you, I have been so worried about him.'

'I will sort this mess out Alice, don't you worry.'

'Getting back to the new you,' she said taking his hand. 'The one that doesn't swear anymore. And this charity work you are doing is mind blowing. Colin filled me in on Waste Not and you wouldn't believe it, but I even run one of the kitchens... just remarkable.'

'Alice, I had to prove my worth first before asking for forgiveness, and swearing is so bad for the soul. It eats at you like a cancer.'

They spent the rest of the day together and as midnight approached, they found themselves exhausted. Alice directed him to a spare room, asking for a little time to adjust to the changes. Daniel however had a lot still to do. There was Frank to find and a multimillion-pound charity with their CEO missing.

The Solicitors in the end decided to retrace his movements from the time when he had been evicted from Manor House. They had to be totally convinced they had the right man. They chartered a small plane and the five suits got to work.

During the journey, they sifted through emails and in date order started to piece together his past.

'Looks like this chap Frank played a big part,' Harvey said after a short while. 'Looks like the venture would never have got off the ground had it not been for him.'

The team of suits arrived in Dresden and got straight to work. They found the charitable trust 'WASTE NOT', but the board of twelve founding members were in different parts of the country. The suits split up and travelled to various headquarters and eventually had all twelve men accounted for. The interviews revealed a common connection between the man called Dan and a photo they showed of a cleaned-up Daniel, even dressed in a suit, with his hair cut made no difference. They were quick to point out that he was the man they had all looked up to as the founder of their charity.

The team of Solicitors traced his movements back to Berlin, then on to Bad Schandau and viewed the caves where they had initially sheltered on the border close to the city. Then returned to Dresden where the twelve had started their publicity cycle to Hamburg via Berlin.

The member called Dirty Dozen number 4 had a recorded phone message. Whereby Dan had asked them to continue without him whilst they were in Berlin. The call made it clear that he had something personal and important to do and Harvey recognised Daniel's voice on the recorded message.

Number 4 had gone on to say that when they reached Hamburg and Daniel failed to arrive, they returned to Berlin and conducted a thorough search. Then alerted the police and the press. That evening the local television and radio stations had run a thirty second appeal, but nobody had seen him.

'It was as if he had just vanished,' the former doctor said, now the charities chief chemist. 'We started to wonder if he really existed or was some sort of messiah sent from heaven.'

'He has changed so many lives he should be declared a saint,' the former bookkeeper added.

The former carpenters, bricklayer and general factory workers all agreed.

When they were told that Daniel, or Dan as they knew him had been found, they were sceptical.

'Somebody is after his wealth,' the doctor speculated.

'It's a charity,' the bookkeeper challenged. 'It is not Dan's money.'

Harvey decided it was time to get Daniel back to Dresden. They asked the twelve what they thought. They were ecstatic and could not wait to see him. Then when they heard he had suffered a traumatic blow to the head and was suffering from selective memory loss, they got together and worked on a plan.

They travelled to Bad Schandau, where they had started their real journey. Daniel was waiting for them there. It was an emotive reunion for the twelve and when they started to cry, he realised how much he must have meant to them.

By the time they reached Dresden, his memory had almost fully returned, but the deciding moment was when they walked into the old Turkish restaurant in Dresden and he reeled back. The smell of the communal eating hall and the surrounding décor made his head spin and brought back a flood of memories.

Was it the sight and smells of the starting point of their Waste Not journey in the old Turkish restaurant that had brought forward this memory return? Nobody knew the answer, but all were delighted at the outcome.

His former colleagues from WASTE NOT stood around like twelve disciples, while Harvey arranged for Alice and Harry to fly to Dresden, where they planned to get the family away for a proper reunion and holiday.

They were about to board a plane when Daniel's phone pinged, and a message came up that he could not ignore.

'Ming here, Frank wants meeting. Be in study of Manor at ten in morning. He says you bring Fischer and his men along.'

He turned to Alice and Harry who stood next to him in the queue.

'Sorry family, but there is something we have to do that is far more important than this holiday.'

Chapter 34
The Sixth Clause

Fischer and his men sat around the desk in the study at Manor House, while Daniel fussed around the kitchen making pots of tea and coffee. Alice said she would feel better taking Harry out for a long walk. There had been a lot going on and the boy needed some fresh air.

There was a strange air of expectancy in the room, as nobody really understood why they were there, other than to meet with the former attic lodger Frank, who was afraid of open spaces, and the Chinese chef's son called Ming. Nobody was any the wiser, but Daniel had a hunch that all was about to be revealed.

They sat looking up at the wall clock as the large hand slowly moved around and the smaller one settled on ten. Then at precisely that moment the doorbell chimed, and Daniel raced to the front entrance.

'Hello Mister Dan,' Ming stood on his own.

'Hello Ming, where is Frank?'

'He is coming now,' the thin Chinese man replied.

Daniel then noticed a neat looking man standing to one side of the entrance, where he had been partially obscured by one of the two large pillars.

'Frank,' he cried out and took a step in his direction. 'You are out in the open.'

'I have had treatment and am not scared of open spaces anymore.'

'Your hair is cut...and you can speak!'

'And I can speak,' Frank added.

When the three men walked into the study Daniel introduced them.

'Gentlemen, this is Ming and the handsome looking figure next to him is Frank.'

Everyone stood up, but Frank took a step back.

'Not Frank Daniel, but Francis. I am your long-lost cousin.'

Order broke down as confusion set in. But after a few hours it was established that Frank was indeed Francis.

'But I have seen the scar on your arm,' Daniel said.

Francis reminded them of how Frederick had scarred his arm as a young boy to further confuse their parents, and that if he had not run from home, Frederick would have come back for him.

For the first time in his entire life Fischer was at a loss for words.

Daniel opened a folder with printed copies of his original emails dating back years.

'This is proof that Frank, or Francis helped me resolve many issues with this house,' he said.

Fischer lent sideways and took a closer look at one of the emails. 'Excuse me, but that email address, I clearly recognize. Where did you get that from?'

'From Frank, or Francis as we now know him.'

Fischer stuttered. 'But... that is the same as the... Undisclosed Person's address... I don't understand.'

Daniel looked from Fischer to Francis and at the row of mouths hanging open around the table.

'I can explain,' Frank started. 'But please call me Francis.' He paused to collect himself. 'After running away, I sheltered with the homeless in dark subways and basement hideouts. Then quite by chance Ming turned up. He had also run from Frederick. My father had the police looking for me and the press ran front page updates for a while, but I was not going to return to Manor House and have Frederick sneak up and torment me again. So I remained in hiding until Ming came up with a plan.'

'I contact his father, but did not give him clue where Francis is hiding,' Ming added.

'You said you went to college and studied IT?' Daniel recalled one of his earlier conversations in the larder room.

'He very good boy,' Ming said. 'I take good care of him. He studies very hard.'

'And the email address?' Fischer asked.

'Initially a postal address,' Francis replied. 'Then email. My father lived in an era without computers. He knew I was alive after I wrote a long letter explaining what had happened to me and that I would never return. I could tell by the response he was not entirely sure what to do and we lost contact. Then a few years later he sent me a message and told me he was dying. He said he had some difficult choices to make and wanted to know that I was going to be taken care of if I ever returned to the old family home. So he installed me in the process of managing his will. While you,' he looked at Fischer, 'made sure everything followed that process. And the prime objective was to have my cousin here,' he then turned to Daniel, 'take ownership of the house.'

'How come he never discovered where your mail was coming from?' Fischer asked.

'I used a P.O. Box and had Ming as cover at first.'

Ming Smiled, revealing a row of crooked teeth. 'We very good at fooling him.'

Fischer asked Daniel, Francis, and Ming to give himself and his suits a while on their own, so that they could confer.

Four hours later they called the three back into the room.

'Everyone here is convinced that you are Francis,' Fischer said, before adding, 'And of course Daniel has already proved his competence.'

348

As they all nodded, he reached for a file in his briefcase. It had THE SIXTH CLAUSE printed on the cover. The final message from Uncle Harry's grave was about to be read.

Fischer broke the seal and pulled out a single sheet of paper and started to read the short, handwritten note.

The fact that this clause is being read would have filled me with more joy than you could imagine.

Obviously, I cannot share in the moment Francis is revealed but want to say how thrilled I would have been.

To have reached this final stage of my bequest is truly my ultimate goal and I want to thank you all.

Always remaining positive, I was hopeful that this would be the outcome. As the reason for this final clause is to ensure that Francis is taken care of, as he did not have the capability to look after himself after leaving home. And that Daniel has matured and can take on the responsible role of managing my affairs. Both Daniel and Francis are to share joint custody of my estate and ensure Ming is given a special place in the family. While JJ Fischer and Partners are to remain as ultimate custodians and act in their best interests at all times.'

Thank you, God bless,

Harry.

Fischer looked at Daniel. 'He would have been so proud of you. To see the charity you built to help all those homeless and vulnerable people. A multi-million-pound charity in two years is a truly remarkable achievement. And the way you have matured into a responsible man, is truly mind boggling,' he said, as he put a hand on Daniels shoulder.

'I couldn't have done it all without Frank or Ming's help,' Daniel replied.

'Francis, if you please,' reminded the man opposite him.

Hours later all the suits departed, leaving the Somersby family to re-establish their kinship. There was so much to talk about that they were still awake at daybreak. Alice had sat silently listening to a replay of the day's events.

They were tired. Daniel offered both Francis and Ming a choice of bedrooms and said they would discuss living arrangements the following day.

'Once we have settled, let us get back to where we left off with the homeless. There is still a lot of work to be done,' Daniel said, as they stood and stretched their legs.

'Thank you, I am so looking forward to working by your side, regardless of what we do,' Francis replied.

'I couldn't have wished for a better outcome,' Alice said.

Daniel hesitated. 'I am sorry Francis, for thinking you may have been Frederick.'

'Don't worry Daniel, I hold no grudges.'

'I even thought it was you who attacked Ming and myself in the subway one night, but it couldn't have been, my assailant had his two front teeth missing and looked as mad as a hatter.'

Francis smiled, revealing a perfect set of canines.

'He always very good Mister Dan,' Ming praised. 'I taught him to brush teeth well when a boy.'

It was late when Francis and Ming headed for the guest rooms, where they were in desperate need of sleep. After all the excitement and emotive reconnections, everyone was exhausted. Alice gave Daniel a hug and told him how proud she was of what he had achieved for the homeless.

Francis turned back down the stairway and called to Daniel. 'I know it is late, but there is just one thing confusing me, and I apologise, but I didn't want to raise it at the meeting.'

Daniel smiled at Alice. 'You head up to bed, while I have a quick chat to Francis. You need to get some sleep.'

He caught up with Francis and rested a hand on his shoulder.

'What's troubling you?' he asked.

'Thank you for being patient, but Fischer said something after reading the letter from my father.' Daniel looked puzzled. 'About how successful the charity for the homeless has been.'

'I am sorry Francis. You should have got most of the credit. If it had not been for you, I would never have got Waste Not off the ground. But don't worry, you have full financial control of the bank account, and I want you to continue with managing that part of the business.'

Francis looked confused. 'Sorry, but I have no idea what you are going on about.'

'Come on Francis, you know what I am talking about. The charity you helped me set up called Waste Not.'

'I know all about the charity. If you remember, I financed you when you were first stuck in Bad Schandau with those twelve dirty men. Then registered the business and rented you the old Turkish restaurant. I even sent you an email after getting the local television station to give you airtime. Then I received a rather distasteful message from you to say stop interfering. It took a while for me to get over that.'

Daniel looked at him in confusion. 'But you kept running the finances for the business, and I most certainly never told you to stop interfering. You called me from your mobile phone, saying your email account had been hacked.'

'It was hacked Daniel, but then when I logged back on, I had a message from you saying you didn't need my help.'

Daniel slumped down onto the stairs, feeling lightheaded and confused.

Francis was exhausted and excused himself before heading upstairs. He paused on the landing and looked back down at his defeated looking cousin. And as he did so, a smile creased his face.

As footsteps faded, Daniel turned back to check all the doors were locked and lights turned off. A blue hue glowed from the study as he walked past, and he realised his computer was still switched on. He reached for the button and was about to press it when he saw an email had just arrived in his inbox.

What caught his attention was the word URGENT.

Tired, and wanting nothing more than to go to bed, even though Alice had asked for him to give her a little space and use a spare room for a few nights. He dithered, as his finger hovered between the read icon and the off key. Trying to decide whether it could wait for the morning.

He tapped the 'Read' key.

The message was from the bank. It said there had been a serious breach of security with the Waste Not account and the entire contents, in the region of seventeen million Euros had been removed. The banks fraud office was working frantically with the charity's accountants to try and trace where the money had gone, and were alerting Daniel to the fact that the police were now involved.

He pulled at a chair and half collapsed into it. His head was spinning as he focused in on the screen. Then as he glanced across at his inbox, he saw an earlier message from Frank.

'That must have been from before he arrived this evening,' he muttered, still confused with the conversation he had just had with Francis.

Hello Dan, its Frank here. Thought, since I have not heard from you in a short while, I would give you an update.

Daniel looked at the time the message was sent and saw it was from a completely different email address, and sent during the family reunion. His eyes darted back to the message.

Due to what I would consider a major threat, I have closed our business account and moved everything to a secure offshore fund, including the final payment received over two years ago from the insurers for the neighbour's house repairs. For reasons I cannot disclose, I have gone into hiding and will not be contactable for the foreseeable future, and would warn you not to try and find me.

Frank.

ACKNOWLEDGEMENTS

First of all, loving thanks to my dear Sue, who gave me the encouragement, support and demonstrated a considerable amount of patience when I took over her study. Her edits were invaluable, and although she never said as much, I know she would have preferred more of a romantic twist. Unfortunately Daniel is far too wicked and self-obsessed for any such thought.

I am profoundly grateful to Alexis Leeks for taking the time and having the courage to read the first draft and give me her honest opinion.

I cannot thank Brian Cackett enough for spending his free time during weekends and evenings reformatting the contents. Forever grateful.

Thank you Lauren. My dearest daughter who lives in Germany and told me a real-life story during a bike ride that inspired this tale.

Then to my dear friends who read early versions of my book, enduring grammatical errors (Mrs Aspline would have kept me in detention for weeks) to give me enough courage to publish in paperback.

For those readers who were wondering how Daniel is managing to cope with his recent news, The Final Twist will be published in the future.

John Russon Saddington is a retired Engineer who emigrated from South Africa to England in the early 1990's. A keen cyclist and when not in the saddle can be found hacking around a golf course.

Born on the South Coast of Natal in a small village called Uvongo Beach, he spent more time during his youth surfing and lifesaving than on academia.

He lives in Lytham Saint Annes in Lancashire with his wife Susan, has two children and retired from a career as a Divisional Managing Director of a Construction Company.

His Grandfather, a Rand Pioneer, was Paul Kruger's personal Saddler. He became friends with I.W. Schlesinger and Edgar Wallace who had an office in the same building as Gandhi and became friends with Sir Patrick Duncan, the sixth Governor General of the Union of South Africa. An explosive opportunity for the author who has written a novel called The Quiver Tree and a sequel to follow. The Quiver Tree will be released in 2021.

Printed in Great Britain
by Amazon